Girls School

Wolf Harbor, Volume 7

L.J. Breedlove

Published by L.J. Breedlove, 2023.

This is a work of fiction. Similarities to real people, places, or events are entirely coincidental.

GIRLS SCHOOL

First edition. November 21, 2023.

ISBN: 979-8223152088

Written by L.J. Breedlove.

Chapter 1

Day 155 of the re-emerged Hat Island pack, Friday, Nov. 8, Vancouver

Benny Garrison was exhausted — emotionally drained by the needs of all the shifters who seemed to be hovering around the dining room table he was using as an intake and counseling center. He didn't think he had anything left to give.

The dining room was in Margarite Lewis's home in Delta, a community just outside Vancouver, B.C. It was a house that looked like any suburban split-level ranch house, albeit bigger than most. Nestled into a property of five acres, it was a much-coveted property now that Delta had better access to Vancouver proper and had attracted well-heeled commuters looking for a place like this. It had served Margarite well for 40 years as her home, the base from which she roamed the world and hosted potluck picnics for neighboring shifters in Vancouver— independents and family packs, not the recognized Vancouver pack. No, the Vancouver pack was its own set of problems.

Not Benny's problems, thank God. He had enough on his plate.

The lines that distinguished all those groups had been blurrier than people realized. Then Benny's Alpha, Abby Stafford, showed up. Now, everyone was in an uproar. Not surprising, Benny thought sourly. Abby had managed to put every pack she'd visited this last month into a tailspin. Then she'd leave a crew to help put things right, while *she* returned to Hat Island.

Benny hadn't liked it much when she'd left Ayta Vuk in Odessa, a small town in eastern Washington, to help that pack figure things out, but he'd accepted it as the smart thing to do. The Odessa pack had Russian roots, and Ayta was a Russian elder, an Alpha in her own right, visiting Hat Island for the winter. Sensible, even if it meant he and Ayta were separated.

It had made sense to leave Okami and Yui Yoshida in Kettle Falls for a week to get that pack back on its feet after Okami killed their former Alpha on Abby's orders.

And Cujo Brown had stayed behind in Hayden Lake to help his father take over the reins of the Hayden Lake pack after Abby killed their Alpha, a man with dementia who was slowly taking his pack into insanity with him. At least that was what Cujo was supposed to be doing there. Benny wasn't sure how Cujo had found time to find one of the missing women, Rose Evans, from the Wolf Harbor serum research and bring Rose and her baby home. That was a story he wanted to hear. Starting with how did Rose even *have* a baby — a cute little girl named Jenna? Rose was one of the women of the cohorts, right? All the cohort test subjects had been chosen for their post-menopausal status — Stefan Lebenev had insisted on it when he set up the serum research. As that thought occurred to him, it was all he could do to stay put in Vancouver. Even shifting to wolf and heading home had appeal, and he'd been uneasy about shifting ever since he got back from Russia.

His wolf whined a bit at that thought. I'm better, he assured the wolf. And he was. He shifted every night here in Vancouver out in the Burns Bog, just a few miles from here. Vancouver and the neighboring communities were blessed with natural wild areas where a wolf could go.

And it was the one guaranteed way to escape questions for a while! Dear God, he even got them when he was sleeping! He set that thought aside for the moment. He lacked any mental privacy in this house to think about things like that. Next run, he promised himself.

Now what had he been thinking about, before that sidetracked him?

Oh yeah, Rose Evans's story. He frowned. Somehow, he thought that story was more important than people had considered it — if they'd had time to consider it at all before they came up here and all hell broke loose.

That's what he was supposed to be doing — collecting stories, making connections, he thought irritably, as he stood up and stretched out his back muscles. He was a Keeper of Stories, and Teacher of the Hat Island boarding school. He wanted to be back there doing that job, not this. And wasn't that a hoot? A man once known as the shifter playboy wanted to be a teacher?

Unfortunately, he was also Dr. Benny Garrison, a licensed psychologist. And there weren't many shifters with degrees in psychology. In fact, most of them were probably here in this room right now.

Margarite's degree might be in social work. Maybe an MSW? He shrugged. No telling. Shifters lived long lives, and as Okami Yoshida was fond of saying, someone might be many things if they lived a very long life. And Okami would know. Benny wasn't sure how old that man was, but he'd been eavesdropping in Abby's mind when Okami admitted to having been a samurai — and called Abby Shogun. It had freaked her out.

Freaked Benny out too. Another necessary story he could be pulling out of one of his packmates, he thought irritably, although he acknowledged he was unlikely to hear it until Okami was good and ready to tell it.

Abby wasn't telling him everything either. He frowned at that. She had a secret, and she was hugging it close to her with such glee. She was happy. Ecstatically happy. His frown softened, and he smiled. It was good to feel her happy. She'd been upset when she'd left here. He'd been worried. He didn't think they knew the complete story of what happened at the Vancouver pack house. And the three people who did know — Abby, security guard Captain Geoff Nickerson, and a once-human wolf named Emily, were now back at Hat Island, and he couldn't corner them and grill them either.

He snorted. He'd gotten used to living in Abby's mind, he thought ruefully. She'd opened up a wide link between the two of them so that he could use her as his encyclopedia to all things Hat Island when he'd lost so many memories in Russia.

Not thinking about Russia, he told himself firmly.

Damn it, the list of things he wasn't thinking about was almost as long as the list of the things he needed to think about!

So yes, he had access to Abby even though he was in Vancouver, and she was on Hat Island, outside Seattle, 200 miles away. He could talk to her, he conceded. But he'd taught her how to lock up thoughts not too long ago. He might come to regret that. She was using it to keep this secret from him. Damn it, she wasn't supposed to use it to keep *him* out!

He smiled ruefully at that. Of course, Abby was entitled to have secrets from him. What worried him was that he thought she was keeping this — whatever *this* was — secret from everybody. Even from her Second, Jake Lewis. And that was dangerous. A pack Second should know everything. If it was making her so happy, why wouldn't she share it with Jake? She should be sharing everything with Jake!

Well, maybe it was a surprise birthday party for the man, Benny chided himself. But it felt big, whatever it was. And that worried him.

Not my problem, he told himself.

No, his problem was 50 or so women who had been forced to become shifters by the former Alpha of the Vancouver pack — kidnapped, attacked and nearly killed, healed by the shifter, and then forced to change to a wolf and back again to finish healing. The old-school way of making humans into shifters.

Benny had been dealing with all the trauma Stefan's serum had caused the human women of the Hat Island cohorts. Waking up to find you now had a wolf was traumatic, no matter how gentle the process or how horrific.

On Hat Island, the women — made-shifters was the term they used for themselves — had been turned over to Stefan's grant funder for rehabilitation and integration into packs. Horrible enough thing to do to a person — uproot them without their permission, change them into a werewolf, and then relocate them? Ugly business.

It was made worse by the fact that the grant funder, Jedediah Jones, now deceased, had sold the women into slavery instead. When Abby Stafford rose to be Alpha and called her pack on Hat Island, she'd killed him, and put a stop to what Jones was doing. And she'd insisted that all of those women would be brought home to Hat Island.

But when Benny had met *these* women he had thought the physical trauma that the women had been through had made it much worse. He wasn't as sure about that now.

The Vancouver women had been brutally changed and then confined to a barracks of sorts, allowed out only to serve the men of the pack. When one of the young men Alpha Chen had been recruiting for his army did something noteworthy, a woman was given to him as an award. Pack standing, a woman, a future in one of the most livable cities in the world — the young men of isolated packs throughout Canada and the northern United States were flocking to Vancouver to do whatever Alpha Chen requested of them.

But truly the trauma seemed to be the same — what the women on Hat Island had gone through was no different than that experienced by these women, and that made him sick to realize.

Benny had been a fitness coach for Stefan Lebenev's serum research. He'd turned the other way when those women were sent off in the care of Jedediah Jones. He'd let it go on.

And the Wolf Harbor women they were rescuing felt betrayed by men they liked and thought liked them. Not just the trauma of being made into a shifter, and then abused, but betrayal.

He might never stop feeling guilty about it. He would always owe them whatever they asked, whatever they needed. All shifters did; their sacrifice probably gave the shifter species a future. But they weren't asked. It was taken from them.

These women, who Vancouver shifters called once-human, knew the men who had kidnapped them and brutally changed them were evil bastards. They didn't feel betrayed by friends and lovers like the Hat Island women did. When they first rescued these women, there had been a sense of relief among the Hat Island leadership — at least we're better than what Vancouver did!

No, Benny had come to realize this week, they were worse. Far worse.

The shifters who ran the Wolf Harbor Resort had betrayed the women's trust.

Benny didn't quite know what to do with that realization, and so he added it to his list of things to think about later.

Whenever later might be. He and his helpers were putting in long hours, interviewing the women and helping to figure out what their path forward should be. They couldn't go back to the lives they once had. Many of them had been decreed dead, buried and mourned for years at this point. None of them looked like the women their friends and family would remember. Becoming a shifter gave them youth, vitality and longevity. So no, they couldn't go back.

Even if the women knew that intellectually, it was still a struggle to accept emotionally. The one good thing Stefan had done was to try to select only women who were elderly and alone. Even that wasn't true in every case, Benny acknowledged, but at least Stefan hadn't disrupted 30-some families in his serum study. Stefan had pulled women from all over the United States; almost none came from the Seattle area so that the disappearances would go unnoticed.

Alpha Chen, on the other hand, had gone for convenience. He and his goons had grabbed women within a two-hour radius of Vancouver. Young, old, married, single, mothers.... Chen hadn't known or cared. And he'd been doing it for 50 years. Spread out like that, no one seemed to notice — and wasn't that a horrific thing in itself? — but in the last few years, he'd started taking more and more women, and Vancouver officials had begun to think there was a serial killer operating in the Vancouver area.

That was why Abby could order Chen's execution. Not for all the horror — by shifter law, the Chairman of the Northwest Council of Alphas didn't have jurisdiction over what happens *within* a pack — but because Chen's actions ran the risk of outing shifters to humans. Vancouver police had approached Chen with questions — the link had been made.

No one knew how far the police had gotten in their investigation. And perhaps now that Chen had 'died of a sudden heart attack,' with a large funeral was slated for tomorrow for all of his large extended family, the police would pursue other 'avenues of inquiry.'

Well, it could be worse, he consoled himself. You could be in charge of cleaning up *that* mess. No, that was the job of the new Vancouver Alpha Gerard Gauthier, an attorney who thought he'd left the pack years ago. Turned out that wasn't quite true.

A lot of things weren't *quite* true.

Let's start with Chen's heart attack brought on by escaping a fire in the gym at the pack house, Benny thought grimly. The fire supposedly had claimed the lives of some 30 other shifters — although most them wouldn't be publicly mourned like Chen. Most of them didn't exist, not in the records of Vancouver bureaucracy. And wasn't that interesting?

That fire worried Benny too. That very convenient fire. He thought the men had to have been dead before the fire even started. Yes, humans might get trapped in a burning building and die of smoke inhalation, but shifters?

He snorted. Hardly.

Not my problem, he told himself firmly.

Again.

But if the police were to discover that many of their missing women — the victims of that possible serial killer — were sitting in Margarite Lewis's dining room, it would not go well. So Benny's problem was discovering enough about these women so that they could be placed in packs away from Vancouver.

Away from anyone they might know.

It didn't help that Chen had used ignorance as one of his methods of control. The women knew very little about being a shifter. Until Abby had rescued them, they hadn't known how to shift!

They weren't pack. They had been slaves.

And that sent his thoughts spiraling back to the Hat Island women. How was he any better? He forced his mind away from that question.

So he was conducting orientation sessions for the women. He had help there. Alefosio, one of Margarite's men, was doing much of the orientation and training sessions. He had a counseling background of some kind, and the women seemed at ease with him. Well, Alefosio was Tongan. Tough warriors, gentle lovers, Alefosio bragged. Benny grinned. Guess he had a point.

The rest of his day was spent interviewing the women for possible placement elsewhere, and doing counseling sessions with those who were struggling the most. Some of the once-human women had been in the pack for 30 years — more accurately, they'd been given to a man who was in the pack. In most cases, the man had never brought the woman into the pack.

In 30 years.

That was a long time for a shifter to be without pack. Benny's eyes burned. He'd been a lone wolf for that long, although by choice, so he knew what it felt like. Now that he was pack again, he would never let anyone take it from him again.

And the Hat Island pack was full of wolves who were just like him.

So he was doing domestic violence counseling, essentially. Did the women want to stay with their shifter man? Some of them had children — a few had grandchildren! Some had integrated into the family structure. One was even a senior wife. She wasn't going anywhere, but even she was benefiting from some counseling.

Margarite Lewis was doing the counseling with the women who did want to stay in the households and families they'd been given into. She knew pack life as a woman better than Benny could ever hope to. And he was grateful she was willing to do it. It wasn't easy on her. Not only was it hard to deal with *their* trauma, it brought up old trauma of hers. Things he didn't think she'd completely resolved herself.

And of course, Margarite had plenty on her plate too. When Alpha Chen died, a lot of the independent wolves — wolves who had been allowed to live independent of the pack — had snapped to her as their Alpha rather than to Alpha Gauthier. Abby had tried to give her a warning, but even with a warning, it wasn't easy.

Margarite Lewis had resisted being an Alpha of a pack for 40 years. Women couldn't be pack Alphas, the powerful World Council of Alphas insisted — ignoring that there had been female Alphas in Russia all along. But in the New World, it was an article of faith — women couldn't be Alphas. Margarite had considered herself a lone wolf — the only known female lone wolf — with a household of men. And she was dominant enough that the powerful Alphas in the Northwest region had let her be.

Women weren't allowed to be lone wolves either, because shifters needed every woman they had, and needed them as mothers. Female shifters were so few, none could be risked. Or so the story went.

Turned out that wasn't completely true either. Discovering the truth behind that lie had cost him his memory. Cost him a lot of things.

Not thinking about that today either, Benny told himself.

But no one was willing to tell Margarite Lewis she had to remain in a pack. No one had ever been able to tell Margarite Lewis much of anything. She was a legend in the Northwest — all over the world really. Jake Lewis, pack Second of Hat Island, was her grandson. He said he encountered stories about Margarite Lewis all over the world.

Benny did need to think about Margarite, his eyes finding her in the room. A young shifter named Jessie Nickerson was helping her with some group therapy. Jessie was a blessing — a member of the Vancouver pack who had just graduated from college in psychology. Then her grandfather, the former pack Second Anthony Nickerson, had decided she needed to be reined in and gave her to the pack Alpha as an additional woman in his household.

Over her objections and even her parents' objections.

Even in spite of her having a fiancé – who was banished from the pack.

Benny knew Jessie was looking for her fiancé, but she hadn't found him, last Benny had heard. He should check on that. So, Jessie had her own trauma to deal with, but she was working long days helping the others cope.

Then there were Benny's two personal charges also seated at Jessie's table — two 14-year-old twins from a Russian pack. Kristina and Taisiya of Michil Bogun's pack were supposed to be on Hat Island attending the boarding school. But Chen had kidnapped them in the midst of all of his other plots last week. Abby had rescued them, along with herself, and the once-human women.

And then Abby returned to Hat Island leaving him here with the twins.

Benny regretted he'd let the twins stay. They needed to be back on Hat Island. And he got the growing dis-ease that he always felt when he let himself consider the two of them. He should have made them go home with Abby.

The twins had formed bonds with the once-human women during their escape last week. And the girls were very protective of them. It helped. The women turned to them gratefully, even if they were only 14. The twins had been teaching them a lot about their wolves. It was actually kind of cute, a feeling he carefully hid from the girls.

But they are in danger, his wolf fretted.

Yes, Benny agreed. And as soon as he found someone to take them home to Hat Island they were going. He hoped it would be him, but a glance around the room made him despair of ever getting out of here.

Some of the newer wolves were so traumatized they couldn't speak. Chen had a thing he did called bringing a woman to heel, a way of breaking a woman. Rare was the woman who was willing to risk going through it twice. So far none of the women could talk about the details.

But there were women who could comfort other women. Cindy, an independent wolf, now part of Margarite's pack, had been through it. She was still struggling with all of it, Alpha Gauthier said. But she'd come out for a few hours each day to just sit with the women. And it helped. Every little bit helped.

Jason appeared in the doorway of the dining room and gestured with his head. Benny sighed and headed toward the door. Jason was handling one of the other problems the former Alpha had left them — a whole herd of young men who had been eager to find a place in Chen's army.

What was Chen going to use his army for?

Not my problem, Benny chanted. What little he knew was sending his intelligencer instincts into overdrive. Another story he should be pursuing instead of counseling women. But that problem was Cujo's.

He frowned. He *thought* Cujo was taking care of that problem. Right? He was the chief of security for the World Council, after all.

"What's up?" Benny asked Jason as they walked outside to the backyard. Truly he was grateful for a chance to breathe the fresh air. It was a crisp fall day — leaves were still falling from the trees around the edge of Margarite's property. Maybe they could make these recruits rake them up, he thought idly.

"What are we going to do with them?" Jason said, gesturing with his head to a horde of young men doing an aggressive workout in the backyard. "I've done everything I can think of. But we've got 30 young men camped in Margarite's back yard. And we've got another 30 of them at the barracks at the Vancouver pack house. What the hell are we supposed to do with them?"

Jason was one of the security team from the Hat Island. He was military trained, and the two of them had been through some shit together — including being buried alive in the Odessa pack's 'man cave.' Benny had never seen him rattled. Jason usually had a half-smile that said he'd seen it all and nothing would surprise him.

He'd lost that smile days ago.

"Why are you asking me?" Benny said with exasperation. "How the hell should I know?"

"Well, who does know?" Jason shot back. "Because we've got to start clearing some people out of here."

"Women too," Margarite said from behind Benny. "Neighbors are beginning to ask questions."

Benny wondered how she had heard that — she hadn't been out of the house in a week. Partially because people needed her. And partially because she wasn't handling this Alpha thing all that well, herself.

Margarite's eyes narrowed slightly.

Shit, Benny thought. She got some of that.

A week ago, during a very fun night, Margarite had started forming pack bonds with her men — the five men who had lived with her for years. And she formed a bond with Abby, because Abby was Chairman of the Council of Alphas and had bonds with all the Alphas in the region — or would, as soon as they finished making the visits to the packs. And somehow, in all of that, Benny had ended up with a bond with Margarite as well.

He hadn't been one of her men in over a decade. And he was Hat Island pack. He'd had a moment of panic when he realized he had a bond with Margarite, worried that he'd somehow switched packs. But no. Thank God. The problem wasn't that bad.

And there were times when he didn't mind the bond. Night time. Sex times. Then it was hotter than hell to have a bond with this woman. Reminded of that, he smiled at her, and saw her soften a bit. She wasn't used to picking up bits and pieces from others. She'd been a lone wolf for a very long time.

A lone wolf with five men. And monthly potlucks. Benny snorted. She'd been a pack Alpha in all but name, so she could just suck it up and deal. And he carefully did not let that thought slip — he liked his head attached to his body, thank you very much.

"So we need to have a meeting of the leadership team," Benny muttered. "Surely someone has an idea of what we do next."

Margarite stiffened. "We don't do leadership teams," she said. "Not in my house — here I'm the boss. And probably not in the Vancouver pack house either. They wanted an autocratic pack Alpha, remember? They threw away an Alpha who would have been happy to have leadership teams — probably *did* have them."

And wasn't that a tragic story? One Benny actually did know. Geoff Nickerson had been pack Alpha here once upon a time — until Chen had challenged him and forced him out. Then Chen had turned the pack from a modern urban one to an autocratic traditional one. He'd banished anyone who disagreed.

Or so he said. Some he'd apparently just ignored — still linked to the pack, but not participants. Benny didn't think it would even occur to most Alphas that could be a thing.

The shifters here hadn't realized that was what he was doing either. Had Chen known? Benny wasn't sure, and the man was dead, so he couldn't ask him.

"Fine," Benny said angrily. "Then decide away, Margarite. You and Gerard Gauthier. Have at it. I'd be happy to get the hell out of here and go home to Hat Island."

The backyard was a tent city. The women were being put up inside. People were worried one of them would decide to go home — or go to the authorities. They had to be getting cabin fever by now, Benny thought, suddenly weary by the magnitude of what they faced.

Or maybe not. From the stories the women told, they'd been cuffed to their beds in their barracks most of the time. His rage burned at the thought. And there was no one left to kill. Abby had already taken care of that. No one had come out and said it, but Benny knew. Deep inside, he knew Abby Stafford had been the cause of those mysterious deaths at the Vancouver pack house. And he thought she'd done it with her mind.

Dear God. How powerful was that woman?

His wolf informed him he would have liked to kill some of those who had kept women cuffed to a bed for hours and hours at a time. And his wolf was fine if Abby had done it for him.

We're no better, Benny thought, and the rage drained from him, changing into self-loathing. What we're doing here? They're still caged in some respects. They still can't go home. They don't see us as any different than the men they'd escaped from at Chen's.

He headed around the house to the street out front. He wanted to get out of here. Maybe he could just keep walking until he hit Hat Island. Be a hell of a walk, he conceded, but he could hitchhike, or go wolf. Damn, if that didn't have appeal.

He felt someone following him, and he checked — it wasn't Margarite. He always knew where she was. And he hated it. She hated it.

"What's going on?" Cujo said quietly from behind him.

Benny shook his head. "I can't stand this," he said miserably. "I can't stand what these women have been put through. And the more I listen, the more I realize, we were worse, Cujo. What we did? Was even worse."

Cujo was silent for a bit. He had probably already figured that out, Benny realized. One of those cohort women on Hat Island was his mate. He'd searched for her for a year before Abby became Alpha and gave him the resources to find and bring her home. And things weren't right there either. Not between the two of them, and not with Cujo.

Cujo was on his list of people he needed to tend to. Abby had added Cujo to Benny's list herself. And neither of them had found time to talk. Really talk. They didn't have it now either.

"I've been out of sorts for days," Benny admitted.

"I need a run," Cujo said. "Can't run as a wolf, not here, and not in daylight even in Burns Bog. But let's go. Two joggers. That OK with you? Because we really need to talk."

Benny looked at what he had on. Black sweatpants, running shoes, a tan T-shirt that said Simon Frasier on it. A university T-shirt. He wondered where he'd gotten it.

Swiped it from someone's laundry, he guessed. They'd only brought stuff for a weekend.

Cujo seemed to assume that his silence was agreement, and he was starting down the road toward town. Benny caught up with him.

The trick to going for a jog was to remember to run like a human. It took focus. And practice. Otherwise, you got inside your own head and when you looked out again, you realized you'd just set a new record for the 5K. But Cujo had passed as human for a long time — almost completely severed from the shifter world. A lone wolf in all ways. Benny had been a lone wolf, separated from his father's pack, but he'd worked for the Northwest Council of Alphas for many of those years. And he'd lived here with Margarite for more of them. It wasn't until he went to Berkeley to get his PhD that he'd lived in the human world strictly as a human. Even then, he wasn't cut off from shifters. He was on good terms with his father: Went home for holidays. Did jobs for him. It was how he'd ended up at Wolf Harbor working with Cujo as a fitness coach on Stefan's serum project.

And he'd been at Wolf Harbor ever since, first as a lone wolf, then as Hat Island pack. So really, the eight years in Berkeley were the only years he'd really lived completely among humans as a human. And let's face it, you'd have to be seriously weird to be so weird that Berkeley noticed. That thought made him laugh a bit.

Cujo glanced at him. "So the school," he began, and then stopped speaking. Benny frowned. Cujo wasn't connected to the boarding school. His mate Olivia was, however.

"Yes?" Benny said warily.

They hit a running trail not far from Margarite's house. Slowly the stress drained from Benny's muscles, and he was moving freely. His wolf approved. Even being in human form there was no excuse for running badly, his wolf informed him. Benny grinned.

"I need to tell you something, and you're not going to like it," Cujo said, morosely. "But when I was in Paris? I got shanghaied into doing a favor for my previous employer."

Cujo's previous employer was the CIA.

"OK," Benny said cautiously. He was picking up serious anxiety here. What was he going to tell him? The Paris trip had been weeks ago!

"They needed a courier into the Sudan region — ransom money. I'd been requested."

Benny looked at him. "Abraham Haile," Benny guessed. Because who else would request Cujo by name in that region? Abraham Haile was the Chairman of the African Council. He was an old wolf, powerful. Benny hadn't ever met him personally, but he knew his rep.

Cujo nodded. "More than the money — and it was a lot of money — he wanted a favor from me," Cujo said. "And it's not wise — or even possible, really — to tell Abraham Haile no."

Benny stopped in the center of the running path and frowned at Cujo. "Go on."

"He had eight girls who are coming of age — puberty and first shift," Cujo said in a rush, "and he wants them to have the serum and to come to the boarding school."

"What?" Benny shouted. "Cujo, the boarding school doesn't really exist! You know that, right? We've got a half-dozen girls from SE Asia who have shown up mysteriously. We've got the twins from Russia — well they're here, but you know what I mean. And we've got Sarah Johannsen, who's a ringleader for all kinds of mischief. But it's not a school!"

"They have teachers, and they learn things, right?" Cujo asked.

Well, yes, he guessed they did. "So tell Haile we'll send the serum to him."

"I tried that," Cujo said. "They're in the middle of the war zone, Benny. And he was going to move his camp to the coast. He wanted the girls to be safe. Can't say I blame him. They were attacked while I was there."

Benny stared at him. And then someone tugged on his mind — on one of the links in his mind. Margarite? Alarmed, he stopped and turned back. "We're needed," he said tersely.

"Wait," Cujo said. "I'm not done telling you...."

"It will have to wait," Benny said. "Margarite just tugged on our link. And she's been in denial that it even exists. Something's wrong."

Cujo shut his mouth and nodded. He turned back and picked up the pace. Not anything to raise eyebrows, but they now looked like they were training for a race, not out for a leisurely jog. Project that, Benny told himself. He'd learned that trick worked. Think of the story you wanted people to believe, tell it to yourself until you believed it, and then project it.

Worked like a charm. He'd been quite smug about it, until he realized he'd learned that trick in graduate school. It was what pathological liars did. And sociopaths.

And wasn't that just grand?

"Do you know what the problem is?" Cujo asked.

Benny shook his head. "Margarite tugged," he said. "Might be just 'it's time for supper.'"

"Unlikely," Cujo observed.

"No, it's not likely," Benny agreed. For Margarite to use it meant something was seriously wrong. "But Cujo, we've got to clear out that backyard ASAP."

"I know," Cujo said. "I think we send most of them — men and women — to Ayta. She's got the facilities there to put up people. And she's a steady Alpha with centuries of experience. She can handle them. But Benny...."

"Can I be the one to take them?" Benny asked hopefully. He'd like to spend some time with Ayta. They'd been lovers until she took on responsibility for the Odessa pack. He missed her.

And he'd better not let that thought seep out to Margarite, he thought ruefully. Or he'd be sitting on the curb without a stitch to his name.

"Benny, you've got to let me finish," Cujo said desperately. "I promised Olivia I'd tell you today."

They rounded the last corner and pulled into sight of Margarite's house. Benny's heart sank.

"Shit," he muttered, as he stared at the motorcycles in front of Margarite's house. "It's going to have to wait, Cujo," Benny said. "We've got trouble." He slowed to a walk as they approached a dozen men who were milling about. Not all of them belonged to the bikes. Some of them were Margarite's men. He could see Seth, Margarite's Second, facing off with someone. Seth had two others of Margarite's men standing with him, and they were between the bikers and the house.

Margarite came striding out of the house toward the men. Benny's only surprise was that she wasn't already in the thick of things.

"What the hell?" he heard Cujo mutter.

Benny sighed. He squared his shoulders, and dropped his filters, letting his own personal dominance show. Most of the time, he was just Benny, an easy-going, charming man. It was easier that way. And he had more fun.

But sometimes, charm didn't get the job done.

"I'm here," he said sourly, pitching his voice to carry to the men ahead of him. "What are you doing here, Ryder?"

The men stilled, and then the bikers parted, leaving one of their own standing there with his arms folded across his chest, and a mocking smile on his face.

"You heard from Dad lately?" he asked.

Benny felt something settle inside of him. Yes, this was the problem that had him on edge so much lately, he conceded to his wolf. Not Ryder. But his father? Yeah. His father was a problem.

"Dad?" he heard Cujo mutter under his breath.

"Come and meet my brother," Benny said with a sigh. "The shit has truly hit the fan, it appears."

Chapter 2

Day 155 of the re-emerged Hat Island pack, Friday, Nov. 8, Hat Island

Abby Stafford had plans for the day. For one whole day, she wasn't going to be Professor Stafford, chair of the anthropology department at Seattle University. She wasn't going to be the mate to Akihiro Tanaka, Alpha of the Tanaka pack, Seattle's large and unwieldly pack. She wasn't even going to be Alpha of the Hat Island pack.

Well, she never completely got away from that last, but she was going to try.

"I want to go out on the boat," she told her pack Second Jake Lewis over breakfast at the lodge. The room was full of pack members, but they didn't intrude. Didn't physically intrude, she amended, because they were always there in her mind. She tried not to let it show that it wore on her. But for a woman who once would go days without talking to anyone but her dogs, having all these people lurking in her brain was hard. Sometimes it seemed impossible to endure one more minute. But there were people depending on her, and so she sucked it up. Jake took her for a boat ride then, or a run on the beach. Or to the University of Washington research libraries. She hadn't been there in a long time. She sighed and put it aside.

"I want to get as far away from the island as necessary to be by ourselves," Abby said. "Think we can do that?"

Jake gave her a half-smile that made her want to jump his bones. The smile was part affection, part amusement — but it did something to her, no lie. Even at 8 a.m. in the morning.

She loved looking at him. He was over 6 feet tall, with brown skin that reflected his mix of heritages — Black, Filipino, and Yakama Indian — and a body that had been sculpted by 40 years in the Marine Corps. Shifter genetics sure had given the Marines something to work with, no lie. He wore his black hair almost military short — mostly because it curled when it got longer, and for some reason that seemed to embarrass him.

All shifters exuded a vitality that came from good genes and healthy bodies. Abby thought she could almost spot a shifter now by that health and well-being. And there was something about their walk — animalistic seemed insulting, maybe predatory? She wondered if she had it now, and she thought maybe she did. That might be what made her colleagues at the university wary of her transformation — she looked younger, but that could be camouflaged by clothing and passed off as a result of a summer at a health spa. And a new lover, she thought with a roll of her eyes. That rumor had spread like wildfire through her department. Nothing like a bunch of old professors for gossip.

But the change in how she moved? That probably did explain a lot. Well, that problem was solved now — one of the things she needed to talk to Jake about.

"Are you done staring at me?" Jake asked, amused. "Did you even hear my answer?"

She started guiltily. No, she hadn't. "No," she admitted. "Was it yes, we can go?"

"Of course, Alpha," he teased. "What other answer would your Second give you but yes?"

Her eyes lowered as she responded to the innuendo in that comment. Maybe they could go back to bed, she thought speculatively. Jake laughed. "No," he said. "You said a day on the boat, and that's where we're going. So eat up."

Abby obediently returned to her breakfast. She needed a lot of food, a lot more than she had ever eaten before. But she was burning a lot of calories, too. She stopped that thought. If she didn't monitor her thoughts, she was going to broadcast her news to the entire pack. And the whole point of today was to talk to Jake first.

She saw his eyes narrow, and she guessed he'd caught that thought. She sighed. She was never alone in her head. That freaked her out more than she wanted anyone to know. She started tightening the barriers in her mind. She sent out a soothing message — mama cares — to the pack so they wouldn't panic. She'd caused a panic a time or two by disappearing from their awareness. She was learning to give them a heads up. If she knew in advance, she did, anyway.

She tightened down the flow to the inner circle, and to all the other bonds and links that lived in her brain. She was especially vigilant about her mate bond with Akihiro — and whatever that link was with Akihiro's Second, Haru Ito. Today was something just for her and Jake.

She did her best with the link to Benny Garrison. Since she wasn't really sure where that link was, it was hard to close off. And didn't that thought sum up the weirdness that was her life these days?

Her link to Okami Yoshida was easy enough to find, but she had no idea how to close off a link that looked more like a wide river bed than the strings the rest of the links and bonds did. But if there was anyone she could trust to keep his mouth shut, it was Okami.

Besides, he probably already knew. His mate was Yui Ito Yoshida, the island's nurse. Among other things. But Abby assumed what Yui knew, Okami did. Actually, she assumed anything *she* knew, Okami probably knew as well.

There was a sense of amusement at that thought — Okami. She often amused him, she feared.

Abby finished her coffee. "Come on," she said happily, her brain as much her own as possible. "I asked for a picnic lunch."

She headed to the kitchen with Jake padding along behind her. She'd grown used to his presence at her back — literally. He walked behind her, just slightly to the left. In the early days, she'd wanted him at her side, but she'd been overruled by Jake and her own wolf. Now, five months later, it felt right. So much had changed in five months, she thought ruefully. But if she had mixed emotions about most of it, this was one thing she was clear about: she loved Jake Lewis and she'd protect their bond with all she had.

She just hoped her news today didn't damage it. She ignored Jake's narrowed focus at her thought. She had planned out how she wanted this to go and having a meltdown — hers or his — in the lodge kitchen wasn't a part of it.

Jake picked up the picnic basket, and they headed down the back pathway to the boathouse. It was a typical western Washington day in November. Cool, overcast, misty. She sighed happily. She'd been born and raised in the Puget Sound area and loved days like this. Oh, sure, warm summer days were good too. But this was a perfect winter day. Not too cold. No wind or heavy rain in the forecast. Just saturated cool air that made her breathe deep and enjoy the feel of it.

And the landscape was turned to shades of green and gray — emerald dark gray for the pine and spruce on the island, a dark, almost polished green on the shrubs below them, and dark blue-gray waters of Puget Sound meeting a lighter blue-gray sky. There were a light frosting of whitecaps on the water — not enough to be a problem in the cruiser, although she wouldn't take a kayak out on them.

She picked up the pace.

The resort cruiser was perfect for an outing like this. The back was open, but there was a cabin as well. They might need that if the weather turned nasty. And it might, in spite of the forecast for a mild day. Especially out on the water, things could change in a heartbeat.

Jake put the picnic basket in the cabin and started up the boat. She could feel his pleasure. He'd spent much time in this boat over the last year, but rarely just to go out for the day. He needed the escape too. She needed to take better care of her Second.

"I'm fine, Alpha," Jake said out loud. "There's no place I'd rather be."

She smiled at him. She was wearing an oversized army jacket that someone had left lying around the lodge. She liked it for its pockets. Women's clothes didn't have enough pockets, damn it. She had on blue jeans, black boat shoes, and a bulky black turtleneck sweater — about the same clothes Jake had on, actually. Pacific Northwest causal, courtesy of REI and Costco.

"How far out do you want to go?" Jake asked.

What she wanted was to run away until they couldn't see land anymore. But that was a long way. Hat Island was tucked in among bigger islands south of Whidbey Island, in what was called Possession Bay — a name that always amused her. Amused only her, apparently. She'd tried to explain that werewolves were thought to be possessed, and wasn't it funny that here they were.... But let's face it — if you had to explain the joke, it wasn't much of one.

So they weren't going to get out of sight of land today. The real ocean was hundreds of miles farther west. "North," she said. She saw the southern bay frequently on her commute into Seattle to teach. "Oak Harbor?"

Jake nodded, and gradually increased the speed of the boat.

She stood next to him topside and smiled with pleasure at the spray as it hit her face. She knew outsiders thought people like her were weird. They bemoaned the wet, damp, rainy days of the Puget Sound. But then there were people like her — born and raised to it. Besides, standing next to Jake while he steered was worth it.

He glanced down at her and smiled. "Yeah, this isn't really the kind of weather I'm used to," he said. "East-sider, here."

Jake had been born and raised on the Yakama reservation in the southcentral part of the state. That area was steppe, high desert. Low rainfall, sagebrush, and cold, windy winters. A much harsher climate indeed.

"And I spent most of my career in the deserts and mountains of places like Afghanistan," he added. "Maybe that's why I enjoy this —

it's refreshing. And different enough that there's no bad memories. But five months of gray wears on me, I'm not going to lie."

Abby nodded. "Oh, I'll be complaining about the gray days too, soon enough," she agreed. "But I need this."

An hour later Abby could see Oak Harbor in the distance. "Here," she decided, and Jake obligingly slowed down. He shut off the motor and dropped anchor.

"OK, lady," he said, tugging her toward the seating area in the back. "Time to spill it. Your thoughts are loud, but not particularly informative." He pulled out cushions from inside the benches, and then tugged her into one of the corners. She settled into his embrace, happily, her head nestled against his shoulder. Maybe she didn't need to tell him today, she thought. Maybe they could just enjoy a peaceful day like this together.

But she knew this was unlikely to happen again anytime soon. And her secret was going to get out. It had been a week. She was surprised it hadn't already leaked.

"Abby," Jake said with exasperation. "Just spit it out."

She laughed. Then took a deep breath, and blurted, "I'm going to have a baby."

When Jake didn't respond, Abby pulled back a bit so she could peer up at him. He was staring at her open-mouthed. She couldn't get a read on him. How was he taking this?

"Jake?" she said uncertainly.

"Are you happy about this? Do you want a baby?" he asked finally.

She smiled and nodded. "I'm very happy about this," she assured him. "I know it will mean many changes lay ahead. I know it affects everything. But yes, I want this baby."

He pulled her onto his lap. She smiled. She was a tall, broad-shouldered woman, and even though she wasn't as heavy as she'd been six months ago, she still wasn't a lightweight. Being held like this was a rare thing in her life, and she treasured the feeling.

"So tell me, then," he invited. "I thought all of the cohorts in Stefan's study had to be post-menopause. Start there? And give me a bit to absorb this! How long have you known?"

"A week," she said. "That spa day last Friday? Yui and Emiyo had it planned — get me relaxed, and then make me take a pregnancy test. Apparently, shifter genes distinguish between menopause as a natural thing, and a hysterectomy as something to be fixed. Remember Rose and Jenna?"

Cujo had brought them back to Hat Island two weeks ago — a rescued made-shifter and her baby.

"And that got them thinking," Jake guessed.

"Yes," Abby replied. "I guess all that energy you all send my way in a crisis does more than rev up my libido — it speeds up my healing as well." She held out her left arm, not that there was anything to see, layered with the sweater and coat. But that was the point. There wasn't anything to see on the arm either. "Remember when my arm was mauled in that dominance fight in Odessa? It would have left me with bad scars and probably damage to the arm's function if I'd been still human. Instead it was almost healed in hours — fast even for a shifter. And now you can't even see that it happened. Yui says that energy did the same thing for my uterus."

Abby peered anxiously at Jake's face. She still couldn't tell what he was feeling.

"It's not something I ever expected," she said, a bit uncertainly. "I knew having children was unlikely even before the car accident that resulted in the hysterectomy."

Well it hadn't been a car accident, although she'd believed it was at the time. A shifter had tried to change her the old-fashioned way but couldn't get her to shift and heal. Believing she was dying, he'd walked away and left her there to die. Even now, knowing much more about all of it, she felt a pang of hurt that a man she thought loved her could do that. She'd made peace with all of it, even with the shifter, she reminded herself. But still....

"After that, I had to face the fact I was never going to have children," Abby said. And quite frankly, she'd been in her 40s anyway. Thinking they were still an option had been denial on her part to start with. "Part of what triggered the depression, I guess."

After the 'car accident' she'd lost interest in a lot of things — in living really.

Four years later, she'd seen an email about a free summer at a fitness spa as part of a research project on a supplement that would make you feel younger, healthier. She'd clutched at it as if it was her last hope. She was 52, and she felt decades older, and life had been kind of gray — not unlike today, she thought with amusement.

Well, things had changed. Life was most certainly not gray and dull now.

"So, I'm pregnant." She said it again, to make it more real. "I'm going to have a baby." She took a deep breath and tackled some of the easier issues first. "I've already put in for a sabbatical at the university — six months to take on a consulting project for a non-profit looking at the role of story-telling in oral cultures."

He smiled at that. That project actually existed. Benny Garrison and a couple of shifters from Russia were experimenting with how to capture the stories that shifters passed down orally — and from mind-to-mind as well, although obviously that part wasn't publicly known. Keepers of Stories like Benny and Ayta were increasingly rare. Abby was fascinated by the whole phenomena and what it meant for shifters, and humans, alike.

"Focus, Abby," Jake said.

She grinned at him, because she had drifted off to think about an intriguing question, completely unrelated to the topic at hand. She did it a lot — that's why they call us absent-minded professors, she thought with amusement. That might even be redundant.

"Abby!" Jake sounded exasperated.

What had she been talking about? Oh, the sabbatical. "Right, sabbatical," she said. "I asked for next semester off. I'll probably get it. The university president has been trying to get me out of there all fall. Now he can. If they won't give it to me paid, I'll take unpaid. Or quit if I have to. I hope I don't have to go that far."

"I guess pregnancy would be hard to hide from your colleagues," he agreed. "Who all knows about this?"

"Yui and Emiyo," she said. "And now you. I wanted you to be the first to know." She looked up at him again, anxious now. "Jake? Are you OK with this?"

He hugged her tight. "Of course, I'm 'OK' with this," he said. "Stunned. And for once, I'm the one who gets to say this — I have questions."

She giggled, because really, that was her usual line. She always had questions. She had a few about this pregnancy — a whole new list just for this. Might as well address some of the biggies.

"So, I don't know who the father is," she said baldly. "I never expected this. Didn't know it was even possible. So no birth control. And Yui said there's no way to test for paternity, not unless Stefan can do it when he gets back from Oregon. She said it's not something shifters do — send off for a paternity test or for the sex of a baby? Too big of a risk that someone would notice the genetic anomalies of a shifter heritage. So, unless Stefan can do it in-house, we're going to learn both of those things the old-fashioned way — at birth."

She took a deep breath and continued steadily. She'd rehearsed this in her mind in the last couple of days, but it still was hard to get out. It made her feel vulnerable. "In those first few days after I called the pack, and we were fighting for our lives, my wolf would show me this picture of you and me," she said. "I wanted a partner and lover, remember? She said Second and... protector." Actually, her wolf had said Second and mate. But that wasn't ever going to be their reality. She regretted that sometimes, but really, they might as well be mated, as tightly bonded as they were — Alpha and Second. And she couldn't love him more. So she'd come to accept this reality, just like she had all the other pieces. Once you fall down the rabbit hole and meet a rabbit with a watch, the caterpillar and mad hatter didn't seem all that strange.

"Can I show you the image?" she asked. He nodded, and she opened up their bond wider and sent through the image of a pregnant Abby, with Jake by her side. "I tried to tell her there would be no cub, but she insisted. I stopped arguing. And it turns out she was right."

"And what does she say about this?" Jake asked, somewhat amused. He and his wolf weren't separate like she was with hers. They didn't talk much. Jake had found it pretty amusing that she and her wolf argued.

Well, her wolf was a snarky bitch, Abby thought. Her wolf felt smug at the description. "She seems uninterested in the paternity issue," Abby said frankly. "Mine, I said. She corrected me, 'ours.' Hers and mine. And yours — as the protector. Are you OK with that?" She asked again, because his silence through their bond was unnerving. She couldn't get a read on him at all.

"I am," he assured her. "I will always be here, Abby. Always your protector. Baby or no baby, I will never be anywhere but at your side. But there are a lot of ramifications here. So be really clear with me. Do you want this baby?"

"More than anything," Abby said fervently. She hesitated. "I imagine a small boy who looks like you," she said softly. "All stubborn and strong. I know the baby might not be yours. And there's no potential father I wouldn't be proud to have a child with. But when I daydream about the future, that's who I see. A small, much loved, Jake Lewis."

Because that was the elephant in the room — she might as well get it out there. The baby could be Jake's. The odds were in his favor, actually, since there were few days when they hadn't had sex, she thought with amusement. She didn't think frequency was what determined paternity. So, it could be Akihiro's. Or it could be Cujo's or even Benny's.

"It will be a much-loved child, no matter who the biological father is," she added.

"Yes," he said. "By me as well as by you. You need to believe that, Abby. Your wolf is right. Your child is my child. Mine to protect — no matter who the actual biological father is."

She thought she might black out with relief. That was what she needed to hear. And she knew he wasn't lying — one of the benefits of their bond. It was almost impossible to lie to each other.

"But it raises all kinds of questions," Jake went on. "Probably a lot of them you don't even know. Call them geo-political questions. Your child will be of interest to a whole lot of people, no matter who the father was. But given the possible fathers? Everyone, and I do mean everyone, will be focused on you and your child, Abby. We will need to discuss that. And to discuss safety issues. I'm glad you're not going to try to continue at the university. That makes it somewhat easier...." He trailed off as if he was thinking about the security issues. So like him, she thought fondly. She just wanted to bask in the pleasure of knowing she was carrying a child, and that this man was going to share that child with her. He was already turning to the practicalities of the situation.

Well, that was why he was pack Second, because he did think security first and foremost. Then she thought about what he had just said. Wait, what? Why would everyone be focused on her child?

"Explain," she ordered, sitting up and looking at him. "Why would anyone care about my child — in what did you call it, 'a geo-political sense?' I mean, the pack will care, right? They'll be happy for me? Won't they?" She was suddenly anxious about all of this. Well, there goes basking in the contentment of a pregnant mother, she thought wryly.

"The pack will be ecstatic," Jake assured her. "An Alpha baby? Of course, they will. Heir to the pack someday. But that's the issue, Abby. Tanaka also has a claim on the child — regardless of whether he is the biological father or not, he's your bonded mate. And Tanaka pack has been needing an heir for a very long time now. Your child? Shifter genetics and dominance is weird." He paused as if he was thinking about how to explain that. She wished he would — he could start with an explanation of her own dominance.

How the hell did she end up this dominant? Her parents weren't — they were human for one thing. And yes, she knew Tanaka's axiom that all women were alpha post-menopause. But she was literally off the charts dominant! She slammed the door on that thought. That wasn't something she thought about, not ever. Not even with all of her links and bonds shut tight like now. She had a locked cabinet in her brain just for that topic.

"So, to some extent, dominance is hereditary," Jake said slowly, as if he was thinking out loud. "I'm very dominant, because my father was. And my grandmother is, right? Which is why pack Alphas are usually succeeded by offspring. But not always. Cujo's family is full of dominant wolves, but not Alphas, at least not until last week."

She nodded. "OK, and I suppose it's like anything else. A person might pop up with dominance unexpectedly."

"Yes," he said. "But that's not the important part of it, Abby. Because dominance is hereditary, and most packs go from an Alpha to one of his offspring, that means an Alpha's offspring is his biggest threat. It's not like a dynasty in medieval Europe or something. Humans have short lives. So a ruler might look to a son as a way to continue power past his own time on the throne. By the time the son is old enough to take power, the ruler is past his own prime and ready to step down. Theoretically anyway. But with shifters? Take Cujo again. His father just became Alpha. He could live another 100 years to reign as Alpha. And Cujo's father isn't even particularly young. Then take Cujo. He's fully mature — in his 60s even — and more than capable of being pack Alpha. And in fact, he's more dominant than his father. His father is always aware that Cujo could take the pack away from him. He has to be. Same with Cujo's brother who became his father's Second. A pack Second is another likely challenger, after all."

"OK," Abby said cautiously. She understood what he was describing. After all it was true of Jake. He'd been banished at 13 — declared a beta wolf — because of his dominance post first shift. He'd been sent off to boarding school and summer camps. His dominance had made him more dominant than his father's acknowledged heir. Probably more dominant than his father. "I get that."

"So Hat Island pack will be thrilled, because we will have a potential heir," Jake said. "And Tanaka will probably be thrilled too — he's wanted to step down for a while, or at least he says he does. I have my doubts, but he's not going to be threatened by a baby, anyway. White Swan pack, my old pack, also has an interest in the child, Abby, because I will be its father — even if not biologically. And a child of ours? Will have dominance off the charts. So that's three packs. If Cujo is the biological father? That's a fourth pack. Or Benny? He's the heir to the Okanogan pack. He doesn't want it, but his father is tired, and wants to lay down the responsibility. If Benny is the biological father? Alpha Garrison could be interested, very interested. And if not the Alphas? Some dissident faction within one of those packs might see a heir as a possible front man for their own causes."

"But that's decades away right?" Abby protested. "I usually don't look much farther into the future than next week."

"You're missing the point," Jake said with a sigh. "I don't want to be the one to alarm you, but here it is. For all of the ones who think they might like to inherit a pack — and that's possibly four packs up for grabs — your baby isn't a potential heir that they might use, he's also a threat to the ambitions of anyone else who is eying those packs. And it's a lot easier to kill a child before first shift, than it is to wait for them to come into their dominance and fight them in a challenge fight someday."

Abby stared at him in horror, her arms wrapping protectively around her belly.

"They would kill a baby?" she whispered. Naive, she chastised herself. She knew better than that. People killed babies all over the world for 'geo-political' reasons.

"Absolutely," Jake said. "And there are plenty of others who would steal that baby because of its potential dominance to raise as their own. And that includes most of the Alphas who will be descending upon Seattle for the World Council meeting in a month, in case you were wondering. Abby, you alone, have upturned a half-dozen packs in the last few months, just by showing up for a meet-and-greet. A baby with your genetics? Coupled with the genetics of any one of those four potential fathers? Dear God, even I quake a bit at the potential."

Abby rocked herself for comfort. Jake pulled her back against him, stretching out along the couch, so that she sat between his legs, and rested against his chest. He wrapped his arms around her, resting them over her own arms still wrapped protectively over her belly. Abby sighed and relaxed. She could spend the rest of her life like this, she thought whimsically.

Her stomach growled. Well, until she got hungry, anyway.

"When are you planning to tell Tanaka?" Jake asked.

"I'd like to wait until after the World Council meeting," she said. "But if what you're describing is remotely true, maybe not."

Jake thought that over. "No, the problem is it might get out before you tell him. And he should hear it from you," he said finally. "But as far as danger goes, the fewer people who know the better."

"And we may need to tell Benny," Abby said, reluctantly. "He's been sending me 'questioning' vibes lately. He's picking up on something, but he's too busy to really grill me over it."

Jake laughed. "He's never that busy," he teased. "He's almost as curious as you are."

"I don't snoop in people's brains!" she protested. Jake laughed harder. "I don't," she grumbled.

"No," Jake agreed. "Because you're curious about ideas and what people think about them. Benny is curious about people. Which is why you're an academic, and he's a psychologist."

Oh, Abby thought. That might be true.

"Maybe the baby will be a girl," she said changing the subject. "And no one will come looking for her for an heir. Except Hat Island's heir."

Jake was silent, just stroking her hair. But she thought he was troubled by that. "They'll want her," he said at last. "Maybe later than a boy. But look at the twins, Abby. If people are kidnapping them because they're supposed to be power batteries or something, what do you think they would do to a daughter of yours?"

"I'd kill them first," Abby said flatly. "All of them. Every damn shifter."

"Abby? Do you think there's something to this power battery thing?" Jake asked.

Abby was silent a moment. Vancouver Alpha Chen had believed some female shifters could act as power batteries that an Alpha could draw on, making him more dominant. He'd thought the twins — one or both of them — were such shifters. So he'd kidnapped them, intending to make them his. She had gotten them free by convincing him that she was such a woman — why go with girls when you could have the real thing? And then she'd proceeded to blast out the minds of 30-plus shifters who were going to gang-rape her — bring her to heel, as shifters called it.

"Okami insisted it was a myth," Abby said. She smiled up at him, but her eyes were troubled. "Can you stand it if I'm an academic for a moment?"

"Always," he promised.

"Well, OK. You know the story of Noah's ark, right?" Abby asked. "People pooh-hooh it and call it a myth. And it is. But, Jake, old cultures all over the world have a similar myth — a great flood that wiped everyone off the earth. Civilizations that never encountered one another. So, a lot of scholars assume that there was some cataclysmic event that people of that period of time explained by a great flood."

"OK," Jake said unencouraging.

"So language is a lot like that," she said. "They tell us things about the past, and the people of the past. Chen had a Chinese word for his power-battery — dònglì diànchí. When Kristina talked to me about it, she had a Russian term for it — *istochnik sily.* Two of the oldest shifter cultures have the concept in their own language. It's not a story they passed to each other, either. It's embedded. So when I got home, I shot off an email to Robert Golde, the Alpha of the Colville pack. He had stories of the pack crossing the land-bridge from Siberia to Russia, remember? I wanted to know if he had ever heard of anything that would translate into power battery, a kind of woman a man could draw dominance from."

She took a deep breath and blew it out. "He called me," she said. "Wanted to know where I'd heard of such a thing. I gave him a brief explanation, and he hung up."

"He what?"

"He hung up, so I called him back, and when he didn't pick up, I called his son," Abby said. This had been Wednesday, and she still didn't know what to make of it. "Tomas promised to check it out and call me back. He had no clue about a power battery and couldn't imagine his father doing that."

"And did he call back?"

"No."

Abby chewed on her cheek. "So I haven't called them again. But I'd say that's an indication that there is a myth that they carried with them — an eon ago. Something. I'm hoping one of them will talk to me but pushing them won't help. So I wait."

"Okami's reaction was similar actually," Jake said, considering it. "He was as forceful as I've ever seen him that it was nothing more than a myth. If it was anyone but Okami, I would have said it scared him."

Abby nodded. "So the Japanese have a 'myth,'" she said steadily. "A myth that the Chinese and Russians have a word for, and a concept that scares the one of the oldest of the Native American shifter packs. So there's something to it. What? I don't know. But a myth doesn't have to be true to be powerful — to be dangerous. People just have to believe it. And to act upon it. Chen had partners — the Chinese Chairman, right? He believes it too. And the two of them were preparing to go to war with Akihiro over the World Council based on their theory that one of the twins is this power battery."

"Didn't someone say that Vuk had tried to breed such a woman?" Jake asked. Anton Vuk — chairman of the World Council for 200-plus years, until Akihiro Tanaka had killed him and stepped into the role four months ago — had been a shifter from the Russian steppe who wanted to rule the world. And for 200 years, he practically had — remaking it into his own image. He'd believed in dominance, and he'd sculpted the pack Alphas of Europe and North America into assholes who believed in it too.

Abby nodded. "And I think there's some truth to that story as well," she said. "I think the twins' mother might have been the woman he bred. A daughter, as a matter of fact. She escaped. And the reason that Chen thought the twins were possibly these power batteries, is because she was their mother." Abby swallowed. She had nightmares about Anton Vuk. She couldn't imagine what the twins' mother had. "And I think Vuk was not only the twins' grandfather but their father," she added quietly.

Jake's jaw muscle spasmed as he clamped down hard on his reaction to that. She had to reach for some self-control herself. Did she think that bastard had raped his own daughter looking to breed some mythical power-battery? Yeah, she did.

"Should we have left the girls in Vancouver then?" Jake asked.

Abby shrugged. "They're at Margarite's with Benny and Cujo. They're as safe there as they would be here — Chen kidnapped them from Hat Island after all."

Jake nodded.

"Hungry?" Abby asked with a forced smile. "And then? Can we just think happy thoughts about a baby?"

"Lunch," Jake agreed. "I might put out a fishing line. And we can sit here for as long as you like."

Chapter 3

Day 155 of the re-emerged Hat Island pack, Friday, Nov. 8, Vancouver, B.C.

"Tell your old lady we're cool here, bro," Ryder Garrison said, deliberately provocative.

Benny got very still. His brother was an idiot to try provoking Margarite's men — or Margarite herself. He looked his brother over. Black biker leathers — pants and jacket over a black T. A silver chain ran from a belt loop to his pants' pockets. He had a silver bracelet on. His brown, nearly black, hair was long and pulled back into a ponytail, but the wind had tugged some of loose. He was standing next to his bike, an Indian, of course. It was new since Benny had last seen his brother — this was an all-black version — a Scout, Benny realized on closer inspection. A cool bike.

Benny focused on Margarite. She was the only one who mattered right now. "Alpha Lewis, I apologize for the uncouth manners of my brother," Benny said formally. "Although if you want to blast him for his rudeness, I'm happy to watch. And if you want someone to teach him some manners, I'll be delighted to assist."

Margarite Lewis was amused, he knew through their bond, although none of it showed. She examined Ryder Garrison as if she was planning to buy livestock. Ryder kept a half-mocking smile on his face, but Benny saw he'd gotten his message — Margarite Lewis was a pack Alpha, and a formidable opponent. Ryder should proceed cautiously.

"Pretty," Margarite said conversationally. Benny choked as his brother flushed. "Well, bring him inside. We'll see if we want to keep him or throw him back until he grows up a bit."

She looked over the other bikers with disfavor. "More unkempt young men? Add them to the collection in back," she ordered. "Cujo? Could you oversee that before joining us inside? Alefosio? Perhaps you could help Cujo escort our guests to the backyard?"

Alefosio nodded. "This way," he said, and headed toward the back yard. "I believe there's some barbeque underway for lunch." Cujo gestured for the bikers to follow. Ryder gave them a brief nod, and the six men went quietly. Two women were left by the bikes, looking after their men uncertainly.

"Perhaps the women could join the other women inside?" Benny suggested before Ryder could invite them along. "The backyard might be a bit much."

Margarite nodded, and Benny walked the two women toward her. "Stay quiet," he said under his breath. "Margarite won't tolerate insolence of any kind."

"She's really an Alpha?" one asked anxiously. "A real pack Alpha? A woman?"

Benny nodded. "She's a real pack Alpha," he assured her. "And she's just as touchy as any others you may have met."

The woman nodded. Both were shifters. Ryder occasionally had humans in his MC, but not today. Not even the women. And six men? That wasn't all of his men. He wondered where the rest of them were, and why only six with him?

Six, he thought sourly. Abby had theories about numbers and their significance in cultures. She said six was important in shifter pack formation — the size of a hunting pack. An Alpha plus six guards could take on almost anything. Four guards were more of an honor guard.

Benny hated when Abby's theories bore out. Why didn't shifters know these things about themselves? Abby said it was instinctive on their part, and Benny didn't like that either.

Margarite was leading the way toward her private sitting room. Benny detoured to the dining room where most of the women were. "These women were turned, some of them recently," he said quietly.

The woman he didn't know flinched. Interesting.

"We're still getting things sorted out for them, he continued. "I'm going to introduce you to a shifter named Jessie. She's been running group therapy and orientation for the women. She may put you to work, if you don't mind."

"What's your name?" Benny asked the one who had flinched. The other one he knew, knew well, as a matter of fact.

"Brenda," the woman replied. They were both looking around the room in curiosity.

Benny smiled at the other. "Maggie, it's good to see you," he said sincerely. She patted his arm. Benny gave them a once over. Tight leather pants, high-heeled black boots, black leather jackets, tight V-neck Ts. He shrugged. They looked good in them — and they looked like what they were, bikers. Jessie would just have to deal. Knowing her, she would probably be delighted.

He made the introductions and left, almost at a run. No telling what mischief Ryder could get up to unsupervised.

Cujo caught him in the hallway. "Brother?" he asked, falling into step with him.

"You didn't think my father had been celibate the last 40 years, did you?" Benny asked.

"I haven't given any thought to your father at all," Cujo said with a shrug. "Much less to his sex life."

Benny snorted. "Ryder is 42," he said. "He rebelled against Dad at 18 and struck out on his own. A year later, he showed back up in Okanogan with a motorcycle club. A mix of shifters — lone wolves — and humans. Dad threw a fit about the humans. Said Ryder risked a first rule violation, and Dad would put him down himself if he did."

Cujo grimaced.

"Yeah," Benny said. "So, I came home, established a few rules for his club, and then rode with him for a year. Dad has changed a couple of men over the years. Oops, as Ryder calls them. That was one of the rules." Then Ryder had decided he needed to go into the military after 9/11. He'd come home changed. And the motorcycle club, MC, was waiting for him.... Since then it expanded; Ryder wasn't the only shifter who had demons chasing him post-war.

"Wait," Cujo said. "You rode with a MC for a year? An outlaw shifter MC? And you never told us?"

Benny rolled his eyes. "Cujo, I've done a lot of shit I don't share," he said. "Not to mention, how should I know what gossip you've heard and what you haven't?"

And wasn't that the truth, he thought as he opened the door.

Benny had ridden with Ryder while he was still an intelligencer for the Northwest Council of Alphas — before he found out what the Council was really doing with the information he collected. He quit the Council, and he'd almost returned to the MC. Margarite had invited him to stay here, and that had seemed like a better option.

But this wasn't the first time Margarite had met Ryder. Benny snorted. She'd turned him away at the gate then, too. When was that? Six years ago? About that. Benny had left for Berkeley and Ryder hadn't known. Then he tried to charm Margarite.... Benny grinned.

"You're sure grumpy these days," Cujo observed. "I think I liked you better as the carefree playboy."

Benny rolled his eyes. "I liked me better as the carefree playboy," he muttered as he opened the door to the sitting room. And he was grumpy, he admitted. And sour and upset. And all kinds of other ugly emotions. He tried to keep it shut away from anyone who might be lurking in his brain.

There had been advantages to those carefree, lone-wolf days. Not that he would go back.

He didn't think so anyway.

Inside the sitting room, Seth was serving wine to anyone who wanted it. It was only lunch time — wine was acceptable, Benny guessed. He might need something stronger to get through this meeting.

"Ryder, why are you here?" Benny asked abruptly, interrupting the silence. Margarite raised one eyebrow but she didn't say anything about his rudeness.

"Do you know where Dad is?" Ryder asked. He sipped the wine, and then set it down on the edge of the bar. Benny saw the back of his jacket had the same colors and patch — Ryder's Wolf Pack. He'd helped design that sucker. A way to tweak the powers that be — including their father.

"No," Benny said, focusing back on Ryder's question. "I don't. And I wish I did. But I haven't wanted to ask too many questions in case his pack didn't know he was gone. He is gone, right?"

"He's gone," Ryder agreed. "And his pack knows. They're freaking out, by the way. The whole region is in an uproar. Some unexplainable wolf attacks. Increased violence. The headlines of the newspaper were full of it."

Benny picked up Ryder's wine and slugged it back. No use letting it go to waste. Seth poured him his own glass, and he took a big swallow of it. Hard to get drunk as a shifter, but he'd give it a try. "Why were you up there?" he asked.

Ryder looked around the room. Benny glanced around. There were two others of Margarite's loose affiliation of a pack — men Jake had termed patriarchs, heads of large family groups — and two others of Margarite's men, John and Harmon. And Cujo. Cujo had staked a position by the door and was slouched against the wall. The others were milling around in the center of the room, while Margarite leaned against the bar. Seth was never more than an arm's distance from her.

And he had positioned himself near her too, Benny realized, as if Ryder was a potential threat. Was he?

Ryder's eyes narrowed as he studied the configuration. Well, Ryder probably had more brawling experience than all of them put together. Even Cujo? Maybe not Cujo, Benny conceded. But assess a crowd in a bar? Yeah, Ryder could do that. And then know just where to toss the match and make the room explode.

Please don't do that here, he pleaded silently.

"I don't know all these people," Ryder said, not challenging, just matter-of-fact. Margarite glanced around the room.

"My people," she said. "I vouch for them."

"And I'm Cujo Brown," Cujo said. "I'm part of the same pack Benny is."

Ryder glanced his way. Recognized the name, did he?

"I'd heard you were part of a pack, now," Ryder said, turning back to Benny. "The one with the female Alpha? Can't imagine doing that myself. What would you do with a female Alpha?" And then he snickered. "Same thing you do with any woman, I guess. Right?"

There was silence. Whelp, there was the match to the fire, Benny thought, torn between being amused and appalled. The two patriarchs were obviously appalled. Margarite's men were livid at the disrespect — even though Benny knew Margarite might make the same crack herself. Benny sighed. Was it possible to get more than one foot in your mouth at a time?

"Did you miss when I introduced Margarite?" Benny asked. "This is her house, her pack, and she is the Alpha here." He was watching Ryder closely. Ryder knew. Deliberate provocation, then.

"You didn't answer my question," Benny said, changing the subject back to that. What was Ryder up to? "Why were you up in the Okanogan?"

"You trust these people with Dad's secrets?" Ryder asked.

Benny nodded. He didn't think most of them would care about their father's secrets at all.

Ryder frowned, and now Benny grew worried. What did Ryder know that Benny didn't?

"Alpha? Could I talk to my brother in my rooms alone?" Benny said, returning to his earlier courteous formal tones. Old wolves could be touchy, and Margarite was a very old wolf.

"Perhaps that would be best," Margarite agreed slowly. "Your father just might have secrets we shouldn't hear."

Benny schooled his face to not show alarm — or curiosity. Did Margarite know his father?

Probably, he conceded. Margarite roamed the Northwest. Roamed the world really. He wondered suddenly what becoming Alpha was going to do to that. But she probably *had* been up in the Okanogan, although she tended to focus on packs with families and women. Hell, she could have met his father in Southeast Asia a century ago. Who knew?

"Perhaps you all will want to head to lunch and we can join you there shortly," Benny suggested. When Margarite gave him a short nod of permission, Benny herded his brother out the door. He gestured with his head to Cujo who fell into place beside him.

"You've got some explaining to do," Benny muttered at his brother.

"Needed to get you alone," Ryder murmured back.

"And you couldn't just say that?" Benny replied with exasperation. Manipulative little bastard.

"She needed to throw us out," Ryder said. "Or she'd be pissy."

He might be right, Benny conceded as he opened the door to the suite he and Cujo shared. He'd moved in here after Abby and Jake had left, even though he often slept in Margarite's rooms. He carefully tightened his own barriers at his link with Margarite.

"Brothers?" Cujo asked once they were inside the suite. "Not the same mother, I take it?"

Ryder snorted. "And what was your first clue?" he asked sardonically. Benny chewed his cheek to keep from laughing at Cujo's expression. He was used to being treated with more deference than that. "No, my mother is Colville," Ryder added.

Benny looked at his younger brother. They might have the same father, but Cujo was right — they looked nothing alike. Benny was slimmer, and he had the soft golden skin tones of his Cambodian mother. She'd died giving birth — not unusual for human women giving birth to a shifter baby. He had memories of a series of Cambodian women who had helped his father raise him. He assumed his mother looked like them — sometimes it was hard to remember it wasn't his mother he was recalling.

But Ryder's mother was Colville. Norma had been Benny's high school guidance counselor — probably the biggest reason Benny had managed to graduate and go to college, as a matter of fact. And Ryder favored her — the dark hair, dark eyes, brown skin. He was taller than most Colvilles, thanks to their father's genes, however. At just 6-foot, both he and Ryder were shorter than Cujo — their father was too, for that matter. But Ryder was broader through the shoulder and chest than Benny. Genetic heritage, mostly, but while Benny practiced Muay Thai, Ryder was more into weights — manhandling a motorcycle took some upper-body strength. Genetics wasn't everything, Benny thought, before pulling his mind back to more important issues.

"So, what's going on?" Benny asked. Cujo got out beers and handed them around, not even bothering to ask.

"I got a call from Mom's neighbor," Ryder said. "So, we went through Omak — we're heading down to California for the winter, right? We swung through. Damned cold to be riding bikes through there now. But...."

Ryder paced restlessly. He tipped the bottle of beer up and chugged it down. "Someone attacked Mom," he said bluntly.

"What? And the pack didn't protect her?" Benny asked. The situation with Norma George Garrison was tricky. Shortly after Ryder went through first shift, their father had 'died' and returned as a nephew to express his condolences and act as a 'big brother' to Ryder.

Norma thought she was a widow. And for all practical purposes she was. She had to be 70, by now, an elderly woman living in a small town on the reservation she grew up on. She lived a quiet life, surrounded by her books, her art, her extended family and tribe, and the visits of generations of students she'd helped. Who the hell would attack her?

"Benny, the attack was *by* a pack member," Ryder said grimly.

Benny stared at him. "Are you sure? Surely, they know she's under the Alpha's protection," he said slowly.

"They know," Ryder said. "Mom was roughed up, but not seriously hurt. But at 70, even that is serious enough. So I tracked the wolf down, and I...." He shrugged.

And he'd killed him, Benny finished silently. Well, he would have too.

"But the pack is out of control," Ryder said. "You know it's unstable at best. And near as I can tell, Dad has been gone six months. No one's sure about that. No one seemed to know much of anything."

"And the pack Second?" Benny asked, which was the question he'd been trying to figure out without actually asking up there. "Is it still Titus Black?"

Ryder nodded. "I couldn't find him," he said. "My pack bond says he's still alive. But I don't know where. He might be with Dad. My bonds don't tell me much more than that they're both alive, and still in power. I think that's part of the problem — no one can challenge

Dad for Alpha, because he's not there. Attacking Mom was a way to flush him out, I think."

Benny considered that and nodded. "Not a good way," he said dryly. "Since the wolf ended up dead."

Ryder shrugged. "Suicide by cop, really," he said. "The shifter was practically insane by the time I found him. He was holed up in a cabin that hadn't been tended to in a long time and trying to drink enough beer to stay comatose. He said without an Alpha he might as well be dead."

Ryder hesitated, then said softly, "I almost didn't recognize him. It was Oscar, Benny."

Benny was silent. He remembered Oscar, a quiet Vietnam vet, who had frequent hallucinations that he was back in Vietnam. Having an Alpha had steadied him, he'd said once.

"Someone else did the planning," Benny said. "No way Oscar came up with that on his own."

Ryder nodded. "He wouldn't say," he said. "He said he was ashamed of what he'd done, and deserved to die, but he wasn't going to rat out his fellow soldiers."

Benny winced. "Fellow soldiers? Hallucination? Or reality?"

"I dunno," Ryder said. "I spent some time visiting others up there. No knows what's going on. Everyone is afraid, Benny. And off kilter. We need to find Dad and get him back. Or you need to go up there and take over as Alpha."

Benny was shaking his head before Ryder even finished that last sentence. "I'm not pack," he pointed out. "Not Okanogan pack, anyway. And I'm never going to be Alpha of any pack, much less that one. You, on the other hand, are Okanogan pack."

Ryder laughed. "Yeah, and how is that going to work? If they can't stand Dad being gone for six months, what would they do when the demons hit hard, and I can't...." He didn't finish the sentence. Ryder went to the small refrigerator and helped himself to another beer. He slugged it back.

"Where is Dad?" Ryder asked, not looking at either of them. That last had been too revealing. "You're the spy. Why don't you know?"

"Intelligencer," Benny corrected. "Ex-intelligencer, at that." He blew out air through his lips and considered the question.

Someone knocked on the door, and Seth stuck his head in. "Margarite says come to lunch, and then you all need to come up with a plan to get those boys out of her backyard. She's at wits' end. The women? Not so bad. But those men?" He shook his head.

Benny wanted to scream. Why was that his problem? He and Cujo stared at each other.

"My men?" Ryder asked, startled. "Are they causing problems?"

"Not particularly," Seth said. "But we've got dozens of other men back there. And another neighbor just called Margarite to ask what the hell was going on?"

Cujo looked like a lightbulb had gone on, however, and Benny grimaced. Cujo's smart ideas were dangerous — literally so, sometimes. And he still needed to know more about what Cujo had been talking about earlier. Girls from Haile's pack coming to school on Hat Island?

Not going to happen.

"I have an idea," Cujo said at the same time as Ryder asked bewildered, "Why do you have dozens of men — shifters I assume — in the backyard?"

"Lunch," Benny said. "And Cujo, you can explain why there are dozens of men in back — before you share your latest bright idea. And don't think I've forgotten about Haile's girls, either."

Cujo actually did a good job of summarizing the destruction of the Vancouver pack, the herd of young men the former pack Alpha had recruited to build into an army, and the women he'd turned into shifters to 'reward' the men. By the time he was done, they'd gone through the buffet line, and were at a table with Seth and Margarite. Not by his choice, but Seth had been determined. And for a man who had been contentedly living with Margarite for decades, the man had more dominance than Benny remembered. Well, Benny had more dominance than he usually showed too.

"So, we've got to move some people," Cujo finished. "And Benny and I have got to get back to Hat Island — today if possible."

They did? Benny glared at Cujo, but he didn't elaborate.

"So, I suggest, we hire Ryder's men to escort Margarite, the new women shifters, and probably a couple of dozen of Chen's recruits to Ayta in Odessa. You could probably take some of the women on up to my mom and sister in Hayden Lake. Having Ryder's men at your command means better control over Chen's recruits."

"Does it?" Margarite asked, looking at Ryder. "Can I trust you and your men?"

Ryder started to answer, but Cujo interrupted. "Not Ryder, unfortunately," he said. "Ryder needs to go talk to Abby."

"I do?" Ryder said. "Why do I need to talk to your female Alpha?"

"Because she's also the Chairman of the Northwest Council of Alphas," Cujo said. "And that problem we were just talking about? That's going to land in her lap."

Ryder frowned. "I thought Johannsen was Chairman?"

"You're out of date," Benny said. "Where have you been?"

"We did the Bike to Prudhoe Bay run this year," Ryder said. At their blank looks, he elaborated, "It's a thing. Bikers from all over the world ride the Dalton Highway from Anchorage to Prudhoe Bay on the Arctic Ocean. Roughest road in the world, some say — mostly because a lot of it is north of the Arctic Circle. It's close to a thousand miles, usually takes a week to do. Some of the most remote and beautiful country in the world. But you can only do it in July and August — or you're likely to get snow."

The rest of them stared at him in appalled silence. "It's a thing," Ryder repeated with a shrug. "So anyway, we've been in Alaska and the Yukon all summer, and we were slowly moving south toward warmer weather when I got that call about Mom."

"Where is the rest of your Club?" Benny asked, absorbing the fact that Ryder probably hadn't heard about anything of significance these last few months. Well, he'd heard about Abby. But Benny didn't think you could get remote enough to not have heard that gossip.

Shifters gossiped. Abby could call it an oral-based culture all she liked, but the truth was, shifters liked to gossip. It wasn't like they could have newspapers or something.

"I left most of them at a campground north of Vancouver," Ryder answered. "I didn't figure showing up with 30 bikers was going to be welcome."

"No shit," Seth muttered, and then reddened a bit, when Margarite raised one eyebrow. "Sorry."

Cujo was looking thoughtful at the number. "That could be useful," he muttered. "So how stable are they?" he asked looking at Ryder.

Ryder looked insulted. "What's that supposed to mean?"

"I mean, how many of them have PTSD and can't be trusted around a bunch of women?" Cujo asked bluntly.

Ryder started to protest, then stopped. He shrugged. "Some," he allowed. "Probably includes me."

Benny snorted. That wasn't a lie. Ryder had some demons riding him from Iraq, although he was pretty sure he could trust him around women. He studied his brother for a moment. Shifter bikers with PTSD? Maybe he should ask the women about the men, not Ryder.

"But if you're hiring us, they'll do as they're told," Ryder continued. He looked at Margarite consideringly, and then at Seth. Seth met his eyes steadily. Margarite had as well, but that went without saying. Margarite had been a dominant wolf before becoming a pack Alpha. Whatever Ryder saw satisfied him, and he nodded shortly. "You're dominant enough to run them," he said to Seth. "I'll send my second with you. How many do you want?"

Benny frowned. "We've got two dozen women," he said slowly. "And I'd like to send some of Chen's recruits too."

"I'm not leaving here until all of Chen's recruits are gone," Margarite said grimly. "Either on the road, or in the ground, makes no difference to me."

Benny nodded that he understood. And he knew Margarite meant that literally. They'd been fearful all week that she'd just kill them. She would have had plenty of help.

There were days when *Benny* would have helped.

So 30 of Chen's recruits. Nearly 40 of Ryder's bikers. Some 25 of the new women shifters. Hell yes, they needed to get them out of here, before the neighbors called the authorities instead of Margarite. "What did you tell the neighbors?" he asked out of curiosity.

"A college reunion," Margarite said tersely. Well, that was one explanation for a lot of people who mostly looked like they were in their 30s. "And that they'd all be gone by Monday."

Benny nodded. He looked at Cujo. Neither of them were good at troop management — they needed Jake for that. Both of them had been solo operators. Ferret out information? Check. Foment trouble? Check. Hell, if you had the money, you could hire Cujo to bring down the government of a third-world country. But logistics for over 100 people?

Not their tool set.

It might be more in his brother's set, actually. Running a motorcycle club of 40-50 people took some serious planning skills. Those weren't weekend warriors.

They had a place in Humboldt County in northern California where they usually spent winters. Benny figured they'd been heading there when they detoured to the Okanogan and then here, because Ryder knew Margarite would probably know where to find him.

"Logistics exercise," Benny said abruptly, looking at his kid brother. "We need to spread out 25 women and 30 young men into packs where they can be safely absorbed. The men are bewildered and resentful. The women know nothing about being shifters and are bewildered and resentful. We've got a stable pack in Odessa."

"Lebenev's?" Ryder said, startled.

"He's dead. A Russian Alpha is the caretaker Alpha there now," Benny said. "Ayta Vuk. She can handle wolves. But we can't flood a small town with strangers either."

"And Hayden Lake," Cujo added. "My father is Alpha there, as of two weeks ago. The last Alpha was sliding into dementia and taking the pack with him."

"And your father took him out," Ryder concluded.

"No, our Alpha did," Benny said. Ryder blinked. Benny laughed and wasn't sure he could stop. "Our Alpha has been a shifter for less than six months. She's now Chairman of the Northwest Council and so far, we've had turnover at the leadership in seven packs."

Ryder blinked. "Unintentional," Cujo assured him.

Not sure that helped, but it was the truth. Really, Abby was chaos personified.

"What about Johannsen's pack? You said he's not Chairman, but he's got a stable pack," Ryder said. He was squinting as if he was visualizing a map.

"Johannsen's dead," Benny said. "And no Abby didn't kill him — Hiro Tanaka did. He's Alpha there now. But you're right, that's a good place to dump a lot of these guys. They're the right age to blend into a college town."

"Any of them Black or Native?" Ryder asked. "What about Craven or Lewis pack?'

"Some," Benny said. "More Asian and white. It's Canada. Not sure about either of those packs, though." He looked at Margarite.

She shook her head. "Lewis pack has enough on their hands right now," she said. "And Craven? The new Alpha isn't the same kind of man as the older one. I most certainly wouldn't leave women there. But the Bellingham pack could take in some women as well as some of Chen's recruits."

Benny didn't comment on her assessment. The Craven Alpha in Roslyn had taken out his uncle 12 years ago — it used to be a well-functioning pack. Guess not anymore. And she was right about the Lewis pack in White Swan. Benny thought it would be a good pack, once the new Alpha cleaned house. But he'd been in power, what, a month?

"I'd think any pack would welcome women," Ryder said, puzzled. "The Okanogan pack sure would."

"These are traumatized women who know nothing about being shifters and aren't going to put up with the crap that shifters hand out to their women," Cujo said baldly. "That's why sending them to Mom make sense. Or Alpha Ayta. But we don't want to send them to some place where they can escape to authorities and start talking about werewolves. And we don't want to send them somewhere they are going to be further traumatized."

Always startled him to hear Cujo championing women like some kind of feminist. Well, Cujo had been through some things these last two years. From playboy mercenary to... whatever he was now. Security chief for the World Council of Alphas and feminist champion? Benny stifled a snicker.

"Your Alpha needs to suck it up and take in these women," Margarite said, and it wasn't the first time, either. Benny reluctantly agreed she was probably right. But they already had two dozen traumatized women of their own.

Well, with Ryder and his men, they had a few more options. He considered that. "OK," Benny said slowly, since it was obvious that they were waiting for him to say something. "We take the most traumatized women to Hat Island. We take the most promising young guys to Hiro in Bellingham. We send the rest of the women to Odessa and Hayden Lake — pretty much their choice. A caravan to Odessa, and those who don't like it there, get a trip on up to Hayden Lake." He grimaced. A bunch of women used to Vancouver, B.C., were going to find both of those places remote. But after what they'd been through at the Vancouver pack house, he doubted it would matter much.

It would work for now. This was a kick the can down the road operation.

"Ryder and enough of his men go with us to get back to Hat Island," Benny said, thinking out loud. "We'll drop off some of Chen's recruits in Bellingham. And we hire the rest of his men to escort you, Alpha, to Odessa and Hayden Lake, with the intent that they should rendezvous in the Okanogan with Ryder and the rest of his Club when they're done."

Seth was scowling thoughtfully. Benny waited. Margarite's Second was considering her safety, he figured. But it was Margarite who decided.

"Done," she said. "I need a trip somewhere — anywhere."

"Tomorrow morning," Benny suggested.

Cujo shook his head. "You and I need to go home today," he said. "Now."

Benny frowned at him. What the hell?

"We still need to talk about finding Dad," Ryder said, somewhat desperately. He wasn't used to this kind of on-the-fly planning. Benny considered that. Not true. But Ryder did it autocratically. He told his Club where they were going and they went. Margarite didn't tell anyone — she just went and told her men she'd be home when she got home.

"Your father is missing?" Margarite asked sharply. "Who's running the pack?"

"No one, apparently," Benny said. But any solution was going to need Abby's involvement. He remembered labeling her as chaos in human form and grimaced inwardly.

Margarite looked worried at that. She glanced toward the table where the twins were, and then back to Benny. He frowned. Why had she looked at them?

"Walk with me," Margarite said abruptly. The men at the table all started to get up. "No, just you, Benny."

Seth started to protest, but he shut up at a glare from Margarite. Benny just shrugged a bit. Seth had to know that if Margarite couldn't protect herself, Benny would lay down his life to protect her. And Benny was no slouch when it came to fighting.

Margarite looked at the other three men. "Figure it out," she ordered. "Rent some RVs and vans. Do whatever it takes. Get these people on the road. I can feel it growing tense."

The men nodded and pulled out cell phones. Benny was happy to escape.

Chapter 4

Margarite headed through her back yard to the path that led to the Burns Bog. Benny doubted they would get all the way there, but it was a nice walk anyway. She really did have a great place. He'd loved living here. Loved living with Margarite. But then he got restless and started to feel trapped. Margarite had told him to go — to Berkeley — and that he'd always be welcome back. But he needed to go.

Benny smiled at the woman walking with him. He had no real clue how old she was — over 100, had to be. Jake was her grandson, and he was in his 60s. She'd lived through some turbulent times, some hard times personally. She was a hard woman — private. And passionate, dominant, a woman who didn't take shit from anyone.

And right now, she was looking around the disaster of her backyard with 30 young men camped out there. And she wasn't happy. He could hardly blame her, especially since she would have disposed of them at the get go if she'd had her way. They'd attacked her guests after all. Chen had ordered them to, and they'd done it. But really, when Benny looked around, he saw a bunch of adolescent pups who had been abandoned by their master. They were hurting, bewildered.

Margarite sighed. "I feel like Akihiro is going to need them," she murmured. "Half-trained though they are. If Hiro Tanaka can mold them into loyal guards? That would be a major win."

And what did she see coming that she thought Akihiro Tanaka, pack Alpha and Chairman of the World Council, was going to need more guards? He already had a passel of them. And Hat Island had hundreds of former beta wolves, most of whom had served in the military, law enforcement, or something like, during their long lives. They'd all be eager to sign up with Tanaka should the need arise.

Benny didn't ask. Margarite might not even know why she felt that way. She got those kinds of feelings. Intuitions, she called them. Not quite visions, just a gut feeling that something needed to happen. Maybe it was just the result of having lived a long time. Or maybe it was something more woo-woo than that. She wasn't the only old shifter he knew who got 'intuitions.'

"If anyone can sort out a bunch of young shifters it's probably Hiro," Benny agreed, as they left the yard. "He's used to all those nerdy young men who seem ubiquitous in the tech fields."

She snorted. "And if he can't, his wolf will take care of it," she agreed.

Not going to argue with that — Hiro was an easy-going man who liked technology. But his wolf was an aggressive, dominant wolf that liked to kill. Benny couldn't think of anyone else who was so different between human and wolf. It was spooky. But it was the wolf that had taken out Johannsen when he came to try and take Tanaka Towers while Akihiro was in Russia.

Johannsen, as Chairman of the Northwest Council, by definition had been the most dominant wolf in the region. Probably not quite true — Benny's father, Akihiro Tanaka, and a couple of others had probably been more dominant, but they didn't want the headache of ruling. But Johannsen had been plenty dominant.

Which put his father back in the forefront of his mind. He was pretty sure that was what Margarite wanted to talk about. "Do you have an idea of where my father might be? Or how to find him?" Benny asked. Of course, then they would have to persuade him to come home. Benny suspected his father knew the pack was destabilizing. So, either he didn't care, or whatever he was doing was deemed more important.

And didn't that scare the bejesus out of him?

"Where do you think he is?" Margarite countered.

"Asia," Benny replied promptly. "That's his territory, right? Really, it's because of the girls who are showing up at the boarding school on Hat Island. They're all from that region. There are others who could be sending them, but they've got paperwork, Margarite.

They've all got visas to study here. That sounds like someone who knows their way around U.S. bureaucracy."

Margarite nodded. "Have you asked them?"

Benny snorted. "They say their English isn't good enough to explain," he said sourly. "As if I wasn't using that line 50 years ago to deflect curious adults! And when I suggest we could discuss it in Thai, Khmer, or even Vietnamese, they just giggle — which is a very effective brushoff, I might add. Not one I used at 12, but damn if it doesn't work."

And that made Margarite laugh. He relaxed and enjoyed the sound of it. She didn't laugh often, and he always wanted to preen when he made her laugh out loud like this. Not a smile, or a smirk, but to laugh freely? Yeah, he loved hearing her. She hadn't been laughing much this last week.

She stopped and grimaced. "It hurts," she muttered. "All these damned voices in my head, always there. They won't go away."

Benny hurt for her. She hadn't wanted to be an Alpha of a pack. She'd clawed out a life for herself that revolved around her household with her men and her travels. And once a month, she threw a potluck for all the shifter families and independent shifters in the area. Her desire to nurture had been satisfied by the aid she gave the women in the remote, and sometimes abusive, packs.

And the potlucks. There was something so mundane and suburban about it that always made him want to laugh.

All Alphas — good ones at least — had that need to nurture, to care for their pack. Benny was convinced that was also the hallmark of an Alpha. Alphas had to have dominance, true, but he knew several wolves who were as dominant as hell and would never be a pack Alpha. They had no desire to care for a pack.

"Are you practicing the visualizations I gave you?" Benny asked. He'd developed some for Abby to teach her how to raise barriers in her mind.

"Yes," Margarite said wearily. "And they do help. But today just seems particularly bad. Just too many damn people. I know I have to go with the women to the packs, but really? I need some time with just my men, and these woods. Time to shift and be a wolf. Peace and quiet. I'd sell my soul for it, if I had any soul left."

Benny frowned slightly at that last, but he didn't pursue it. He thought about it for a bit, and then hesitantly offered, "If you let me, I can probably help. Akihiro threw up a barricade in Abby's mind when she inherited the links of the Northwest Council. They were overwhelming her. He used their mate bond to create the barrier until she could deal with them. I think I could do the same thing through our link."

"We're not mates!" Margarite sounded horrified at the idea. Benny grinned.

"No," he reassured her. "We're not mates. But maybe, old friends?"

She smiled at that. "Well, old friend, if you think you can give me some relief, I would consider it a great favor."

"It won't last," he warned her. "It's for temporary relief, but let me see if I can do it."

It was weird to walk into someone else's brain. At least that was his visualization of what he was doing. He wasn't sure he'd ever initiated it before — Abby had pulled him into her head a couple of times. Invited him to dinner — that had been weird. Usually they used their link just to talk.

And in Russia and when they'd returned, he'd leaned on her to fill in all the missing gaps in his memories. His encyclopedia Hat Island.

But this was different than talking, or emotional exchange. He visualized throwing up a plexiglass shield between Margarite's wolf and the links to her pack. That was how Abby had described the barrier Akihiro had created for her — like bullet-proof glass in an observation chamber.

He watched Margarite's face. She wasn't an expressive person — she kept her feelings well-shielded. But he saw her shoulders drop, and her face relax a bit, and he delicately detached himself from the link that joined them.

"How is that even possible?" Margarite asked. "I've never heard of such a thing."

"The joke in the Hat Island pack is that Abby can do a lot of things simply because no one has had the time to tell her it's impossible," Benny said, rolling his eyes. "But once we see what she's done, it opens up ideas of what we might do. Mostly just within her inner circle. But these links...." He trailed off and shrugged. "They aren't bonds as we have understood them," he continued. "I don't know what they are, to be honest. I'd like to spend the next decade studying them, but that's not going to happen."

Margarite was laughing again. "No," she agreed. "Probably not." Benny grinned at her.

They walked companionably forward, and Benny loathed to interrupt the peace and serenity of the walk. But damn it, he was worried about his father.

And even more, about the Okanogan pack. He had this feeling that time was running out.

"Dad?" he prompted. "You know him?"

Margarite nodded. "Sometimes it feels like I know most shifters," she admitted. "I don't, of course. But most of the major players? I've probably met them at some point in my wandering. And I met your father a long time ago. But I've also seen him fairly recently."

She stopped and thought for a moment. "Maybe six months ago? I was in Laos, and we crossed paths. He was on the move, and so was I, but we were going in different directions. And it felt like he was on a mission — there was such purpose to his movements, whereas with me, I was just satisfying an itch to explore."

She paused. "Will I have to give that up?" she asked quietly. "It scares me that I might."

Benny considered that. He wanted to pursue her tale about his father, but he owed her whatever succor he could give her. She had taken him in at the lowest point of his life, and he would never forget that.

"I don't know," he said honestly. "Most Alphas are closely tied to their pack and territory. But Abby was able to go to Russia. Even Tanaka did — although he had a harder time of it. But something I noticed with Tanaka? When he reached a critical mass of his people — people he had direct links to — he was able to function better. And damn it, it had been six people." He said the last morosely, because it did bug him.

Margarite snickered at his expression. "So I might want to take people with me?"

"Maybe," Benny said. "Abby says four works for her. But Margarite, you've been Alpha for the scattered families and independents for decades in all but the name. They're fairly autonomous, right? And you've traveled during all of that time. It feels more like you host the pack rather than dominate it. It seems it's about people more than territory. So you may be able to travel just fine. Talk to Ayta about it. She was worried about being so far from her pack for so long, but it doesn't seem to be a problem."

"I look forward to meeting her," Margarite agreed.

"I wish I was going with you," Benny said. "I miss her."

Margarite raised an eyebrow but didn't comment. And on second thought, Benny thought he'd change the subject right now. Talking about Ayta wasn't going to win him any points.

"So Dad? You thought you might have an idea where to find him?"

She was silent for a while. Then she sighed. "He wasn't alone," she said finally. "A woman — a shifter. A very powerful one, it felt like." She walked on, and Benny could tell she was troubled about something.

"Those girls? What do you know about them?" she asked abruptly.

Benny frowned. The twins? "They were raised by the St. Petersburg pack," he said slowly. "A woman came to them in distress, and they hid her until she gave birth. And then she left — she said she was a danger to them, both the pack and the babies. The pack — a bunch of Russian monks if you can believe it — raised them, passing them off as boys, I think. When puberty and first shift made that harder to do, there was talk. So, they asked if Abby would take them. She was reluctant; I'm not sure why, actually. But she agreed and made them pack. Not wards of the pack, but actually members. They're powerful. Smart. And you know the rest of the story — that Chen kidnapped them because of some crazy myth about power batteries. They helped Abby rescue the women, and then asked to stay to help. I should have sent them back to the school — they're only 14, after all — but we needed help, and the women seem to look to them."

Margarite nodded. "They're spooky. But in spite of what Okami insists, the dònglì diànchí was a real thing. Women so powerful they could change the course of a war, but who could be subdued by a dominant man and used as a resource for power."

Benny stopped and stared at her.

"There were great battles on the steppes of what is now Russia and China," she said. "Barely remembered at all now. But I've seen the paintings of those battles — myths and stories, people will tell you, not real. I think they *are* real. And you'll often see a woman dressed in white on the edge of it — her hair is always flying out from her head as if electrified. Okami knows the old stories. He may deny them, but his furious insistence that they are just myths is because they scare him. And so they should. They should scare us all."

"And you think the girls are dònglì diànchí?" Benny asked, using the Chinese word for it. There had been a Russian word too, but he couldn't remember it.

"Chen thought they might be," Margarite said. "And he wasn't a stupid man. Crazy. But not stupid. I wish we knew which Chinese Alpha he was aligning himself with."

"I do too," Benny agreed. There were two who claimed to be the Chairman of the Chinese Council of Alphas. Like the human world — one was in mainland China, the other was in Taiwan. Most of the packs in Southeast Asia looked to the Taiwanese Council Chairman. All that Jessie Nickerson had been able to tell them was that the Chairman who Chen was plotting with spoke Chinese and no English, and that Chen referred to him as the Chinese Alpha.

Jessie had been quite the little eavesdropper. Benny approved.

But they'd been plotting an attack on Tanaka and the World Council. Benny thought Chen's death might be a blow, but he suspected the Chinese Alpha was still out there, plotting something.

"There was a rumor that Chairman Vuk was trying to breed for a dònglì diànchí," Margarite said, referring to the former Chairman of the World Council. "Russians called it istochnik sily, for what it's worth. This is pure speculation on my part, but I think the woman who was with your father — and I just caught a glimpse of her — was the product of Vuk's attempt to create an istochnik sily. She looked like Anton Vuk."

Margarite took a deep breath. "And I think she's the one the St. Petersburg pack gave refuge to. And those are her daughters, in my house. They look remarkably like her — like Anton Vuk."

Probably because Anton Vuk wasn't only their grandfather, but their father, Benny thought, sickened at the idea. He'd heard parts of this story before.

"The twins' mother was my second guess at the source of the girls coming to the boarding school," Benny offered when Margarite fell silent. "But having the proper paperwork persuaded me that my father was more likely. Didn't occur to me they might be working together."

Margarite nodded. "So, two things, and then we should head back. I can feel Seth — it's like he's pacing."

Benny grinned at that, and she smiled.

"But one, I think the girls have a tight link with their mother — they have a strong bond with each other, and I think they have a similar one with her. They could probably contact her, and if she's still with your father, persuade them both to come to Hat Island."

"Worth trying," Benny agreed, considering it.

"But here's the thing that worries me," Margarite said. "I doubt your father has spent the last six months in Southeast Asia just to recruit for your boarding school. And that scares me. If he's working on behalf of someone? His skill set isn't for making tea and crumpets. And if he's working on his own? That might be even worse, Benny. Your father is a scary man."

"Did he really have something to do with Pol Pot's downfall?" Benny blurted.

"He was the CIA station chief in Cambodia," Margarite said flatly. "And he didn't leave until after Pol Pot was overthrown by the Vietnamese. What do you think?"

Benny had spent a lot of time recently trying not to think about that question at all. He'd never thought about it until Hat Island. But several of the betas who had served in Vietnam and afterwards had laughed when he'd expressed surprise at the idea.

Took a lot to make him feel naïve. Not surprising it was his father's past that did it, however.

Margarite let the question hang there as she turned around and headed back to the house. They were almost within sight of the house, when Benny slowed down. He glanced at Margarite with a frown. Something. She nodded. She felt it too.

Benny let his wolf surge closer to the surface. His senses sharpened. There were more smells on the slight breeze — a breeze he hadn't even really noticed before.

And his hearing told them someone was nearby. He took a deep breath and focused — a shifter. More than one, he thought. He sent a message to Margarite to tug on Seth's link. He tugged on Cujo's.

Then five men jumped out at them. It was a good spot for an ambush — some large boulders narrowed the path, giving them both something to hide behind, and acting like a funnel for their victims.

Benny barely registered what they looked like — it was where they were and how they moved that mattered. He exploded into a roundhouse kick, leaping slightly to make the kick snap the neck of his first attacker. The man went down — his neck was broken; Benny didn't even bother to check. He could make it permanent in a moment.

He let the momentum of the kick carry him around, to where another attacker approached — his leg still extended, perpendicular to the ground. This was why he practiced Muay Thai, it was lethal, but it was also about balance and movement. Almost a form of ballet — a very lethal form of ballet.

He connected with the second assailant, but the man had seen it coming and pulled his head back, and it wasn't the neck-breaking kick Benny had wanted. He allowed his leg to pull him around and lunged into the attacker. Clenching with the man, Benny jerked his head upward under the man's chin. The man's head snapped back with an audible crack. Benny dropped the body.

He glanced at Margarite who was struggling between two men. She twisted and kneed one man in the groin, and the man screamed and dropped her. Yeah, he bet that hurt. Margarite turned to the other man and was moving in for the kill. Tai chi, Benny thought, assessing her moves. She'd take him down no problem.

But Benny thought there had been a fifth man. Where was he? He turned around, arms and legs loose to mount an attack, looking for the man. A shifter in wolf form leaped up from a crouch from the bushes just past the boulders. Benny dodged him, and then shifted. This shouldn't happen, he thought grimly. Two wolves fighting in the mid-afternoon on the walk to Burns Bog? Well, he'd take the wolf down first, and then handle the consequences.

The wolf was bigger than Benny, but that didn't worry him. His wolf was eager for the fight, and Benny just let him take over. His wolf had become powerful in Russia — to the point where it scared Benny most of the time. He was scared that if he shifted, the wolf wouldn't let him shift back. Scared of what the wolf might do when Benny wasn't in control. But this was his wolf's forte — to take out an attacking wolf. To protect Margarite.

He was still persuading his wolf to let him shift back to human and to stop eating the fifth assailant when Cujo and Seth came at a run.

Cujo took one look at Benny-wolf, and ordered, "Shift."

Benny's wolf grumbled. He's the dominant, Benny pointed out. The wolf sighed and shifted. Benny pulled on his sweatpants without looking at anyone. It was embarrassing to need help shifting back to human like he was 13 not 63. Cujo was more dominant with his own wolf than he was, Benny thought sourly. His wolf whined at that. He didn't have the energy to argue.

Since when did he have to argue anyway? He'd thought it was a leftover effect from losing himself to the wolf while he was in Russia. Now he wasn't so sure. Snarky wolves? When did that happen?

His wolf flashed a series of images of Abby-wolf playing follow the leader. Benny smiled and relaxed a bit. Was Abby-wolf teaching the wolves bad manners?

Holy shit, he thought as that idea sank in. Was Abby's wolf teaching their wolves to be more self-aware? To develop personalities of their own? Abby described her wolf as if it was a separate being — a snarky bitch, she said fondly. "Is your wolf developing more of its own personality?" he asked Cujo under his breath.

Cujo glanced at him. "Yes," he said shortly. "And I blame you. Mine really likes the phrase stupid shit."

Caught off guard, Benny choked on his laughter. OK, he thought, maybe it wasn't the problem he thought it was. He looked at the bodies around them, and grimaced. Cleanup time. His three were all dead — one in wolf form. But given the moans that Margarite's two were making, they were still alive for questioning.

"Do you recognize them?" Cujo asked, looking at Margarite who was standing close to Seth, her arms wrapped around herself. She glanced at her two attackers and frowned. Then she walked over to the two dead. "Familiar," she said briefly. "I think they're from the Penticton pack. Not much of that pack was left after Akihiro Tanaka got through with it. But they've rebuilt in the last 15 years. But they have that look. Why would that pack want me dead?"

Cujo scowled. "Penticton? How far is that from the Okanogan? Not far, right?"

Margarite and Benny looked at each other. "You think the attack might have been on me, not Margarite?" Benny asked slowly. He tried to think back. Had it been?

"Ryder!" Benny said with alarm and started toward Margarite's house at a run. Then he stopped and looked at the mess on the pathway.

"Go," Cujo said. "Margarite, if you would have your Second escort you back to the house? Could you send Jason and a team of recruits here to help with cleanup? I think I'd like to have a conversation with these two men."

Benny didn't hesitate any longer. He ran.

Behind him he could feel Margarite and Seth, although they weren't trying to keep up with him. And farther behind, he heard Cujo say, "So which one of you wants to talk? I only need one of you, you realize that, right?"

Benny winced, but he didn't slow down.

Chapter 5

Benny could tell there was a problem somewhere as soon as he entered Margarite's backyard from the Burns Bog pathway. What had felt like a well-ordered, if crowed, camp now resembled more of a kicked beehive. Chen's recruits were milling around in agitation — some were arguing with Jason. Even Jason looked grim — someone was going to get punched if the idiots didn't back off.

But he didn't see any of Ryder's men. Not good.

"Jason," Benny called. "Ryder?"

"In the house," he said. "There's trouble." He glanced at Benny's bare chest, and said, "I gather you met some too?"

"Yeah," Benny said. As usual, his sweatshirt hadn't made it through the shift. He'd left the tatters back at the attack site. "Cujo wants you — take a squad of these guys with you." He looked around for others he recognized. "Harmon? You're in charge here. John? Go with Jason — Margarite and Seth are about 5 minutes behind me. I don't think there's more trouble out there, but let's be safe."

By the time he'd finished calling out instructions, he was at the backdoor of the house, far enough away that he could ignore the questions they were asking him. As if he had answers?

Inside, he pulled out another sweatshirt from the lockers in the mudroom. He thought you could probably guess you were in a shifters' home simply from this — stashes of sweats, strategically placed, for the residents and possible visitors.

Did humans have similar closets? He didn't know. He wasn't sure he'd ever been inside a human home. He paused for a moment. Well, women's homes, he conceded. But he hadn't been there to explore closets.

He shook his head briefly and moved quietly through the house, listening for his brother's voice. Damn it, what was going on?

Jessie Nickerson was standing outside the dining room where the women were. She was frowning in the direction of the front door.

"What's going on? Do you know?" Benny paused to ask.

She shook her head briefly. "Not sure," she said. "I'm trying to hear, but I don't want to leave this room untended. But I think someone called the cops, and they want to come inside."

Benny winced. His worst nightmare for this situation. Damn it, it was deteriorating rapidly. They'd gotten complacent. Things had been stable and going well enough that they thought they had time. Obviously that was no longer true.

"Thanks," he said, and tried to give her a reassuring smile. She didn't buy it, he saw. "Don't let the women out of there, Jessie," he warned, probably needlessly. She knew — they all knew — of the danger of the women getting a chance to talk to law enforcement.

He glanced down at what he was wearing and winced again. Hardly imposing — gray sweats, the pants a bit worse for the wear, and running shoes. Well, even authoritative men might go for a run, he encouraged himself. He squared his shoulders and lengthened his stride. I'm here to take charge, he chanted, and he dropped his nearly-automatic filters that hid his dominance again.

He was having to drop those filters so often these days he might as well dispose of them.

Like Jessie, he could hear the voices from the front of the house. But the front door was down half-a-flight of stairs — typical of a split-level house like this — and the sounds were muffled. He let his senses expand. Three shifters were at the door talking to an unknown number of humans on the front steps. At the top of the stairwell were more men — Ryder's men, Benny thought. He rounded the last corner and saw them standing there in a line, arms folded across their chests. Yup, there they were. And as long as they didn't start a fight themselves, he was glad to see them. No one was coming past that defensive line.

To his surprise, Randall was with them. Randall was almost a submissive wolf, and usually didn't mingle outside of Margarite's household. Benny wondered what had pulled him out here? And to stand guard with Ryder's men?

Interesting.

He stopped beside him. "What's up?" he asked under his breath.

"Someone called the cops apparently," Randall murmured, his eyes fixed on the top of the open front door — all that was visible really from here. "Alefosio went to answer the door, and I followed to stand guard up here."

Benny nodded. Standard protocol here — one to answer, one who could send for backup if necessary.

"They demanded to come inside. Something about a wellness check? And they wanted to know who owned all the bikes. Your brother showed up about then, with these men." He gestured with his head. "So we've been standing here together." He rolled his eyes a bit at that. Benny grinned at him.

"How long?"

"Not long, 5 minutes? A confrontation always seems longer than it is."

No lie, Benny thought. "All right, the cavalry is here." He glanced at Ryder's men.

"You and you." He pointed at random. "Margarite and Seth are headed back this way. Go tell them they're needed."

One man started to protest, and Benny just stared at him.

The other man nodded and pushed at the protester. "Let's go."

Benny turned back to the front door, wondering what to do next. He chewed on the corner of his mouth. Then he shrugged. He took the stairs down to the entry landing, loudly enough so they could all hear him coming. Taking someone by surprise in a situation like this was not a good thing. Definitely not a good thing.

"Gentlemen?" he said pleasantly. "Can I be of service?"

Alefosio glanced back at him and relaxed just a bit. Yes, backup was here. Such as it was. Ryder looked more relaxed than Alefosio, with that half-amused smirk of his, but he was lethally poised to explode. Benny recognized the signs.

"These gentlemen are responding to a neighbor's concern for Margarite's wellbeing," Alefosio said. "I've explained to them that she went for a run. But they want to come inside and look around."

It would be a cold day in hell, Benny thought grimly. "She should be back shortly," Benny said. "Do you really want to wait? We could have her call the station when she gets in, if you'd rather."

"We want to come in and see for ourselves that everything is OK," one officer said belligerently. There was always one, Benny thought. In any group of men, there was always one who was just looking for a fight. Cops were apparently no different. He glanced at his brother. Ryder was often that one, although he seemed to be holding it together. For now.

"I'm sure that Margarite will be pleased that her neighbors and local police take her wellbeing so seriously," Benny said, and he saw a second officer flinch. Yeah, there was a cop who knew Margarite. "But she also values her privacy. And since she's currently hosting a college reunion of friends, I'm afraid having police come inside would be perceived negatively."

"And you're going to stop us?" the belligerent cop asked.

"Who do the bikes belong to?" a third cop asked.

Three cops? Benny frowned. He peered over the officers' shoulders. Two cars. A fourth officer was leaning against the hood of a car, arms folded, watching. Backup. This wasn't a wellness call.

He studied the street scene. The house was set back from the street, with the ubiquitous suburban lawn in front. At the street was a graveled parking area for guests — where Ryder's crew had left their bikes. A paved driveway led to the two-car garage to Benny's right. There was another two-car garage discreetly tucked off to the side.

One police car was parked in the driveway. The second blocked in the bikes. It was that one the fourth officer leaned against as he looked over the bikes. Had he ran the plates? Benny wondered if he'd gotten any hits. Probably not, or this would be a different conversation.

"As I explained earlier, the bikes belong to me and some friends," Ryder said. "We've been in Alaska for the run to Prudhoe Bay, and we're heading south ahead of the snow. We stopped here this morning — Margarite Lewis is an old friend of mine. To our surprise, she's having a house party. She's invited us to stay, but we probably will head out later — or maybe in the morning, depending on the weather forecast."

Nicely done, Benny thought with approval. But he thought Ryder had already said it before. So why were the police still here? He kept searching the street. It was like one of those games: Can you spot the differences? He compared it to the street scene from earlier when he and Cujo had gone for a run.

There, he thought. That beige van. It screamed soccer mom, but it hadn't been there this morning. He didn't remember seeing it before either. Did it belong to their assailants on the trail? Was there anyone in it?

He thought there was. Benny let his senses expand. It was odd, this ability to know if there were shifters about. It didn't appear linked to any particular body part. Eyes saw. Tongue tasted. But what sensed shifters? He didn't know — although he did usually take in a deep breath. Maybe there was a subliminal scent? So shifters beside him, shifters behind him, and yes, shifters in front. But they were too far away to get a sense of the numbers.

He needed to get the humans out of here. If there was going to be a shifter fight, he didn't want human cops to be unintended collateral damage. "So, should I have Margarite call you?" Benny asked again.

"I don't know you," the belligerent cop said.

"No, I don't think we've met," Benny agreed. He didn't volunteer anything more. The cop scowled.

"I'm here," Margarite said from the top of the stairs. "What is the meaning of this? Harold? Is that you on my front porch?"

"Yes, ma'am," the officer who had winced earlier said. "We got a call from a neighbor concerned for your wellbeing. And about the motorcycle club."

Margarite came half-way down the stairs — staying out of the sight of anyone outside. The cops could see her, but no one else could. Benny approved.

"Well other than having my run interrupted because cops were trying to interrogate my guests, I'm doing well," Margarite said dryly. "How's the baby?"

"She's got her first tooth," Harold said proudly. Everyone was starting to relax now, even the belligerent cop. But Benny was watching the van. Someone got out. Oh, oh. Here we go. He tugged on the link to Margarite.

She didn't blink. "Well, now that you can see I'm fine, you must have better things to do," Margarite said, dryly. "And you can reassure that busybody next door too."

"I still think we should come in and check," belligerent cop began.

Two more people got out of the van. Benny tugged on Cujo's link too. He wished he had a family link with Ryder, but they never had developed one. He didn't know why.

"Check what?" Alefosio asked. "If you want to check on whether we've got houseguests that seem quite comfortable to stay forever? I can tell you that much."

Benny forced himself to grin at the man. "I can take a hint," he said humorously. "Time for us to be gone, I take it?"

"You're always welcome here," Margarite said firmly. "For as long as you want to stay. Officers? If there are no other questions, I do need to get back to those houseguests."

"Of course, Ms. Lewis," Harold said, and he turned, urging his fellow officers off the step. "You have a nice rest of the day."

"You too," Margarite replied. "Benny? Perhaps you and Alefosio would walk them out?"

Benny and Alefosio stepped outside, herding the cops ahead of them.

Benny felt someone fall in step just behind him. He glanced back — Ryder. He was a good man to have at your back, Benny acknowledged, in part because it meant he wasn't in front of you starting shit. But Benny kept most of his attention on the five men who had gotten out the van and were heading across the lawn to the back of the house.

Cujo stood at the side of the house and watched them come.

"Whoa," one of the officers said softly. "That's a man I wouldn't want to meet in an alley at night."

Benny glanced at the officer and then up at Cujo, who stood with his arms loose, hands at his side. His feet were shoulder-width apart and he was poised up on the balls of his feet. Benny labeled the stance 'spoiling for a fight.'

Cujo was pissed.

The shifters approaching him were in a phalanx formation.

Benny gritted his teeth. They were minutes away from a rumble, and there were cops here.

No way this timing hadn't been planned. Benny couldn't see why or who would benefit. But he didn't believe in coincidences — not like this.

"He's a good man to have as a bouncer," Benny replied to the officer with a laugh. "But he might be getting low on patience at this point."

The cop Margarite had seemed to know grinned. "Every party should have a bouncer like that," he agreed. He hesitated. "You tell Ms. Lewis I'm sorry we seemed aggressive. But we worry about the people we respect."

"I'll tell her," Benny promised, thinking, now just go away!

"Who was the neighbor that called it in?" Alefosio asked. "I'm sure Margarite will want to thank them personally."

Harold snorted. "I don't believe that for a second," he said with a laugh. "But he didn't give his name. Just said there was trouble at the Lewis house and he was worried for her safety. He hadn't seen her out and about lately."

"Well, no, because she's got guests?" Benny said. "And the running path out to the Burns Bog is sweet."

The one police car was already heading out of the cul-de-sac. Benny wanted these men out of here too.

"Call us if you need us," Harold said as he got into the passenger seat. Apparently, he was the designated speaker now that intimidation wasn't the point. Good cop, bad cop? Benny stopped himself from rolling his eyes.

"Stay here and make sure they leave," Benny muttered to Alefosio. "Ryder? You're with me." He turned and headed across the lawn with Ryder at his heels.

"What the hell is going on?" Ryder asked.

"No clue," Benny said. "Let's see if these new shifters have some answers."

It was almost as if these shifters were setting up a first rule violation, Benny thought grimly. And that made no sense! Something was going on that he couldn't see.

They were 15 feet away when the strangers rushed Cujo. He stood his ground and let them come. Benny almost wanted to hang back and watch — Cujo seemed confident that he could take all five of them. Really?

Maybe he could, Benny conceded. Or maybe he'd learned something from the attacker he'd questioned that made him so furious he didn't care.

Or he was so frustrated that pounding on someone sounded good. In which case, Benny was just glad it wasn't him.

But Ryder appeared to want in on the fight and he rushed in. Benny sighed and followed. He'd already had his fill of fighting today — literally, he thought with a mental grimace. He and his wolf had different views of how to take out your opponent.

His wolf huffed.

Benny grinned. He flexed his hands, and then he grabbed the nearest attacker and flung him to the ground.

The fight didn't take long. Benny kept an eye out front as he and Ryder shoved the attackers toward Cujo and the back yard, but the police didn't return. He had questions for these men, he thought grimly. "One lives," he warned the other two men.

"Got it," Ryder said, and punched a man in the gut. "So the others go down?"

"I want to question them all," Cujo said grimly. "We need some answers."

One man broke free and tried to run for the van. Benny took him down and twisted his neck like a pepper grinder. "Oops," he said. "You'll have to make do without him, Cujo."

That made one attacker glance at the dead man on the ground, and he flung up his hands. "I submit," he said.

Cujo punched him in the gut anyway. Benny's eyebrows arched. Well, that was interesting. Cujo grabbed another and knocked him out. Not dead, but unconscious. With five attackers and only three of them, two 'bad guys' had to be eliminated from the fight right away. Each of them grabbed one of the attackers, at that point, and manhandled them toward the backdoor that lead to the mudroom.

And the basement. Apparently that was where they were headed.

"Harmon? Can you have a couple of men grab those two bodies?" Benny called as he walked his captive through the back door. "Careful, one's still alive."

He followed Ryder and Cujo into the basement. The other attacker from earlier was down there already, tied up with what looked to be a clothesline. Did people still hang clothes out on clotheslines?

Cujo looked at the two of them. "I don't need witnesses," he said grimly. "Give me a bit."

Ryder started to say something, but Benny waved him off with a slight shake of his head. Cujo was not in a mood to be argued with. "I'll position a guard at the top of the stairs," he said quietly. "Holler if you need backup."

Cujo nodded once, and Benny pushed Ryder up the stairs ahead of him. Harmon was bringing the dead body inside, followed by a young man carrying the live man over his shoulder. Well, he had been alive, Benny amended.

"He tried to run," was all Harmon said. Benny nodded and held the door for the two of them.

"Can you post a guard up here?" Benny asked. "Cujo will call you if he needs backup. I want to talk to Margarite."

"I'll stand guard," Harmon said.

Benny headed back into the house, using his link with Margarite to find her. She was in her sitting room, he realized. He knocked lightly on the door and entered when she invited him inside.

She was sitting in the dark with Seth. He pulled up a chair to the table and joined them. "Cujo is getting answers," he said. "But those cops said a man called in and didn't leave his name. Sounds like a setup. But why? Why bring cops into the picture when they were going to attack us?"

"Coincidence?" Seth suggested. "I mean, two different groups? There are the attackers — which came from Penticton apparently. But someone else might be monitoring us."

Benny gave a half-shrug in agreement. But he was mostly worried about Margarite. She had a bruised look around her eyes. The attack? Maybe, but Benny had never known Margarite to be upset about defending herself. She was pretty ruthless. He got up and went to the bar and fixed himself a drink. "Margarite?" he asked.

"Coffee, actually," she answered. Benny made some, glad to have something to do while they waited for Cujo.

She smiled gratefully when he put the cup in front of her — black, as she always drank it. He started to sit down again. "Would you mind?" Margarite said. "We need Ryder and Alefosio here, and Cujo, if he's done with his questions."

Benny nodded and headed for the door. Wasn't hard to find Ryder. He was out in the backyard with his men on the patio. It had started to drizzle. Benny grimaced. It would probably continue to drizzle from now until May. "Have you seen Alefosio?" he asked.

"The Tongan?" Ryder said. "Last I saw him he was still in the front entryway keeping an eye out for more visitors like those cops."

"Margarite would like you to join her for a conversation about what to do next," Benny told him, and turned to go back to the house.

Ryder walked beside him. "This is going to be a clusterfuck if we don't get ahead of it," he said under his breath.

Benny nodded. "That's what's on the agenda," he agreed. "As soon as Cujo has some answers."

"That is one scary dude," Ryder said. "You hear the stories, but watching him?" He shook his head and then grinned. "Kind of makes me want to take him on, see what happens."

"Don't," Benny warned. "Especially not when he's in this mood. He'll eat your lunch."

Ryder gave him that half-smile. "I can be a scary dude too."

"Yeah, but people paid Cujo millions to be scary," Benny said grimly. "And he's pissed. However, we have smokers regularly. Try him then."

"You mean like fighting competitions?" Ryder said incredulously. "How do you keep people from killing each other?"

"Okami Yoshida," Benny said. He didn't bother to explain more — Ryder would know Okami's rep, if not the man himself. Ryder stayed abreast of shifter politics more than most people. Apple didn't fall far from the tree. Collecting intelligence seemed to be a family trait. "And Cujo. And Jake Lewis? You know that name?"

"I know Jake," Ryder said. Benny glanced at him, but Ryder didn't say anything more.

Benny paused inside the door; Harmon was leaning against the wall next to the door to the basement. "I'll wait for Cujo," Benny said. "Would you go get Alefosio? Margarite is in her sitting room."

Ryder nodded and headed into the house. Benny sighed, and made his shoulders relax.

"So I didn't get the whole story, but I gather someone attacked you and Margarite on the trail," Harmon said. He was a quiet man. Benny had known him for years and didn't know a damn thing about him — not even his last name, he realized. But Margarite's household was like that. However the men found her, once they were here, the past was just that — the past. It had felt like he had been suspended in time. No past, just the present.

No future either. And that was what had finally driven Benny out of here.

"Yeah," Benny said. "I thought it might be a holdover from the fight for the Vancouver pack, but Margarite thought they were from Penticton. That makes no sense. Why would they be attacking Margarite?"

"Might be after you," Harmon said, after considering the issue. "They're not far from your dad's pack."

"Been nearly 40 years since I was a part of that pack," Benny pointed out.

"And your brother?"

Benny nodded. "He's still pack," he admitted. "So maybe. But attacking Margarite Lewis because they want my brother? No one is going to like that. Margarite is legendary."

Harmon made an equivocating gesture with his head. "She gets an attacker every now and then," he said. "Maybe one a year? Here. I don't know if she gets attacks when she travels or not. She's never said."

Benny frowned slightly. Margarite was getting attackers? He didn't remember that from his years here. That had been, what 15 years ago? Something like that. "Is that new?" he asked.

Harmon started to answer, but then they heard steps coming up the stairs from the basement. Cujo opened the door, glanced at Harmon. "You'll need to dispose of the bodies," he said. "I assume you have a method?"

Harmon grimaced. "Yes, but usually not 10 of them."

Cujo shrugged. "Your problem," he said brusquely. He rotated his shoulders. "I need a shower. Margarite wants a meeting, I take it?"

Benny nodded and fell into step with Cujo as they walked back to their suite silently. Cujo disappeared into the shower. Benny paced the room waiting.

And waiting. He frowned. How long did it take for Cujo to shower?

He tapped on the door. No response. The shower was still running. Benny grimaced. He checked his pack bonds, but they told him nothing. Fine. They got bleed through all the time when it was rude or embarrassing, but now when he could really use a heads up? Nada.

Well, he'd done embarrassing things before. At least he thought he had — if he could remember. He rolled his eyes and pushed open the door.

"You OK?" he asked quietly.

Cujo turned off the water and stepped out. He reached for a towel and wrapped it around his waist, avoiding looking at Benny. Benny waited.

"I liked being a fitness coach," Cujo said finally. "I liked being a student, with a mate, and a job as security for a non-profit promoting world peace."

Benny grinned at that. The World Council really was that — a non-profit promoting world peace — in the larger human world. Who said Vuk didn't have a sense of humor? Although that might be the only evidence for it that Benny had heard of.

"I called Haru Ito to tell him what I learned from your attackers," Cujo said. He toweled his hair dry and went to look for clean sweats. Good luck with that, Benny thought as he trailed along behind him. "And he chewed me out. Said I needed to get my head in the game and be who I am — chief of security for the World Council. Said I needed to get this solved and get home because there were other problems to deal with. And he's right. I just...."

Benny was sympathetic. He felt the same way about a number of things — psychologist, Keeper of Stories, Teacher. He'd liked being a carefree playboy and fitness coach too. And this load of responsibility sucked.

"I get it," Benny said quietly. "But Cujo, those skills of yours are keeping this place safe. And that matters to me. A lot of the people I care about in the world are here."

"I know," Cujo said wearily. "It's just that I thought I was leaving all that behind. I want to grow tomatoes on Hat Island. Instead I just tortured and killed a bunch of shifters, and I'd do it again if need be."

Benny snorted. Cujo and his obsession with tomatoes. But he got it. Everyone had some touchstone for the ideal life they wanted. That was Cujo's.

"Tortured?" Benny asked. "Or used your dominance to make them talk?"

Cujo shrugged. "Is there a difference?" he asked. "Have you ever been forced to talk? Yeah, I glared at them, and they felt compelled to tell me everything. And then I killed them."

"Alpha's question," Benny said. Pack Alphas could compel a pack member to answer truthfully in an inquiry. But Cujo wasn't their pack Alpha. Or Alpha of any pack.

"Something like," Cujo agreed. "How that works for me, I have no clue."

"Dominance," Benny said. "We're finding out that few things about shifters work like we thought they did when most packs were small and isolated." Which reminded him of his spider web nightmare. He needed to think about that. It had been disturbing, he acknowledged. But it might have been his brain trying to tell him something too.

Later, he told himself, and focused on the man beside him.

"Let's go," Cujo said. "I need to talk to Margarite. And then we've got to get out of here." He straightened his shoulders, tipped his chin up. It was as if he was morphing back to Cujo the mercenary before his eyes. Benny frowned a bit as they left the suite and headed toward Margarite's sitting a room. He wasn't sure the Pacific Northwest was ready for Cujo the mercenary.

Cujo Brown, easy-going pack third, had been scary enough.

Chapter 6

They were gathered around the table in Margarite's sitting room. Jessie had brought in sandwiches for everyone and didn't seem inclined to leave. No one said anything to her about leaving either. Benny grinned at her. She was very good at being where she needed to be to gain information. She ignored him and continued to lean against the wall by the door.

Margarite looked withdrawn, focused inward on something. Benny could have checked their bonds for why, but he didn't. He wouldn't have hesitated with Abby, but Margarite valued her privacy and protected it fiercely. He wasn't going to invade her mind just for curiosity sake.

Seth sat to her left, just the strong steady presence he'd always been. He might have a title now of pack Second, but that was all that had changed. He had Margarite's back. He always had. Alefosio sat on her other side. He usually had a sense of amusement about him; that was gone. Warrior, not lover, today.

And the fourth at the table was his brother.

Ryder was moving his beer glass around in the condensation on the table. Benny didn't know where his thoughts were, but they weren't on anything in this room. Benny sat down next to him.

"I called Haru Ito," Cujo said. People looked up, surprised by the change they all sensed in him. He wasn't tamping down his dominance — and he was easily more dominant than anyone here, even Margarite. Well, that was why he had been cast out as a beta. And why most pack Alphas still wouldn't want him around. He could probably successfully challenge any Alpha on the West Coast for their pack. Maybe not Tanaka, Benny conceded. But the word 'maybe' was telling.

Cujo's voice was different. Colder. He looked bigger. This was the man the cop had seen earlier — a man no one wanted to meet in a dark alley. A great bouncer, though, Benny grinned inwardly at that.

Cujo was no bouncer at a house party now. He was terrifying. Benny swallowed. Haru, I hope you know what you've unleashed. And he wondered why Haru had.

"So the Hat Island pack's plane is coming to pick up Benny and me," Cujo said. "Ryder? You need to come with us. We'll have to take the twins along, and that leaves seven seats for women who are the most in need of care and supervision."

"There are more than seven," Jessie interjected quietly.

"We'll get to that," Cujo promised her. "So Margarite? I'm assuming you planned to take the women through Canada and then drop down into the States at Oroville?"

She nodded, started to say something, then stopped. Benny thought what she finally said wasn't what she'd been thinking about. "But those were Penticton wolves?"

Cujo nodded. "And that makes it too risky to take the women along that route. They'll have to go down I-5 with Chen's recruits. And we need a better term for them than that."

Cujo was still standing. Benny handed Cujo a sandwich from the platter in the center of the table and took one for himself. Roast beef. He wondered how much roast beef they'd gone through this past week? His mantra was no hungry wolves. He might make that his mission until they got home — making sure Cujo's wolf wasn't hungry. He was scary enough as it was.

"What is going on with the Penticton pack?" Margarite asked. "I haven't heard much out of them since Okami went through there on his mission of vengeance over a decade ago."

Cujo swallowed a bite of sandwich, and then finished the rest of it off in short order. "So, here's the scoop. Okami did take out a lot of that pack — and Haru Ito and some others went back and finished the job a few months later after he healed up. But they didn't take out the pack Alpha — neither of them wanted to be Alpha of what Ito called 'a bunch of mangy wolves in the backwoods of British Columbia.' But that allowed the Alpha to lick his wounds and rebuild his pack. Of course, now he's not just an Alpha who did Anton Vuk's bidding years ago — he's also bitter and angry."

Benny handed Cujo another sandwich and looked at Jessie with raised eyebrows. She grimaced and slipped out for more food. He would owe her the whole story, he promised her silently.

"And just to the south of him is the Okanogan pack," Cujo continued. Ryder jerked his head up at that. "That pack seems leaderless. So he's decided he can take it — gain wolves and territory. He'd be a force to be reckoned with then, he reasoned. There's a lot of gossip, Margarite, about what happened here in Vancouver, and I'm afraid we've made you a nice fat target. That's one of the reasons we've got to get out of here. But the Penticton Alpha hears that Benny's here. And he figures he can take out one of the heirs to the Okanogan pack, and check out what's going on. Maybe pick up some men for the pack. Maybe even some women."

"Me?" Benny said, startled. "I haven't been part of the pack in 40 years."

"You've said yourself that your father would turn over the pack to you in a heartbeat if you returned and wanted it," Cujo pointed out. "But the interesting question is how did he know you were here?"

Benny grimaced. "And did you get an answer to that?"

"I think it's pretty obvious," Cujo said. "One of Chen's recruits told him. I'd guess some of those young men are from Penticton, and one of them, at least, has a cell phone."

"Don't know that we even thought to check," Alefosio said in the silence.

"Probably not," Cujo agreed. "Things were pretty chaotic."

And wasn't that an understatement?

"And it makes a person wonder who else we've got out back," Seth said.

More silence as they absorbed that thought.

"So the Penticton men get here, and they see the bikes," Cujo continued. "And they realize that they've got the other Okanogan heir here too. So they... used their initiative."

People grinned. They'd all run enough missions of various kinds to know that phrase. Abby was the only leader Benny knew who thought that was a *good* thing.

"They thought they could get into the backyard, get some help from the men there, stage a coup, and take out both Benny and Ryder. And their Alpha would be so proud," Cujo summarized sardonically. "Of course, it went south fast. Benny and Margarite took out that first team. They delayed too long up front when their distraction with the police fizzled, giving me time to get into position. They never even reached the backyard where they could have gained support."

Benny frowned though. That could have worked. It was only Cujo's ruthlessness that prevented it. If he hadn't taken that second team down fast and hard, the coup would have worked.

"What was their original goal?" Benny asked, while everyone else seemed to be brooding.

"The twins," Cujo said flatly. "They wanted the twins. Oh, the wanted the men — whoever wanted to go back with them. And they figured they'd grab some of the women. But the mission they were charged with? Get the twins. Kill you."

He glanced at Ryder. Ryder was still brooding, but Benny thought he wasn't surprised about Cujo's description. Interesting. Looked like Ryder had already come to the same conclusions.

"Well, that does create a problem," Margarite said. "You're right. I was thinking of taking the women to Odessa through Canada." She started to add something else, but Cujo replied first.

"You're going to have to go down I-5," Cujo said. "Haru Ito said he would talk to Hiro Tanaka about taking on some of the recruits in Bellingham. There's a campground just north of the pack territory — you all can set up camp there. Let Hiro vet some of the men, and take them in. Then you come on down into Seattle. We might get Tanaka to take on some of the other men and even some of the women. You can pick up I-90 and head east. You'll actually make better time than going through Penticton."

"Better time, but you're talking about the most populated area of the Northwest," Margarite pointed out. "A lot of opportunities for people to disappear from the caravan. And for the caravan to get noticed. How are we doing for transportation anyway?"

"Well, some good news there," Alefosio said. "I talked to a friend of mine from the city softball league."

Benny blinked at that. Margarite's men played city league softball? Suburbia at its finest. He wanted to snicker, but after one look at Margarite's stone face, he schooled his own.

"His church has a bus they'll loan us," Alefosio said. "I told him all about a basketball team we were sponsoring of homeless young men and a series of tournaments we were scheduled to participate in — Bellingham, Yakima and Spokane — over the next two weeks. He was very impressed and glad they could help. So we've got a bus. It says First Baptist on it, and he suggested we add a banner that said Delta Basketball to it."

Alefosio was trying not to laugh, and Benny grinned at him. "Perfect," he said out loud.

"It is," Cujo said with a laugh. "And the women?"

"We've got two vans and two RVs lined up," Alefosio said. "They're delivering them here this afternoon."

"Good job," Cujo said. And his approval mattered, Benny saw. Well, well. This was interesting. Scary but interesting.

"I can't go," Margarite said abruptly. She shook her head. She was so tense, it was painful to watch. "I want to. I wanted to get out of here and roam a bit. Prove to myself I could. But then those shifters came and invaded my territory. And I'm outraged. My wolf is outraged. And I can't go. It's almost visceral, this need to stay and defend my territory." She looked at Benny. "You said you thought my pack was more about people than turf, and I think — thought — you were right. But being attacked? This small bit of land matters to me very much."

"As it should," Cujo assured her, and she relaxed a bit. "We can't lose this place, Margarite. We can't lose your hold on the pack — all these independents and families? No, you have to stay and make a stand if need be. Whatever it takes. So if you think you have to stay, then you stay. And we'll defend you and your place here."

Benny couldn't read the expressions that moved across Margarite's face, but she was relieved? Grateful? And still upset. He looked at her gently until she met his eyes. "Close your eyes," he said. "I want you to visualize being rooted here, in this place. Claim it. It's yours."

She closed her eyes, and Benny continued, "Seth stands with you. That's a given. Now find the edges of your territory. Who do you need to secure this place and be safe? Think about your household, Alpha. Who among them can go? Who can you let assist moving all these people?"

Silence. It was almost as if they were holding their breath waiting for her answer. Seth reached over and put his hand on her clenched fists in her lap. Finally, she opened her eyes. She clasped Seth's hand, and held it tightly. Then she looked at Alefosio. "Will you?" she asked. "Will you represent me and this pack and take the women and recruits to safety? I can think of no one I trust more for this job."

Alefosio nodded. "I will," he promised. "I will not let you down, Alpha."

Margarite smiled. "There is no question in my mind that you would."

Cujo nodded once in approval. Jessie passed around another platter of sandwiches, and it broke the tension a bit, as they all helped themselves. "Good," Cujo approved. "Can you hold your territory, Alpha? Do you need us to leave more defenders? Jason?"

Benny flinched. Jason was going to kill Cujo if he had to stay behind. Well, he could try, Benny amended.

But Margarite shook her head. "You're going to need every man you've got. There are plenty in Delta pack who would come to my defense if necessary. We'll be fine if you just get all of those ornery boys out of my backyard!"

Cujo grinned at her, and Benny could feel Margarite respond to him through their bond. Respond sexually. He hadn't felt any interest in Cujo from her before. Benny was fascinated by the reactions to Cujo's increased dominance.

Interesting. He wanted to think about it some more. Add it to my list, he thought sourly.

"Ryder?" Cujo asked. He frowned. "Is that your real name? Seems awfully appropriate."

Ryder blinked. "That's what you want to know? Now?" he asked. He shook his head. "No, it's the name I gave myself at 18. Dad was concerned. He didn't like the notion that I was going out on a motorcycle as it was. But he worried that using my real name would bring too much attention to me. He has enemies — both in the shifter world and among humans. Garrison is a dangerous name to own. Benny hasn't helped any either."

"Me?" Benny said startled. Then he reconsidered. He'd been an intelligencer for the Northwest Council when Ryder went on his first ride. He might be right.

"So Ryder Garrison is somehow better?" Cujo asked.

"Just Ryder," he replied. "No one has called me anything but Ryder in decades. And Garrison isn't my legal last name either."

Cujo nodded at that. Benny wondered what he was thinking. Well, he'd ask later — if he remembered.

"We need you at Hat Island to talk to our Alpha about the Okanogan," Cujo told Ryder. "Do you have a Second who can be hired for guard duty for this caravan?"

Ryder shook his head. "Not for something this complex," he answered. "We're talking about a bus, a couple of vans, two RVs, and the rest of my club — don't forget them. I've 40 more wolves camped out south of the city. That's a lot to shepherd down I-5. No I'll have to be with them. It's going to take my dominance. My knowledge. We can do it, I think. And not even be conspicuous. But that's a delicate dance — secured transport vs. inconspicuous transport. I'm going to have to be on a bike. Your Alpha will have to wait until I can get there by bike."

Cujo considered that. Then he nodded. "We'll have to make it work," he decided. "It's not like we're talking huge distances here. The campground is an hour away. Hat Island is two hours from there. You get everyone set up at the campground. And tomorrow, we can either bring you into Hat Island, or bring the Alpha to you."

Ryder nodded. He looked at Jessie. "You said you thought there were more than seven who needed high-security transport?"

Ryder's past was coming out too, Benny thought. Military lingo. He wasn't sure if that was a good thing or not. Ryder had come back from Iraq a hard, cold man. He returned to the road as if his memories were chasing him. Benny didn't understand what the road and the club gave his brother, but he recognized that it gave him something — something that stabilized him, soothed him. His father saw it too.

Like to like, Benny thought. His father and his brother were both molded by their military experiences. His father had gone to ground to deal with his. His brother? Still fleeing them on the road.

Well, their father *had* gone to ground, Benny thought sourly. Where the hell was he now?

Jessie hesitated and then nodded. "I can give you names," she said slowly. "But I'd say 10? Even the idea that they would be in an RV campground makes me cringe." She considered that, then nodded. "And I need to go with you."

"What?" Benny asked startled. "I figured you'd be glad to be free of all of this. To look for your missing fiancé?"

Jessie shrugged. "I've looked in the Vancouver area," she pointed out. "The word is out among shifters. If he is here, he'd know and come for me by now. He hasn't. So I think he's gone farther afield. And this gives me a chance to go farther as well."

Jessie's grandfather had ordered her engagement broken so he could place her in Alpha Chen's household. Her fiancé was banished. That had been months ago. During all of the chaos last week, Jessie had just walked out of Chen's household, and hitchhiked down here with just Margarite's name. If you're ever in trouble, go to Margarite — the women of the packs passed that message among themselves. And so Jessie, 23, battered but determined, had done just that — she'd showed up here while they were planning to rescue Abby. She'd helped with the planning of that, and she'd been instrumental in working with the changed-wolves since then.

"I think you should let Kristina and Taisiya go with me in the RVs," Jessie continued. "That would free up two more spots on the plane. And if Ryder is on a bike, that's a third spot. And that gives us 10 for women who really shouldn't be out in the real world yet."

"What?" Benny said startled. "No way. Kristina and Taisiya need to be safely back at the school. They were targeted here!" He was sure of that. He didn't know why, but he did know that those two should not be where they were at risk.

"Benny, they're really good with the women," Jessie insisted. "The women trust them — see them as their rescuers. And we're going to have all of Ryder's men as guards. They couldn't be safer!"

And who was going to protect them from Ryder's men? Benny grimaced, but he managed not to blurt that out. Ryder would find it insulting, even if it might be true. Kristina and Taisiya were 14. They should be safe — they were children still. But they were at that age where they didn't look like children. He hesitated, torn between wanting to protect them, and knowing they could protect themselves. They were downright scary, to be honest.

"Acceptable," Cujo pronounced. Benny glared at him. Who did he think he was? They were Benny's charges, not his.

Security Chief for the World Council, a voice in his head suggested. Benny was pretty sure that voice was his own, but it bothered him that he couldn't be sure. He had that flash of a spider web expanding again, ring by ring, connection by connection. Was he supposed to be the spider making the web? Or the fly trapped in someone else's web?

Spiders had a nasty meaning in shifter terms, but Benny didn't think his nightmare referred to that. No, it was more literal in a way. All these shifters, living too close together, were connecting, building a web that joined one to another, allowing them to experience each other's feelings. In some cases, they could communicate — like Abby and her inner circle. That had been seen as a rarity, but Benny was beginning to wonder if it might be more common than people thought. All you had to do was put a bunch of shifters in a confined space....

He wrenched his thoughts back to the reality of this closed room. Stop thinking about it, he told himself, or you're going to run out of here screaming, and won't that be a disaster? Benny schooled his thoughts, ignored the sharp glance from Margarite, and focused on the caravan details.

"Is Jason going on the caravan?" he asked. "Or do you need him here, Margarite? You're still going to have some of the women stay, right?"

"We shouldn't need Jason," Margarite replied. "And the women who are staying with me are the ones who are connected to shifter families and partners. They'll move out of here when we agree it's safe for them to do so."

She meant when she was sure they wouldn't go screaming to the police that there were monsters in the closet. Benny could interpret that just fine.

Cujo glanced at the clock on the wall. "Then we need to prepare those women who are flying out of here for the trip to the airport," he said crisply. "Benny? That's your job — Jessie can help. Whoever else you need. Ryder? What do you need to organize the caravan?"

"Money?" Ryder cracked. "A contract?"

"You have my word," Cujo said. "Name your sum. The World Council will pay for it."

Ryder nodded. "A debit card then," he suggested. "Gas, campground fees, food...."

"I'll get you one," Cujo promised. "What else?"

People brainstormed ideas and suggestions, but Benny gestured to Jessie and they slipped out of the room quietly.

"I'm worried about the twins going with you," Benny said as they went toward the dining room where the women were.

Jessie shrugged. "They're pretty level-headed," she pointed out. "And they are a godsend with the women. I don't get it, really. But the women look to them for... protection? guidance? Whatever it is, it works."

Interesting, Benny thought. Worth exploring? Later, he decided. Like everything else of interest.

He pulled the twins aside first and asked if they were willing to travel with the women. Taisiya nodded, and Kristina didn't contradict her. "Taisiya? You have a bond with the Alpha, right?" Benny said slowly. She nodded once. "So you can reach out to her if there is trouble on the road?"

"Yes," the girl said.

Benny hesitated, feeling his way along with his questions. "Do you have a similar bond with your mother?" he asked softly. "Because I have reason to believe she might be traveling with my father. And we need to reach them ASAP. There's trouble."

Taisiya chewed on her cheek. "Mom reaches out to us," she said, barely making any sound at all. "I don't know if I can initiate. I haven't heard from her in a while now. I've been worried."

"Have you tried to reach out to her?"

"Yes," she said. "But maybe.... I reach the Alpha in a different way. I have been thinking about trying that with Mom. But she's always been very stern with us. It isn't safe."

Benny frowned at that. "It isn't safe in what way? Can it hurt you?"

Taisiya shook her head slightly. "It doesn't hurt with the Alpha," she said uncertainly.

"I think she's worried we will be exposed for what we are," Kristina said.

For what they were? Benny frowned. Did they know of the legends? This wasn't the place or time to ask. "If you get the chance, you might send an SOS message to your mother," he said finally. "I need my father to call me."

The girls grinned at that, and Benny rolled his eyes at them. They giggled. "I will try," Taisiya promised. "Mom usually reaches us at night, when we're about to sleep. So I'll try tonight."

Benny nodded. They should probably wait until they were safely back at Hat Island, but for some reason he felt a sense of urgency. He really needed to talk to his father as soon as possible.

He changed the subject and instead, described the plans to drive south of town, and camp out overnight. The girls were intrigued. "But remember, it's important that none of the women reach out to humans," he cautioned them. "You know that, right?"

They nodded. Well, they'd grown up in secrecy; he supposed they did know. "But, if you want to fly home with me, I'll make that happen," he added.

The two grinned at him. "We'll stay with the women, it will be fun!" Kristina said excitedly. "I've never camped out before."

Benny laughed, and told them to have a good time, shelving his own misgivings. He had so many misgivings about so many things, he could barely sort through any of it anyway.

It turned out it wasn't hard to convince the most traumatized women to fly to Hat Island after all.

They were happy to go, one said. Abby was quite the attraction.

"She taught us to shift," another said shyly. "She introduced us to our wolves."

Benny nodded. Had he known that? He guessed he did. The women didn't have much — for most of them, a change of clothes was all. He left Jessie to take care of those details and escaped back to Margarite's sitting room. He bumped into Cujo coming out of the room. "Are you sure about us leaving all these people in Ryder's care?" Benny asked him.

Cujo shrugged. "Yes? First of all, he has more experience with on-the-road caravans than you or I do. The hardest part will be getting everyone out the door. And I suspect Margarite will take care of that part. She's likely to just shoot anyone who is still here at sunset."

Benny snickered. True enough.

"And it's only an hour to the campground," Cujo continued. "They'll be fine. And we have got to get back, Benny."

Benny started to ask about that, when Harmon came around the corner from the front door. "We're loading up everyone for the airport," he announced.

Benny grabbed his backpack from their suite and went to say goodbye to Margarite. It was an affectionate goodbye, he thought with a grin as he dashed outside when someone honked a horn. The bright side of this past week had been spending time with Margarite and her household — something that might not happen again in the near future.

He grabbed a seat behind the driver. "Remind me why you're all the sudden in a rush to get back?" Benny asked Cujo. "Not arguing, but we could have gone days ago."

"I told you," Cujo said. "Haile is sending his girls to the boarding school."

"Yes?" Benny said slowly. "When?" Then the realization hit. "Cujo! Are you telling me these girls are arriving today? And you're just now telling me about it?"

"I told you!"

"Today," Benny argued. "You only told me earlier this morning that Haile was sending girls from his pack. And you neglected to mention that they were coming *today*. How long have you known this? Weeks?"

Cujo shrugged. He had, Benny thought sourly.

"Olivia and Okami are meeting them at the airport this evening," Cujo said. "She said I had better have you at the school to receive them when they arrive."

Benny stared at the man. He'd move heaven and earth to get back too — Olivia Trainer was not someone to cross. "We're not prepared for something like this! Do they even speak English?"

"Of course they do," Cujo said impatiently. "Do you really think Haile would send his girls into the world unprepared? English, Italian, Farsi, and their own language. Probably French, too."

"You have a school?" a woman said hoarsely. Benny glanced at her. Leslie, he thought her name was. It was the first time he'd heard her speak. "I was a teacher."

"Welcome then," Benny said, gentling his voice. "We need you. Yes, it's a boarding school for girls. An international boarding school apparently." He focused on Cujo again. "How many girls, Cujo?"

Cujo rolled his eyes. "Eight."

"Eight girls. That doubles our enrollment! Nearly anyway."

"Benny?" Cujo said. "Suck it up. You know I couldn't say no to Abraham Haile. He knew about the school. He knew about the serum. And he told me I either took the girls out on the helicopter with me, or I could walk out with the pack — out of the contested region of Eritrea next to the Sudan all the way to the coast — while Olivia sat in Monte Carlo. So I took the girls. They've been in Monte Carlo while Kent found them chaperones for the trip. And now they're soon to arrive here."

Benny flopped back against his seat.

"What serum?" Leslie asked.

It was Cujo who answered. "Eighty percent of our girls die during first shift," he said bluntly. There was a murmur of horror from all the women in the van. "A scientist who is a member of Hat Island pack developed a serum that helps girls to survive the transition. But it's been resisted in some parts of the world — here in the Northwest, particularly. In other places, like Haile's pack in Africa, it's seen as a godsend that will let their girls live."

"We could have sent the serum to them," Benny grumbled.

"Benny? The bigger question is how did Haile even know about the school and serum?" Cujo said. "I'll give you one guess."

Benny groaned. "Dad."

Cujo shrugged. "That would be my guess, yes."

"Could you tell us more about the boarding school?" Leslie asked timidly. "And the serum?"

"Go on, Keeper of Stories," Cujo said, with barely hidden amusement. "Tell them the story."

Benny rolled his eyes. but he straightened up to tell the story right. "This is the story of Dr. Stefan Lebenev," he began. "He was determined to find a cure for the deaths of shifter girls facing first shift after his twin died decades ago...."

The women listened intently.

Chapter 7

Day 155 of the re-emerged Hat Island pack, Friday, Nov. 8, Vancouver, B.C.

Ryder thought he should probably have himself committed for a 30-day involuntary hold in a mental institution for agreeing to take a caravan of men and women 200 miles across Washington state. Hell, he wasn't even sure what he'd agreed to do!

He went to find Alefosio. Alefosio was going on this trip — surely he had a better idea of exactly what they were doing. He stalked through the hallway looking for the man — how hard could it be to find a Tongan the size of a small mountain?

Instead he bumped into the young woman who had been lurking around all the various meetings he'd been in today. She usually brought in food, so no one had questioned her attendance. Smart, he thought, amused. She was of medium height and slim, with dark brown hair. He thought there was Chinese ancestry somewhere, although he couldn't pinpoint why. Maybe her eyes.

She was casually dressed in jeans and a loose sweater. Dressed to not call attention to herself, Ryder thought. It didn't work. She was an attractive young woman.

Emphasis on young, he reminded himself. If he wanted a woman, there were several in the club who were more than willing. He didn't need to be eyeing this one.

He couldn't even remember her name, if he'd even been told it. "I'm looking for Alefosio," he said brusquely. He didn't want to engage in chitchat with a chit, he thought amused at his own word puns.

Well, it beat the thoughts that usually pounded away at him in his skull.

"He's with Margarite," she said, falling into step with him. "You don't want to interrupt."

He snorted at that. "And who *are* you?" he asked, stopping in the hallway. They were near the kitchen, he thought. A good a place as any to go if he couldn't talk to his 'partner' in this trip. "And what role do you play here?"

She smiled briefly at his bluntness, but it didn't seem to faze her. Good.

"I'm Jessie Nickerson," she said. "And I've been working with the made-wolves, the women who were changed by the former Alpha."

"You're talking about Alpha Chen?" he asked. "He's the *former* Alpha? Who's Alpha of the Vancouver pack now?" Damn it, he goes up north for a summer and all hell breaks loose.

"An attorney named Gerard Gauthier," Jessie said. "He took over after Alpha Chen died."

"Died," he said flatly. People took over after they killed an Alpha. Alphas didn't just die.

She smiled again, that same brief, small smile. It didn't reach her eyes, and he didn't believe it. "Abby Stafford killed him," she replied, and frowned. "I think. It got weird up there, and no one seems to know exactly what happened. I hope it's true. I hope he died, knowing it was at the hands of a woman."

The last was said so fiercely that Ryder jumped. What the hell had Chen done to this girl? That had been real hate he heard in her voice. He recognized it easily. He had a few hate buttons himself. He was glad her hate wasn't directed at him. Ryder studied the girl for a moment — and she was just a girl, he decided, maybe in her early 20s. "You're going with us, right?"

He thought he had that much right.

She nodded. "I'll go with the women," she said quietly. "They need me."

"How bad off are they?" he asked abruptly. That was crass, he supposed, but he needed to know. Exactly what was he taking down the road? An insane asylum? Because made-wolves.... That didn't sound good. Jessie didn't answer. "Jessie," he said softly, but with some real force behind his words, "Tell me what happened. And what condition are these women in? Why are we taking them to Odessa, of all places? And who are these guys everyone calls Chen's recruits? And if Chen is dead, why are they his?"

Jessie laughed. It sounded bitter, and if he was any judge, exhausted. "Come on. Let's raid the kitchen, and I'll tell you."

Jessie pulled out a large beef roast that appeared to have been grilled and started slicing it. "There's bread in the cupboard," she said, gesturing with her head. "And brown mustard in the refrigerator."

Bemused at being given orders in the kitchen, Ryder pulled out bread, mustard, cheese, and onions. There wasn't a woman in the club who would think of asking him to help make sandwiches. He was used to being served, thank you very much. He had a brief flash of being young and making sandwiches with his mother. And he let it go.

Making sandwiches wouldn't hurt him. And there was no one around to get any ideas that he'd gone soft.

They took the sandwiches to a kitchen table, and Ryder took a bite before saying, "So tell me."

And Jessie did. Told him about the women Alpha Chen had changed so he could reward his new 'recruits' for the jobs they did for him. About Abby Stafford — Benny's Alpha, apparently — and what she'd done to rescue the women. And how a second pack had coalesced around Margarite Lewis, who wasn't happy about it — at all.

That part Ryder had figured out. "And you?" he asked when she ran out of words.

She closed down. "Come on," she said. "Let's see if your brother got his women to the airport and if Harmon is back with the van. If we're going to get to Bellingham before dark, we need to move."

Ryder let it go. He nodded and followed her out of the kitchen. Interesting woman.

Down boy, he told himself. She's too young for the likes of you.

But she'd been through some shit, and that always interested him — messed up though that was. But some happy-go-lucky princess could never handle the darkness in his brain.

He couldn't handle it sometimes.

That's what a bike was for. Get on it, ride like a demon from hell. Feel nothing but the wind, the bike, and the road — not the pain, anger and fear that haunted him. Hear nothing but the sounds of the bike and road — not the shelling, the gunshots, the screams of people dying in the streets.

He shook his head. Iraq had fucked him up, he admitted privately. Southeast Asia had screwed over his father and much of the Okanogan pack, and they'd found solace in the quiet woods of the Okanogan. They'd gone to ground, so to speak. And it worked for them. But it didn't work for him. He got restless, and he needed to run. And when running as a wolf didn't get the job done, he'd ridden a bike out again, like he had when he was 18.

Ryder grimaced. He should have listened to his father and stayed out of the military. But no, he was infected with patriotism post-9/11 and signed up. Turned out, Iraq had nothing to do with 9/11. A lot of people died because a president had something to prove to his daddy.

Well, Ryder could relate to that. Looking back, he thought his enlistment had more to do with proving something to his father than patriotism. His father had almost myth-like status among the shifters, and even among the old human veterans. He'd heard all the stories growing up — stories of Vietnam rescues and undercover work in Cambodia, and all the rest. Not from his father. His father didn't talk about the past. But from the pack? Yeah, they'd talked.

Shifters told stories. Gossiped, really.

And one of the people they gossiped about was Tom Garrison.

They gossiped about Benny Garrison too — more for his exploits as a playboy than as an intelligencer. Even the psychotic wolves of the Okanogan pack knew it wasn't good to gossip about the intelligencers and enforcers of the Northwest Council of Alphas. But Benny was always just the big brother who came home, intervened with his father, and then went out on the road with him. And Benny let him be the dominant in that first ride — let him assemble a club and run it. Benny was just along to have fun, he'd said.

Ryder shook his head. He couldn't do that. If he was in the group, he was going to run that group — and that had probably been true dating back to kindergarten sandboxes.

So he'd gotten out of the Army, bitter, disillusioned and hurting. He healed up in the Okanogan, and then took off again with a small group of wolves attracted to the idea of an open road.

Wasn't a small group now. There were 32 men and 8 women riding with him. All shifters. They occasionally picked up human riders, but for the trip up the Alaskan Haul Road, he had only wanted shifters, so they could go for runs as wolves.

A trip of a lifetime. His shoulders lost their hunched tension as he thought of it. The ride. The open land. The runs as wolves. They'd stayed and played, until the snow chased them out.

Bikes weren't good in snow.

So they headed south, planning to go to their place in northern California for the winter. And they'd get there eventually. Settle back into human society for a while. But he'd gotten a call from a pack member about his mother, and he'd detoured to the Okanogan.

He took care of that and put out feelers to find his brother. There was trouble coming, and Benny needed to do something about it. Now he was ass deep in this mess of Benny's, and he really hadn't had a chance to tell Benny the whole story.

He grimaced.

"Are Brenda and Maggie going with us?" Jessie asked, interrupting his thoughts. "They're working out great with the women right now. It helps to have female wolves who can answer questions. Can they drive the RVs, maybe?"

Ryder considered it and nodded. "That works," he agreed. "Alefosio can drive the bus full of guys. Will you drive the van then?"

She hesitated. "If it's not a stick-shift," she said slowly. "I haven't driven very much."

Ryder frowned briefly. Was she younger than he thought? Why wouldn't she have driven much? "Do you think a male driver would work?"

"Alefosio maybe," she said dubiously. "But he's driving the bus? I guess it will have to be me."

Ryder nodded. "How old are you?" he asked bluntly.

She flinched — he didn't know why, except she didn't like talking about herself much. "I'm 23," she said, and she sounded defensive.

"Just a kid," he teased. "Come on, we'll see if the van is back from the airport, and make sure you can reach the pedals."

She huffed a bit, but then laughed. "I might need to drive it around the block — make sure I remember how to drive at all."

"And then we can find Alefosio — and I don't care if we interrupt something or not," Ryder said. "Are the women ready to move out?"

"More or less," Jessie said. "They know we're leaving, but they don't have much to take with them. A backpack of clothes. Some of them are excited and interested. Some of them are still...." She trailed off. "They don't seem to give a shit about anything," she blurted out. "Not where they are, not what the eat or wear, or anything. I worry about them."

He nodded. "PTSD," he said. "They've been through some bad stuff. We'll take it easy, but getting out of here and into new experiences might help."

"If they don't wander off and decide to tell someone everything, or wander off and just get lost, or wander off and try to kill themselves," Jessie said, and he could hear that exhaustion in her voice. Was she the one responsible for all of these women's mental health issues?

When he asked, though, she shook her head. "No, Benny has been shouldering most of it," she answered. "I just listen to the ones who want to talk. Some do. Some talk to me — some talk to the twins. I worry most about the ones who don't want to talk. We sent the most traumatized on the plane. But they're all traumatized. It's almost like being free is harder on them than being a captive."

Ryder flinched. "Yeah," he said softly. "That can be true."

Jessie looked at him sharply. "You were in the Army?" she asked.

Ryder shrugged. "I was Army," he agreed. "That's why Benny just turned over all this to me. Military transport is something I did. Although this is much more of a hippy-dippy caravan than anything I ever organized." He considered that. Thought about the convoy out of Mosul of Iraqi families.... A lot of those people had walked out with their children and what few things they could carry on their backs. The vehicles had been reserved for the injured who couldn't walk. Iraqi families. Military personnel from more than one country. One long line of refugees hoping for a better place down the road.

Of course there hadn't been a better place. He hoped there would be for this caravan. Which reminded him. "Why are you taking them to Lebenev's pack?" he asked abruptly, shutting down the sounds of bomb bursting behind him as he directed those refugees onward out of Mosul. "Alpha Lebenev's the last person I'd take shell-shocked new wolves to."

"The Alpha there now is a woman," Jessie answered. "They call her a caretaker Alpha. She's actually an Alpha of a pack in Russia. And she's really old. Ayta Vuk. I really want to meet her."

"What happened to the old Alpha?" he asked. This was all making his head hurt. How could so much change happen in six months? He couldn't remember the last time there'd been a change in Alphas! He thought about it. Craven pack, he decided, and that happened just about the time he got home from Iraq, nearly 20 years ago. Margarite Lewis had listed that as a pack to avoid, he recalled. Well, add Penticton and Okanogan to the list.

"He was going to kill the girls in his pack," Jessie said indignantly. "And Abby Stafford wasn't going to let that happen."

He rubbed his forehead between his eyes. What? He wanted to meet this female Alpha. She was marching through the Northwest packs like General Sherman through the South!

Not his problem.

His task was to get these people pointed in the right direction, and to a campground north of Bellingham tonight. And then he needed to track down his brother — and this female Alpha — and talk to them about Dad and the pack. He considered the information about the Penticton pack making inroads and decided not to worry about it. It might solve his problems, actually, and if it didn't, and Penticton bit off more than they could chew — his prediction — well, that solved everyone's problem.

One of their problems. He took a deep breath and gave the girl beside him a reassuring smile. She watched him without expression. "The twins?" he asked. "Those the two teenagers I've seen with the women?"

She nodded but didn't volunteer anything more.

"And they're riding with you?"

"One in each of the RVs," Jessie decided. "Because...." She stopped. When he raised one eyebrow, she just shook her head. "The women find the twins comforting," she said at last. "They helped them escape while Abby Stafford was taking out Chen."

"What are they age 14 or 15? And they're the protectors?"

Jessie nodded.

He'd seen teenagers fight to protect younger siblings and even their mothers. Something like that, he supposed. Teens could be ferocious fighters. They didn't believe in their own deaths yet.

They learned. In Mosul they'd learned. Those who lived, anyway.

Every question seemed to raise more questions, though.

So, stop asking questions, he told himself, and they went out to check on the transport they had available.

Ryder sent two of his men to get the rest of the club moving south. He gave them one of the debit cards Cujo had given him and told them to buy food for a campout for 30 men, 15 women, and the 40 members of the club. "Shifters," he warned. "And we need supper tonight, and breakfast in the morning." The two men just nodded as if doubling the size of the club was no big deal.

And maybe it wasn't.

The van had an automatic transmission, and he told Jessie drive it around the block a few times. She came back and nodded that it was OK. Really it wasn't going to be difficult for even an inexperienced driver. They could pick up I-5 south near here and stay on it. Until the border. He paused. "Passports?"

"That's what the men have been working on all week," Jessie assured him. "Everyone's got papers of some kind. Jason would know more."

Jason. Oh, right. The ex-military guard that Cujo had left them. Now there was an interesting shifter. And Cujo wasn't even pack Second?

Well, he was security chief for the World Council. That might be why not. And he had a fistful of debit cards in his wallet? Interesting.

Focus, he commanded himself. "Let's find Jason then," he said out loud. "And Alefosio."

And two hours later he had everyone loaded, to his surprise. It helped to have Margarite Lewis stand there with her arms crossed and glower at everyone. She'd run out of hospitality apparently. Being attacked would do that. Although, he'd not found her all that hospitable the last time he'd come looking for Benny here.

He snorted. That had been a clusterfuck — his father again. Benny disappeared. How the hell had that become his problem? He found Benny — in Berkeley of all places — let his father know and went for a ride. By himself.

He stood near Margarite on the steps for a bit. "We might get this done," he observed.

She nodded, but her body was tensed up, and her face was somber. "Maybe," she agreed. "You've got some ticking time bombs, there, though, Ryder."

He jumped a bit at her use of his name — as if they were partners in this. Whatever this was. He turned to look where she was looking. And oddly, it wasn't at the bus load of disaffected young men, or the women standing in silence by the RVs. She was looking at those twins.

He glanced at her, intending to ask her about them, but she was looking at him with this appraising smile, and he lost his train of thought. That smile did something to him, no lie. Whether it was something good, he couldn't tell. His cock seemed to think so.

His wolf wasn't so sure. She wants something, the wolf insisted.

Probably.

"You grew up," she observed.

He snorted. "Maybe you won't throw me off the property if I show up next time."

She laughed. "Maybe not. But I wouldn't count on it."

She tapped him lightly on the butt. Astounded, he glared at her, and she laughed again. "Take care of my people, Ryder," she said. "And Alefosio had better come home to me in one piece. You hear?"

"I think he can take care of himself," Ryder said, his eyes seeking out the man.

"We all need someone at our back, even him," she replied.

He nodded. True enough. He hesitated, then blurted out, "We're being watched."

"I think so too," she said. She took a deep breath, her nose flaring slightly with the inhale. She shook her head. "Too many people, not all of them mine," she said. "I can't tell."

Ryder agreed. He'd tried sensing for shifters on the edges and he couldn't get a read either. "Do you have enough protection?" he asked. "I can leave a couple of men, if you want."

"No," she said. "I'll call in some of the pack once you're gone. I'd just as soon they didn't see you go. But they'll come, and we'll be fine. Maybe even get that backyard cleaned up."

The last was a bit sour, and he grinned. Yeah, she was salty about that backyard.

"Take care, Alpha," Ryder said seriously, and found it wasn't as hard as he'd expected to give her the respect of that title. Huh.

He walked down the sidewalk to the street parking area and started to get people moving out of there.

"I want you to take the RVs out of here," he told the two women from his club. They nodded. They'd ridden pinion coming in, so there weren't extra bikes to be left behind, thankfully. "Keep each other in sight, go the speed limit if you can. Those things handle like lumbering oxen. The van will keep you in sight — you don't worry about it. You know that campground, so head there. The rest of the club should beat you there and be setting up camp. Pull in, use the RVs to partition the camp into a boys and girls division."

"Got it, boss," Maggie said cheerfully.

He snorted. "Then get out of here."

He sent Jessie out in the van next. "Use your phone for a map," he said. "Have a woman copilot for you. Take the direct route to the I-5 freeway. Get on, keep the RVs in view, but don't try to follow close. It's about an hour drive south. Follow them to the campground. Pull up on the side of the RVs where there aren't a bunch of bikers." He grinned at her. "Don't worry, they'll be on their best behavior. To be honest, I'm more concerned about the guys on the bus."

Jessie nodded. "We've kept them pretty separate," she said. "But we aren't going to be able to do that forever."

"No," Ryder agreed. "But my men will make short work of those boys if they get out of line. Just scream my name."

She frowned. "Will you be there ahead of us?"

He laughed. "Trust me, it won't matter. You scream my name, and you'll have 20 men and a few women rushing to your rescue."

She smiled. "OK. We're off then."

He sent Alefosio out a different way. "You know the area," he said seriously. "Take the bus out as if you're going to Vancouver, then circle around and head south. Ignore the van and the RVs. We do not want to look like a caravan. When you get to the campground, you pull in alongside the bikes. We're going to keep people segregated."

Alefosio nodded seriously. "We're being watched, you know."

"I know," Ryder said. "Every neighbor on this street has been watching every move all day. And we still don't know who called the cops — not for sure. But that could have been very bad."

"It could have," Alefosio agreed. "But you're not worried about nosy neighbors."

"Not worried about *just* nosy neighbors," he corrected. "But I can feel it, can't you? Feel there's someone watching."

Alefosio paused and studied him for a moment. "Yes," he said. "I feel it. Paranoia I hope, because otherwise we're leaving my Alpha exposed here."

Ryder considered that, looking back at the house. "I'll talk to her again before I head out," he promised. "I offered to leave a couple of men, but she said no."

"That would be a help," Alefosio said gratefully. "I know why she wants me to go, and I really am the only one who can. But I can't say I'm happy about it."

Ryder nodded. "I understand. Clear out, then. Head north, then circle around to the south. You'll probably see me and my men here. Ignore us. Drive the speed limit and take your time."

"On it, boss," Alefosio said with a grin, proving he'd heard Maggie's cheeky response. Ryder forced himself to smile. Not convincingly, apparently. Alefosio straightened his face, nodded, and climbed into the bus's driver seat. He drove away from the house slowly.

Nothing wrong with that humor, Ryder told himself. But his wolf didn't like it, coming from someone not in the club. And Ryder tried not to set off his wolf.

In the end he didn't ask Margarite about leaving a couple of men. He couldn't figure out how to raise the issue, since she'd already refused. Instead, he just left two of his remaining men there. "Keep an eye out," he instructed them. "Watch for anyone heading out after us or any shifters who approach the house. The Alpha said she was calling in some of her people, so you can't assume anyone is a problem. But still, it won't hurt to have some backup. If nothing happens in the next hour, head out. If you see someone following me out of here, give Maggie a call. And if something looks off here, you should seek out Seth, her Second."

He stopped and stared at both of the men, until they bared their neck to him. Satisfied, he continued, "And don't piss her off! She holds grudges."

The two men snickered and relaxed. Ryder nodded once, and he and four others rode out. Damn it felt good, he thought. He glanced back over his shoulder at the two he'd left behind. Don't get into trouble you can't get out of, he wished them. And then he focused on the ride ahead, and the campground. Hopefully they'd have it all set up and food on the grill by the time he got there.

Chapter 8

Day 155 of the re-emerged Hat Island pack, Friday, Nov. 8, Hat Island

Abby stood next to Jake at the wheel as he piloted the boat back into the boathouse. She was wind-blown: her hair in her face, covered with salt spray, and damp from the mist that had turned to rain 30 minutes ago. And she hadn't felt better in months.

Jake glanced at her with a smile. "Good," he said, responding to her feelings. She smiled up at him and tucked one hand under his arm.

"Uh oh," Jake said, with a nod forward. Abby peered ahead.

Yui Yoshida was waiting for them on the dock. Abby grimaced. That was not a good sign.

Yui stood quietly, with no show of emotion on her face. An attractive woman of Japanese descent, she looked to be in her late 20s. She was older, in her 80s, but she'd often been mistaken for her children's nanny when Hat Island was still a mixed community of humans and shifters.

But Abby picked out signs of stress. Yui's body was a bit too stiff, her hands were clenched into fists at her side. What had happened? They hadn't been gone that long!

She dropped the barriers in her mind and ran a brief check across the bonds and links she carried. Nothing seemed too terribly amiss. Well, that was good, she guessed. Either whatever was wrong wasn't that big of a deal or the pack hadn't learned of it yet.

Abby hopped out of the boat and grabbed the mooring line to snug the boat up to the dock. Then she turned to Yui. "What's wrong?"

Yui smiled briefly. "Not sure where to begin," she said. But the story she told was mostly coherent, Abby thought, if somewhat unmoored from the here and now. She listened to Yui's complete summary while Jake secured the boat and got two salmon out of the ice chest. Fresh salmon for dinner tonight!

"OK," Abby said when Yui seemed to have run out of words. "So let me see if I've got this straight. Some Alpha in Africa forced Cujo to take his pre-shift girls to safety, and Cujo promised to bring them here to the boarding school for the serum. And Cujo didn't tell anyone?"

"It's not some Alpha in Africa," Jake interjected as he urged her forward toward the lodge. "Abraham Haile is the Chairman of the African Council of Alphas. He's an extremely powerful wolf — been in power for a century or more. And he'll be here for the World Council meeting next month, by the way."

"Fine," Abby said. "But I'm more interested in why Cujo didn't say anything?"

"Olivia is annoyed with him about that very thing," Yui said, amusement in her voice. "But it is true things have been a bit hectic here. So this morning, Olivia got a call from someone who told her the girls and their human chaperones and shifter guards are on their way. And Olivia chewed out Cujo, telling him he needed to get back here, with Benny, before the girls landed this evening. And then she came to see Okami and Michil Bogun."

"Is Michil in charge of getting things ready for these new students?" Abby asked somewhat appalled at the notion. She liked the man, but he would fit right in with her collection of absent-minded professors on campus.

"No, Emma is taking care of that," Yui assured her. Abby nodded. Emma had been a high school teacher in Oakland before she came to Hat Island in Stefan's last cohort — her own cohort. She was a good choice, although she usually ran the Beach House hotel with King Davis these days.

"OK," Abby said cautiously. "Sounds like it's all under control then?"

"Well, kind of," Yui said. "Cujo called Geoff and told him they'd need the plane if he was going to get Benny back here in time to welcome the girls. So Geoff sent the plane. But it's coming back full, Abby. Apparently, Margarite has had enough, and she wants the women and those young lads, as Okami calls them, gone. So they're headed here."

And that's where Abby lost the plot. "Not all of them would fit on the plane," she said. "That must be 60 people!"

Yui shook her head. They'd reached the back steps to the lodge's kitchen door. Jake ducked inside to hand off the salmon. Abby went through the back door into the mudroom and started stripping of wet clothes. Yui rummaged in the lockers and found her some dry sweats.

"No, of course not," she said, answering Abby's point. "And I'm not sure I understand this part — Okami got it from Geoff who seemed confused by it all as well. But apparently most of the women and the young men are headed down to Bellingham in some kind of caravan. Only the 10 most damaged of the women made-wolves are on the plane."

Abby nodded. She found a towel and dried her hair. She wanted a shower — salt spray made a sticky mess of her hair. As if her curly red hair wasn't a mess at the best of times.

"So the pilots, Benny and Cujo and 10 women," Abby said. "When are they getting here? Before Okami and Olivia get back with the new students, I take it?"

"Oh yes," Yui said with amusement. "Olivia was quite clear." The two women grinned at each other. Olivia was a bitch, to be candid, but she got things done. Abby thought she'd like her if the other woman gave her a chance. She didn't know why there was this wariness.

Her wolf flashed her a picture of two female dogs circling warily at a dog park. Well, maybe, she conceded. How do you know about dog parks, anyway? We haven't taken the dogs to one since I became a shifter! Her wolf just laughed at her, making Abby smile.

"But Abby, there is only room for 12 on that plane," Yui said troubled. Abby raised an eyebrow. "So 10 women, Benny and Cujo? Where are the twins? Okami was concerned, but he didn't have time to inquire. Olivia was quite insistent they meet that plane at Sea-Tac."

"And so she should," Abby assured her friend. She considered the matter. How concerned was she that the twins weren't with Benny? Moderately, she conceded. But they were either with this caravan, or with Margarite.

"Do we have rooms for the women?" Abby asked. She headed to the kitchen. She was going to need a sandwich — maybe two — to deal with all of this!

"Yes, Emiyo and Mei moved people around and freed up rooms up here in the lodge — above the spa," Yui answered. "Not everyone is pleased, of course. But it was thought that having the women here where they could be monitored and protected would be good."

Abby nodded. A cook handed her a roast-beef sandwich. Abby took a big bite out of it and smiled her thanks. It was good, but then she expected no less in the kitchen run by Okami Yoshida. There were benefits to having your kitchen run by a notorious assassin.

"OK," Abby said. "It sounds like everything is handled?"

"Except for this caravan of people heading our way," Yui said. She grabbed an apple from a bowl on the table and thrust it at Abby. "You need to eat more."

"Yes, Mom," Abby muttered, but she smiled and took the apple. "So this caravan? Are they coming here? Tonight?"

"No," Yui said, somewhat doubtfully. "Something was said about a campground outside of the Bellingham pack territory? Cujo told Geoff he was going to talk to Uncle Haru about talking to Hiro Tanaka about it?"

Abby snorted. OK, that was clear — not. "And who is in charge of that?"

Yui shook her head. "I do not know." She glanced at a clock on the wall. "But the plane will be here shortly. Perhaps they will have more answers."

"And more questions," Abby muttered. She knew her people. "OK, if you would? Find Alice, Emily and Betsy, will you? They should meet the plane with us. They know the women, at least some of them, right?"

Yui looked relieved to have Abby giving directions. The three women had also been some of Chen's victims. Alice was a nurse. Emily was Hat Island's first female security guard. And Betsy? Betsy had been determined not to be left behind, and Abby couldn't say no. But she had said no to the other two dozen women — and the dozens of young men who had been part of Chen's guards. So what were they doing on her doorstep anyway?

"You said this island would be a sanctuary for those who needed it," Jake said quietly, responding to her thoughts. "Has that changed?"

"No," Abby said. "But these women need serious help, Jake! We don't have the resources they need."

"Oh," Jake said. "You mean you only wanted to give sanctuary to people who don't need help?"

Abby paused. OK, she conceded. That was stupid. She sighed. "Point," she said ruefully. "But still. Jake, we don't have the resources they need!"

Jake nodded. "Then we'd better find them," he said. "Because there's going to be more traumatized people coming behind them."

Abby looked at him puzzled by that comment. But he didn't elaborate. Instead, Jake asked, "So when Dawson is making his inventory of people's skills, does he ask?"

"Ask what?"

"Ask if they have counseling skills? I know he asks about a medical background, but what exactly is he asking them to check off?" Jake asked. "Does he ask about teaching? Or just construction and security? We're only going to know if we ask."

"That is a very good point," Abby said slowly. She looked at Yui who was still standing there listening to them. "Yui? Do you want to follow up? What skills is Peter inventorying? And what should be added to his list?"

Yui nodded. "I will ask," she promised. "And I will find the three from Vancouver. But you need to be there to meet the plane, and I think they're about to land."

"No time for a shower?" Abby asked, not expecting that she would. She looked down at herself — pack sweats, which meant black pants, a gray sweatshirt, both a bit too big on her. Her own sneakers, which were damp with salt water. Her hair was frizzed by the mist and needed a brush — if not shampoo and a wash. She didn't look like an Alpha, she thought mournfully. She pictured Margarite, who always looked put together. Or Akihiro Tanaka who was impeccably dressed — whether business suit, workout clothes, or casual wear.

They didn't look like something the cat dragged in.

"No self-respecting cat would touch you," Jake said lightly. "Come on. Grab another sandwich. You can meet the women, and then corner Cujo and Benny for the rest of the story about those girls. And whatever the hell is going on with the caravan. Because if they're here, who's with them?"

And that was a very good question, Abby thought, as she did what he ordered: she grabbed another sandwich, and headed through the lodge, out the front door, and across the lawn to the path that led to the Beach House and the airstrip. Yui walked out with them, detouring toward the boarding house where the three Vancouver women lived.

Abby walked in silence focused on getting to the airstrip. It wasn't far. Nothing was far on Hat Island. It was a 5-mile run around the island, after all. The fact that they had provided homes for 500 people was a testament to their architect's vision of what a high-density neighborhood could look like.

And to all those wolves with construction skills that Peter Dawson had identified. Construction was frantically trying to meet demand. But wolves didn't do well alone anyway — so tight quarters wasn't necessarily bad.

She thought of her own Retreat House. She loved it. Loved having the space to be private, just her and Jake. She kept rooms at the Beach House for when Akihiro and Haru came over —they didn't come all that often. Akihiro had told her once that being in another shifter's territory was difficult. It didn't bother her, but it did him. So she stayed at Tanaka Towers more often than he came out here. But then, she still taught at Seattle University just a mile from Tanaka Towers. So she went over on Sunday nights or Monday morning, came home Thursday after work.

It made her treasure her days here on the Island to have so few of them, she acknowledged to herself. She felt a guilty relief that she would soon be quitting that commute. It was just for a while, she reassured herself. She'd go back to work next fall with none the wiser.

She hoped she could, but realistically, she wasn't sure about it. The pack needed more than a part-time Alpha.

"They need a happy Alpha," Jake said. "And if that means you need to commute and teach to be happy, we'll make it happen for you, Abby."

"You're answering my thoughts today," Abby observed. "Are my barricades too low?"

"Depends," he said. She looked back at him, and he was smiling. "It's useful for me to hear your thoughts, but if you're going to chew out Cujo without everyone on the island knowing about it, you might want to raise them a tad."

Abby laughed, and obligingly took a new assessment of her barriers. She'd lowered them to check on problems that might send Yui to the boathouse dock and hadn't raise them again. She should have, she thought. She really didn't want this latest crisis bleeding out to the pack at large.

Was it a crisis? Her gut said yes, but she wasn't sure what the crisis was, exactly: these women in need of serious care, the students from Africa, or this mysterious caravan. "Is Jason in charge of the caravan?" she asked Jake.

"Don't know," he answered. "But I wouldn't think that was something he would take on willingly. He must be with the caravan, though, or maybe he stayed behind at Margarite's?"

Something to consider. The rest of the security team had come home on Wednesday to Brighton's relief. Benjamin Brighton, chief of security, was getting ready to head down to San Mateo with Synde, Rick and Terry — Benjamin's partner. Geoff would be stepping up from assistant chief to chief. Abby wondered if Benjamin had told Geoff that yet. She snickered to herself. She should sell tickets. Bring popcorn.

But in the end, Synde and her team would be heading to San Mateo in a week, and Geoff would be security chief for the Hat Island pack.

Benjamin had wanted his security guards home. He was always paranoid about having too few here to defend the island. And he had reason to be, she conceded. But she wondered why now? It seemed quiet.

Didn't it? Then why was Jake worried about more traumatized people heading their way? And why did her gut say there was a looming crisis?

Something wicked this way comes, by the pricking of my thumbs, she thought soberly. Shakespeare had it right. So did Bradbury, for that matter.

She tried to think if there had been clues of stress at Akihiro's, but she'd been so focused on not letting any of her secrets get out, she didn't think she would have noticed if there had been. They'd talked about Chen, and his mysterious partner who might be planning a coup at the World Council. And they'd talked about Margarite, the situation with two packs in the larger Vancouver area, and even about what to do with all those young men.

She considered that issue for a moment. Thirty young men had attacked Margarite and her collection of independent and family packs because Abby was there for the girls to get the serum. It had been Abby who had intervened to leave them alive. Margarite would have killed them all. But it hadn't set right with Abby, and it still didn't. If shifters were to survive as a species, they had to stop killing off their young — killing off young girls at first shift, killing off young men in stupid dominance fights.

But there had been an additional 20 who survived the takedown of Chen as Alpha at the Vancouver pack house. She didn't know how many died in that battle. But what had Chen been planning to do with his army of 100 young shifter men? Men who had left their isolated home packs for the promise of a better life — an urban pack, a woman, status. Just how many disaffected young shifters were there? And what was she going to do with them?

Something occurred to her, and she stopped in her tracks. Jake went on alert. "What?" he asked in a low voice.

Abby shook her head. "Nothing alarming," she assured him. "I just had an idea."

"Alpha, if you come to a dead stop every time you have an idea, we'll never get to where we're going," Jake said with amusement. "Care to share?"

"I need to think about it," she said. "But do we have any loggers, farmers, fishermen?"

"Okami," Jake said, as they started moving forward. "He's got a team of fishermen. I don't know about loggers and farmers. Why?"

"Later," Abby said. "I need to let this idea ferment a bit first."

"Like yeast?" he teased.

"Exactly like yeast," she said seriously. Would it work? Maybe. She set it aside as they reached the Beach House, and then the airstrip. It wasn't much — a strip created by a man who refused to be dependent on the ferry only to find out that winter weather grounded him all too often. The strip had fallen into disuse, until Jedediah Jones bought land and built the outlandish house that was now the hotel they called the Beach House. And of course, he too thought he needed a landing strip. So when they took possession of the house, they got the strip as well. Not that they needed one. Well, not until Abby became the Chairman of the Northwest Council, and they became possessors of two aircraft — and one very large ship. Abby stilled at the thought of that ship and added it to her ball of string — mixing my metaphors, she thought ruefully. Can a ball of string ferment?

Alice, Emily and Betsy were already at the strip with Yui. Abby had an idea — yes another one, she thought grumpily. She felt Jake's amusement at their link and smiled. But these women would be a perfect project for Betsy. She needed something to do, Abby thought, and this was something that needed to be done.

"So we've got 10 women who need mentoring and counseling," Abby said when she reached the other women. "Betsy? You're going to be point on this. Emiyo and Mei have rooms in the lodge ready for them. But someone needs to be their big sister, so to speak. Show them around, get them involved in the classes at the gym, make sure they know about the lodge and the dining area — all those kinds of things. That's your job."

"What?" Betsy squeaked a bit. "I've only been here a week!"

"So?" Abby said with amusement. "I'd only been here a week when I howled at the moon and became Alpha of a new pack. So suck it up."

Jake started laughing as the other women just stared at each other. Abby shrugged. It was true. She wasn't going to listen to that as an excuse. "But seriously," Abby added. "You've explored and learned where things are, and how things work, right? Now you just have to cajole all of them into joining you."

"Ten is too many," Alice said. "She needs a partner in this."

Abby nodded. "Find her one," she ordered. "You've been working with the other women on the island. Who do you recommend?"

Alice considered that. "Maria?" she said. "If we're going for a motherly figure. But if we want someone who needs to come out of her own shell — the shell-shocked helping the shell-shocked — then I'd say Rose Evans."

Abby looked at Yui. Rose and her baby had been living with them. "What do you think?"

Yui tipped her head to the side considering it. "Yes," she said finally. "She needs to connect with other people. But Maria too. Maria, Betsy and Rose would be a good team."

"Done," Abby said. "Yui, you get to be the one to tell Maria she's got a job — and Rose, too."

Yui just nodded. "I will do that," she said seriously. "What about the others? The women at this campground?"

"One thing at a time," Abby muttered, her eyes searching for the plane. "One thing at a time."

Jake was amused, she could feel it. "What?" she demanded.

"Nothing, Alpha," he said, and she could hear the barely suppressed amusement in his voice too. "Glad to see you delegating."

She snorted. At least she could just order it done here. At the university, that kind of decision would take a week of cajoling people. Even bribery might be needed. There were advantages to being a dictator.

Was she? A dictator? Yes, she realized uncomfortably. A benevolent one, she hoped. But she had a hard time getting the inner circle to discuss a proposal! It was why she valued Benny so much. He could tackle a proposal and discuss it in such a way that others could disagree and debate the subject. But they wouldn't challenge her.

No wonder Alphas started thinking they were gods. They were, in some ways. It bothered her, for any number of reasons.

"There they are," Yui said, nodding toward a series of lights in the sky. "Good, because Okami is getting closer too."

Abby glanced at her, and just nodded. Mates. She knew where Akihiro was too. Of course, he mostly stayed in Tanaka Towers. She could guess that much. If she looked at the map in her head, though, she could track most of her inner circle. Most of her pack, really. And if she wasn't careful, her map would populate with every shifter in Seattle — thousands of little dots showing up and overwhelming her.

She'd learned early to keep the map cropped tight, as she thought of it. It was useful then, not overwhelming. The map had probably saved the pack that first weekend. But she still shuddered at the memory of the first time she'd accidentally opened it up.

The plane landed and taxied up to the small building that served as a hangar. They opened the door and dropped the steps. Cujo was the first one out. Then a line of women slowly followed. Benny brought up the rear. Abby waited for them to reach her.

"Welcome," she said with a smile. "I'm glad you're here."

"So you can abandon us again?" some woman said. Abby was taken aback. Had they felt abandoned when she left them at Margarite's? Possibly.

"No, this is my home, and you're welcomed here," Abby reassured them. "This is now your home too. I'm sorry you felt like I abandoned you — usually women think Benny and Cujo are sufficient!"

There were some giggles at that, and a shy smile in Benny's direction on one women's face. "I'm Betsy," Betsy introduced herself. "I'm the one who had a hard time shifting? Now I can shift easily! But I'm your guide for the time being. After all, I've been here all of a week."

More laughter, although Abby picked out a few who seemed totally disengaged from their surroundings. Well, Yui said these were the most traumatized of the women. Benny would know what they needed.

She hoped.

"Food?" Abby suggested. "Food is always good."

"I eat so much!" a woman marveled. "And I think I'm losing weight anyway!"

"We'll do a weigh-in tomorrow," Yui said. "I'm Yui, and I run the medical center and the women's spa. Your rooms are right above the spa, so you'll have easy access. Massages, pedicures, women's spa days...."

"And how are we supposed to pay for that?" Abby thought it was the same woman who had asked about being abandoned. "On our backs?"

There was a moment of appalled silence. But really after all these women had gone through, the woman had reason to ask, Abby thought compassionately. "No," Abby said. "There is no charge for the services at the spa. Or for your meals. If you're willing to wear pack sweats, all your clothes are provided for. You are owed compensation for what the Vancouver pack put you through. At some point you'll find something to do here — a job or a hobby or a passion. And a lot of the women here have been through what you've been through. They find they want something to do. But there is no rush. Your first task is to become used to being a shifter. And that's a big enough job by itself."

"So food?" Betsy said, persevering. Abby wanted to laugh. The woman really didn't take no for an answer. "I'm hungry, and you probably are too. And then we'll find Emiyo and figure out rooms. That's plenty for your first evening, don't you think?"

Betsy started moving them all toward the lodge, still talking. She was telling them about her first days at Hat Island and pointing out landmarks as she walked. The women followed her — some reluctantly, but they all trailed along. Abby was relieved. She looked at Yui. "You better call Maria and Rose," she said.

Benny and Cujo started to follow them. "Un uh," Abby said. "You two have some explaining to do."

"Okami is putting in at the ferry dock," Yui said. She pulled out her phone and stepped away to call Maria.

"Did he take the ferry over?" Abby asked with a laugh. She headed in that direction.

"You had the cruiser," Yui said. "So it was either the ferry or the fishing boat."

Abby laughed. Well, for a bunch of girls from Africa, the ferry would be fun. Hell, *she* thought it was fun. It was basically a tug boat with a cabin for passengers during bad weather. Someone — a decade ago from the looks of the boat — had painted it in different shades of blue and turquoise. It probably needed another paint job, Abby thought with amusement as she watched the ferry put in. Surely there was someone who wanted to take that on.

"So give me the quick and dirty," Abby ordered as they all started toward the ferry terminal.

"Cujo finally got around to telling me that he's doubling the size of the school," Benny said sourly. "Today. Today, he told me. Today!"

"And we'll get to that," Abby said soothingly. "But, he's only increasing it by 25 percent, Benny. The number of girls arriving from the Southeast Asia has increased. It's daily now. I told Pi to stop sneaking around and just use the ferry and go get them. Benjamin assigned him a guard and driver."

"What the hell?" Benny exclaimed. "Is this my father's doing? Which I need to talk to you about, by the way."

"I don't know," Abby said. "I got home, heard about it from Michil Bogun, talked to Pi, and then went into Seattle to the University. But Michil sent me an update each day. We've got two dozen girls — plus Pi — and now eight more."

"I need more teachers," Benny said morosely.

"Get with Peter Dawson," Abby said. "See who might have teaching skills. But a lot of the women do, Benny. And it would be good for them. They can teach the girls math. The girls can teach them languages, and they can all learn about shifting together."

"Joy," Benny said. He took a deep breath. "On it, boss."

Abby laughed. "Come on, let's meet these girls, get them settled in, and then? You and Cujo are coming to the Retreat House for a debriefing."

She felt Jake smile at her usage of the term debriefing. Abby grinned back at him. She did get a bit of fun out of using debrief and brief correctly, she acknowledged.

"Olivia," Cujo began.

"Olivia is going to be busy with those human chaperones," Yui interjected. "I have them booked at the Beach House. She said she'll wine and dine them, and then they can be taken back to the airport tomorrow. Apparently they wanted to see where the girls were going to be staying. I approve."

"Yes," Abby agreed. "What about the shifter guards?"

"Well, that's a problem," Yui said. "I'm not sure I got it straight, so we'll have to wait until someone explains it. I don't think Olivia was sure that she had it straight."

Cujo snorted. "Well, she'll straighten it all out," he said. "So yes, Alpha, I am at your disposal. And after you get through chewing me out — and Olivia has a go at me — Haru Ito wants a chunk of my ass too. And he's already chewed me out once today."

"I'd be careful about that phrasing around Haru," Benny murmured. "He might take it literally."

"Benny!" Abby scolded.

"What?" Benny said with mock innocence. "I wouldn't put it past that old wolf to nip a man's butt to get him in gear."

"I wouldn't put it past that old wolf to nip a man, period," Cujo muttered.

"Some men would pay big bucks for that experience," Benny replied.

"Enough," Abby ordered, but it made her laugh to envision Haru Ito's wolf nipping her men to get them moving. Then Benny sent an image through their bond, of a naked Haru and Cujo entwined. *Benny,* she said scandalized, sending her own image back to him. Benny bent over laughing.

Cujo just plodded on, resigned, toward the boat. Abby worried about him. Well, she'd pry it out of him shortly.

They watched in silence as Okami brought the ferry into dock. Jake and Cujo caught the lines and tied it up, and then helped the girls and women off the boat. Okami and two other men jumped off behind them.

Olivia brought them all up to introduce them. Abby was introduced as the superintendent of the school and a professor at Seattle University. She smiled at the girls and shook the hands of the chaperones. "Thank you for bringing them to us," she said sincerely.

The two women smiled. "They are a pleasure," one of them said. Abby thought she had a French accent, something about the way she phrased it? The girls were introduced to her by name, and there were shy smiles. Abby nodded and smiled at each and shook their hands too. That brought giggles, and Abby grinned at them.

Benny was introduced as Teacher Garrison, and the girls' eyes widened at that. Abby wondered what that term meant to them. She hoped someone would tell her, because it was an interesting reaction. Benny smiled at the women chaperones and shook their hands, holding them, really, Abby thought with amusement. The women melted.

Maybe we can have our meeting tomorrow? Benny suggested through their bond. *It would seem a shame for these two women to dine alone.*

Abby responded, *Not alone. I believe Olivia was going to take care of it.*

I don't think Olivia's their type, Benny replied, his eyes still holding the gaze of one of the women.

If you debrief quickly, you can invite yourself down for a nightcap, Abby suggested dryly.

Deal, Benny said promptly. *I get to go first.*

Abby snorted. *Olivia might want to weigh in on that — sounds like she and Cujo have some things to sort out.*

I called dibs first, he replied.

Abby struggled to keep a straight face as their backchat continued. The humans would think she was a maniac if she started giggling out loud about Benny's mental snark.

"We can all walk up to the school," Abby said. "I'm sure you'd like to see it. And then I believe Olivia has made arrangements for you all to stay at the Beach House, a hotel on the island. Will you be returning tomorrow?"

The women nodded. "We must," one of them said. Abby had forgotten her name already. "It is too bad. I would have liked to have taken my vacation and stayed. But that could not be arranged."

"If you ever decide to vacation here in the future, you are welcome to come back," Abby said. "We will not forget your generosity in bringing these girls to us."

Michil and Emma were waiting for them. The girls brightened to see a Black woman. And they were introduced to Sarah Johannsen, who at 17, was the de facto leader of the girls. There was chatter as the girls were shepherded inside.

"We'd give you a tour if you'd like," Benny offered. "But you might be too tired, and prefer to go to the hotel and settle in. I think Okami had your bags taken there. And Olivia is hosting you all at dinner."

"I am," Olivia said with a smile.

"And if you're willing, I'll join you later, for a nightcap," Benny said smoothly. Cujo looked at him sourly. Jake just seemed amused by it all.

"That would be charming," the one woman said. She seemed to be speaking for both of them.

It's going well, Abby thought. Almost like we've rehearsed it, rather than cobbled it together on a minute's notice. But she hadn't realized how much of a shifter territory the island had become until two humans were introduced into it. Making sure they only saw what they should see was a taxing proposition.

And then she staggered as Taisiya's mind voice hit her. *Alpha! The bad men are here! We must run. We must hide. Save us.*

And then Taisiya was gone.

Chapter 9

Day 155 of the re-emerged Hat Island pack, Friday, Nov. 8, Hat Island.

"Get me out of here," Abby murmured to Jake as quietly as she could. Damn, that girl packed a mental punch. "Now. Benny and Cujo too. And Okami."

"We're going to be late," Jake said, smiling at Abby, although his eyes showed his worry. "Okami? You and Yui ready to go? Cujo? Benny? Let's move it."

Olivia started to say something, and then she studied Jake with her eyes narrowed. She nodded shortly. "Come on," she said to the visitors. "You'll really like the Beach House." She lead them away, talking about the island and the hotel.

Jake urged Abby toward the lodge, but she just shook her head, waiting until she couldn't hear Olivia. Good enough. "I just got a mind blast from Taisiya," she said tersely. "She says the bad guys are there, and they must run and hide."

"What?" Benny exclaimed. He looked accusingly at Cujo. Cujo just looked sick.

"Benny? Cujo? Who's with the women?" Abby asked.

"Jessie," Benny answered. "And some of Ryder's women are driving the RVs."

"Ryder?" Abby asked, frowning. Was she supposed to know who that was?

"My brother," Benny said. "He and his motorcycle club are escorting the women and Chen's recruits to a campground just outside of the Bellingham pack territory."

"You have a brother?" Abby asked, diverted for a moment. "And he's a biker?" She considered that, then shook her head. It could wait. She *hoped* it could wait. "Jessie Nickerson? She's not enough to protect the women."

"Didn't think she'd have to," Cujo answered. "That's what the bikers are for."

Abby absorbed that, as much as she could. "OK." She started handing out orders. "Benny, call Jessie. I want a cell phone in Kristina's hands ASAP. Have her call me directly."

Benny nodded and was already paging through his phone directory. "Kristina? Not Taisiya?"

"Taisiya has more power. But it's Kristina who is the grounded one. She looks after Taisiya more often than not. I want to talk to her."

"How do you know that when I didn't?" Benny asked. He punched a number.

"Chen's pack house," Abby said. Benny didn't ask for more details. He turned away and started talking — to Jessie, Abby presumed.

"So who is with the caravan?" Abby asked Cujo. "Of our people?"

"Jason Wahlberg and David White — the medic," Cujo said. "That was the last of our people. Alefosio, one of Margarite's men, was coming along too."

"Not Margarite?" Abby asked, startled. "I thought she was planning on taking the women to Ayta herself."

"It's been a hell of a day, Alpha," Cujo said wearily. "Margarite and Benny were attacked on the Burns Bog trail. And then a team from Penticton attacked her pack house. She didn't feel she could leave. I don't blame her."

"Penticton," Okami said flatly.

Cujo nodded.

Abby looked at the two of them. "You can explain that later too."

"Alpha? Here's Kristina," Benny said, handing her the phone.

Abby took a deep breath and gentled her voice. "Hi, honey," she said, making sure to pace her words so that she didn't sound as panicked as she was. "I got a mind blast from Taisiya. What's going on? Are you under attack? She seemed worried that you were."

"I don't know what's going on," Kristina wailed. "She says we are. But we aren't. She wants us to run and hide, but I tell her we are hidden. That we are safe. But it's like she can't hear me."

Abby put her on speaker. "Tell me," she ordered. "Start at the beginning."

Kristina said Taisiya had been intrigued by Benny's suggestion that she contact their mother. She hadn't ever tried to be the one to initiate — her mother always contacted them. So when they got to the campground, she curled up on the RV bed, and tried it. And it worked!

"I didn't mean to do it now!" Benny muttered. Abby rolled her eyes.

"Did your mother say where she was?" Abby asked Kristina. "What did she say?"

No, her mother hadn't said that. She just ordered Taisiya to run and hide because the bad men were coming. "I don't think Mom meant right this minute," Kristina said, fretfully. "I mean she doesn't know where we are. I think we're safe here, but I want to come back to the island — that's hiding right?"

"Yes," Abby said. "You're safe here. I think you're safe there too." She hoped.

"But Mom's voice is really powerful," Kristina said. "And when she ordered Taisiya to run and hide, Taisiya wanted to do it right now. I won't let her. I locked her in the RV. But she's broadcasting her panic and anxiety, Alpha. And it's infecting the other women. They all want to run and hide. Jessie and I are trying to keep it under control, but Taisiya is more powerful than we are."

Abby swallowed. "I'm going to get you some help," she promised the girl.

"Can you come?" Kristina said in a small voice. "Please?"

"Yes," Abby said calmly. "But we're nearly three hours away, Kristina. So you've got to hang on, OK? You focus on calming Taisiya down." Abby considered that. Bikers? "Kristina? See if some of the bikers have some weed. Edibles would be good. But, get Taisiya to smoke it, eat it, inhale it. It will help. Is David White there? See if he's got a sedative he can give her."

Benny was doubled over, laughing about the weed, she guessed. Abby ignored him. It had worked for the Hayden Lake pack, hadn't it?

"I'll ask," Kristina said.

"Good," Abby approved. "Now let me talk to Jessie again. You stay with Taisiya, Kristina. You're safe. And you need to make her feel safe too."

There was a mumbled shuffle of voices, and then Jessie said, "Alpha? What do I do?"

"Find Alefosio and Jason," Abby said. "And David White. Get a sedative into her — weed will do it, by the way, if any of the bikers have some of that."

"I thought about Alefosio," Jessie said. "But the women are picking up on Taisiya's fear that the bad men are coming. I'm afraid they'll flee any man at this point." She took a deep breath and exhaled. "It's all I can do not to run, myself. I want to hide."

"It's not real," Abby said quietly. "Think of it as if she's trapped in a nightmare, OK? Tell the other women. It's a nightmare, and she's projecting it. She doesn't mean to alarm anyone. Does that help?"

There was a sigh of relief. "Yes," Jessie said gratefully. "That helps. I'll tell the others. But I don't think having men come into this part of the camp is a good idea."

"You're the one on the ground," Abby said. "I trust your judgment. Benny said something about women in the motorcycle club? Are they shifters? Can you get them to help you? You need to keep the women in the camp, Jessie. Don't let them scatter and hide. And you need someone to give Kristina some sedatives for Taisiya. Those two things. Focus on them. Is Benny's brother in the camp?"

"I don't think so," Jessie said, worry in her voice. "Ryder was bringing up the rear. But I don't think he's here yet."

"OK," Abby encouraged her. "You're doing good. Hold on. Help is on the way."

"You're coming here? Kristina said you were."

"We are," Abby said. Okami turned back to the ferry to get it started up. Jake moved to help him. "But we've got to cross over to Everett, and then drive up. It's going to take us nearly three hours. So you're going to have try to keep things under control until we get there. Call me back if you need to, OK?"

"I'll try," she promised with a shaky voice. Abby ended the call and handed Benny his phone back.

"Jessie doesn't think your brother is there yet," she said. "See if you can find him. And call Alefosio and fill him in. Cujo? Call Jason, tell him what we know."

Abby looked at Yui who was standing quietly beside her. "You need to stay here if you would," Abby said. "Tell Pete and Maria, they've got the island. Let Benjamin and Geoff know what's going on. Tell Olivia and Michil they're in charge of the school — Emma can help with the new girls."

"We'll be fine, Alpha," Yui said. "We've got the island. Go."

Abby nodded. She trusted her people. Remember that, she chided herself. It wasn't their first crisis after all. She almost had hysterics at that thought. She hopped onto the ferry, followed by Benny. Cujo was still standing on the dock, looking undecided about something.

"He's not picking up," Benny said with worry. "May just be he's on his bike."

"And I really want to know this story," Abby said. "A brother named Ryder who has a MC?" She shook her head. Priorities! she told herself. She turned to Cujo.

"Cujo? Why are they at a campground outside of Bellingham?"

Cujo started telling her the events of the day and how they'd gotten to this point. "So, Haru Ito called Hiro Tanaka about taking in some of the young men, put them into college or something. Hiro isn't thrilled, as you can imagine. No one wants these young men — which is why Chen's call was so attractive to them in the first place," Cujo wrapped up. "But Hiro was going to go out and meet with the men and see what he thought."

"Why not the women?" Abby muttered. "They might be a better fit for college than those young idiots." She considered her own students. "Well maybe not. Young idiots do just fine on a campus." Benny snorted at that.

"So, call Hiro Tanaka," Abby ordered Cujo. "Who is best to talk to him about this? Cujo?"

"I will call him," Okami said from the helm. "But he will need to hear from you, Alpha."

"Hear what, exactly?" Abby asked, but she nodded. "I'll talk to him."

Jake took over the ferry, and Okami came down to the main deck, talking to someone on his phone quietly. Abby waited. "Alpha Hiro Tanaka," Okami said. "Alpha Abby Stafford." He handed her the phone.

"Alpha," Abby said. "We've met before. I'm sorry that this visit will be under such uncertain circumstances."

"Rumor has it, all of your site visits have created 'uncertain circumstances,'" Hiro Tanaka said. He was Akihiro's nephew, a tech giant in his own right, if Abby understood things correctly. And now Alpha of the Johannsen pack — the Bellingham pack — by right of challenge. It hadn't been easy to walk into a hostile pack and make it his own. He appeared to be doing it — a testament to the strength of his wolf.

"Not by my intent," Abby replied. "But this does seem to be a time of change. As you have proved, yourself."

There was a pause, and then Hiro sighed. "Do you know why I have a bunch of shifters camped on my doorstep?"

"Not completely, no," Abby said, forcing herself to laugh. "Margarite was going to take the women victims of Chen's pack, along with the young men he recruited to be his soldiers, to Ayta in Odessa. She was planning to go through Penticton. But Penticton attacked her this morning. She's feeling the need to defend her territory and couldn't come as their escort. And it wasn't deemed safe to go through Penticton. So they started south. I believe the hope was that you might find room in your pack for some of those who might see college as an option."

"This makes my head hurt," Hiro muttered. "And I've already heard the explanation from Haru, *and* from Okami. All right, I will speak to the wolves. Anything else?"

"Well, yes," Abby said. "I just got a mind blast from one of the young wolves there. She's panicking — saying the bad guys are coming, and they must run and hide. And it's infecting everyone. We're hoping your presence will give them a sense of security and prevent the women from scattering."

Another silence, longer this time. "A mind blast," Hiro said, his voice carefully neutral. "Like what mates might do?"

"Something like," Abby agreed. "She's telepathic and has skills off the charts."

"There is no such thing as telepathy," Hiro said flatly. "What are you saying?"

Abby paused, looking around for Okami. He was frowning, but he didn't help her out. She was pretty sure Okami had used his links and bonds to communicate when Tanaka Towers had been under attack. Had Hiro not been one of the recipients?

"What do you call it when mates can speak to each other through a bond?" she asked, a bit helplessly.

"A myth?" Hiro asked sardonically. And in that moment, he reminded her of Akihiro, not necessarily a point in his favor.

She chuckled and hoped it didn't sound as forced as it felt. "Well, it is possible. And it can be done through other kinds of bonds and links as well," Abby said. She didn't mention spiders and whisperers and all the other things that went bump in the night. "But in this case, it's like the young woman is having a waking nightmare, and she's pulling others into it. We hope that a strong Alpha such as yourself can calm things down. The thing is, part of what she's broadcasting is that there are bad men coming — run and hide."

Hiro grunted. "My arrival with my guards is not likely to inspire faith then, is it?"

"Do you have a woman — a powerful woman — in the pack you could take along?"

"You have the two women closest to that, Alpha. My daughter. And the daughter of the former Alpha, Sarah Johannsen," Hiro said.

"Mei?" Abby considered that. Sarah was needed here with the new girls, and she couldn't get up there any faster than Abby herself could. "Is she that strong?"

Yes, Cujo sent. She hadn't been aware he was eavesdropping.

"Stronger than any women I have here," Hiro answered. "Johannsen didn't exactly welcome strong women."

Abby bet there were strong women in the pack that Hiro had dismissed — just like there had been in all the packs she'd visited.

Well, not the Vancouver pack. She stopped herself from thinking what that pack had done to strong women. She'd be in the fetal position having a meltdown instead of just fighting hysterical laughter if she let herself dwell on that.

"I'll get Mei on the road ahead of me," Abby promised. "She's still over an hour out, but she's 40 minutes ahead of us. That will help. But I wanted you to be apprised of the situation."

"For all the good it does me, I thank you," he said. "I look forward to your arrival."

Abby ended the call and handed it back to Okami. She found her own phone in her jacket pocket and looked for Mei's phone address.

"Alpha, I can't go," Cujo said somewhat desperately. He was still on the dock. "I've got to stay here."

"Why?" Abby asked. She tapped on Mei's number and waited for her to pick up.

"That was Kent Frasier who came with the girls," Cujo said. "And Tighe."

Who? Abby asked of Benny through their link. She watched Jake continue to untie ropes and move smoothly through the tasks of getting the ferry back out to sea. She could feel him listening, but he didn't pause in his tasks.

Kent Frasier is Cujo's manager in Monte Carlo, Benny answered. *No clue who Tighe is.*

"So?" Abby asked when Cujo didn't continue. "Wait," she ordered when Mei picked up. She explained to Mei what she needed.

"And you think I can reassure one of the twins?" Mei asked, incredulously. "Have you been around them? They're incredibly strong!"

She can, Cujo said. *She's stronger than she knows.*

That was interesting, Abby thought. She was learning all kinds of interesting things tonight — or getting interesting questions to pursue, at least.

"Yes," Abby said. "I know how powerful they are, and yes, I think they will find your presence comforting. Besides I promised your father."

She snorted at that. "On it, boss," she said wryly and hung up.

"So Kent wouldn't leave Monte Carlo unless something big is up," Cujo said, picking up that conversation as if they hadn't been interrupted. "And Tighe? He's linked to Olivia." He saw Abby's expression, and elaborated. "Like an employment bond? Or like Margarite without the sex."

Abby blinked. "Olivia has men linked to her like Margarite does?"

Cujo nodded. "It's a long story, and I don't even understand how it happened, myself," he said. "But yes. Kent and three others formed links with her when they came under attack while they were in Monte Carlo and I was in Africa."

Abby rubbed her forehead between her eyes. "I knew I should have made you tell me what had happened on that trip," she muttered.

"Things got a bit busy," Cujo said. Abby wanted to laugh at that; she was still fighting hysterics. "But I need to know why they're here, Abby."

"So call Kent and ask," Abby said. "But I need you on this ferry, Cujo. I'm sorry, but I do."

Cujo swallowed hard and nodded. "And I had better give Haru Ito a heads up, too," he muttered. "He chewed my ass this morning over waffling about killing the attackers."

He killed attackers? Abby asked Benny, not wanting to interfere with Cujo's phone call.

Well, I killed three, and Margarite disabled two. They attacked us when we were on the trail. Cujo killed the last one after he questioned him. But then another team came at us. Cujo killed them after he questioned them too. Left them for one of Margarite's men to dispose of. He's gone back to mercenary mode, Alpha. It was scary to watch.

Abby just bet it was. She'd seen glimpses of that Cujo when they'd gone to Russia. But mostly she worried about Cujo. That wasn't the man he wanted to be.

That's what he said too, Benny agreed, eavesdropping on her thoughts. *But apparently Haru Ito said Cujo needed to step up and be the World Council security chief, not some fitness coach at a health spa.*

Abby winced at that.

"Benjamin wants to send guards," Jake said, looking away from his own phone. "He thinks this is a lot of leadership in one place for there to be no guards."

Abby looked around. Jake, Benny, Cujo, and Okami? She'd be willing to invade Japan with this team.

"If we take guards, we're not going to have room for the girls coming back," Abby said. "And if we take two vans, we're still undefended. Besides, we've got outsiders on the island. I want him to have every guard at his disposal."

Jake nodded and turned back to his phone. Abby stood on the deck of the ferry and fretted. What didn't she know? What did she need to know? She shook her head. She hated this on-the-fly stuff.

She felt Jake's amusement. *What?*

You are very good at managing several different conversations and decision threads at the same time, he said. *It's a pleasure to watch you.*

Abby grimaced. *Doesn't feel like I'm managing anything.*

"Let's go," Jake said out loud. They pulled away from the dock slowly. At the last minute, Cujo hopped onto the ferry, his phone still to his ear.

Abby wanted to start grilling people, but really the diesel engine of the ferry, coupled with the wind that had picked up, made it impossible. And she suspected everyone needed to hear it all — another reason she was glad there were no guards going along. She looked around at Cujo's and Benny's stressed faces, at Okami's grim expression, and Jake's alertness. It was going to take a while for them to tell her what the hell had happened this morning. She sighed.

The van was still dockside, fortunately. Jake took the driver's seat and started it up. Abby slid into the seat next to him. The other three men sat in back, Okami in the farthest back seat.

"All right," Abby said. "Who wants to start? Benny? Have you found your brother yet?"

"He's not picking up," Benny said, worry in his voice. "I can't figure out why he wouldn't be there already."

"Keep trying," Abby said. "And tell us about this brother? I didn't know you had one. Why is he shepherding this caravan anyway?"

Benny told her about Ryder. "He did a lot of transport work in the Army," Benny finished. "He was in Iraq. Brought a refugee convoy out of Mosul. So when he showed up at Margarite's it made sense. I mean if he can get refugees out of Mosul, this should be a piece of cake."

"Should be," Jake agreed. His voice was grim. "Mosul was bad news."

"Yeah," Benny said. "Messed him up some. He doesn't talk about it. He came back a different man than the one who left. Dad and I both tried to talk him out of enlisting, but it was right after 9/11. He was one of the first in. I'm not sure what happened in Mosul. But he couldn't settle back into the pack. He took to the road again, this time with some of the pack and some human vets like him. It's almost like a pack, or a mobile section of Dad's pack, I guess."

He hit redial on his phone.

"So he and the MC went up to Alaska for the ride to Prudhoe Bay — I guess it's a big deal," Benny said.

"I've heard of it," Abby said with a nod. She'd spent some time in Alaska, researching what happened in Native Alaskan communities as they came into contact with outsiders.

"And they had a good time," Benny continued. "They stayed until the weather chased them out. They were headed to their winter home in northern California, when Ryder got a call about his mother. Someone had roughed her up. She's near 70 now. She's under the Alpha's protection — she doesn't know that, of course. So Ryder detoured to the Okanogan to see what was up. He took care of it, and then he came looking for me. Starting at Margarite's."

"So he knew to look for you there?" And what did 'take care of it' mean? Stupid question, really, she thought. It meant someone died for it. Duh.

"Ryder knew she'd probably know where he should go to look for me," Benny amended. "He kept saying things had gotten crazy during the last six months. That he went away, and things went to hell?"

Benny snickered, and everyone laughed too. Didn't that sum things up?

Well maybe not to hell, exactly, Abby thought. But changed, most certainly there was change.

"Hey, bro, where are you?" Benny said into his phone. "There's a problem at the campground."

"Yeah, well I'm kind of in a situation myself," Ryder responded. Benny put him on speaker phone.

"We're headed north, where are you?" Benny asked.

"I'm trapped in the rest stop just south of the border," Ryder said. "Got herded off the road, then the bastards fired at me. Cleaned the rest stop out right quick. But now I've got two flat tires, a bike for a barricade, and some assholes shooting at me. So how is your day going?"

There was silence in the car. "Well that sucks," Benny agreed. "One of the twins connected to her mother telepathically, and her mother told her to run and hide — bad men were coming. And she's blasting it to everyone in the camp. We've got 15 women about to bolt."

"I'd ask you to repeat that, but it wouldn't make any more sense if I heard it again," Ryder muttered.

"Look, you need to wrap up your problem and get down there," Benny said with more seriousness. "Alpha Hiro Tanaka is on his way there, and someone needs to meet him. And someone needs to reassure everyone that they don't need to run and hide."

"And you think I can do that?" Ryder said incredulously. "Even if I got down there, what exactly am I supposed to do? You've got a psycho inflaming the paranoia of a bunch of traumatized women, and I'm supposed to reassure them that the bad men aren't coming? Bro, they think I am the bad man!"

Abby grinned. That about summed it up.

"Not to mention I'm held down under gun fire, and I have two flat tires!" Ryder was on a rant.

"Ryder, this is Abby Stafford," Abby introduced herself. "Are your attackers shifters or humans?"

There was a pause. "Shifters," he said finally. "I double-checked."

"Jake Lewis here," Jake said, letting the phone pick him up. "Are you truly alone in the rest stop? No humans around? No police on their way? And is their vehicle in the lot?"

"Sir," Ryder said. Abby thought it was said seriously, but it was hard to tell. Jake didn't comment. "There are no humans. No police, either, which is odd now that you mention it. But I won't question a gift from the gods, because cops will assume I'm at fault. But there's no vehicle here either. So they came in on foot — two or four — and that's a problem too. I can't take them out and leave the bodies for cops to find. Not with my bike sitting here."

"Understood," Jake said. "Stay alive, soldier. We'll send someone to help."

Jake nodded and Abby ended the call.

"You're not sure he isn't having a flashback," Cujo observed.

"Well, he's got a bike with two flat tires, and someone is shooting at him," Jake said. "But whether he's still tethered to the here and now? You tell me."

There was silence in the van. "Why?" Benny began. He stopped. "What makes you question it?"

Jake didn't look back but stayed focused on the road. Abby noticed that he'd inched up his speed, however. "The details don't add up," Jake said. "Something Ryder noticed too. And the 'sir' worries me."

"Which is why you called him soldier," Abby observed thoughtfully.

"It would be reassuring no matter what he's facing," Jake said. "He's got a commanding officer on his way. Trust me, knowing that may be all he needs to solve this. But we need to get him some backup ASAP. Because if he solves it by killing them, we need to get him and his bike out of there fast."

Abby considered the challenge. Not just people, but a rig big enough for a motorcycle. What she really wanted to know was why. Who would be good too. But both questions could wait. She sighed, and pulled out her own phone, and called Jessie back. What the hell had they done before cell phones?

Rhetorical question, she told herself. Not to be added to any list.

"Hey there," she said when Jessie picked up. "You all good?"

"Hanging in there," Jessie replied. "No one has bolted yet. You know that once one goes, we're going to see them scatter, right?"

"We're on our way," Abby reassured her. "But we've got a problem. You know Ryder? He's under attack at the rest stop just south of the border. You know the one?"

"We came past it," Jessie said. She sounded worried. "Under attack by who?"

"That's a good question," Abby said, forcing herself to laugh. "And I don't know for sure. Shifters. But they shot out his tires, so even if he runs them off, he needs a ride home. That's got to be you."

"Me?" Jessie yelped. "Alpha, if I leave here, the women will freak."

"I want you to take the twins with you," Abby said, ignoring that. "That will reduce their panic. Take the RV they're in. Explain to the other women what's going on and drive away."

There was silence — both on the phone from Jessie, and in the van. Yes, this was a bit out there even for her 'creative problem solving approach,' she thought with amusement.

"I can't drive the RV," Jessie said finally. "I could barely manage the van. Ryder let me practice with it before we left for here. But the RV? One of the women in his MC drove."

Good, they were discussing how, not if. Always a good thing, Abby told herself. "So, find the woman who drove it, and get her to drive it now. With Ryder in jeopardy, you shouldn't have any problem convincing her to help. But be sure someone trustworthy stays with the women!"

"I'll call you right back." Jessie ended the call.

Abby nodded once, then called Kristina. "How is it going? You find any sedative yet for your sister?"

"No sedative, but someone had some pot gummies." Kristina giggled. "I just find it funny that these big, bad bikers had gummies."

Abby laughed. "Sampled them, did you?" she teased.

"Both of us had some," Kristina agreed. "And yes, it helps."

Probably a good thing, Abby thought. If Kristina stayed calm it would help the women outside the RV and it would help Taisiya. Win-win.

And she should be shot for telling 14-year-olds to get stoned.

"OK, on a different note, there's a problem," Abby began.

"You think?"

No filters, Abby thought, amused. But Benny choked behind her and started coughing.

"Ryder — you know who he is? — he's under attack at the last rest stop. I want Jessie to take the two of you there to back him up. The bad guys are shifters. And they shot out his tires. So he's trapped."

"Taisiya is going to freak," Kristina said uncertainly.

"That's where you come in," Abby said frankly. "You need to make her understand that Ryder is on your side — on *our* side — and that you're going after the bad guys. Do you understand the phrase 'the best defense is a good offense?'"

Kristina giggled. "That's a sports saying, isn't it?"

"How about get him before he gets you?" Cujo interjected.

"Yes," Kristina said. "I understand that one."

Abby knew she did. She mourned that a 14-year-old girl knew about killing a man before he killed her. But Kristina did. And there was no going back from that.

"Good," Abby said. "Then you need to know, that's what you're doing. You're going to go after the bad guys before they come for you. Because I'm very afraid that in the end, you're who they want."

Abby could hear a muffled conversation — Kristina and Taisiya, she supposed. Kristina returned. "Yes," she said. "Taisiya thinks that's a good idea."

Abby swallowed hard. That scared her more than anything else had. "Remember, Ryder is on your side," she warned again. "He is not one of the bad guys, he's a good guy, a protector."

"We've got this, Alpha," Kristina said confidently. "Jessie's here. And Maggie. So we're heading out. Brenda is staying with the other women, and they understand. We're going after the men Taisiya is worried about."

The call ended. Abby chewed on her lower lip, wondering what she'd just done.

"Well, that should be interesting," Benny said dryly. "Do you want to call Ryder back and tell him he's about to be rescued by teenaged girls, or do I get the pleasure?" He started laughing.

"Oh shut up, Benny," Abby said, laughing herself. "Go for it. I need to call Mei and warn her."

"Warn her about what?" Cujo asked, and it sounded like he was just curious — an academic question worth exploring.

Abby snorted. "Good question, I'm not completely sure," she said, then dialed Mei's number.

Chapter 10

Day 155 of the re-emerged Hat Island pack, Friday, Nov. 8, I-5 North to Bellingham

Mei Tanaka ended the call from Abby Stafford and shook her head. How the hell did she get roped into these things?

She was the manager of the lodge at Wolf Harbor, which was supposed to be a fitness resort, but had become a research lab for Stefan Lebenev and then home to 500-plus werewolves. Not all of them lived in the lodge, but many of them did. And even more of them ate there regularly. Wolves were communal, given a choice. And so even those who owned a house on the island or lived in one of the cabins or the dormitory, usually ate at least one meal a day at the lodge. They socialized there, or in the attached gym. She ran that too.

Truth was she was good at running things. Now if she could just convince her father and her great uncle of that. She rolled her eyes. They saw her as a 15-year-old girl not the competent 25- year-old woman, and probably always would.

All of the business offices were still at the lodge for both the pack and its various business entities. They were bursting at the seams. There was a civic center and business offices in the plans for the island — down by the ferry terminal. Soon, she hoped.

Thank God, she didn't have to deal with most of the business aspects — Peter Dawson did. And he was good at it. She so liked competent people.

Mei mostly ran the lodge by mediating disputes between housekeeping, the kitchen, the spa, the research staff, and the business office. She actually liked solving all the problems that arose. She also ran the office on the docks in Everett — the public face of the resort, the pack, and its businesses. And because she was the person who was most often there, she seemed to be in control of travel arrangements. She liked that too — it meant she was in on whatever was going on in the pack. If they wanted to go somewhere, they usually had to go through her.

Except for Cujo. He had his own vehicles — including a very nice new black pickup that was sitting in the parking lot by the dock office. So even with him, she knew whether he was on the island or not.

Not that she cared about what Cujo was up to, she assured herself. She was just snoopy.

But this harebrained exercise? What were they thinking?

Abby said, go north. You're the strongest female shifter in the area. We're right behind you. But something is going on with Taisiya, and Kristina needs your help.

OK, Mei wasn't sure how strong she was, but if Kristina was having to cope with Taisiya, she definitely would need help. So Mei agreed to drive up and help out. Besides, let's face it, she was curious. Benny had a brother, and he was a biker? With an MC and everything? She wondered if he had tats....

Wolves didn't, as a rule, although some packs practiced scarification, which sounded like it would really hurt. That was the point, Michil Bogun had told her when they were talking about it one day. She didn't remember how it came up. Something about Anton Vuk. Apparently he had a lot of ritual scarification — they looked like tattoos, she'd heard, but they weren't.

How had she heard about that? Well that question was easy. A spa day with the other women. She didn't even have to think about that. Probably Synde had gotten it from Abby and shared it with the rest of them.

She pulled her mind back to the real world of driving up I-5 in the rain. It had been misty all day, but it turned to rain around sunset. Just her favorite thing — driving in the dark, in the rain, to go rescue a bunch of paranoid wolves. She pulled into a Starbucks drive-through in Marysville and got a venti black coffee. It was just an hour drive. Well, probably a little more in the rain.

Mei's phone rang again, as she reached Bellingham. "Answer," she said out loud. She glanced at her phone — Abby again. Really, she needed them to leave her alone so she could follow the directions to the campsite on Google maps.

"There's a problem," Abby said. She told her about Ryder being trapped at the rest area south of Blaine, and that the twins and Jessie had gone to rescue him. Mei rolled her eyes. Wouldn't it have been better to send her? Then she looked around at the interior of her Prius. Well, maybe not. Might be hard to fit a motorcycle in here. "So I don't know exactly what you're going to be walking into at the campground, Mei," Abby said. "I just wanted to give you a heads up. You need to take charge of whatever is going on and don't let it turn into a first-rule violation situation."

Mei knew what she meant by that — don't let the boys get huffy and go wolfy.

"Me?" she protested, startled. "You think I can prevent anyone from doing anything?"

There was a moment of silence. "Your father seems to think so," Abby said. "He said you were the strongest female wolf in the area when I asked him to take his strongest woman with him. You just have to control things until he gets there. You're going to be about 20 minutes ahead of him, I think."

Her father thought what?

"Abby," she began to protest, then Cujo took the phone.

"Mei, listen to me," he said calmly — as if she had a choice. "Remember on the beach? I told you to go back to the cabin, and you stood there and argued with me. Remember?"

Mei saw the exit to the campgrounds at Tennant Lake and took it. "Yes, I remember," she told Cujo. "You didn't have a good reason. You can't just order me around, Cujo!"

"Well, I *can* order most people around, actually," Cujo said. "The number of people who wouldn't have to obey me when given a direct order are very few. Most of them are in this van, to be honest. And you."

Mei paused at that. Dominance, he was talking about dominance. But if she had to obey every stupid male in her life, how would she ever get anything done?

"So what? I pull in and start issuing orders?" she asked sarcastically.

It was Abby who answered, taking her question seriously. "Basically, yes," she said. "Take a moment, Mei. Let it sink in. You're the most dominant wolf in the area. Those are your wolves to command. Keep repeating that to yourself until you believe it. You need to find Jason Wahlberg and David White. They're Hat Island pack. And Alefosio — he's a Tongan, it'll be easy to spot him. He's the size of a small mountain."

"Does he have tattoos?" Mei asked. So she had a thing about tattoos, sue her.

"Benny says yes," Abby answered with amusement. "So protect the women. Calm them down. Take charge. I know you can. I've seen you do it."

OK then. Think of it as mediating between Okami and Stefan, while protecting the wolves who cleaned the lodge. She could do this. "Got to go," she said. "I just arrived at the campsite."

She pulled up to an RV that was dividing a large gathering of people — it reminded her painfully of middle school dances — the women were in the RV and the van next to it, the men were on the other side of the RV. And in between were a handful of women and three men.

Mei grimaced. She didn't think dancing was what the men intended. She could feel the hostile intent even in the car. She let her senses expand outward. All shifters. She didn't sense any humans in the area. Well, a rainy November night wasn't likely to draw many campers. That was good. And anyone with any sense would feel the tension out there and move on.

She would turn around and drive off, if she had a choice.

Mei studied the handful of women standing aggressively at the nose of the RV. Mei didn't recognize them. Standing just in front of them, though, was Jason Wahlberg. She did recognize him, he worked for Hat Island's security; and that was David White next to him. The rather large man — and even for a shifter he was large, well, more broad than large, she guessed — must be Alefosio.

Confronting them was a bunch of hostile young men. Holy shit, there were a lot of young men! She hadn't expected that.

Beyond the confrontation, she could see a covered pavilion where there looked to be a barbeque going. A bus was pulled up next to it — a rather elderly yellow school bus that said Delta First Baptist on it. There was a banner beneath that, but she couldn't make out the words. She shook her head in disbelief.

How the hell did she get herself into these things?

Cujo, usually. She was going to blame him for this escapade too.

Mei took a deep breath and let it out slowly, centering herself. A second breath, and her shoulders dropped, and she tipped her chin up. These were her people, hers! Who did those unruly boys think they were? Her wolf huffed and rose closer to the surface. Right?

Mei got out of the car, beeped it locked, and dropped the fob into her jacket pocket. And then she stomped forward. She could smell good meat on the grill — why were they letting it burn, for God's sake? She nodded to the women who were standing by the RV. "Thanks," she said. "Just stay firm."

"They want the women," one of them murmured. "And Ryder isn't here. They saw the other RV head out, and it was like a wall of power dropped. We didn't even know it was there until it was gone. And suddenly that one guy says, 'we should invite the women to party with us, don't you think?' Those three men said no. And here we are."

Mei picked out the man she was talking about. "One of yours?" she asked.

"One of the men they call Chen's recruits," the same woman answered. "But our men are being stupid shits too."

Mei glanced at her. "Do you know Benny Garrison, by chance?" she asked then shook her head. "Never mind."

"Yeah, Benny's ridden with us before," the woman said with amusement. "You recognize the phrase, I gather."

"I do," Mei assured her. "Well, let me go deal with those stupid shits."

Confidence, she reminded herself. Never let them see you flinch. And she walked up to the leader, a young man who looked to be her age. If she had the story right, he actually *was* her age. Of course Jason looked to be not much older than she was, and he was her father's age.

"Go back and eat," she ordered the ringleader. "You're letting good meat burn."

She felt, rather than heard, Jason's laughter. She did like the man.

"I'd rather play with a little bitch like you," the young man said. He reached for her. Mei centered herself and kicked him in the balls.

Somehow, she reached out, connecting to Jason and to David, and maybe even to Alefosio? She wasn't sure. But then, she wasn't sure what she meant by connecting either. It centered her to know they were there, and she felt energized by it too.

The ringleader doubled over and howled. She kicked him again. And again. Over and over she kicked him ruthlessly until he was on the ground in the fetal position not moving. He'd recover eventually, but wouldn't be a threat to women for quite a while. She didn't bother to look at him. She'd been taught self-defense by Haru Ito. When she put a man down, he stayed down.

She had a flash of the man she'd killed not that long ago and swallowed. It had been necessary, she told herself. And she would kill this man if it became necessary too.

She looked at the now-silent men in front of her. "Did you hear me?" she asked levelly, keeping her voice low but projecting it outward so that all could hear. She'd watched Cujo do that. Very effective. "Go rescue the meat. And leave the women alone. Have you no manners?"

She felt Jason move into place at her right shoulder. David was standing to her left with Alefosio. It felt right to have them there.

"Yes, ma'am," a young man said quietly. "We didn't mean no harm."

Yes they had, but she sensed that now they didn't. The man at her feet had been stirring them up somehow.

"You'll need to eat first," Jason said softly, just loud enough so she could hear and no one else. "You've declared yourself the dominant wolf here. You have to act like it."

Mei grimaced, but she gave a quick nod. She looked around. "You three," she said, pointing at random. "I want that food line ready to go ASAP. I'm hungry. And you two? Take this piece of shit lying on the ground and tie him up. The Alpha will deal with him when she gets here."

No one moved. "Well?" she demanded. "Move! I'm hungry."

And they moved.

"You OK?" she asked the three men who hadn't left her side.

"We're fine," Jason assured her. "We were minutes away from being in a world of hurt, but that asshole didn't quite have enough dominance to get it done. Not with the three of us united against him. But what the hell did you just do?"

Mei looked up at him. She barely reached his shoulder. Jason was a strong, confident man who did a lot of pack security work. She knew him and liked him. He was very competent, and there was no drama with him. But she had no idea what he was talking about. "I told them to go get supper," she said, bewildered.

He started to say something else, but then he just shook his head. "Then we should go eat supper, don't you think?" he said, smiling down at her.

Mei smiled back uncertainly. She'd missed something. Well, it would come out sooner or later. "What about the women?"

One of the women who had stood with her men — and when had they become her men? — answered her. "We were fixing food in the RV. Then we saw them heading our way and knew there was trouble. We'll finish getting dinner ready now."

"Good enough," Mei said smiling at her. "I'll join you just as soon as I make sure these boys remember their manners."

The woman laughed. "That was as nice a takedown as I've ever seen," she said. "I'm Brenda. You ever want to go honkytonking with me and the other women, you just let me know."

Mei forced a grin, still not completely sure what she'd done — besides destroy that man's ability to father children. She knew exactly what she'd done there. "You're on," she said lightly.

Headlights showed at the park entrance. She checked her family links — it was her father getting closer. "Dad," she said, and continued to the food line. All the men were waiting patiently.

"Go first," Jason urged her quietly.

Mei picked up a plate, held it out to the man at the grill. "Medium rare, if any meat survived that grilling," she said lightly.

"Yes, ma'am," the man said. "I'm sorry about Micky. He shouldn't have done that."

"No, he shouldn't have," Mei said levelly. "I won't tolerate that kind of disrespect to me, or to the other women."

"No, ma'am," he said and meant it.

Mei wanted answers, but she didn't want to look weak either. She nodded decisively and moved down the line. She took a piece of pizza — see, Okami? I'm eating some vegetables! And grabbed a can of Coke. She wanted some of the iced tea, but she wasn't about to drink from an open container. Just think of this as one big frat party and you'll be fine, she told herself, trying not to fall into hysterics.

She staked out a table away from the RV, pulling the focus of all these men with her. Jason seated her, and took a chair next to her, with his own heaping plate of food. Alefosio and David sat down as well. "You're doing just fine," Jason reassured her. She nodded shortly. She didn't know what was up, not really. And being the focus of all these men was unnerving. But if they were focused on her, the other women could eat in peace.

She saw her father approach, then, and she stood up to greet him. He gave her a brief hug, using it as an opportunity to ask, "Is everything under control?"

"Seems to be now," she answered. "Could have used you a half-hour ago."

Hiro Tanaka stepped back and looked around the camp space. Men were quietly filling their plates, finding places to eat. "So where is the MC leader, Ryder?" he asked. "And who speaks for all these men?" He glanced toward the RV. "And women?"

"Abby is on her way," Mei started, when one of the men looked up from the nearby table.

"She does, sir," he said, and nodded toward Mei. Mei stared at him, flummoxed by the comment. "We accept her as our spokeswoman."

Hiro raised an eyebrow at his daughter. "What have you done?"

Mei shook her head. "I have no clue."

***

Maggie drove the RV into the rest stop parking area at a faster speed than the sign recommended. Jessie looked around. She hadn't admitted it to Ryder earlier, but she really hadn't gotten out Vancouver for more than a couple of short trips to Victoria and Prince George. She didn't think she'd ever been to any roadside rest area before. This one was deserted, except for a motorcycle laying on its side near a concrete block building. Restrooms, Jessie guessed.

It was designed for a lot of vehicles. Even on a rainy Friday night, it seemed disturbing that it was deserted like this. Maggie honked the horn, and she pulled alongside the sidewalk, ignoring the lines for diagonal parking.

And then they sat there. Nothing moved. Maggie grimaced. "Now what?"

Taisiya had been in the bedroom at the back of the RV, but she came forward now. Kristina trailed behind her. She looked haggard, like she needed a couple of good meals. Jessie worried about her. She found Taisiya terrifying, although she couldn't have said why. Well, couldn't have said why *yesterday*. Feeling the panic and paranoia the young woman had been broadcasting outward in waves, she knew *now* why she was wary. Why her wolf was wary, Jessie amended. Her wolf had known how powerful Taisiya was.

Listen to your wolf, her mother had told her, when things started to go bad with her grandfather and Alpha Chen. Your wolf knows.

Well yeah, her wolf knew, but there had been fuck all either of them could do about it.

Jessie stopped those thoughts. Nightmares lay down that road, and she couldn't fight her own nightmares and Taisiya's nightmares at the same time.

"They're out there," Taisiya said. "The bad guys. I can feel them."

Jessie swallowed, her throat suddenly dry. "Can you feel Ryder?" she asked, trying to keep her voice even. "You met him, right?"

Taisiya nodded. "Teacher Garrison's brother." She took a deep breath and let it out. Then she nodded again. "I can find him." And she darted for the door before either Jessie or Kristina could stop her.

"Wait," Maggie said with alarm. But Taisiya didn't listen to her either. Kristina just scrambled after her. Jessie looked at Maggie.

"Stay with the vehicle," Jessie said, and she ran after the twins. To be honest, she didn't think Maggie had any intention of leaving the RV.

Smart woman.

Taisiya was headed up the hill behind the bathrooms. Kristina was just a few steps behind her. Jessie tried to catch up with them. They only had a 10-second head start! How could they be out of reach?

Fortunately they slowed down, and Jessie joined them. "Where?" she asked. "And did the others leave?"

She immediately wished she hadn't asked that question. Taisiya was caught in her own world, she thought, worried about the girl. Taisiya tipped up her face as if she was scenting the breeze, and then she growled. "They're still here," she said. "Take care of the good man. I'm going after the bad men."

"Wait!" Jessie said desperately. "Where is the good man?"

Kristina gestured to their left. "He's over there," she said softly. "He's injured. I'm not sure...." She glanced at her sister who was stripping off her clothes. "No, Taisiya!"

Taisiya ignored her and shifted. She blended into the rainy night, now. Jessie could barely see her — a dark gray wolf.

"Take care of Ryder, Jessie," Kristina said. And she stripped and shifted as well. Then there were two young wolves staring at her. Two wild wolves, Jessie thought. She wasn't sure the human was in control at all. Either of them.

Jessie stayed very still until they turned in unison and headed northeast. Cleaning up this mess was going to require more than an RV, she thought. Not her problem. She was not going to be responsible for what those girls did to the men who had come here hunting Ryder.

Jessie turned to her left, going where Kristina had gestured. About 20 paces, she found Ryder, curled up behind some kind of shrub. Even with her wolf's eyesight she could barely see him as she knelt down beside him.

"It's Jessie," she said softly, reaching out to touch him on the arm. "Are you hurt?"

"Hell, yes," he growled. "Do you think I'm curled up under some fucking rosebush for the fun of it?"

Jessie snatched her hand back and jumped back a bit.

"Sorry, sorry," he chanted. "I'm sorry, girl. They shot me. But the bullet didn't go through, and my body keeps healing around it, and then I move, and it moves, and I can't breathe...." Ryder paused.

"Where am I?" he asked. She could hear the paranoia and suspicion in his voice, and it scared her.

"You're at a rest stop," she answered, worried.

"A rest stop." He paused. "Where?"

Alarmed now, she kept her distance from him as she answered, "Just south of the Washington-Canada border? Where do you think you are?"

Ryder's breathing was heavy and uneven. She didn't like the sound of it at all.

"Who are you?" he asked suddenly.

"Jessie," she said quietly, wondering what was going on. "Remember me? You met me at Margarite's house." She smiled briefly. "Taught me how to drive that van."

"You didn't know how to drive it?" Ryder asked incredulously. "Margarite's. I remember now. I'm not in Iraq, I'm in Washington."

Jessie swallowed hard. A flashback? She couldn't say she blamed him. "Not Iraq," she assured him. "You were escorting a bunch of shifters south, and you were forced off the road here and attacked. You talked to your brother, Benny? And he sent reinforcements."

"You? You're my backup? You can't even drive a car!" Ryder sounded outraged. Well, she supposed she could hardly blame him.

"Maggie drove the RV here," she said. "And the twins? They're out there. Chasing down the bad guys. I think."

"And you're stuck here with a guy who isn't sure what country it is, or what decade? Lucky you."

She snickered a bit and saw a flash of a smile on his face.

He lay there for a bit, and she knelt down beside him and rested her hand on his shoulder to comfort him, more secure now that he was back in touch with the here and now. "So what's your story?" he asked. "Talk to me."

"We should get you down to the RV and out of here," she said hedging.

"How?" he asked. "You can't carry me, and I can't walk out. Not yet."

"Where is the bullet?" she asked, concerned.

"Spine," he answered. "Went through my chest, nicked a lung, and lodged up against my spine. The bastards."

Jessie frowned. "Your lungs aren't healing."

"They will," he replied. "I think."

"We need to get it out," Jessie said slowly. "The bullet."

"You got a knife?" Ryder was caustic. "Or are you planning to do it with your teeth?"

She ignored the attitude. "You can't heal with it in there," she said slowly, reasoning it out. "And you can't walk with it lodged against your spine. And your body heals a bit; then if you move, you reopen the wound."

"Yes," he said. "And I can't shift, because I'm afraid of what damage will be done in the process. I don't think...." he trailed off. "So talk to me. Why were you at Margarite's? You're not one of the wolves Chen made."

She snorted. "No," she said. "I'm a shifter princess, don't you know?" She said it bitterly, self-mocking. "My grandfather was the pack Second. I was golden. I had just graduated from college, and I was engaged to be married. And then I overheard something I shouldn't have."

"You listen," he agreed. "Every time I looked around, there you were, listening."

"Yeah," Jessie said. "That's me. And so, my grandfather decided I needed to be under tighter control. He broke off my engagement and gave me to Alpha Chen to be a woman in his household."

"And your family let him do that?" Ryder sounded outraged.

"And how were they going to stop him?" she snapped. "The Alpha threatened to kill my entire family if I refused. And then he made me watch what they did to women who were rebellious." She was silent. "There aren't many rebellious women in the Vancouver pack. Not anymore."

"But you got out."

She nodded, even though she thought it was probably too dark for him to see her. "Word among the women of the packs is that if you needed help, go to Margarite in Delta. So when the chaos started, I walked out through the forest and then hitchhiked down to Delta, then asked where Margarite could be found. Everyone there knew Margarite. I got there just as they were planning to go back and bust Alpha Stafford out of Chen's pack house."

"Chaos?"

"Abby Stafford came for her site visit as Chairman of the Northwest Council, and to bring the serum to the girls of the pack and the independent families," she said. She didn't think he was tracking all that well, but maybe her voice was better than the dark and the silence. She wondered what had happened in Iraq. Something like this? Had he been trapped there waiting for the bad guys to come and finish him off? She flinched at the thought and returned to her story. She didn't mind talking about Abby Stafford, it was the horrible months that had preceded Abby's visit that she struggled to talk about.

And as a psychology major, she knew that wasn't good.

"Chen captured her — Abby," Jessie said. "He'd already sent a team to kidnap the twins. But he wasn't powerful enough to hold the twins, or to hold Alpha Stafford. And he died."

She said the last viciously. "Died at the hands of a woman. I hope he knew, and that he raged against it. I hope he died hard."

There was silence. "And then you stayed to help the other victims," Ryder said. "Good for you."

"Yeah," she said, suddenly tired. "Good for me."

Jessie listened — was that a howl? She thought it was. She pictured those two wolves trotting off toward the hillside and shook her head.

"So we've got to get that bullet out," she said, practically. "I can go down and see what we've got in the RV."

"Not safe to move," he said immediately. "They're still out there with a rifle."

"I think the twins are taking care of that," she said. She wasn't worried about the rifle. There were scarier things out in the dark than a rifle.

"Until you're sure, don't go and get shot yourself," he said. "Talk to me. What did you study in school?"

"Psychology," she said. "People are interesting, you know? Did you go to college?"

"No," he said. "Too restless. Too young and stupid."

Jessie ran her hand over his chest, found where the bullet went in by the bloody and torn shirt. She visualized the trajectory it must have taken. "Were they shooting down at you?"

"Yeah," he said. "I should know better. Never fight against someone who has an uphill advantage."

She didn't know what that meant exactly, but it sounded like he knew what he was talking about. She reached around him, her hands working their way behind him, pulling up his shirt. His skin was soft, she thought absently. She had expected it to be rougher.

"Jessie, what are you doing?" he demanded.

"I'm going to shift," she said. "And then I'm going to open up your back. I'll shift back and dig out that bullet."

There was silence. "I think waiting until you can get a knife might be a better plan, don't you?" he asked.

"No," she said. "It needs to come out, before it does permanent damage. And I need to get you out of here before the twins come back down."

"Why?"

"You hear the howling?" she said tensely, as she started stripping. "They're in wolf form. And I don't think they remember that there are good guys out here. Not you, probably not even me."

"Then go," he ordered. "Leave me and get out of here."

Jessie ignored him. No one was going to leave anybody behind. Besides, she didn't want the twins to live with having killed an innocent. They were just young girls, after all. Sometimes it seemed like people forgot that.

She shifted and unleashed her claws while he was still giving orders.

She ignored his scream. Ignored the sound of the wolves getting closer. She'd been worried about the twins, but now she worried about what was coming at them ahead of the twins. She shifted back. "What the hell, girl?" Ryder shouted at her.

"Those aren't just the twins howling," she replied. "My wolf knows the sound of their wolves. And that's not them. Well, not just them."

Jessie probed the open wound she'd made, her fingers searching for something out of place, something that wasn't blood and muscle.

She ignored his swearing. He should be glad it hurt — it meant he could feel it and wasn't paralyzed. And then she felt the bullet, just a bit of cool, smooth metal, and teased it out. There were better ways to do surgery, she thought wildly. But whatever got the job done.

"Heal," she ordered in a whisper. "Shift."

Suddenly a black wolf lay under her hands. She petted him, enjoying the feel of the wolf's pelt. He shifted back, and she was stroking a man's bare back. She snatched her hands back. "Don't stop on my account," he said huskily. He rolled over onto his back and tugged her down beside him.

"Behave," she said severely, keeping her hands to herself. But she had to acknowledge a whisper of interest in the man. She wasn't going to act on it, she assured herself, but it was almost reassuring to know that she could feel interest at all. She hadn't thought she ever would.

It had worried her. What if her fiancé came back, and she couldn't stand his touch? What if she never could stand to touch him again?

But maybe it would be OK, she told herself, taking heart. Maybe she could heal after all. She just had to find Bjorn. Maybe it would be OK.

Ryder reached up and touched her cheek, stroking it gently. "Stop me if you don't want this," he said huskily. He slowly brought her head down toward him and kissed her.

She tensed, but she didn't protest. It was such a gentle kiss, she thought with wonder. His lips were soft, open, inviting her to explore. Tentatively she tasted him, running the tip of her tongue over his lips. She could taste the salt there, a tang of blood. He'd bit his lip to keep from crying out in pain and giving his position away at some point, she thought. Maybe more than once.

It undid her, that taste of salt. She kissed him again, pressing her lips against his. She wasn't sure quite what to do next. Making out underneath rosebushes hadn't been part of her sexual history. She smiled at that thought. Not even with Bjorn.

Ryder released her, and she pulled back. She should say something, but she wasn't sure what. Ryder touched her lips gently with one finger, silencing her words. She just stared at him, her eyes big in the dark.

In the distance, wolves howled. They were getting closer.

"It's OK," Ryder said, pulling her back down so that her head rested on his chest. "Just the sound of wolves."

"That doesn't worry you?"

"No," Ryder said. "Not when you've laid out like this in a war zone with your guts hanging out and listened to bombs going off and the screams of people fleeing. And the sounds of Army transport trucks rolling over the roads below, and you know you can't call out for help — not even from your own side, if they are on your side — because they'll kill you, or worse, put you in a research lab somewhere, for your ability to heal."

"Iraq," Jessie guessed. She probably should be able to pinpoint it better than that, but this probably happened before she was born. Or close to it. She wondered how old Ryder was.

"Iraq," he agreed.

And then Ryder changed back to his wolf and nudged her. She shifted too.

Time to get out of here. Because whatever was coming down that hill wasn't good — whether it was two enraged teenagers, or the wolves they were chasing. At this point, Jessie wasn't sure which would be worse.

But she hugged that kiss close. It had been a very nice kiss.

They raced down the hill toward the RV where Maggie had used some debris to form a ramp and was walking the motorcycle up it. At least Jessie hoped it had been debris. She ran up the ramp into the RV and headed into the back bedroom to get on some sweats. Just because she could endure a wet November night in the nude, didn't mean she enjoyed it. She grabbed an extra set and a towel and came back out to where Ryder was talking to Maggie outside of the RV. If nothing else identified them all as shifters, this ease with being naked did.

Although Jessie admitted she wasn't as comfortable with it as Ryder seemed to be. It had been a while since she was comfortable with her own body, naked or clothed. She firmly shut that thought in the locked room of her mind along with all the other such thoughts that had occurred in the last six months. Some day she would have to clean house, but today was not that day.

She tossed the towel to Ryder, and he dried off before stepping into the RV. She handed him the sweats, and he pulled them on with a quick nod of thanks.

"Help me pull this ramp out of here," Maggie said. "Last thing we need is Ryder reopening his wounds straining over a piece of plywood."

Jessie nodded, and together they pulled the wood back over to a pair of posts. Jessie grimaced — guess the improvised ramp hadn't started out as debris. Well it was now.

"The twins?" Maggie asked in a low tone.

Jessie gestured with her head toward the hillside. "They're still out there. I don't think they're done hunting."

Maggie grimaced. "Ryder says you saved his life. Thank you. We owe you one."

"You don't owe me anything," Jessie protested, startled. "Anyone would have done the same."

Maggie snorted. "Ryder's got more enemies than friends, girlfriend," she said. "He's amazed when anyone does anything nice for him. Oh, he covers it up — tries to accept it as his due. He's really our pack Alpha, you know. We're not an official pack. He's Okanogan pack, and so are probably a dozen of the other wolves. The rest are lone wolves. Or like me — I belong to a pack that ignores that I'm riding with Ryder instead of settling down and raising a passel of kids."

Jessie felt a bit wistful at the notion of settling down and raising some kids. Didn't sound all that bad to her. Well, it might not sound that bad to Maggie someday. Shifters had time. That was what they all said. You've got time. When you were living in hell, that wasn't a positive. People, even her family, had told her that. Give it time, this will pass, you're young yet. And all those phrases had sounded like a death sentence. Worse than a death sentence. Enduring the unspeakable.

Jessie took a deep breath. Time to wrap this up and get everyone back to the campsite. It worried her what might have happened after they left. The men they called Chen's recruits worried her. And she wasn't sure about the motorcycle club either.

Maggie and Brenda had been great, though.

She shrugged and put her fingers to her mouth and let out a piercing whistle. Maggie clapped her hands over her ears. "A bit of warning, girl!"

"Sorry," Jessie said, laughing. Maggie grinned.

"Will it work?"

Jessie shrugged, and scanned the hillside, watching for movement. It might. Or it might have just been the equivalent of turning on the flashing blue light at K-Mart. Now serving sitting ducks....

Get a grip she admonished herself, but she couldn't help but grin at that image.

"There," Maggie said, pointing. "Are those two ours? Or the bad guys?"

Jessie wasn't completely sure there was a difference. She squinted at the two moving shapes until they resolved into the wolves she recognized. "Ours," she said. "Let's get them loaded up."

The two women returned to the RV and stood at the open door. Taisiya-wolf and Kristina-wolf came racing up and leaped into the RV, heading back to the bedroom. Jessie climbed inside, and Maggie went around to the driver's seat. Ryder was sitting in the passenger's seat. Jessie sat at the table where she could see Ryder. She liked watching him, she admitted. He was watching the rest area, and the surrounding hillside now. Not tense, just alert.

"Let's get out of here," Maggie said, then started up the big rig, and headed for the exit. "We'll need to send a cleanup team."

"How many were out there, Ryder?" Jessie asked. "How did they trap you, anyway?"

An 18-wheeler forced me off the road," Ryder said sourly, glancing back at her. "Conveniently right at the exit to this rest area. I took it. It was that or get run over. I was planning on just running right through, but they were waiting for me. Shot the tires out as I went by. I managed to ditch the bike by the restrooms. But then I was trapped with no cell service. So I moved up the hill to get service, and to avoid them."

"How many were there?" Jessie repeated her other question.

"Six," he replied. "Fewer now."

Jessie grinned at the satisfaction in his voice. She glanced back at the RV's bedroom; she needed to check on the girls. "Benny says his Alpha has a theory about numbers," Jessie said. "Six is a hunting squad. Four is a ceremonial unit. So an Alpha plus four. Or an Alpha plus six guards. And I saw that at the Vancouver pack house. It seems to be the way shifters — at least shifter men — organize themselves. So if that holds true, there was another somewhere, probably the squad commander."

"Women are different?" Maggie asked.

Jessie shrugged. "Didn't see that with the women at Margarite's," she said. "But that's the only time I've been around a large group of shifter women. Be interesting to ask Alpha Stafford that."

"So you think there's a squad leader still out here somewhere?" Ryder asked, ignoring the rest of it. He considered the theory. "Makes sense. They have to have transportation somewhere."

Jessie shrugged. "I'll ask the girls, but I say let the cleanup be his problem."

Ryder grunted with amusement. "Might need to check and make sure in the morning," he said. "Hard to explain six dead wolves. Especially 200-pound ones."

"Not easy to explain a funeral pyre either," Jessie replied, getting up to go back and check on the twins. "Ask me how I know."

Neither of them asked.

Jessie got up and went into the bedroom. The two wolves were curled up on the bed in wolf form. Jessie assumed they were asleep until one of them opened her eyes — Taisiya, she thought, although they were as similar in wolf form as they were in human. Maybe more so; she didn't have a problem telling the two of them apart in human form.

"You did good," Jessie said softly. "You got the bad guys."

Taisiya closed her eyes again. But Jessie thought she heard Taisiya in her head: *There are more bad guys out there. A lot more. We need to hide.*

Jessie answered the voice as if it were really Taisiya, because who knew? It might be. The girl was spooky, no lie. *Or we need to fight back.*

There was a pause. *Or we fight back*, the voice agreed. Jessie closed the door softly and returned to the front of the RV.

Chapter 11

Day 155 of the re-emerged Hat Island pack, Friday, Nov. 8, I-5 north to Bellingham.

"OK, which one of you wants to go first?" Abby asked her van full of men. She was going to get some answers, and a road trip up I-5 might be as private a time as any. "Benny? You have a brother? And you say he took care of whoever roughed up his mother in Okanogan. Does that mean what I think it does? What's going on up there? Does he know?"

Benny sighed. "Well, Naomi moved back onto the reservation when Dad 'died,'" he said. "That was shortly after Ryder successfully went through first shift. So 30 years ago? Dad reinvented himself as a younger nephew who was willing to be there for the now-fatherless son. It gets damned difficult, you know? Keeping all of that straight. I was working for the Council by then and had been declared a lone wolf. Ryder is still part of the pack, however."

"You're rambling," Cujo said. "Could you get to the point about why the Penticton pack would be interested in the Okanogan? I can't say that either place has that much to offer."

Benny snorted. "Rugged mountains that draw hikers and hunters, that's about it," he said. "I don't know why the Penticton Alpha would want to expand, but it looks like he does. And he saw the chance with Dad gone."

"Your Dad's been gone for what? Four months?" Abby asked. "Where is his pack Second?"

"I'm guessing he's dead," Benny replied. "It's really the only way any of this makes sense. I think Dad left him in charge of the pack when he went off to do whatever the hell he's doing. And someone took him out. Penticton would be my guess, at this point. As for why?" Benny shrugged. "The Alpha there is looking for revenge and power. But he's not all that smart. I'm guessing someone else is doing the thinking."

"That's a lot of guessing," Jake observed.

"Yeah," Benny said with a sigh. "And as a former intelligencer, that's a painful admission."

"That's what happened last time," Okami said from the far back seat. "We should have killed him, Haru and I. But neither of us had any desire to be Alpha of a no-account pack hundreds of miles from any place we wanted to be. So we let him live. A mistake obviously."

"He was involved in kidnapping Yui and Haru," Abby said, enlightened.

"Yes," Okami said. "I do not believe it was his idea. He just supplied the manpower. It was actually a fairly large pack back then — it's a perfect place for a pack. Remote, plenty of room to run, but a good-sized town for jobs and supplies. Chairman Johannsen and Anton Vuk were behind the plot, although we didn't have enough proof to accuse them. But we decimated that pack. The Alpha probably sees taking the wolves of the Okanogan as a way to regroup. But I'm sure someone else suggested it."

"I agree," Benny said. "And some of Chen's recruits are probably young men from that pack as well. I think one of them tipped off the Penticton men who attacked us that we were at Margarite's."

"But why?" Abby asked. "Cujo? You questioned the attackers?"

"Yes," Cujo said. "They're expanding, they said, and they deserved to be recognized as the power they really were. And they had some plan — they were hazy about this — that required being able to cross the border freely. But the Alpha — a man named John McKenzie, by the way — had been one of Chen's partners in whatever scheme he had to seize power on the World Council. So McKenzie thinks he can pick up where Chen left off. And he's opened up his pack to the young men left leaderless following Chen's death."

"A number of whom we have contained in a campground near Bellingham," Abby said. "What exactly do we have there, Cujo?"

"I'm not sure," Cujo answered. "I think most of them are what we think they are — young men from shifter families and isolated packs who were looking for the opportunities Chen held out to them. A lot more young male shifters than I realized seem to fall into that category, but I think that's truly what they are. Probably pulled from all over Canada and the Pacific Northwest. But some of them may have allegiances to McKenzie. It's a dangerous situation."

"No shit," Abby muttered. "And we just sent Mei Tanaka to deal with it?"

"Mei is very dominant," Cujo said slowly. "She's more dominant than her father, as a matter of fact —something Akihiro Tanaka has known since Mei was 15, by the way. Her father ordered her to do something, and she looked him in the eye and refused. Shocked the hell out of Hiro, I understand. So the pack leadership started watching for potential matches. The theory was, that any man who could control her, was a potential heir to be pack Alpha someday. And the pack is short on heirs — especially now that Hiro has his own pack in Bellingham. Unfortunately, ambitious young men spotted what they were doing, and saw Mei as a quick opportunity for advancement. Two years ago, one of them tried to rape her, and she killed him without hesitation."

"Cujo!" Abby exclaimed. "What were they thinking? Akihiro and Haru, I mean."

"I'm not sure they *were* thinking," Okami answered for him. "Cujo and I became involved because she needed us to dispose of the body. Unfortunately, he was a scion of a prominent family, and it got messy. However, Alpha Tanaka — both of them — has since backed off and left Mei alone. Although, if Cujo ever expressed an interest, or if Mei ever expressed an interest in Cujo, Haru Ito would gladly remove any barriers to their ascendance as heirs to the pack leadership."

"I've made it clear to him that won't be happening," Cujo said grimly. "I've a mate — anything happens to her, and I'll see who is the uglier fighter, Haru or me. He knows that. And Mei has made it clear that she thinks I'm bad husband material. Demonstrates her intelligence. But in the mess that Okami refers to, as a test, I ordered Mei to return to the beach cabin. Did it with full dominance. And she stood there and looked me in the eye, and asked me 'why?'"

"Sounds like they should forget about which man can top her dominance, and just make her the heir," Abby muttered.

There was silence.

"I do not think that has occurred to Alpha Tanaka or to Second Ito," Okami said slowly. Abby thought he was smiling as he said it. When Okami smiled, she immediately became wary. The man had a lethal sense of humor. In this case, perhaps literally so.

"Remember, until six months ago," Okami continued, "no one believed a woman could become a pack Alpha. And then you became an Alpha and called a pack."

"Tanaka would have a cow," Benny said irreverently. "But I wouldn't mention it to him, unless Mei gives you the OK."

"No," Abby said. "I don't intend to. Although I'd like to be there when it dawns on him that he's been looking for an heir and he has one — a young woman whose competence is outright scary."

Benny snickered.

"So that explains Mei," Abby continued. "Back to the Okanogan. Benny? Are you saying your father doesn't know about his Second's death? That's hard for me to imagine."

Benny considered that. "True," he said slowly. "And his Second has been in that position since the pack formed. No, you're right. His Second has to be alive. But I don't think he's with Dad, and I don't think he's in the Okanogan."

"Penticton," Okami said grimly.

There was silence. "Possibly," Benny agreed. "Someone will have to investigate that."

There was a pause, and then Benny got it. "Oh, hell no," he protested. "It's not going to be me."

"Who else?" Abby asked reasonably. "You and Ryder together? No one else can. We'd be attacked, and you know it. The whole region would explode. Your father's pack is unstable — without him there, it makes Hayden Lake look like a high tea party for the queen."

"I thought you wanted me to run a girls boarding school! How can I do that, when I'm never there?" Benny protested. "And what do you know about high tea parties for the queen?"

"Delegation," Jake said, with amusement in his voice. "Isn't that what you're always telling Abby? And to be honest, it seems like you've got the school delegated just fine."

Benny grunted. "I'll talk to Ryder," he said with resignation in his voice. "Shit."

There was sympathetic laughter. "OK, next question," Abby said, ignoring the diversion into talking about high tea parties. "Cujo. What did Kent say? Why is he here?"

Cujo sobered. "That's a bit more involved question than you might think. And you're not going to like it. So first. I've been working for Ito since I quit as security chief for the Wolf Harbor Resort — two years now. Contract jobs. When you proposed I become security chief for the World Council, that made it fulltime. But I'd been doing jobs all along."

"And you didn't think to share this?" Jake sounded pissed.

"I know," Cujo said. "But it was as if I had two lives — and I've always had two lives. There was my life in the pack, where I hoped to go to college and grow tomatoes. And there was the mercenary, still active. So Haru Ito would need something, and I'd do it, and come back to my other life on Hat Island. You can kick my butt later," Cujo added when Jake started to say something. "And I deserve it. But let me finish this first. It gets worse."

"Doesn't it always?" Benny muttered.

"Not helping," Jake said, sounding like he was forcing out the words through clenched teeth.

Cujo ignored both of them. "So you need to know — and I've thought you should know for some time now — humans know about us, about shifters. And not just that tech billionaire from San Mateo. About two years ago, an old CIA buddy of mine showed up to tell me there was a research project underway. A black ops was looking into the possibility that there was a subspecies of humans that lived extraordinarily long lives. They had a list of suspects. My name was on it — the first name my friend had recognized, and somewhat trusted. So he came to find me. He was worried about the project. Worried it might be true, and that it would result in a witch hunt like the world has never seen."

"I know some of this," Abby said quietly. "Ricci told us." Benny had been there for that conversation, too. But not Jake or Cujo? She tried to recall if she'd told them about Ricci's points about the serum benefiting human women only. Damn it. Things were happening too fast and she couldn't keep up!

It's OK, Alpha, Jake sent through their bond, reacting to her disturbed emotions. *We'll get it figured out. We've got time.*

But that was the problem, she didn't think they did. Shifters had a 'time will tell' philosophy, but time was running out. They weren't going to be a secret much longer.

Apparently they weren't much of one now.

"Yeah, Ricci's the one who put my name on the list, back when he was working for Jones, the bastard. He thought it would be funny," Cujo said sourly. "But Tanaka's and Ito's names were there too. I've had a look at the list. At least two-thirds really were shifter names — family names that even I recognized. And wouldn't we like to know how they're spotting us? Although, we may have a lead on that too. Later," he added hastily, when Abby started to ask about that. She subsided. They knew her too well. "So my friend gives me updates. And we're his backup. Jake, you *were* told that."

"I was," Jake conceded. "Not why, just that we should render all aid necessary. That was before the pack formed, actually."

Cujo nodded. "But the black ops research program doesn't know about the wolf. Just the longevity part. And there's a bunch of moving pieces to that story...." He trailed off. "Maybe conversation for the return trip."

Jake snorted. Abby glanced at him, and he subsided. "Go on," she said. "Kent?"

"Yeah, so this goes back to the man Jedediah Jones sold Olivia to," Cujo said. "A human named Bastion. Richer than god. Sadistic, untouchable, and he's got a human menagerie. Women who are held captive for his display and pleasure. And Jones sold Olivia and two other women to him. Bastion knew what he had, too. He was keeping the three of them in cages when we busted them out of there."

"I remember," Abby said.

"So, he's pissed about losing his prizes," Cujo continued. "And this is the part you don't know. When I was in Paris, he tried to have Olivia re-taken for his menagerie. Turns out he is part of a consortium of club owners. Olivia stopped the kidnapping, and later that night I killed the men who tried — humans. But I got to thinking about it, and I couldn't see how it could happen without the club owner knowing and participating. So the next day, I paid him a visit. And nearly got trapped by a CIA team. I killed the club owner. Killed the lead CIA agent. And got us all the hell out of Paris."

Cujo paused for breath. Abby suspected he was sorting what parts of the story to share. "Was this before or after you rescued the girls from Africa?" Benny asked, tongue-in-cheek. "Seems like you had a busy trip."

"After the rescue, *and* after the side-trip to Scotland — just before we flew home. But before the side-trip to Canada," Cujo said tiredly. "It *was* a busy trip. I grilled the agent — didn't have a lot of time, but he was chatty. He was supposedly rogue from the CIA black ops research my friend is involved in. And he'd been contacted by Olivia's former captor with information to trade. Information about our wolves. In exchange, Bastion wanted Olivia back. And me dead."

"Shit," Benny said under his breath.

"Yeah," Cujo agreed. "But I don't know how much the rogue agent had been telling the CIA. He may have really been rogue. My friend in the black ops research end doesn't seem to know about the wolf. Or at least he hasn't mention it."

"So Kent?" Abby prompted. They were almost to Bellingham, and she wanted to hear the end of this story before they got out to the Tennant Lake campground.

"I'm getting there," Cujo said grumpily. Jake glanced in the rearview mirror in warning. Cujo straightened up. "So, we've known we were going to have to go in after that bastard. We can't have a human blabbing to authorities about werewolves! But there are protocols to be followed. The Chairman of the European Council had to be consulted, right? He about shit his pants that he might be expected to take on the man — he owns half of Liechtenstein."

"The whole country," Benny said neutrally. "Tell me you're exaggerating?"

"Not by much," Cujo answered. "Filthy rich bastard. So it's back in the World Council's lap — fine by me. I don't trust anyone else to get this done, to be honest. But Jake? I may need you for this. You and a task force of our best beta wolves. It's going to be sticky."

"For what exactly?" Jake asked.

"To take the man out, Cujo said matter-of-factly. "So, backtracking a bit, the man behind much of the problems in Hayden Lake was one of Jedediah Jones's key men — a man Haru and I used to call the accountant. He's the one who kept track of all the women sold and who they were sold to. He used Rose Evans as a bartering chip to create a bolt-hole for himself in Hayden Lake. And then set out to recreate the pack more to his liking."

"OK, I knew some of this," Benny said. "The whisperer. Did you get him?"

"We did," Cujo answered. "Ito flew out and took him into custody." He paused to consider the timeline. "That was Halloween."

"And he still has him?" Abby asked. Halloween? Haru and Akihiro had been out to the island that night. And Haru hadn't even mentioned a trip to Idaho!

Of course not, she thought sourly. Why would he do that?

"Ito interrogated him," Cujo said. "He's dead by now." He paused. "I think."

"Go on," Abby said grimly. "Kent?"

"So Elliot Bastion — the man in Liechtenstein — got word that we had the accountant in custody, apparently," Cujo said. "And he sent a team to Monte Carlo to go after Kent — and no, I don't know how he made that connection. Max and Tighe and some others there fought Bastion's team off. But they were worried about the girls — Bastion's team weren't all killed, and they'd take the word back. A man like Bastion would do just about anything to have one of those girls, Abby. And Max was worried about Kent, I suspect, although Kent didn't say that. So, Kent upped what he was willing to pay for chaperones — even I flinched at what those two women are making — and they flew out this morning."

Abby was silent, thinking that through. Did she know who Max was? Maybe it wasn't Cujo she needed to talk to — she and *Olivia* needed to compare notes. "Cujo, those two women know the girls are on Hat Island," she said slowly.

"I know. And I'm not sure what to do about that," Cujo said. "They're Parisian teachers — from a private girl's school. If they return to Paris and keep their trip confidential as they're being paid to do, they should be fine. If they start talking and Bastion hears of it, their days are numbered."

"And Bastion will come for us," Abby finished.

"And Bastion will come for Hat Island," Cujo agreed. "He's got a bounty on me, dead or alive. And one on Olivia — alive. He's furious that we stole his 'prize pets' as he called them. And then he lost his CIA contact. He's beyond angry. Insanely so."

Abby sighed. "We can't let those two women go back to Paris," she said. "Too risky. Benny, I guess you're going to get two new teachers."

She picked up her phone, called Olivia and updated her. Jake paused at the entrance to the campground, while Abby talked to her. She put Olivia on speaker phone so they could all hear her response. Abby grinned appreciatively. Olivia had a mouth on her.

"All right," Olivia said. "I'll talk to them. See if I can woo them into staying for a while longer. But then we've got humans to worry about."

"Not for long," Benny said. "We'll have to change them."

"Without their permission?" Olivia asked ominously. "No, that's not acceptable. And if we offer them a choice? What do we do if they don't accept it?"

"That's the question Wolf Harbor has faced from the beginning," Abby agreed. "Ideas?"

"Let me think about it," Olivia said. "Personally, I'm inclined to let them go back to Paris. Put a watch on them for a while. Max can arrange that. Tighe would volunteer, I think," she said, laughing. "Does this mean Kent is staying?"

"Ask Kent," Cujo replied. "He's your man, not mine."

"Damn it, Cujo," Olivia said without any real heat. "All right. I'll see what they all say."

The call ended, and Jake started up the van, easing down the entrance road to the campground. It wasn't hard to spot their people — they were the only campsite with vehicles. Was that a church bus? Abby peered into the gloom. It was. She shook her head. "And we'll talk about those links on the way home, Cujo."

Cujo sighed.

"I might have things to say about that topic," Benny said uncomfortably. "I don't think we've been looking at pack bonds and links in the right way."

"Well that's a hell of a note to end a conversation on," Jake said into the silence. "But that's Hiro Tanaka out there. And I see Jason and Alefosio. So Mei and David are probably there too. Unless you want to include all of them in your discussion, we'd better table it for now."

"After all, there's a two-hour trip home," Abby said, somewhat maliciously. "And I can't *wait* to hear what Benny has to say about links and bonds."

"Joy," Benny muttered. "Maybe Ryder and I can just head to the Okanogan from here and skip that conversation."

Chapter 12

Day 155 of the re-emerged Hat Island pack, Friday, Nov. 8, Tennant Lake campground

Abby got out of their van and surveyed the campsite. She waited while Jake came around the van and stood in his usual spot, just to the left and behind. Cujo, Benny and Okami got out of the van and joined them. Benny whistled soundlessly.

"Looks like a church cookout — even has the church bus," Benny observed. "I thought there was supposed to be trouble brewing?"

Abby pursed her lips as she considered the scene. Didn't look like trouble, she conceded. Even both RVs were here. Women were milling around between the two RVs, and the van had been parked to make a back wall. They seemed to be moving around the area between the motorhomes with plates of food. No one seemed unduly stressed.

On the east side of the RV setup, men were at the grills under the pavilion, and others filled the picnic tables. They didn't seem particularly hostile either. Subdued, really. Less anger pouring off of them than the last time she'd seen them at Margarite's.

"What the hell?" Cujo murmured.

Which about summed it up. She spotted Mei and her father walking toward them, and she just watched them come. The whole camp scene had the feel of entering someone's pack territory, she thought, disturbed by the idea. Were they in the Bellingham pack territory? She hadn't thought so.

More like Margarite's backyard felt before she raised a pack, Benny commented in her mind. *Turf, maybe, not territory.*

Abby considered that, and yes, it did feel like the potluck in Margarite's backyard. *Did Hiro establish 'turf' here for some reason? To quell a fight?*

Benny was silent for a moment. She glanced at him. He was standing there with his lips parted just a bit, as if he was tasting the air. Finally he replied, *If it's anybody's turf, I'd say it's Mei's.*

Abby stared at him, and then she turned to greet Mei and her father. Jason was right behind Mei.

Standing as if he were her Second? And behind the three of them were Alefosio, David White, Jessie, and a man she didn't know.

Ryder, Benny supplied. *Where are the twins?*

Abby lessened her sluice gates at the links she had with the twins. *Sleeping in the RV farthest from us,* she replied. She frowned for a moment. *They're in wolf form.*

Benny didn't comment.

"Alpha Tanaka," Abby said with a smile. "Thank you for coming out here."

"Odd place for a site visit," Hiro said, taking her hand. It wasn't quite a shake, and not quite holding it. But it felt welcoming, and Abby only took her hand back when it went on long enough to be awkward.

"It is," Abby said, with a smile. "Perhaps we can do a more formal visit at your pack house soon."

Hiro Tanaka nodded once, an almost bow. Hiro looked like the man he was named for, Akihiro Tanaka. He was a compact but well-muscled man of about her own height. He had dark hair, cut professionally short, and looked like the successful Japanese-American businessman that he was — even though he was dressed in black sweats instead of a suit right now. Well, they were expensive sweats, Abby noted, unlike her own which came from Costco. The pack bought them in bulk.

Mei resembled him, although she was slimmer and shorter. Abby reconsidered. It wasn't so much their looks, beyond their shared Japanese heritage, as it was the way she was standing — she was balanced on the balls of her feet, poised to pivot and fight if necessary. What had brought that stance to the forefront for her?

"As you know, these women are the victims of Alpha Chen's plot to recruit men for his own personal army," Abby began. "And these are some of the men he recruited. Most of them are lone wolves and have no pack to return to."

She saw Hiro's eyes narrow at her emphasis on most. Good. A glance at Mei showed she was barely tracking — she looked... shell-shocked? What the hell had happened here?

"Most of the men — and some of the women as well — are of college age, or close to it," Abby continued. "It is my hope as Chairman of the Northwest Council of Alphas that your pack might take some of them in." Surely some of them would have college aspirations. Right?

"I'd rather take vipers into my home," Hiro muttered, and earned himself a sharp glance from Mei. She must be paying more attention than it appeared. "But it is something we can discuss. There is meat on the grill in back, Alpha, if you'd like to join us."

"I would," Abby said, walking beside him, toward the food. "We weren't planning on this trip, and I haven't had dinner."

Hiro grunted. "I don't think anyone had this excursion on their calendar."

Abby preceded Hiro through the food line. She was the Chairman of the Council after all, she reminded herself. These displays of dominance didn't come automatically for her as it did for the born-shifters. To be honest, she hoped they never did. But at least dominance displays were becoming more comfortable.

They ate silently and quickly. Abby, Hiro, Mei, Jake, Hiro's Second who hadn't been introduced, and Ryder. Interesting that he was included.

He's essentially the Alpha of the motorcycle club, Benny told her. *And since he speaks for them, Hiro is treating him as a visiting Alpha. Generous of him, really.*

Abby finished her food and sat back. "Mei? Perhaps you'd join me in a visit to the women's side of the camp? I have to say I feel like I'm at a middle-school dance with the boys awkwardly on one side and the girls on the other."

"Gawd, do not remind me of those days," Hiro said, with a short laugh. "I think I'll get dessert instead. Whoever provisioned this camp included pineapple upside-down cake."

"It is one of our staples," Ryder said. "We find that most grocery stores can manage a passable version of it. I'll join you, if I may. And I know it's one of Benny's favorites."

"Any dessert is fine with me," Benny said, and the three of them headed back to the food line, with the rest of the men following behind. And weren't they all on their best behavior? Abby rolled her eyes.

Jake didn't go, which Abby expected.

Neither did Jason, which was unexpected.

"Get me out of here, before I have a melt-down and blow this charade to pieces," Mei said under her breath.

"Let's go, then," Abby replied. "I bet the women's camp has dessert too."

It did. More pineapple upside-down cake. A woman who introduced herself to them as Brenda dished up large servings. "Jessie is in that one, if you're looking for her," she said, gesturing to the RV they'd just walked past. "But the twins are sleeping in the other, and we're trying to keep it that way. No one wants a repeat of the earlier episode."

Abby assumed she was referring to Taisiya broadcasting her fear and desire to run and hide. "Maybe we could use the van for a meeting room?" she asked, and then added, because the woman seemed to think Jessie should be included — and wasn't that interesting? "And maybe Jessie could join us there?"

"I'll get her," Brenda agreed, and then she smiled. "And we have coffee."

"Bless you," Abby said fervently. She was damp and getting damper. A good cup of coffee was just what she needed. Even a cup of bad coffee would suffice.

It was good coffee. Jessie came to the van with a coffee pot and enough cups for everyone.

"OK," Abby said, as the women crowded around the pulldown table. Jake and Jason took up guard posts by the door. "Who wants to go first? Jessie?"

Jessie told them the story of her night's outing to rescue Ryder at the rest area. "So we're back, the twins are sleeping, and hopefully that continues until we get them to Hat Island where they will be safe," she finished. "And I hope someone — maybe Alpha Hiro Tanaka — has a cleanup crew I suspect there was at least one survivor. He should clean up after himself."

"Ryder was injured?" Abby asked with a frown. "It wasn't noticeable."

Jessie flushed, and Abby wondered what she wasn't telling them. Later.

"I turned wolf, dug out the bullet," Jessie mumbled. "And his body was able to heal from there."

She what? Abby blinked. She had never considered that possibility.

"But appearances are deceiving," Jessie continued, growing indignant. "He's still hurting. He most certainly shouldn't be riding a bike anywhere in the morning!"

Abby suspected that was a repeat of an argument she'd already had with Ryder. And lost, if Abby had to guess.

Well, they could always come up with a reason why everyone should remain here another day — so Hiro could decide who he would take in, for instance.

"Sounds like you did quite well," Abby approved. She looked at Mei. "OK, girlfriend. Spill it. We thought we were sending you into the lions' den, and instead you've got complacent pussycats."

"I don't know what happened!" Mei wailed. "Dad is upset with me, and I don't know why. Jason is hovering, and although I'm not adverse to Jason, it feels significant. And I don't know why. And when Dad asked who spoke for the recruits, one of them said I did. Why me?"

Abby sorted through that outburst. It sounded remarkably like Margarite's place, actually.

It does, Benny agreed. *See what your map tells you about links. I'm guessing you're going to see a fairly strong link to Jason and David. And maybe Alefosio. He's not talking, but he feels off-kilter to me. And then there may be radiating spokes from her to these other young men. I don't think she grabbed the motorcycle club. God, I hope not.*

Abby said flatly: *You think she formed a pack?*

Benny: *Not quite. I think the young man was right — she's their chosen speaker. But it could become a pack. I can almost feel it.*

Abby stopped the mental conversation. Mei was almost hyperventilating. "Easy girl," Abby soothed. "You did good. Let's get Jason in here. He might be able to tell us more about what happened before you got here."

Mei nodded jerkily.

"Hey Jason?" Abby called. "You and Jake come on inside. I know you're listening anyway. And I want to hear what happened between when Jessie left with the twins and Mei arrived."

Both men ducked inside but remained standing. Military men at rest, Abby thought amused. Jason had served in Vietnam; Jake had served in Desert Storm, then Iraq and Afghanistan. But the posture was there. Drilled into both of them.

"So what happened?" she prompted.

Jason shook his head in amazement. "I'm not sure which woman was doing it, probably the twins," he started. "But someone had built an invisible barrier between the men and women. And when they left to go rescue Ryder, the barrier came down. It didn't take long before the men noticed. And one asshole said, we should invite the women to party with us. He'd spent the last week with them at Margarite's! He knew they wouldn't want to 'party.' But he didn't plan to give them a choice, if I read him right."

Jason paused for breath. "Some of the women from the motorcycle club stood in their way. Amazing really, that they could resist the wave of dominance coming from the asshole and his buddies. We've got the ringleader tied up for you to question, by the way. Anyway, Alefosio, David and I joined the women protectors. And we had enough dominance among all of us to push back. But we were at a standstill, and it was growing uglier by the minute. And they had the numbers — although I'd bet on these women being vicious fighters if pushed."

"I would too," Abby said quietly. She thought it would turn feral, actually, in all the meanings of the word. They'd dodged a bullet there. "So Mei shows up?"

"She does," Jason said with a laugh. "Pulls up in that little blue Prius, and gets out as cool as a daisy, and says 'I'm hungry. Why are you all letting the meat burn?' The ringleader challenged her, and reached out to touch her, and she kicked him in the balls. And then she proceeded to kick the shit out of him. He's going to take a while to recover." Jason smiled fondly at Mei, who smiled timidly back. "And then she sent everyone to eat, and they went. I made her go through the line first — dominance displays matter, especially when you're dealing with a horde of young men, ask any Army sergeant —

and we all ate. We were still eating when Alpha Tanaka showed up. He asked for Ryder, who wasn't here yet. He was a bit annoyed by that — as if it was Ryder's choice. And Hiro said, 'so who speaks for these men?' And one of the men nodded towards Mei and says, 'she does, sir.' The men around him agreed, and everyone continued eating as if it was no big deal."

"And that's when Maggie brought Ryder and the twins back," Mei added. "And Jessie. We were just catching up on that story when you arrived. But Abby, I don't want to be responsible for all these men!"

"Does it feel like you are?" Abby asked. She did as Benny suggested and looked closer at the links on the map that connected Mei to others. There was Mei's pack bond to the main Tanaka pack, and Mei's employment bond to her. And then there were other links. It was like looking at a dandelion burst. But there was a strong link to Jason, and she was willing to bet that hadn't been there this morning. She studied the map, spotting other links that surprised her — one to Cujo and one to Okami and Yui. It was almost like one link to the bonded pair. Interesting. She wondered what Benny would make of this — and what he wanted to talk about regarding links and bonds.

"It does," Mei said in a troubled voice. "Someone should be, don't you think? They need someone to care for them. But I've never heard of such a thing!"

"Yes you have," Abby said, smiling at her. "It's exactly like Margarite's household — before she reached critical mass and it evolved into a pack. But even as a pack, it feels like a household plus neighbors who drop by for monthly potlucks. Weirdest thing ever."

"A household," Mei repeated, ignoring the evolution part. "You think I'm creating a household like Margarite's?" She flushed. "Minus the sex?" she added hastily.

Jason snickered, and Mei glared at him. But Abby noted the bright red spots on her cheeks. Well, well, she thought.

"You've got family links, right?" Abby said calmly. "Can you visualize them?"

"Yes," Mei said, getting an inward look on her face.

"And there's your pack bond to Tanaka, and your employment bond to me," Abby continued. "Can you see them? Feel them? Some people can see actual lines. Others, just feel the connection."

Mei nodded. "I feel them," she said quietly.

"And then you should see a couple of lines leading to Jason and David. Maybe to a few others as well," Abby said, not bringing up Cujo, or the Yoshidas, out loud. They could discuss those connections if Mei saw them and said something.

Mei walks in dreams, Okami said through their link — also a unique link. Benny was right — shifters had a larger repertoire of connections than they acknowledged. *She's been in Yui's dreams a couple of times, and in Cujo's. She doesn't seem to have any control over it.*

Thank you, Abby responded. She got the sensation of a short bow, and then he faded from her consciousness. Not from her brain. Like Benny, Okami was there most of the time.

She tamped down on the dis-ease that thought created. Not now. Right now she needed to keep Mei stable and let her deal with this new responsibility. Good luck with that, her snide inner voice said.

It's either her or me, she thought. And I vote for her.

"So then there should be a bunch of faint lines, connections if you will, and they reach out toward the men who are over there eating pineapple upside-down cake," Abby continued. "Can you see them?"

"Yes," Mei said, a bit doubtfully. "As if I've somehow acquired a bunch of young cousins."

"Exactly," Abby said with approval, and Mei relaxed a bit. "Do the lines extend to the women over here?" And that was an important question, maybe the most important one. Abby tried not to let it show.

Mei frowned. "No," she said slowly. "But it's almost like there could be? All I would have to do is reach out and... connect? Is that the word you used?"

"Good to know," Abby said. "But don't reach out quite yet. Let's talk about it first."

"No," Mei said faintly. "I won't." She opened her eyes and looked at Abby, a bit horrified. "I don't want any of this!"

Abby smiled at her. "Really? Are you sure you don't? You just defended them — said they needed someone to care for them. Are you sure you don't want to be that person?"

Mei didn't say anything for a bit. Then she burst out, "What do I do with them? They're hardly a puppy that I can say, 'Dad, he followed me home, can I keep him?' There's dozens of them for one thing!"

Abby laughed at the image of Mei coming back to her apartment complex with 30 young men in tow.

And a dozen women, if she managed this correctly. All Mei's responsibility and not hers. She felt almost giddy.

"If you were to speak for them, what do you want for them?" Abby asked gently, and she was truly curious.

Mei considered the question seriously. She looked at Jason for a long minute, and then back at Abby. For the first time Abby realized Mei could meet her eyes — and always had been able to. There were very few people who did these days — human or shifters. Humans might not know why, but shifters did.

Dominance.

Cujo was right, Abby thought. Mei's dominance *was* off the charts. Well, that shouldn't surprise anyone. Look at who her father was. And her great-uncle. What did they expect?

They expected her to marry the next Alpha, not be one, she thought, revising the old joke. Don't laugh, she admonished herself. This is serious.

Her wolf rolled her eyes. Her wolf took few things so seriously that a bit of snark wasn't appreciated.

"They need a place to belong, someone to belong to," Mei said slowly. "They've been adrift. First from their birth packs, then from the Vancouver Alpha. And wolves don't do well that way."

"No they don't," Jason said. "But how do we create that for them? Is there a pack that will take them in? They're a mess. Chen turned them into weapons, and he was planning on using them against Tanaka. Would Tanaka pack take them in? How could they trust them? Either of the Tanaka packs. And they don't have any skills. Margarite's got more than she can handle as it is — she's working with a dozen women who were more integrated into the Vancouver pack and didn't want to leave it. And the Vancouver pack did take a dozen or so of the young men — but Lord what that man is dealing with! Odessa seems like a good fit. But it's a dead end, really. Just more wolves in isolated rural packs. If they'd wanted that, they could have stayed in their birth packs."

That might be as long a speech as Abby had heard from Jason. She wondered what part of that analysis resonated with his own personal experience? Probably why he'd gone into the military. "Military has been the answer for previous generations of wolves wanting out of those kinds of packs," Abby said.

"It has," Jake said. Well, he would know. "But the world has changed, Abby. And so has the military. It wouldn't be as easy for these young men to enlist. I doubt they've got the paperwork for one thing. And it's harder to stay hidden. We're not at war. No cannon fodder needed."

The last came out bitter. She looked at him and raised an eyebrow. Jake just shook his head.

Later, he sent. She nodded.

"College," Abby said. "That's also been a traditional way out of poverty and isolation."

Mei nodded thoughtfully. "Can we send all of them — the men and the women both — to college? Who would fund it?"

Abby shrugged. "The Northwest Council of Alphas will," she said. "This is a problem caused by all the packs and should be solved by all of them. Scholarships for community college. Learn a trade, start an academic career, pursue a passion. They get jobs, like any college student. Is that what they want? Or, what you want for them?"

"I'll ask them," Mei said. "And I'll talk to Dad. He owns my apartment building. It's secure. If we move the women in, they'll be safe. And we can move the men in as well."

Abby hesitated. "You know that the men participated in the abuse of these women," she warned. "And that they were promised the women as rewards for their service to Chen."

Mei flinched, but she gave it some thought before answering. "Then we reteach the men — women's choice — isn't that what Wolf Harbor Resort said? If they want to be chosen, then they become someone worthy of choosing."

Women's choice about everything except becoming a shifter, Benny said bitterly. *And about being given to Jones for his abuse.*

Abby was startled by Benny's emotions. She labeled it bitterness, but it was more complex than that. It worried her. Not that he was wrong, she thought, but there was a feeling of self-loathing in it. And that was never healthy.

I'm fine, Alpha, Benny said. *It's just that I had some hard truths to face while dealing with the women at Margarite's. But I like Mei's idea of housing the women in Everett. We can continue therapy sessions there.*

Abby sent him comfort and added him to her list of people she was concerned about. A growing list. It troubled her, just how long that list was.

"My concern is that the women might talk," Abby said out loud. "That was why we were taking them to Odessa."

Mei considered that too. "You've taken the most broken women to Hat Island already," she said, borrowing a term from Yui's plaintive song. *We are all broken,* the lyrics said. Truth. "We can ask the women. Give them a choice. Explain why they cannot go to humans and say we're 'werewolves!'"

Abby snorted. "I don't know which would go worse — if they're believed, or if they aren't," she agreed.

"It would just take one of them changing in front of human authorities, and they'd be believed," Jake warned. Abby didn't think he was opposed to giving the women a choice, just raising the issue. A valid one.

"Jessie?" Abby asked. "What do you think? You've been working closely with the women."

Jessie frowned thoughtfully. "Offering them college to begin a new life might be attractive," she said. "And you can do it is as an Alpha's question, can't you? And then you'd know who would take advantage of the offer, and who would most likely try to go to authorities. And the second group we take on to Odessa."

Alpha's question. Almost impossible for a shifter to lie to an Alpha. But that had many shades of gray. It was impossible really for a shifter to lie to their own pack Alpha. But these shifters weren't her pack. Still she'd compelled honesty before. She had a flash of the recruits who had come to Hat Island after Geoff. She'd interrogated before they went to Vancouver. They'd talked. And then Brighton had killed them — the penalty for attacking the pack on its own territory.

She didn't ever want to do that again. It was why she was determined to find a better way for these men. As for the women, they were Chen's victims, and they were owed.

"We can do that," Abby agreed. "Mei, you can talk to the men yourself. If you find men you're wary of, we'll separate them out for further questioning. The ringleader might not be the only one of them with loyalties to the Penticton Alpha — if that was even his problem."

Mei nodded, not even questioning her assignment. Abby watched her, wondering what she was becoming. Another female Alpha? Is this how women became an Alpha? They were given people to care for, and then they became their protector? Abby had felt like that about the women in her cohort before she called the Hat Island pack. Abby wished she could talk to Margarite about it. But Margarite was prickly, and still in denial about her own status as a new pack Alpha.

Well someday. They had time.

She hoped.

"So we'll camp here tonight," Abby continued. "And tomorrow we sort them all out. Mei, you might talk to your father tonight about that apartment building. It's not empty after all."

Mei nodded. "He owns a lot of property, however," she said. "It might take a couple of weeks to give them notice and offer other rental options. But it can be done. I manage the books for building."

Abby wasn't surprised. Her father was no fool — *of course* he used his daughter's talents as a manager.

"Let's walk through the men," Abby said. "And we need to talk to that ringleader. I'm worried about the possibility of other Penticton wolves too."

"And I want to talk to Ryder," Jake said grimly. "We need to know more about the attack on him."

And we need to talk about the Okanogan, Benny sent. *With Ryder. But first? Could you send Jessie out? I need her.*

A lot of talking to do, Abby thought. And then she wanted a motel room for the night. She would be damned if she slept out here in the rain.

"Jessie? Would you go see what Benny is up to?" Abby said, without explanation. Jessie looked surprised, but she nodded and went.

"And let's go check out the boys side," she said to Mei. "We need to talk to your father."

***

Jessie watched. Ryder had caught her at it, and he had been amused. But he wasn't bad at watching himself. Every time she looked over at him, he was watching — watching Alpha Stafford, watching his brother, watching Mei Tanaka and her father.

And watching her.

It did something to her to meet his eyes when she caught him watching her. Something she wasn't sure she liked. She wasn't even sure what it was!

He finally came over to her. "Come," Ryder said. "I want you to walk through the men. Tell me what you sense."

Jessie frowned, puzzled. Why would she sense anything? But she was curious, and so she strolled around the men's picnic area with him. He led her in a big figure eight and they ended up near his brother. "Who do they belong to?" Ryder asked.

Jessie stared at him. "How would I know?" she asked, but then realized she kind of did. "There are lone wolves," she said slowly. "Many of them I feel are connected to me — so I think they were Vancouver pack maybe, like I was."

Benny's eyes sharpened at that. "Interesting," he commented. "That's the question of the evening, you know. Who belongs to whom, and what does that even mean? We used to think there was pack, and there were lone wolves. Simple, right? But...." He looked around the area.

Jessie did too. Some of the bikers were setting up music under the pavilion. It was beginning to feel like a party. She didn't know if that was good or bad. Well, at least wolves couldn't get drunk and obnoxious. Just obnoxious, she thought ruefully.

"So, there are connections forming," Benny said. "Not quite pack bonds. But it's as if these men want to belong so badly, they're connecting to each other, and Mei Tanaka seems to be the focus of those connections."

Jessie nodded. That agreed with what she'd heard the Alpha saying. And she could feel that hunger. It tugged at her too. She frowned. It was coming from.... She looked up at Ryder who was watching her intently with a half-smile.

"You feel it, don't you?" he murmured.

She flushed.

"No!" She said sharply. Ryder laughed.

Benny rolled his eyes. "Later, kids," he said. "So what I want to identify are the men who aren't connecting to Mei, because they already have connections — pack bonds or employment links — to someone else. Maybe to someone who isn't here."

Oh. Jessie thought that was an interesting question. "Ryder's men — and women — are linked to him," she said slowly. Benny was watching her carefully, and she didn't know why. But he nodded encouragingly. "And Ryder is linked to someone — are you pack?" she asked him.

Ryder nodded, his eyes also watchful. "I'm still Okanogan pack," he agreed. "Dad has never banished me. I'm not sure why."

"He learns from his mistakes," Benny said. "Banishing me set me free of the pack, and he regrets that. He has wanted me to come home and take over as Alpha. It isn't going to happen. Not now, especially. But even before the Hat Island pack rose, I wasn't going back. And he had no way of compelling me to."

Ryder stared at him. "And you think I'm going to take up the reins?" he demanded. "Hell, no."

Benny chuckled. "Dad is a conniving son of a bitch, Ryder. Do not underestimate him." He looked back at Jessie. "You see things," he said. "What other connections are you sensing?"

Jessie thought he wasn't telling her everything, but that didn't surprise her. She'd worked with him all week — speaking of a conniving son of a bitch. She surveyed the men again. "Those over there," she said, and used her chin to point to a group who were hanging out in the shadows by the bus. "They're linked, aren't they? Maybe to the man you all tied up?"

Benny chewed on his cheek. "Why do you think that?"

Jessie didn't know really. She considered it. "They mirror each other's movements," she blurted out. "Watch the man toward the back. And then watch the others reactions to him."

The two brothers looked at the man she pointed out and then stared at each other for a moment, and Jessie got uncomfortable. "It's true," she insisted.

"It is," Benny agreed. "Good job spotting it. Anything else?"

"Those two over there," Jessie said, nodding toward two men who were by the women's RV. "They're not part of the other group, and I don't know that they're a danger. But something is off."

"OK," Benny said, and his eyes tagged them. "Anything else?"

She looked around. "No, the rest of them seem like Mei's Lost Boys."

Ryder snorted at her name for them, and she felt defensive. "No," he soothed. "It's an apt description."

Benny looked at his brother. "Any way to see if they're Penticton pack? Either set?"

Ryder shrugged. "Walk over, see if they throw a punch?"

Benny snorted. "Don't know that you'd do well getting into a fight tonight."

Jessie looked at Ryder triumphantly. "See?" she said. "You are *not* fully healed."

"No, I'm not," Ryder said, and he smiled at her. "But I'm a whole lot better off than I would be if you hadn't removed the bullet when you did."

Jessie subsided.

"Do I want to know what you did?" Benny asked, looking from one to the other.

"Surgery by wolf," Ryder said. "She sliced me open with her claws, then changed back, and reached in and pulled out the bullet."

Benny stared at her. "Guess it worked," he said finally. Ryder and Jessie grinned at each other. Not much caused Benny to lose his words, she thought laughing.

Jessie saw Cujo approaching and tensed a bit. He was downright intimidating.

"You know there's nothing to be afraid of with him, right?" Benny asked in a soft voice. "He'd die to protect you — to protect any one of you."

She nodded. She did know that. But.... Well, it had been a rough year.

"You're looking at those guys, too," Cujo said.

Benny nodded. "Jessie thinks they're pack — and not our pack. Penticton, I'm thinking."

Cujo frowned. "Then so is our ringleader from earlier. They're getting ready to break him out of here."

Jessie was surprised he knew that, then realized shifter hearing. He'd been eavesdropping.

"Does the name Bjorn mean anything to any of you?" Cujo continued. "They keep saying his name. Who is the pack Second for Penticton these days?"

Jessie flinched. "They say who?"

"Bjorn," Cujo repeated. "British Columbia has a fair number of Scandinavians — just like the Puget Sound. But I don't associate them with remote places like Penticton."

"Penticton isn't that small," Benny objected. "There's probably 30,000 people there."

"And, your point?" Cujo replied.

Jessie ignored their bickering. She stared at the cluster of men standing by the bus. They knew Bjorn.

It was the first solid lead she'd had since he'd been banished.

"Jessie?" Ryder said quietly. "What's going on?"

"My former fiancé that I've been looking for?" she said. Her mouth was dry, and she could hardly force words out. "I think I've found him. Bjorn Hansen. What are the chances that there are two shifters named Bjorn in British Columbia?"

The three men stared at her.

"You thought he might have headed south," Benny said at last.

She nodded. "His mother said Chen banished him when he took me into his household four months ago. I've been searching the Vancouver area since I got out of there," she said numbly. "I didn't find any trace of him. Nothing. His family aren't talking — not to me, at least. They were Chen loyalists. They took the banishment hard and blame me."

Ryder put his arm around her shoulders and gave her a light hug. She closed her eyes briefly to prevent tears, but then she opened them and squared her shoulders. She would not break down over this. She'd shed all the tears she was going to about her broken engagement and missing lover.

But what the hell was he doing in Penticton? Was he involved in the earlier attack on Margarite's place? That had been Penticton pack, right? It was hard to think logically about all this. Her heart hurt.

"Beta?" Cujo asked. "Not just a lone wolf?"

Jessie chewed on her cheek, thinking about that. "Not dominant enough to challenge Alpha Chen," she said at last. "But among our generation, he was a leader."

Cujo blew out air between his lips. "Well, shit." He considered that. "I came to tell you that Abby wants to talk about the Okanogan pack. But maybe we should question the ringleader from earlier first. And start with questions about the Penticton pack."

"You going to do the interrogation?" Benny asked. "Or do you want me to do it?"

"No, Abby is," Cujo said grimly. "Alpha's question."

Benny nodded slowly. "Well, that will do it. Do we get to listen?"

"Yes," Cujo said. "She wants to do it publicly — under the pavilion. She says justice should be doled out in public."

Benny swore under his breath. "And that cluster of his supporters?"

Cujo's grin was savage. "They're mine."

Jessie looked at him with pure vengeance in her eyes. "And mine."

Chapter 13

Day 156 of the re-emerged Hat Island pack, Saturday, Nov. 9, Tennant Lake campground

Benny Garrison was up early in search of coffee. This was a well-run camp, surely there was coffee somewhere. He needed to have a talk with Ryder, and he wasn't about to do it without coffee.

The camp was quiet. He glanced at his watch: 6 a.m. It was barely dawn, although it would be hard to tell — another rainy, overcast day in the Puget Sound. He shook his head. He'd lived on the rainy side of Washington most of his life. And Lord knew Thailand got pretty damn wet during the monsoon seasons. But those few dry-weather years in the Okanogan? He yearned for weather like that, all winter, every winter.

Not enough to go back, mind you. Which was what he needed to talk to Ryder about.

Last night had been a revelation in so many ways. Abby had questioned the ringleader — a 28-year-old named Micky something — about what he had been doing. He tried to claim he just wanted to invite the women to join them for dinner and fun. Abby didn't accept the answer. And the story got uglier as Micky was forced to tell the truth: he wanted a disaster, one loud enough and bad enough that cops would get called. And he figured attacking women who had already been victimized by Chen was the way to do it.

"Why did you want the cops involved? Do you want a first-rule violation?" Abby asked.

He wanted to split up the caravan. He wanted to bust his men out of here. Maybe with some of the women. He had a place where they'd be welcome.

"Were you planning on asking the women if they wanted to go?" Abby asked then.

No, he wasn't. Of course he wasn't, Benny thought savagely. Damn it. Chen had turned these young men into thugs who took what they wanted and didn't see women as people. He wasn't sure they saw *anyone* but themselves as people, to be honest. He'd mentally eavesdropped on Abby and Mei's conversation before the Alpha's question. And while he approved of their good intentions, he wasn't sure these men *were* redeemable.

There was an old analogy about dogs. Take a pup and raise him in a loving environment and he'd be loyal to you forever. Oddly enough, you could take a dog and raise him in a brutal environment and get a fiercely loyal dog too. But take a dog and put him in an environment where brutality and love rotated randomly? You got a feral dog that couldn't be trusted — ever.

These shifters were like that. He didn't know if they could ever be trusted. It hurt to acknowledge that. And he thought it would break Abby and Mei's heart if it turned out to be true. He sighed.

A problem for down the road — a phrase that made him scowl. He suddenly wondered if he had misread Abby's plans for the men — not in the near future, but down the road. There had been something....

Were the women any better? Benny wasn't sure. He had his eye on a couple who he thought would bolt for human authorities if given a chance. But really, he could hardly blame them. It had to be prevented, of course, but it wasn't irrational. He was surprised, really, that someone hadn't tried that already. Of course, if they did, they'd end up in a research lab somewhere....

So the Alpha's question had actually worked. Benny could feel the crowd of men withdrawing from the ringleader. Most of them, at least. And that was good. Okami had taken Micky away, and the only question Benny was left with was what did Okami do with the body?

Another dead homeless drug addict, so sad.

Benny shook his head.

He wandered over to the women's side of the campground, and sure enough, he'd found his coffee.

He'd also found Cujo, Ryder, and to his surprise, Jessie. He wondered how Cujo's interrogation had gone, and whether there were more bodies to be disposed of. And what about Ryder's attackers? They were leaving quite the string of bodies along the I-5 corridor — and they weren't moving on very fast either.

Jessie poured a cup of coffee and handed it to him. "You're late," she teased.

Benny grunted. He gulped half the cup down and held it out for a refill. It took a fair amount of caffeine to give a shifter much of a jolt. And he needed the boost. She topped off his cup.

"Thanks," he said gratefully.

"So Abby and Jake went into Bellingham with Hiro Tanaka. Okami went with them. Mei is here somewhere, with Jason and David trailing along," Cujo said conversationally. "And we've got another alpha female with connections to her men. Does anyone else wonder if that's why shifter women are kept on such a short leash? Was it known at one time that powerfully dominant women can form households like Margarite's? And often did?"

"So much we don't know about ourselves," Benny agreed. He was almost through his second cup. He'd be able to think coherently soon. But in the meantime, talking about women who had links to men was interesting. "What about Olivia? Did you say she's got a link to Kent?"

"She does," Cujo agreed. "And to Tighe and two others who are in Monte Carlo. I likened them to employment bonds."

Were they sexual links, Benny wondered, but didn't ask. Not because of Cujo's possible feelings — he wasn't sure Cujo had feelings the way most people did — but because he was afraid he'd embarrass Jessie, and she seemed fragile after last night.

"Is that how Mei would describe them?" Jessie asked. Benny couldn't tell if she was actually interested or just doing her part to keep the conversation going.

Cujo snorted. "She is in denial about Jason and David all together and likens the links to the Lost Boys as having inherited a passel of young cousins to care for."

"How did she take what happened last night?" Ryder asked. "You killed those men, right?"

Cujo stopped for a moment. "What would you have me do?" he asked. "Pat them on the head and give them another chance? We've got no room for second chances — and these men are far beyond a second chance."

Ryder shook his head. "No, I'm not arguing against their deaths," he said. "I wondered if it affected Mei, that's all."

Cujo looked at him as if trying to determine if he was being honest. Benny thought he was. Ryder could be brutal, explosively so. Benny had seen him beat a man to death, and Benny hadn't even been sure what the man had done. Staying the Alpha of a motorcycle club was rough — and of a motorcycle club of shifters, rougher yet. No, Ryder wouldn't lose any sleep over the deaths of a bunch of men who were planning to destroy this camp, grab women and head off to take over the Okanogan territory into the expanded Penticton pack. The sheer stupidity of that plan was reason enough to kill a few of them.

"Mei said the conspiracy plotters didn't have a connection to her," Cujo said finally. "I asked her first. Apparently because they were connected in some fashion to Penticton, they didn't get swept up in whatever she did yesterday."

Ryder nodded, he didn't look up from his own coffee mug.

"Glad they're all too old for the boarding school," Benny muttered, which reminded him of the students he did have. He sighed. "Jessie? The twins?"

"They're still asleep. They changed back to human form sometime during the night though."

Benny nodded. He needed to talk to them before....

Well, before he and Ryder left for the Okanogan. Let's just be blunt about what had to happen next.

The pack's van pulled up. Jake and Abby had arrived. No Okami? That was odd.

He's having words with Hiro Tanaka, Abby said with amusement. *Hiro only wants to take a few of the women, and none of the men. Okami is 'negotiating.'*

Benny snorted. Good luck, Hiro. Just do as Okami tells you like a good boy — like the rest of us do. He felt not only Abby's amusement, but Jake's. He carefully raised his barriers. Some of his thoughts were best not shared. At the same time, he didn't want them asking why was he barricading his thoughts.

Sometimes this shit was hard. He thought briefly of his lone-wolf days and sighed.

He refilled his cup of coffee and walked over to the RV where the twins had spent the night. One of Ryder's wolves, a woman named Maggie, blocked his entrance. "No," she said simply. "Not even you, Benny."

"It's all right," a voice said softly from behind her. "He's the Teacher."

Maggie raised an eyebrow, skeptical of this announcement. He didn't blame her. "Things have changed since you last rode pillion behind me on a bike," he said with a sigh.

She laughed. "Guess so," she agreed. "Teacher."

Benny grinned at her. "I'm running a boarding school for teenaged girls these days, Maggie."

"That's a story I'd like to hear," she agreed. She moved aside and let him in.

"I'm sorry, Teacher Garrison," Taisiya said, before he could even get seated. "I didn't mean to scare everyone."

Benny wanted to laugh. She sounded like she'd jumped out and said 'boo' to some younger kids or something. Instead she'd panicked a couple dozen adult wolves to the point that they could hardly stop from fleeing.

"Tell me what happened," he suggested. "I heard some of it from Kristina."

There wasn't anything new really. Taisiya had reached her mother through their bond. Her mother had been scared. "Run, hide, the bad men are coming," Taisiya said. "Kristina says she doesn't think Mom meant right this minute. But there were bad guys out there, weren't there? And then more bad guys came after your brother, Teacher. And Jessie took us there to help him. So Mom wasn't wrong?" The last was said almost pleadingly. Taisiya put a great deal of stock in her mother being right. Well, she was only 14, and had been in the custody of a pack of Russian shifter monks her whole life. And she had a strong bond with her sister and mother.

"Your mother wasn't wrong," Benny agreed. "There are always bad guys out there, Taisiya, and there always will be. But panic rarely helps. If you had fled to hide and had caused the other women to do so as well, the women would have been at risk. Women band together to protect each other. Which you all did."

"That was Jessie," Kristina said. "She said we are protectors, and we can't flee. And we can't protect the others if our panic makes them afraid and they run."

"Jessie is a very smart woman," Benny said. He was so out of his depth! "So, tell me, does your mother have a name? I can hardly call her Mom, now can I?"

The girls giggled. "Nadia," Kristina said.

"And her last name?" Benny held his breath, not sure they'd give him that detail. Not sure that they trusted him that much.

And they did hesitate, and then looked at each other. He sensed they were communicating through their link. He waited. Kristina looked at Maggie still standing behind him. "Don't tell anyone?" she asked the woman.

Maggie shook her head. "I wouldn't tell," she promised. "But I'll step outside so I don't hear. Some secrets are supposed to remain private."

Kristina nodded, and the twins waited until she closed the door behind her. "Our mother is Nadia Vuk, daughter of Anton Vuk," she said steadily. "And we are Vuks too. The Vuk daughters of a Vuk woman."

"There's a prophecy," Taisiya said. "That's why we aren't supposed to tell. But I think Mom is coming here. I think that's what she meant. She's coming to Hat Island for sanctuary because the bad guys are closing in."

Benny bowed to them. "Thank you," he said seriously. "I think you might be right. And she will be given sanctuary. The Alpha has promised that."

"Even if there are bad guys?" Taisiya asked anxiously.

"Especially if there are bad guys," Benny said. "And if she contacts you, you must tell her that. We will protect her with our lives on Hat Island."

The two girls looked at each other, and then back to him. They nodded.

"I have one last question," Benny said, "And then I think you need to go with the Alpha back to Hat Island yourselves. You've had quite the adventure."

"Teacher? Did we do wrong to kill the men who attacked your brother?" Taisiya asked. "They were bad guys right? Jessie said that instead of hiding, we should be fighting. Was that OK?"

"You defended my brother, and I am grateful," he said, choosing his words carefully. He didn't want to create vigilantes here!

Or maybe he should? He would have to think about that.

"But it's always good to think if there is another way besides death," Benny said. "But last night? Death was the right answer."

"We didn't get them all, though," Kristina said doubtfully.

"That's OK too," Benny assured her. "It means the leader has to clean up his own mess, and not us."

They giggled at that, and he grinned at them. "So my question," he said slowly. "Did you set up some kind of mental barrier to protect the women from the men yesterday? Mei thought there was one, and that it came down when you left."

They shook their heads. "Not us, Teacher," Kristina said seriously. "That was Jessie. She said she needed to protect the women, and we couldn't make them afraid, because then it was harder for her to protect them."

Benny blinked at that answer. It wasn't what he expected.

"Come out and have breakfast," he said with a reassuring smile. "And pack your things. You can finish your trip with the Alpha when she leaves, OK?"

They nodded, and he escorted them out of the RV.

Jessie? Jessie had built that wall?

Well, wasn't that interesting?

Mei had joined the Hat Island coffee club when Benny returned with the twins. The girls made a beeline for the other RV where Benny assumed they would find breakfast. Maggie just nodded at him and followed them inside. Self-appointed guard and chaperone? Well they could do worse.

"Take them home," he said to Abby quietly. "I think we missed a question last night. It terrifies me that the women the ringleader actually wanted are those two girls. They'd be prime bargaining chips for the Penticton Alpha if he's looking to step into Chen's place."

Abby frowned. "Is that what you think is happening?"

Benny shrugged.

"Intelligencer!" she said sharply. "Give me your assessment."

The others fell quiet and looked at him. He looked at them all. They could all be mistaken for a homeless camp, he thought, him included. Or upscale yuppies from the city with REI jackets and rain gear. In the Pacific Northwest it was often hard to tell the difference. Jessie handed him another cup of coffee, and he wondered what he'd done with the first cup. He blew on the coffee lightly.

Stop trying to buy time and answer the woman, he told himself.

"Ryder and I need to go find out," he said abruptly. Ryder didn't even look up. So he'd figured that out as well. "I think they've got the Okanogan pack Second. And since he's still alive, Dad may not even know how much trouble there is in the Okanogan. So we're going to have to go in, get him out, and restore some order to the Okanogan — and Penticton — before the whole place blows sky high."

Ryder nodded. "After we finish escorting the caravan to its destination," he said. Benny started to object, but Ryder wasn't finished. "Six of my men," he said abruptly. "Benny and me. If we can't do it? Send in the Marines," he said with a wry smile at Jake. Jake just grimaced.

"And me," Jessie said. "I'm going too."

"No," Benny said, and then wished he hadn't. There was a better way to handle it. He wasn't sure what, but telling her no wasn't going to work.

"Why?" Ryder asked her.

"They mentioned Bjorn," she said quietly. "I promised I would find him, and now I have a place to look. So I'm going too."

"You realize you may not like what you find," Ryder warned.

"I know," she said. "But I have to find out. I have to know. I have to know why he didn't come for me."

"Or maybe he did," Ryder countered, meeting her eyes steadily. "Have you thought about that? That team from Penticton at Margarite's place might have been sent by him to rescue you."

Benny hadn't thought of that. And he didn't like the thought now either.

Jessie swallowed hard. "Whatever is going on in Penticton, we need to figure it out," she said quietly. "And I may be the best chance of learning anything meaningful."

Ryder stared at her, and she met his eyes without flinching. "Come on," he said. "Let's go for a walk. We need to talk about this."

Benny wondered what his chances were of getting included in that talk. Not much, he thought, as the two of them walked away, both of them with their hands jammed into their pockets, and not even allowing shoulders to touch. Their heads were bowed slightly in the rain.

"Well!" Benny said brightly. "I hope someone is in charge of breakfast?"

Chapter 14

Day 156 of the re-emerged Hat Island pack, Saturday, Nov. 9, Tennant Lake campground

Jessie walked alongside Ryder without comment. He seemed to be making a circle around the campsites in the campground. She wondered what he saw? She saw a bunch of bikers setting up grills for food under the pavilion. They nodded to him as they walked back, carefully ignoring her. She lacked status, she thought, and until that was decided, she was nigh invisible. The church bus was being loaded by some of the young men — no longer Chen's recruits, but Mei's cousins? She hoped they would have a better life than what Chen promised. They looked subdued and didn't meet Ryder's eyes. Nor hers, for that matter. Well, after last night, she could hardly blame them.

An insurrection — maybe two insurrections if you counted what happened at the rest area north of here — had been put down brutally. The fact that Ryder didn't do the actual killing, meant little to these men. They probably had a fine sense of dominance developed by now.

"If you go, you ride behind me," Ryder said abruptly. "My men will treat you with respect, because they'll see you as my woman — a woman under my protection," he corrected himself. "Benny can take care of himself, and he's ridden with us before. But we don't welcome outsiders, Jessie. And for all that, they've been respectful and polite here to you and the others here, that could change."

"Why?" she asked, curious about what he was trying to tell her. He looked at her with a raised eyebrow. "Why would they be respectful now, but change?"

"The motorcycle club functions like a pack," he said and they continued their path around the campground. Apparently they were going to canvass the whole place — the whole lakeside campground.

It seemed empty to her, even to her expanding senses, but Ryder didn't appear to make assumptions like that. "And this is a pack of men who have been through rough times. Some weren't stable to begin with. Some came back from the war with PTSD and issues that make it hard for them to stay in one place. Hell, I fit that description. All of them are just one step away from losing control. And they rely on me to provide them that control when they're going to lose it. To control them brutally, if necessary."

She waited, letting him think it through. It was as if explaining it to her helped him explain it to himself. "So sometimes they challenge me — challenge each other too. They want reassurance that I will do what is necessary to protect them. Even from themselves. Cujo understands that. So does Jake Lewis. But Jake had the structures of the military to assist him in maintaining control. Cujo and I? We do it when the only structure is our ability, and willingness to kill."

She flinched a bit at the bluntness of that word, but she thought it was probably why Cujo intimidated her. She'd seen him willing and able to kill in the last few days. He'd barely flinched.

Strangely she didn't see Ryder like that. Did Ryder see himself like Cujo? Apparently so. But the reality was that she felt safe with Ryder. "All right," she said, a conclusion based on that acknowledgement that she was safe with this man. "I get that. What does that mean for me?"

He smiled briefly, but he didn't look at her. "You'll be the only woman going in," he said. "My Second will be in charge of the majority of the club, and if necessary, he will take the club all the way to northern California for the winter."

"Not to Odessa?" she asked.

"That's a conversation for the larger Hat Island group. We'll get everyone safely to this apartment complex that Mei is talking about," Ryder said. "I won't let a convoy entrusted to my care stop short of its destination. But if Hat Island needs to send people further, they've got people who can escort that silly church bus and the RVs and whoever else over the mountain pass." They grinned at each other. That church bus had been inspired, but it did look silly. A church bus full of shifters pretending to play in a basketball tournament.

Not that she was going to tell Alefosio that.

"They might not need me," Ryder said. "But if they do, I'll see everyone safely to Odessa, or wherever. That's just a part of who I am."

Jessie didn't ask about the convoy he'd mentioned before. The one in Iraq — Mosul? She wondered if she should ask Jake Lewis about that. She thought he would know. Or maybe she'd wait and see if Ryder was willing to tell her more. She considered the proposed trip.

"But you're going to Penticton on bikes?" she asked.

He grinned, and she was stunned at how good looking it made him. "It will be a good ride for us in a small group — if it doesn't snow. We know Penticton — we stop there on the way down to the Okanogan, usually once, sometimes twice, a year. We've been through there twice in the last few weeks." He considered that. "I didn't sense anything wrong, but I was focused on getting through there as fast as possible. Sometimes going through pack territory can be risky for us. We don't want to be a challenge some podunk Alpha — and end up stuck as an Alpha of some small town pack? Hell no. But pack Alphas are a paranoid bunch as a rule. So, unless we have reason, we stay clear. And I was focused on getting to Mom, and then, the second time, getting back to Vancouver, to find Benny."

She nodded, and waited. She didn't think he was done talking. But it occurred to her that the Penticton pack might have followed him into Vancouver, if he'd just been there. She filed that away. Things were too volatile to share that little nugget.

"Anyway, there's a bar in Penticton — a biker bar. We're known there — not as shifters, you understand, but as bikers," he continued.

He considered something, then went on, "That's part of the problem with you traveling with us. There's shifter culture and there's biker culture. And women are in jeopardy in both — but maybe differently."

"That makes sense," Jessie agreed. And it did. Just as there had been shifter culture and Bjorn's frat culture. She was at risk in both, but differently.

She just hadn't realized that she was at risk from her own grandfather.

Dead, she reminded herself. He's dead. And Alpha Chen is dead.

And I'm not.

Ryder was still talking, and Jessie refocused on what he was saying. "If we hit that bar on a Friday or Saturday night, we'll learn all that we need to know. We can spend the night in town and then move on before the Penticton pack really knows we're there. We'll probably camp then. And it won't be a nice camp like this one. You're not used to living rough."

"No," she agreed. "I'm a city girl."

She considered it. Could she do it?

"No shame if you want to reconsider," Ryder said. "And, if you have second thoughts, we can leave you in Odessa with the women if we go that route. Or on Hat Island. But once we approach Penticton, you've got to be willing to obey the rules. And they're not always explicit...." He ran his hand through his hair. "Shit, I should have made Benny have this conversation with you. I'm not good with words like he is."

"Just tell me," she said quietly. "Tell me what you need from me. I've been through worse."

He snorted. "I guess you have," he said. "And I don't even know what all happened to you."

They'd made most of the big loop around the campground. All the tidy firepits, and pavilions, the gravel pullouts, all empty except for the four spaces that they were stretched across. Camping rough wouldn't be like this, she thought, although she didn't know what it would be like. But this was camping for city people like her who wanted to get out in the woods for a weekend, and then built walking paths so that their feet wouldn't get wet.

"You'll be my woman," he said bluntly at last. "I'm not saying you owe me sex, or anything like that. But you can't flirt with someone else. You'll be expected to fetch me a beer at the bar if I want one. You dish up a plate of food for me before eating yourself. You focus on me. Not even Benny."

She frowned at the last addition. "I'm not interested in Benny," she said, then flushed, because the implication was right there. She was interested in Ryder. He didn't tease her about it. Didn't comment at all.

She thought about what he was describing. She got it, she thought. Well, probably she was missing much of the nuance, but she got the big picture. It felt familiar somehow. She frowned.

He was describing how Bjorn had expected her to behave when they were with his friends at his college frat house, she thought. Arm candy, he called it. It had made her bristle then — weren't they her friends too? No, he'd said, they're not. You don't have friends, you don't, you hear me? I do. And I have a fiancée. And my fiancée doesn't need anyone but me.

It had been a memorable fight.

But yes, she knew how to behave like this. Was she willing to do it for Ryder? Was she willing to do it for *anyone* after what she'd been through the last four months?

The time in the Alpha's household had changed her. But freeing herself, and then working with Hat Island to rescue Abby — although Abby had pretty much rescued herself — and then working with the women Chen had victimized, all of that had changed her too. Made her realize who she was, and that she had value. She wasn't going to let anyone put her back in a box like Chen's household.

But that wasn't really the issue here. The issue was could she act in a certain way for the good of the team? A short-term thing. And it was her choice. That was important. She could choose to do this, or not.

Finally she nodded. "Yes," she said. "I can handle that. All of that."

Ryder didn't look at her. He just said, "Let's go talk to the others. I think Benny wants to go after Penticton right now," he said emphasizing *right now* as if he were talking about a toddler. She grinned. "But we've got to see the caravan to safety first. Hopefully that's just to Seattle. But if it's farther, then that's what we do. I said I would."

They turned back into the picnic area where the Hat Island leaders were sitting. Jessie thought about Ryder's dogged determination about seeing the caravan to safety. She might have to sit on Benny. It was important to Ryder for some personal reason. And she thought he was right — the women deserved that. Even Mei's Lost Boys deserved it. She snickered to herself, wondering if she could get that name to catch on? It was better than Chen's recruits, at least. The faster they left Chen behind the better.

"We need to leave for Penticton as soon as possible," Benny said when they got back to the table. "We could be there tonight if we get a move on."

Ryder shook his head. "I have an obligation to see these women and these guys to their safe place," he said. "That comes first. Whatever is happening in Penticton and the Okanogan has been brewing for months. It can wait until we finish this job. I don't abandon a convoy."

Jessie caught Jake Lewis's sharp look at that. She was right, she thought. Something in Ryder's military experience was driving this. But he wasn't wrong either. They weren't safe yet.

Benny started to argue, but Jessie intervened. "Benny, you're thinking like an intelligencer," she said, stumbling over the term a bit. "You want to go find out what's going on. But Ryder? He's in protector mode. Like an Alpha, I guess." She saw that comment hit Benny, who started to smile, like it meant something special to him. She wondered what, but she continued on before she lost her nerve. Who was she to be lecturing Benny Garrison? Or any of these people?

"It's important to him to see these people to safety, because he said he would. And he's right," she added firmly. "We aren't to a safe place yet. Maybe that's Seattle. If so, great. But it may be Odessa. And that's what matters first. Get the women and these Lost Boys of Mei's to a safe place where they heal and flourish. Bring some stability to their lives — and to the region. That's what you and I have been working toward all week."

"Like an Alpha, hey?" Benny said softly, looking at Ryder. Ryder just stared back without expression. "All right," Benny conceded. "You're right. These women are still hurting, and they do need a safe place. And these guys too, I suppose."

"I wish you all would quit talking about them as if they're a begrudging afterthought," Mei said heatedly. "They're as much victims of Chen's drive for power and prestige as the women are."

"They willingly signed up for it," Benny pointed out.

"Did they know what they were signing up for?" Mei asked. "Was there any way out if they wanted out? And just what about shifter packs would have told them that what Chen wanted was wrong? Benny Garrison! You know more about the packs and families those guys came from than the rest of us put together. Tell me, what would have prepared them to know it was wrong and to know how to get out of it?"

Benny considered that. Jessie liked that about him. He listened and he took in what the other person was saying, and he could even change his mind. She didn't know too many male shifters who would change their minds because some woman told him he was wrong.

"OK," he said. "I think it *is* different, but you're right. Once in Chen's army, they'd either do or die. And I can say I would rather die, but I'm not 20, fresh off the farm, being offered everything shifter men are told to want: a pack, position of respect, a woman to start a family with. And the fact that the women were kidnapped and coerced? Well, you're right, I'm too aware of the marriage practices of some of those small packs and family packs to say they should have known it was wrong."

Abby looked at him sharply at that, but she didn't question him. Jessie thought she might later. She'd heard that Abby Stafford never stopped questioning everything.

Which was probably why she was a college professor, and chairman of her department! Jessie was in awe of the woman — regardless of her status as an Alpha.

"Good," Mei said decisively. "I've been talking to everyone. About half of the men and a third of the women are intrigued by the offer of college and a meaningful fresh start. There are choices here — and it's not too late for them to settle in and start school in January. I'm thinking that the men who are interested would do well with my father. But the women should continue into Everett and stay in my apartment complex. That means finding places for them to live until the apartments open up. There are a few open now; a few more will be ready Dec. 1."

"That solves the problem of separating the women and these men," Abby said thoughtfully. "At least some of the men. Although I want to hear you tell your father what you have planned." There was some laughter at that.

"What about the others?" Abby continued.

Mei shrugged gracefully. Jessie envied the woman who seemed so poised. Not like herself — she was a mess, both physically and emotionally. "I think the men should go out to Odessa," Mei said. "Give them a job, preferably a physically taxing one. Then ask them about college in a year."

There was more laughter. "If *that's* what you want, we should take them to Mendoza," Cujo said. "Those men know hard work."

"Doubt these kids could keep up," Jake said. Both he and Cujo had grown up in eastern Washington packs, Jessie knew — at least she thought that was right. Was Mendoza a migrant labor pack? Did that exist?

Cujo grunted his agreement. "I could run them out there, though," he said thoughtfully. "I'd like to check on my nephew anyway. Maybe not," he added hastily when Abby opened her mouth to berate him. Jessie giggled. So did Mei, and then they grinned at each other. Jessie felt better about how together she was.

Abby shook her head. "You've got a death wish, Cujo," she muttered. "Weren't you just saying Ito needs you?"

"I know, I know," he said, trying to sound contrite. He wasn't doing that great of a job of it, in Jessie's opinion. From the look on her face, Abby didn't think so either.

"OK," Abby said, and people quieted. Jessie realized they'd been debating and arguing with each other in front of her, and no one deferred to her particularly. No one had confronted her, but they'd argued with each other. That was interesting. She couldn't picture anyone doing that to Alpha Chen, nor her grandfather. And dear God, not Margarite! She might like hanging out at the Hat Island pack to watch this female Alpha. If they'd let her. She resolutely refused to think about her future. Just one day at a time, she told herself.

She thought Benny would make sure she had a roof over her head, or at least a bus ticket back to Vancouver.

But suddenly she knew she didn't want to go back. She was angry at the Vancouver pack for what had been allowed to happen. Angry at her own family. And even Margarite — she'd known, hadn't she? Known that Chen was mistreating women, at least.

And they'd all looked the other way, because Chen was the Alpha.

She looked at the people at this table. Somehow she didn't think they would give an Alpha a pass like that. And even more? She didn't think Abby Stafford would want one.

No, she decided. She wasn't going back to Vancouver. And something she hadn't told anyone was that no one could make her. She wasn't pack. She didn't belong to the Vancouver pack, nor to Margarite's pack in Delta. When Chen had died, her pack bond broke, and it didn't re-establish with the new Alpha. That had been true for a lot of people. But she didn't bond to Margarite either. She wondered how many shifters in the greater Vancouver area were in the same boat. Well, if they wanted a pack bond — and most did — they could just ask one of the two Alphas, she supposed.

But Jessie knew she wasn't going to seek out a bond with either pack. She was a lone wolf. A female lone wolf. She gave herself a mental hug, and something gleeful bubbled up inside her. She liked that notion. She liked it a lot.

Chapter 15

Day 156 of the re-emerged Hat Island pack, Saturday, Nov. 9, Tennant Lake campground

Abby called Okami on the phone and told him what Mei had decided. There was silence. Abby tried not to laugh, but she was afraid Okami knew it — if not because he was a smart man, then because he could sense it through their bond.

"Mei needs to call her father, then," Okami said at last. "I will wait here until he has finished raging, and then we will make plans for the young men. How many did she say?"

Abby wasn't sure, but better to leave fewer than expected instead of more. "Twenty-five?" she hazarded.

Okami grunted. "Have her call Hiro right away."

Abby gave Mei the message and watched with amusement as the younger woman winced. Mei just nodded and moved off to make the call privately. Abby thought Okami had the right of it, however. Hiro would rant a bit, and then welcome his daughter's proteges to his pack house, and farm them out somewhere. She snickered at Okami's characterization, and then refocused on the table. Ryder and Jessie weren't back from their walk and talk, and really, Ryder needed to be part of the discussion about the Okanogan. Benny was pacing and drinking coffee. She watched him for a moment. Was there anything she needed to do?

Abby couldn't think of anything. "Breakfast," she announced, and she got up and headed around the RV to the men's pavilion to get a plate of the meat she could smell on the grill. Bacon, ham, sausage? Yes. And maybe some toast.

She was too focused on the smell of breakfast that she missed the wolf — in wolf form! — bearing down on her until it was almost too late. And then it took a second blink to understand what she was seeing. Really? In wolf form?

Abby heard shouts and knew that Jake was just two steps behind her. She knew where all of her people were, actually, but none of them were between her and the wolf coming at her. She widened her stance a bit, bracing herself for impact, and then she let her wolf surge closer to the surface, and shifted her hands.

Still, the impact of a 200-pound animal staggered her. He was going for her throat, and that was his mistake. Should have gone for her gut, she thought, a bit grim that she'd become such an expert in this. She didn't make the same mistake — she raked his belly with her claws, opening him up. And then she danced backward, to avoid his bite. What big teeth you have, grandmother, she thought, a bit hysterically.

And then Cujo had the wolf in his own hands, and Jake had put himself between her and her attacker. "Make him shift," Abby ordered. Cujo nodded. He said something to the wolf, and then there was a naked man on the ground, guts leaking out of him. Abby grimaced.

"Name, and pack," Cujo growled. Abby worried he was close to losing control of his own wolf. And if this group of men needed to know what a terrifying alpha wolf was like, they were about to get a demonstration.

Easy, she sent. *We're all fine.* Cujo took a steadying breath and nodded.

The man mumbled something. Cujo rocked back on his heels. "Penticton," he said. "With your permission, Alpha, I have a few more questions for him."

"He's all yours," she said, and turned away. She didn't need to watch that.

Ryder was standing behind her, in guard over the women. Smart, she approved. It could have been a feint — draw her and her protectors into a battle here, and then raid the unprotected women. That second attack didn't happen.

Abby considered it. The wolf who had attacked her might have been the commander of the guards who had attacked Ryder last night.

"We need to get out of here," Ryder said to her. Jessie appeared and handed her a cup of coffee and a napkin loaded up with bacon. Bless the girl, Abby thought gratefully. She attacked the bacon. A partial shift took a lot of energy.

And it was bacon.

"They know where we are," Ryder was saying. "We're sitting ducks."

Abby nodded. "Mei is negotiating with her father," she said, looking around. Mei was still on the phone. The attack hadn't taken very long.

I'm sorry Abby, Jake said through their link. *I shouldn't have been caught off guard like that.*

Not your fault, she assured him. *I didn't think. I should have warned you I was on a straight-line march toward breakfast.*

Jake snorted. *Ryder's right, though. We've been here too long.*

"So we're going to have to split up," she continued out loud. "Mei and a team will take some of the young men into Bellingham and out to her father's pack house. The rest of us head down to Everett and out to Hat Island. We'll have to house all these people until Mei makes arrangements at her apartment complex. Suggestions?"

Ryder looked around the campground, as if he were evaluating numbers of people, and transportation options. "We'll use the two vans to take Mei's young men to her father," he decided. "We'll put you and Jake on a bike." He looked at Jake. "I'm guessing you haven't forgotten how to ride one?"

Jake grinned. "I remember."

Abby looked at him. He knew how to ride a bike? Now was not the time to grill him — he was studying the bikes parked beyond the church bus. "Someone going to loan me one?"

Ryder nodded. "We'll get you one." He looked at Cujo who had joined them, wiping his hands on some napkins. "I'd like to put you on a bike too with Mei riding behind you. You good with that?"

"Better ask her," Cujo advised. "But yeah, that works for me."

"I'll send a half-dozen of my men as your escort," Ryder continued. His eyes narrowed thoughtfully. "Maggie and Brenda can continue driving the RVs. Alefosio drives the bus. Van drivers?"

"Jason and David," Cujo said promptly.

Ryder just nodded. "That works," he decided. "Then another half-dozen of mine will follow the RVs. Diego will take the bulk of my wolves on south to home. We've got more bikers than is good for us. But we need to talk about who goes on to Odessa — if anyone — and who guards."

"On Hat Island," Jake said. "This place isn't secure. They know we're here."

"Do we know who 'they' are?" Abby asked.

"Penticton," Cujo said. "Apparently, a number of Chen's people fled there, and they're regrouping under the leadership of the Penticton Alpha, and his new pack Second."

Abby saw Ryder's quick glance in Cujo's direction. Something about that statement meant something to the man. She wished she had a link to him so she could ask what. But the whole camp felt precarious. She didn't ask questions that would hold them up.

Mei came back. "We're good," she announced. "Dad's expecting us."

Abby caught Cujo's amusement — a wisp in her mind, and a crinkling of his eyes. Mei had better not get wind of it, or he'd pay, she warned him mentally.

Cujo just looked more amused.

Men, Abby thought, torn between amusement and disgust. Did he want to wind up Mei? *Why*?

More amusement. She rolled her eyes.

"Brenda, get the Alpha a helmet," Ryder ordered. "Since you're driving an RV, tell Inky that you need your bike back — Jake can use it."

Brenda nodded, and ducked inside the RV — the one where the twins weren't, Abby noted. A woman named Maggie had staked out that one. Jake took the helmet from Brenda and she showed him a motorbike. Abby watched with narrowed eyes. She'd never ridden one before.

"You'll need a warmer jacket," Benny said softly at her side. He'd stepped up when Jake had gone to check out the bike — and he was methodically going over the bike inch by inch. Abby was used to his paranoia, she glanced at Brenda and Carl. They just looked amused. Abby guessed paranoia was nothing new to them either.

"I've never ridden one," she confessed to Benny. "I don't know how."

Benny grinned. "Easy," he said. "You sit behind Jake, wrap your arms around him so tight he can't breathe. Then you lean when he leans. Think of yourself as one body....." He considered that. "Actually with your bond, that might be interesting."

Of course, he found it interesting, Abby thought with some sourness. Benny found everything interesting.

And you don't? Benny demanded in her brain.

She ignored that.

And then she just waited, while Ryder organized things to his liking. "He's good," she said to Jake, who had returned to her side, carrying two helmets.

Jake nodded. "A lot of running a motorcycle club is just this — logistics. But if he's who I think he is, he did this in the Army too. Transport."

Abby thought transport meant trucks, but it seemed to mean something more to Jake. She was missing something, she thought.

Jake had been a Marine — a Lt. Colonel at that. Why would he know anything about an Army enlisted man?

She started to ask, when there was trouble. Jake started to put her behind him but stopped when she glared at him. She could take care of herself, hadn't she just demonstrated that?

You shouldn't have to, Jake argued. But he stayed at her back.

Besides, the biker wasn't coming at her. He came for Ryder.

"Why are we doing this?" he shouted. "We should be heading home. Hell, we should be home by now. Instead we're babysitting this bunch? It's not like they're some presidential candidate. Get us out of here."

Don't tell me Ryder's a Biker for POTUS, Abby said to Benny, truly appalled at the idea.

No, not him, or any of his pack, Benny said with amusement. But his attention remained on Ryder, and the confrontation. Abby stopped distracting him.

People backed away, giving Ryder room. He rushed the man, grabbed his fist, and twisted his arm behind his back. The man yelped.

"We're doing it because I said so," Ryder said calmly, but his voice carried. He intended it to, Abby thought. "That it. That's all the reason you need to know. I gave my word. Unless you're challenging me, Timms? You want to lead this sorry bunch of bikers?"

"No, Ryder," the man's voice was softer now. "I'm sorry. I need to ride. That's all."

"And if you stop interfering with me getting things organized, we'll all be on the road faster," Ryder said. The crowd snickered a bit. Crisis over, Abby thought, fascinated by the dynamics. Ryder still had the man's arm twisted up behind him, and they stood chest to chest. Control, she thought. He's controlling him physically, but he's also giving him a chance to regain self-control.

Yes, Benny sent. *They rely on him to be able to do that. He's demonstrating that he is in control, of the club, of himself, and of them. And even when one of them loses it, he will still be in control of them.*

More than that, Abby thought back. *Look how he's doing it. He's up close. Body to body, in a way that heterosexual men don't do. I mean he could have just given him a hug.*

Benny was snickering at that. *No, bikers don't have group hugs,* he agreed.

Abby grinned, but her eyes were on the two men still standing in the center of the ring of people, mostly other bikers, but her people too. *So he caused pain, but not damage,* Abby went on. *He'll feel it every time he uses that arm — the whole ride, I suspect — but he's not damaged. The club doesn't have to wait until he heals or leave him behind.*

Benny considered that. *Interesting.*

Abby nodded. *And he's controlling him so that he can't do something so stupid Ryder can't overlook — like challenge him. He's letting him get his own control back before he releases him.*

And there he goes, Benny agreed, as Ryder stepped back from the man.

"We're doing this, because that's my brother," Ryder said. "And because I took the job. And I'd rather help out victims of abuse than some no-account politician, and so would you."

There was laughter.

"And we're doing this, because it's the right thing to do," Ryder said quietly. "And sometimes, even a bunch of bad-ass shifter bikers ought to do the right thing. But none of that matters really. We're doing it, because I said so. And if you don't like it? You know the rules. Ride out, and don't come back. Or challenge me."

"Got it," someone said.

Ryder nodded, looking around, meeting people's eyes. And then he walked over to Abby. "I'd like you to get started down I-5," he said. "We'll send others after you. But...."

Abby smiled at him. "But the Alpha leads," she finished for him. "Get me headed to the barn and the rest of the cows will follow."

"Something like that," Ryder agreed with a grin.

Jake nodded then fastened Abby's helmet on her head, and checked for fit, and then swung one leg over the bike like he did indeed know how to ride one. Ryder helped Abby get on behind him. "Snuggle up tight," he said, "and wrap your arms around him. The tighter you are, the easier it is for you to feel his body move and move with it."

He grinned at her. And Abby just laughed. She wasn't going to touch that. She heard the sexual innuendo loud and clear.

"I'll be bringing up the rear," Ryder said. "No one gets left behind."

Jake looked at him. "Ryder?"

Ryder stopped, but didn't turn back to look at them.

"You were the soldier at Mosul, weren't you?"

"I was," he said, but didn't look at them. "But I couldn't get them all out to safety."

"More lived than would have without you," Jake said. "Sometimes it's good to remember that too."

Ryder did glance around at that. "Got your own nightmares, do you, Marine?"

Jake grunted. "Yeah, I do." He started the motorcycle, and Abby wrapped her arms around him as instructed. Then she realized where her hands were resting and snatched them back.

No, that's how you know you're holding on tight enough, Jake said with amusement. *Just keep your hands where they were, and press those breasts against my back, and we're good.*

He started slowly down the exit road toward the freeway. *Really good,* he added.

Abby laughed.

The trick is to not think of other things, however, Jake said. *No day-dreaming! No chats with Benny about links and bonds. You need to be present in your body. Let your body sync with mine. Ryder's not wrong — it's a lot like making love.*

Abby paused, because she had been going to do exactly that — think about what Benny had said about links and bonds. *I can't think?* she asked, wondering if she could even do that for 90 minutes.

Jake was amused, and it came clearly through their bond. *Just feel, Alpha. Just feel.*

Well, she'd try. Abby pressed her breasts tightly against Jake's back, and let her hands rest just below his belt buckle. She felt his body respond. OK, she thought with a grin. Just feel, might be fine.

Chapter 16

Day 156 of the re-emerged Hat Island pack, Saturday, Nov. 9, Tennant Lake campground

Ryder watched Jake and Abby slowly leave the campground. "All right!" he shouted. "Let's move this camp out of here. Brenda? You and Maggie get the RVs headed out. Benny? You and those six of mine, need to be behind your Alpha ASAP."

Benny had gotten Maggie's bike back from whoever had brought it down this far. Ryder hadn't noticed. But Benny was already on the bike and heading after Jake. He wasn't going to let them out of sight, apparently. His team of men followed closely behind him. Benny was known and Ryder had chosen men who'd been with him a while for that very reason.

"Alefosio, you get that embarrassing bus loaded up and get out of here too."

Alefosio grinned and made short work out of getting the men loaded. All the gear was already stowed.

He turned to his second in command. "Close one, boss," Diego said softly.

Ryder grunted. It could have gone bad, he acknowledged to himself. Timms was a brawler. He would have been willing to fight just for the hell of it, and then realized too late that he had gone too far. And he needed to know Ryder wouldn't let that happen.

"Take Timms with you," Ryder said. "Make sure he realizes he isn't being banished, and I'm not mad. But he's too hotheaded for this kind of work. Hell, I'm too hotheaded. But he'll be better off in Horse Creek."

"Will do," Diego said. "How many are you taking with you?"

"I need another six to go with Mei and Cujo and the two vans," Ryder said. "And you get all the others. Lucky you."

Diego laughed and went to sort out their people.

Jessie was standing there waiting for him. "You're riding with me," he said gruffly. "Just hang tight. If you really want to go with us to Penticton, this will give you a taste of what it's like."

Jessie just nodded. Ryder turned to Cujo and Mei Tanaka. She kept the stillest face, he thought, fascinated a bit. Even with all of that chaos, she was just watching him, as if she found him a mildly interesting bug on the sidewalk.

"I'm going to put you on a bike too," he told her. "Just like Abby. You lead out, your two vans and an escort follows you. Cujo? You riding the bike?"

"Sure," Cujo said, smiling. "I'd love to."

Mei shook her head. "You don't even bother to ask if I can ride a bike, or who I might want to ride behind? Men, I declare."

The two men stared at her. "Well, you can ride the bike of you want, and I'll ride pillion behind you," Cujo offered. She laughed, and relaxed.

"You would too," she said. "No, I'll ride pillion. And my car?"

"Can you ride?" Ryder asked, confused by the exchange.

Mei grinned at him. "You'll never know, now," she teased. "You coming with me, or going after the Alpha?"

"After the Alpha. I'll have one of your Lost Boys drive the Prius," Ryder said, setting the other issue aside. Let Cujo deal with her, and good luck with that. "You two have it under control, right?"

Mei nodded. She handed him her key fob. "I'll get things situated at my father's place, and then we'll head for Hat Island. I've got this itchy feeling things aren't right."

Ryder took that feeling seriously. "Can you pinpoint it?" he asked, trying to keep his voice casual. "A problem with the men you're taking to your father? The ones headed to Hat Island? Or the women?"

Mei considered the list. She shook her head. "Maybe it's nothing," she decided. She smiled at Cujo. "Let's see what you know about riding a bike."

Ryder watched the two of them walk off to the bike waiting for them. He glanced around to make sure someone wasn't left bikeless — nope, his people were all good. Were Cujo and Mei a couple? He hadn't thought so. He shook his head. Not his problem.

He spotted Diego, who was cleaning up the campground. Or rather, he was supervising the cleanup of the campground. Good enough. "Come on," he said to Jessie. "Let's get you a helmet."

She followed him silently, and he worried about it a bit. It had been a while since a woman had interested him as much as she did. He always had a woman when he wanted one. And usually even when he didn't much care, there was a woman available. But this was a woman who had come for him, pried a bullet out of him, and got him to safety. And who was fiercely determined to go after her man. He frowned at the last. Was that what she was doing? Did she even know?

He explained the basics of riding pillion, and she listened intently. He didn't think she'd been on a bike before, and he wasn't used to novices. "Just hang on tightly," he finished his instructions. "The trick is to move as one body." He didn't play any of the innuendo games he had with Abby Stafford. He wasn't sure why, except that Jessie seemed vulnerable. And he didn't want to hurt her, or even make her uncomfortable.

He couldn't remember the last time he worried about a woman like this. He wasn't sure he ever had. She's too young, he reminded himself. Yes, age wasn't the same issue for shifters that it was for humans. But truth was, he'd been raised by a human mother, in a mostly human world — except for the slightly surreal weekends with his father and his pack in the hills. So to him, they might look the same age, but they weren't. He was in his 40s. And she was what? Half that? He shook his head.

Someone in the pack had repaired his tires, he noted. He'd have to see about getting new ones in Seattle. He didn't trust a patched tire, not on a bike. He hesitated. Did he trust the patch enough to even go that far? What was it, an hour? He could take the back roads and go slower.... Might find a shop in Marysville, but hell, by the time he got to Marysville, he was almost to Everett.

And he had Jessie to consider. Having a blow out at 70 mph was a death sentence, even for wolves, if they landed wrong.

"Hey Diego!" he called. "Someone swap bikes with me. I've got a woman riding pillion with me — and patched tires. That's no way to treat a lady."

There was laughter, and some rude comments, which Jessie ignored, although there were two bright red spots on her cheeks. It was Timms who rolled his own bike out to him — an apology, of sorts. Ryder just nodded and they swapped the two bikes. It wasn't his bike, but it was a good one.

Timms stayed to help Jessie get on behind him, and something settled inside of him. He always felt better on a bike. He wasn't trapped anywhere when he was on a bike. His wolf flashed him an image of Jessie. And yes, he'd admit it to his wolf, and only to his wolf, it felt good to feel that woman's arms wrap around him tightly, her hands against his ribs. He grinned, because that wasn't exactly where Jake had positioned Abby's hands. He wanted to snicker, but then he might have to explain....

He felt Jessie press tightly against his back, her face turned to rest between his shoulder blades. Yes, all right, he told his wolf. She feels right, too. His wolf felt smug. Another image: one of Jessie's wolf, clawing his back open. Bloodthirsty wench, Ryder told his wolf. And then he rode out of the campground.

***

Mei was holding on tightly to Cujo. It felt good, she thought privately. She firmed her lips. No point in thinking about it.

It does feel good.

Mei frowned. *Cujo? Are you talking in my brain?*

There was a feeling of laughter. *Should have kept silent and just eavesdropped,* he teased. *But yes, up close like this? I can hear you through that link.*

What link, she wondered. She focused inwardly like Abby had taught her yesterday. There was the dandelion burst, and damned if it didn't look like that. Her pack bond. Her employment bond to Abby. Her family links. She could see them all clearer today than last night, as if they'd become more solid. Or maybe she was just looking now and she hadn't before. Because there were some other links.

She frowned. She tapped one lightly — the one that looked the strongest. *That's the one you have with me,* Cujo agreed. *Not sure who else you're linked to. Yui? Or you wouldn't have been able to experience her nightmares like you did. And when you created that dandelion burst, you grabbed Jason and David. So you've got links with them some place. I don't know if you can talk to them like this. Maybe if they're up close? Because we're really close right now.*

Mei wanted to lean back, away from him a bit, but she really did know something about riding a bike and leaning back was the absolute wrong thing to do. *We're not mates,* she said definitively. *So what are we doing with a bond?*

Benny says shifters have a wider variety of bonds and links to choose from than we're taught growing up. Maybe it's just that people don't know. But he didn't elaborate. I think Abby was planning to grill him on the way home in the van, but well, here we are.

Mei made a mental note to corner Benny herself. What did he mean there were more kinds of links and bonds? She'd decided the links— the dandelion burst — to the young men were temporary. And she'd carefully not allowed any links to form to the women.

But a bond with Cujo? She sighed. *I missed you,* she confessed.

Missed you too, Cujo replied. *But you made your 'no' clear, and I can accept a no, Mei.*

You have a mate! Mei said, and she was all riled up again. This man infuriated her! And she sensed he was amused by that thought. Was she like an open book to him?

Kind of, Cujo admitted. *You'd better have Benny teach you how to block your links when you want to. Mei, Olivia and I have a mate bond, but we're not monogamous. And even if we were, we could still be friends. But Olivia has a lover. More than one actually. And she's not my only partner either.*

Mei thought about that. Mates who weren't monogamous? She didn't think she'd like that very much. But what did she know? She knew four mated couples. Well, five, counting Synde and Ricci, and wasn't that a headache of a concept? But Abby and Alpha Tanaka weren't monogamous. Her parents were. And Yui and Okami were. She thought they were at least.

She could almost feel Cujo lurking in her brain. *Well, are they?* she demanded.

Far as I know, Cujo answered, laughing at her. Although she picked up something, a wisp of a memory. She frowned.

Cujo?

No, he assured her. *Yui and I have never been lovers.*

Mei discovered she was relieved by that. *I wish we still had that beach cabin.*

Cujo was silent for a moment. *We could restore it,* he said slowly. *Now that Ricci is going to San Mateo with Synde, we could fumigate it. Make it ours again.*

She giggled at the fumigate part.

Mei? Cujo said tentatively. *Be very clear here. Are you asking me to share your bed again? Sometimes, maybe?*

Was she? Every bone in her body — well more like a very important muscle in her body — was screaming yes.

Olivia wouldn't care? she asked.

I told you, she has lovers, Mei. I'm fine with that. They make her happy. Why wouldn't I want her to be happy? There was a pause, and Mei got a feeling Cujo was amused. *Of course, I think she would be even happier if I were jealous about it.*

Mei grinned. She bet Olivia would be, too. Olivia was a possessive bitch. She liked her. But she walked wary around her.

But yes, I'll reclaim the cabin if you want.

Mei thought about it as she gave Cujo instructions to her father's new house up in the hills above Bellingham. As they were pulling into the driveway, she decided. *Yes. Reclaim the cabin.*

Mei hopped off the bike, glad to put a bit of distance between her and Cujo. She didn't know *what* she wanted, she admitted to herself. Dear God, was she supposed to ride all the way to Seattle like that? She shook her whole body, like a wolf shaking water out of its fur, and told herself to focus. She turned to look behind them. The two vans were pulling in with six bikers rolling in behind them.

"Better have them wait out here, until your father welcomes them inside," Cujo suggested.

"I guess you do know my father," Mei said, laughing up at him.

He looked a little grim. "Yeah, we know each other."

Mei blinked a bit; she'd actually thought they were friends of a sort — although she thought her father was a decade or more older than Cujo. But she didn't have time to sort that out. Not right now. She hung her helmet over one of the bike's handlebars, and walked up to Jason who was getting out of the first van. "You're in charge," Mei informed him, probably needlessly, but she'd say it anyway. Jason was generally in charge no matter who thought they were running the show. "Keep everyone in the vehicles, and the bikers quiet until I talk to my father."

Jason nodded. "Take Cujo in with you."

Mei looked at him, quizzically, but he didn't elaborate. Did he think she was in danger in her father's house?

No, if there was one place she was safe it was here. She had a mental flash of a dinner party where her father had set her up with a young man. A man she had to kill later that night. She'd never talked about it with her father. Suddenly she wondered if *Cujo* and her father had talked about it?

Men. They always thought they knew better than you did, and yet most of the problems were caused by men. How did that compute?

It didn't.

Mei squared her shoulders and walked confidently up the stairs to her father's home. Well, really it was her parents' house, wasn't it? Strange how she never thought of it that way. But her father was larger than life, and her mother was a quiet woman, a successful artist, but one who rarely said anything, preferring to let her mate be the interface with the rest of the world. Her mother spoke to the world though her art. It was where Mei got her own creative instincts.

Both of them greeted her at the door, with Okami visible behind them. Mei raised her eyebrows slightly at him, but he didn't give her any signs. She mentally shrugged and hugged her mother hello. She bowed slightly to her father and let him initiate the hug. They were careful with each other these last couple of years. Mei didn't quite know why. She had another flash of the man she'd killed.

When the man's family came after her, it was Cujo and Okami who protected her. She set that aside.

"So I have a gift for you," she announced. "Sixteen young men, eager to work and to learn. They're all yours."

Her father closed his eyes, as if his head hurt, and then he sighed. "Well, take me out and introduce me. We've arranged rooms in the men's hall out back. I gather you're going to take the women into Everett?"

She nodded. "We decided it might aid the women's healing if they didn't have to deal with these young men any longer," she said carefully. "The remaining young men didn't want a college education, so we're sending them out to Odessa. Alpha Stafford seems to think that the Odessa or Mendoza packs would, ah, 'inspire a change of heart.'" She snickered, and even her father laughed at that. "She believes in education, obviously."

"Yes, I can see why she would," her father agreed.

Mei looked around for Cujo, but he was standing back at the house looking at something with her mother — some of her mother's art? No, that was actually one of her own pieces that hung inside the door. She wondered what that was about, and then focused on Jason instead. "Dad, this is Jason Wahlberg," she said. "He's an assistant security chief for Hat Island. The other driver is David White, one of our medics."

More head nods. No offers to shake hands, however, unlike with Cujo. Her father had shaken his hand. Interesting.

Two men came around the corner of the house, and Jason tensed slightly. "My pack Second, and my pack master," her father said. "I seem to have inherited a number of young male wolves in the pack changeover. A pack master is a must."

Pete Craven had become the de facto Hat Island's pack master — a steady influence on hot-headed young wolves. Although in Hat Island's pack, the hot-heads weren't young wolves, just a lot of lone wolves who were having a tough time adjusting to pack life again. Pete was their... teacher? Pack master, Mei thought with a shrug.

"Then these young men should fit right in," Mei agreed.

Her father looked at Mei sourly, but she just grinned at him. "We need to get going. Okami-san? Are you coming with us?"

He nodded. "I will ride with Jason. Are you riding with Cujo or with us?"

Mei hesitated. Cujo had turned away to take a call. She frowned. What was so important that he would answer his phone in her father's presence. Well, if she rode behind him, she'd find out. "I'm riding on the bike," she said lightly. "Been a few years since I had the chance."

Her father started to say something, but after a stern look from her mother, he shut his mouth. Mei grinned again.

"We need to go, unfortunately," Cujo said, returning to the main group. "Moving this many people turns out to be more challenging that I expected when we left yesterday."

"Not surprised," her father said.

More hugs. Mei put her gloves and helmet back on and waited for Cujo to start the bike. She slid on behind him, and he eased the bike down the driveway, driving for all the world like a date wanting to show her father he was a responsible driver.

Exactly like that, Cujo agreed with amusement.

So tell me, Mei demanded. *What's going on?*

That was Ryder. He's worried about high ground.

Mei frowned. *What does that mean?*

It means something has triggered his military instincts, Cujo said grimly. *And I don't know if he's in the here and now, or if he's having a flashback and he's back in Iraq. Either way, we're about 30 minutes too late to do anything about it. But I'm sure as hell going to try.*

Mei tightened her grip on him. *Got it. Bat-out-of-hell time.*

Cujo increased their speed.

Chapter 17

Day 156 of the re-emerged Hat Island pack, Saturday, Nov. 9, I-5 Southbound

Ryder sunk into the joy of riding. He didn't even mind the misty day; he was just thankful it wasn't raining. He was used to riding in rain or sun or even snow. But he wanted Jessie to enjoy her first ride, and rain sucked. It wasn't so much the rain coming down — helmets and slickers and coats took care of that. It was the puddles that formed, even on a freeway, and sprayed upwards when you went through them. And it didn't take much more than a gloss of a puddle to do it either. And then your crotch was soaked.

But today the pavement was bare, and the mist didn't even qualify as rain. A misty day. Trust the Pacific Northwest to have a dozen different ways to describe an overcast, winter day.

He wasn't sure how far behind the RVs he was. Or behind the bus. The bus might even be moving slower than the RVs. And his guard unit better be weaving in between them and the Alpha. Especially around the Alpha. That attack this morning worried him. Well, Benny was leading them. He'd keep things moving. Still, Ryder was uneasy. Mei had been uneasy too, he remembered.

He took the next exit and went up the ramp to the overpass. And there he paused, bracing his legs to steady the bike as his inexperienced passenger wobbled a bit before putting her own legs down. "What's up?" she shouted in his ear. He winced. Didn't need to be quite that loud, but he didn't say anything. She'd figure it out on her own, and it would go better than him correcting her.

His mother didn't raise no fool.

"I wanted to take a look at the convoy," he said, then corrected himself. "The caravan. Best view is always high ground."

It was that phrase that did it. High ground. There were a lot of exit ramps like this one: Exit up, and an entrance back down to I-5.

An overpass to his left across the freeway, and matching ramps down the other side.

And a sniper could be positioned on any one of them.

"You've said that before," Jessie said neutrally. "Don't carry a fight to the enemy when they have the high-ground advantage."

"Did I?" he said absently. "Probably. I learned that lesson the hard way. And there's probably a dozen of these between here and Marysville. Some of them are pretty remote. You could sit up here, watch for a biker that smelled like a shifter, and fire a shot."

He looked at her. "You got a phone number for Cujo?" It was a wild shot, but he'd try.

She nodded, elaborating when he looked surprised. "He gave it to me when we went to take out Alpha Chen. He made sure I had his, Benny's and Jake's cell numbers."

"Good," he said. "Let me use your phone, if you don't mind."

She brought up the directory, punched in the number, and handed the phone to him. And then she studied the freeway while he talked. He'd be willing to bet she could repeat every word, for all that she didn't look like she was paying attention.

She listened, after all. Wasn't that what she said?

"I wish I'd told Jake to take every exit up and over," Ryder said to the other man. He chewed his lip. "If there is someone waiting for us, they'll be gunning for her."

"Why do you think that?" Cujo asked. He was at the Tanaka pack house apparently; Ryder was glad to have caught him there.

"The wolf this morning," Ryder said, reasoning it out. "He came for her. Not me, not just someone random. The night before, they wanted me. But that changed when Abby joined us."

"Makes sense," Cujo agreed. "All right. This is top secret, don't even admit to anyone you know anything. But Abby has a way of establishing links with her closest wolves — her inner circle, she calls them. I think I should be able to reach her — or maybe Jake — depending on how barricaded she is right now. Might be Benny."

"Like what Mei created with the recruits?" Ryder said, frowning as he tried to make sense of that. "Except you can talk through them?"

"Benny says Abby is able to do things because no one has had the time to tell her they're impossible," Cujo said lightly. Ryder didn't buy the tone, but he let it go. "To her, the bonds in her head look like telephone wires. And so she uses them like that."

"And she's in your head." Ryder shuddered at the thought of it. Although it raised all kinds of interesting questions — as long as it wasn't his head they were talking about.

"You learn to build barricades," Cujo said. "But that all can wait for a later conversation too. I need to get off this call and get on the road. I'll see if I can catch up. And see if I can reach one of them. Tell them to take the high road."

"Yeah," Ryder said. "Paranoid, I know. But better safe than sorry." The two men said the last together, and Ryder grinned. Nothing like working with a professional paranoid.

He ought to know.

Ryder handed Jessie her phone back. He thought if there was anything else he could do besides ride out of here faster than he'd planned. "Can he really do that?" Jessie demanded. He raised his eyebrow at her. "Talk to someone through their bonds? I mean there are myths that mates can, but I've never known anyone...."

Jessie paused. "Well, Margarite can communicate with her men, I think." She blushed a bit. Ryder grinned. He'd like to know what she'd observed to make her blush. Sex, probably. He'd heard stories about Margarite and her men his entire life — the old vets of the Okanogan pack hadn't been all that careful about what they talked about in front of the teenaged son of their Alpha. And Margarite and her men had been a topic of much consideration.

"I don't know," Ryder said. "But if Cujo says he can hear voices in his head, I'm not going to argue. I'm going to say, 'Yes, sir!' and figure he hears voices in his head."

Jessie nodded, and put her helmet back on. "He scares me," she admitted.

"Shows you've got good sense," Ryder assured her. She laughed and hung onto him tightly as he started down the ramp back onto the freeway.

***

Cujo was trying to go as fast as he could legally, maybe even a little faster, and reach out to the so-called inner circle at the same time. It was frustrating. He rarely initiated with anyone but Olivia. And usually the inner circle had to be a flooding rice field for him to hear Benny or Jake — Abby's metaphor.

Well, it made sense to her.

He tried visualizing Abby. He tried looking inward, but it was hard to do while he was supposed to be driving a bike!

What do you need?

Cujo frowned, trying to place the voice in his head.

Okami. The voice said. *What do you need!*

Cujo kept it simple and told him what Ryder had said.

Do you think this is a possibility?

Did he? He repeated what he and Ryder had agreed on earlier: *Better safe than sorry.*

Okami grunted. Now how did he know that? And there was nothing more. Cujo took a deep breath and slowed down a bit. That had given him a headache. He didn't think he'd ever spoken to Okami in his brain before. He frowned. Did he have a link to the man? Guess he did.

The inner-circle links?

Benny was right. They needed to talk about pack bonds and links. It was more complicated than they realized.

You OK? Mei's mental voice was soft with concern.

Okami. His mental voice is like a sledge hammer.

There was a pause. *Do you realize how weird that sounds? Do you want me to drive?*

You really do know how? Cujo asked.

There was the soothing sound of Mei's laughter. He grinned and pulled over. Ride pillion behind Mei Tanaka? Of course he would.

***

Okami woke Abby from her near-bliss state of just holding Jake and moving when he moved. *What?* she demanded more rudely than was her norm with the man. *Jake says no mind-talk, just focus on staying in the moment and moving with him.*

She felt Okami's laughter. Strange how he rarely laughed like that in the real world.

There is concern, Okami sent. *Tell Jake to take each exit and look ahead. And beware of snipers — the overpasses are high ground. He'll understand. Ryder is concerned. Cujo is concerned. So we will all drive faster and get closer to each other.*

Abby blinked a bit about all that *concern*, and then she relayed the information to Jake.

Understood. Abby, do you have a way of passing that on to the twins? To tell the RV driver they're to do the same?

Abby grimaced. Taisiya gave her a headache. Kristina was easier, but Taisiya was stronger. She reached for them both and relayed the message. *Tell Maggie this.*

Yes, Alpha, Taisiya replied. *Are there more bad men?*

There are always going to be more bad men, Abby answered, striving to be truthful, and yet not set off the panic-and-hide response Taisiya had yesterday. *But we are strong, too. Tell Maggie.*

There was no response, but she didn't sense any panic in the links either.

She passed the message on to Benny as well.

Well, shit, Benny said.

Tell Benny to stay on the freeway with the bus and other RV, Jake said.

Abby sighed, and let down the floodgates and flooded the field. *Tell him yourself.*

***

"Miss Maggie?" Taisiya said timidly.

Maggie Beaumont glanced back at the teenager. "Something wrong?" She liked the girls. They were damned powerful shifters, she acknowledged. But they were also nice kids. And the way they looked after the other women, these poor battered women, was sweet.

"Alpha Stafford says to take the exits at each overpass?" The girl sounded like she wasn't sure what that meant. "That there could be trouble — high-ground advantage?"

That sounded like Ryder. He had a thing about high-ground advantage. She understood why. It made her flinch too. But how were these girls using his phrase? What did she mean Alpha Stafford told her? Had she called them?

Not from the back of a bike, she hadn't.

"Honey? How did Alpha Stafford tell you that?" she asked carefully, not taking her eyes off the road. She could see the Alpha's bike up ahead. And yes, there was an overpass coming up. And whoever thought about the dangers of those things wasn't wrong. If she was going to try to take out someone, she'd be up there waiting in ambush.

Still wouldn't be easy, she conceded. But a shifter with a high-powered rifle and shifter eye-sight might be able to take out a tire. Or a rider. Or the gas tank....

Or an RV.

"Taisiya?" she prompted.

"I'm pack," Taisiya said, a bit proudly. Understandable. She was a 14-year-old girl, and not born to this pack either. "And Alpha Stafford, she can use the pack bond to talk to me."

Maggie frowned. Was that possible? Well, she didn't know about the Alpha, but she'd believe just about anything after that mind blast yesterday from this kid. And a female Alpha? A recently changed shifter at that? She'd have to be pretty formidable to do that.

Act as if, she decided. The advice wasn't bad advice.

But if they went up that exit ramp and someone was there — what then? And why did the Alpha want *them* to go up the exit ramp with them? Was everyone going? She doubted that. They were taking some pains to not look like an organized caravan. Just part of the traffic heading south on I-5. This motley collection of vehicles all exiting and then re-entering the freeway would be noticeable, to say the least.

Maggie had been military. She came from a small southern pack where most young shifters served in the military, even the women. The few the pack had. That was how she knew Ryder after all. They'd fought in Iraq together.

She'd been at Mosul.

Not thinking about that, she reminded herself, as she did almost daily. Mosul had been a nightmare. She didn't need to trigger a flashback here and now.

She'd stayed in eight years. But when she returned to her pack, they couldn't understand her bitterness and disillusionment. Their own government had betrayed them! How could they not understand that? Their own government had lied. Lied to the public, which didn't surprise anyone, not really. But lied to their own troops? There had been no weapons of mass destruction there. There had been no links to the destruction of the World Trade Center. There had only been bewildered, and then enraged, Iraqis who fought the invaders — the United States — like their lives and their freedom depended up on it. And there was nothing fiercer than a people fighting for their homes.

Fighting her. She'd invaded a country for no reason. And people, some of whom she had cared about a lot, had died. Many innocent people had died.

Oh, she knew not everyone saw it like that, not even now. Her pack treated her like she was a hero when she came home. All the vets in the pack were treated like that. But she wasn't a hero.

The Vietnam vets understood. They didn't talk about it, but she could see it in their eyes. Oh yeah, they understood all right.

When the rage got to be too much, she'd ride out. But she was a risk — a risk to her pack, to shifters in general. She drank and got into fights. And she was a first-rule violation just waiting to happen.

Her Alpha was a good man, a veteran himself — World I and II. He tried to balance her need to run — and she was honest, that was what she was trying to do, run away from her memories — with the pack's need to keep her close.

But it wasn't working. One day, she remembered Ryder's invitation to come find him when she got out. Okanogan pack in Washington state. He'd see her there, he said.

So she went. She found him there — with an outlaw motorcycle club of shifters? Wasn't that wild? She'd known him under a different name, in Iraq, but he was the same man. And she joined up. Been over a decade now. She shook her head.

She was still pack, oddly enough. Her Alpha figured a stable Maggie on the West Coast was better than a Maggie teetering on an explosion back home. After all, there was time. Time for Maggie to come back if she wanted. Smart man, her Alpha.

So she'd seen things, riding with Ryder. Ryder's father was a scary man to start with. Looked at you with those cold eyes, and you wanted to blab everything you'd ever done. They didn't look alike. Ryder was brown and warm, for all that he had a cold streak in his heart. But then Ryder's mama was a local Native American woman. She'd met her, actually.

So, go up that ramp? And then what? If the bad guys were there? What then?

"Anyone know how to drive one of these things?" she asked the women in the RV. They were too silent. Women cooped up like this would talk.

One woman spoke up. She had a low husky voice that sounded like she hadn't used it much of late. "I can," she said. "Why?"

"There might be trouble ahead," Maggie said, still wondering why the Alpha was worried about this vehicle especially. She glanced at the twins who were perched on a bench right behind her so that they could see out. Might be why, she conceded.

"If there is trouble, I want to be in the passenger's seat," she continued. "You willing to drive?"

The woman nodded and moved forward. Maggie slid into the passenger's seat, and the woman took the wheel. "I'm Wilma," she said. "My husband I had one of these RV's. We were spending our retirement years traveling." There was sorrow and anger in her voice. Maggie didn't ask about her husband. She could guess. She'd heard enough talk to get the picture — that bastard of an Alpha had been kidnapping human women and changing them. Then he gave them to his men as rewards for jobs well done.

"Maggie," she replied, although she thought they all knew. Maggie quick-stepped into the back of the RV, swaying with the motion of the vehicle. Damn thing was huge. She'd lived in apartments smaller than this. In fact, her cabin at Horse Creek wasn't much bigger. She knelt down and pulled out a locked box from under the seating area. Everyone watched her silently.

The silence was beginning to bug her, no lie.

She opened up the box, and took out a sawed-off shotgun, and pushed the box back under the seat. It was the first thing she'd packed into the RV when they were provisioning it. And it would be the last thing she took from it. She didn't go far without it. Fangs and claws were good for up-close-and-personal work, but there was nothing like a shotgun to make sure that she didn't have engage close in like that.

"Bit short, isn't it?" a woman asked.

Maggie looked at her and grinned. "Interesting you would know that," she said, and the woman laughed.

"I know," the woman said. "What's going on?"

"May be a problem," Maggie said. Her first instinct was to protect them from it, but she changed her plan for that. They'd been moved from place to place without any consultation for a week now, from what she'd heard. Time they got some control over their own lives.

"So listen up," Maggie said, and she heard the military tones creep back into her voice. "There's concern that we may come under attack at one of the overpasses. So we're going to go up the exit ramps and down again on each one — our own private rollercoaster ride. We're following Alpha Stafford's lead here. But it worries me. I don't think this RV and her bike are the only targets — high priority ones, maybe, but not the only ones. So I need someone who can watch out the back, and others on the sides. This rig isn't built for views as we travel."

The women laughed at that, but they were looking at each other, as if they were communicating silently. Not spooky shit like the twins and the Alpha, just normal women evaluating each other's faces for the messages there. "We can do that," said the woman who had known about shotguns. "I'm Carol, by the way."

"Good," Maggie said. "So here are the ones I think might be targets too. Benny Garrison. You all know Benny?"

"We know Benny," the women agreed. She could hear the amusement in their voices. That man sure got around. She had a brief bit of nostalgia for when she'd ridden behind him — ridden him other places too, she thought with a grin.

"He's on a bike. Blue helmet. And the bus. To be honest? I'm more anxious that those young men will stage a rebellion from within than it getting attacked from without."

"Good thinking," Carol said. "Those boys aren't right."

Maggie grinned at her. She could hear the South in her voice, made her homesick. How did she end up trapped in a Canadian pack? Maybe she'd tell her one day.

"And Ryder. They came for him yesterday, remember? He'd probably dismiss the danger, but I think he's still a target. He wears a black helmet, and he's got that girl, Jessie, riding with him. She's got a black helmet on too."

"They're going to be farther back," Carol said, considering the matter.

"Yeah, but he won't stay back there, not if there's trouble," Maggie said. "Rushing in where angels fear to trod was a prophecy for that guy."

More laughter. Maggie grinned at them. "So here's what I'm going to do. I'm going to sit with this shotgun. If there's no problem at the top, we go down the other side. But if there is a problem, we're going to slow down, I hop out. I use this barely legal shotgun loaded with buckshot, and then run down the ramp. You all will be waiting for me at the merge sign. And we repeat, if necessary on the next overpass."

"Do we know who?" a woman asked.

Maggie shook her head. "Shifter politics. That bastard who imprisoned you had allies. And I hear they'd like you back." Probably shouldn't have said that, she supposed. But they needed to know what the stakes are for them — why should they care about shifter politics otherwise? She slanted her eyes toward the twins, and she saw the other women nod. They got it. It was about the girls too.

"All right," Maggie said, returning to the front seat. She was pleased with the caliber of women she saw in the back of the RV. They might be licking their wounds, but she thought they were sound.

"Ms. Maggie?" Taisiya said timidly. "Okami says don't stop. No matter what, keep moving. Harder to hit us that way."

They were a pretty big target, moving or not, but whoever this Okami was, he wasn't wrong. She considered that, then nodded decisively. "We won't stop," she agreed. Then she smiled. "But we might slow down at the top."

Her driver gave her a quick grin. "Got it," Wilma said cheerfully. "Here we go."

Chapter 18

Day 156 of the re-emerged Hat Island pack, Saturday, Nov. 9, I-5 Southbound

The bad guys weren't at the first overpass. Jake took Abby up the ramp and down the other side without a pause. They weren't at the second one, either. Abby began to hope it was a false alarm — or an excess of caution, which she couldn't fault. Hell, they'd sent a wolf into a public campground after her this morning!

She shook her head. The Pacific Northwest region was becoming more and more unstable. Too much change, she feared. And she was driving that, in large part. Just her sheer presence as a female Alpha of a new pack seemed to be doing that. Add in her ascension to Chairman of the Northwest Council?

And add in Akihiro's ascension to Chairman of the World Council, she thought suddenly. This song isn't about you — not completely, anyway. She wondered just how much of the turmoil was caused by *Akihiro* — the traditionalists feared what he gave his pack. Would it spark unrest in their own packs? And they resisted change in any form to start with.

Listening to the radio, Okami told her. She set aside her questions to focus on his message. *There's an accident ahead. All southbound traffic is backed up from Marysville almost to Arlington.*

Setting us up? Or coincidence? Abby asked.

My assessment is that they want to force us off the freeway to a more isolated route, Okami replied. *Or leave us stuck in traffic where we're sitting ducks.*

Abby considered their options. *Pull over,* she told Jake. *We've got to figure this out.*

He slowed down and pulled off to the side of the road. She put her feet down to steady herself and got out her phone to look at a map. "Most likely route to take would be to get off at the Arlington airport exit, go east, and then continue south. We could pick up I-5 at Marysville," she said. She'd grown up out here — in a small town to the east called Darrington. Her parents still lived there. She had a brief moment of grief — she would never see them again. She called them regularly. They were talking about her coming home for Thanksgiving or Christmas. She'd have to make up some excuse. She stopped that thought, locked it in the storage closet of her brain, and refocused on her map. "There's a 10-mile stretch in there that's pretty quiet. That's where they'd set up."

She frowned, thoughtfully. "But we could go west instead. Head out to Lake Goodwin, and then down to Tulalip."

"You're thinking we could go by boat down from there," Jake said slowly. "Take a while for our boats to get up there."

Abby nodded. "Gives us time for lunch," she said with a quick grin. "Maybe not everyone," she added. "The women. Benny, Cujo, Ryder, Okami. Ryder's club continues south as planned — no way to reach them anyway. Benny's guard group continues with the bus full of men on I-5. Won't hurt them to sit in traffic. I'm worried a bit about Alefosio — what if there's still a plant from the Penticton pack in there?"

Benny pulled up alongside them. "What gives?" he asked.

Abby told him. He considered it as his team of bikers pulled over too. They were getting noticeable, she worried. Or maybe not. Eight bikers looking at a map? Nothing to see here, she projected. The projection might not matter, but it helped her feel more in character.

"I'd like to send a couple of my group down the east route," Benny said slowly. "See if they really have a trap set there. We might have created an enemy in our own minds." He looked around. "Abe, you willing to take a couple of others and go down the east stretch? Might find yourselves a fight," he warned.

A man grinned. "I wouldn't mind a fight," he said. "Sure, I'm down with that. We'll call you from Marysville?"

Benny nodded. "And then join up with the bus again, and we'll see you in Everett. Park at the Wolf Harbor Resort office. Someone will be there to greet the bus, and you all."

"Can do," Abe agreed.

"Head out then," Abby said. She waited until they were back on their bikes and on their way, before she used her phone to call Okami. He listened to her plan silently, and then paused to consider it. She took a deep breath and let it out to a count of 10. Silence was still hard, she thought ruefully. There was this tendency of all Americans, white Americans in particular, to fill in the pauses. And she knew better!

"I think that's sound," Okami said finally. "I will call the harbormaster. You do not plan to take the RVs down by boat?"

"No, they're rentals," Abby said. "Brighton can send someone up to return them. Same with the vans." She considered the vans. "Maybe have the second van go down I-5? Who's driving it?"

"David," Okami answered. "We're empty, both of us, after leaving the young men at Alpha Hiro's place."

So that was to be the distinction in names? Worked for her. It had been getting awkward distinguishing between the two Alpha Tanakas.

"I'm worried about having no guards around the bus, however," Okami added.

Abby thought about that. She could leave Cujo and Mei on I-5. Or Ryder. No, she worried that Ryder was a target. As was Benny. And Cujo would have to guard Mei, not the bus.

"We will have to make do," she decided. "Benny? Call Alefosio and see what he thinks. If he needs guards, we could get some started toward him from Hat Island and meet him in Marysville."

Benny nodded and turned away to call him.

"Okami? Could you call David and let him know the plan? He should probably try to catch up with the bus as well," Abby delegated. She would have to be the one to contact Cujo.

"Alefosio says the men have been in good spirits, and it feels pretty settled," Benny reported. "If you ask me, having Mei as their 'speaker' is what they needed."

"Well, that and the fact we weeded out a half-dozen of the bad guys," Abby said dryly. The phrase 'bad guys' made her remember the RV. "Call the RV drivers, and talk to them, too, Benny? I saw them go by us, just a bit ago. They need to know to take that exit and turn west."

Benny nodded and made the second call.

"And Ryder?" Jake asked. Abby grimaced.

"I'll wait here," Benny said, looking away from his phone call. "Catch him when he gets here and send him after you. I think we've got too few guards with you, Alpha. You're assuming you'll surprise them. But we don't know how many are involved in this. It seems like a major effort — and I don't even know why they'd do this at all."

"Then you follow to Tulalip with Ryder," Abby said.

"Better," he agreed.

"Let's go," Abby said to Jake. "I'll talk to Cujo on the way."

You should talk to Tanaka, too, Jake said. *I think there's an extended family pack in the Tulalip area. They look to Tanaka but aren't Tanaka pack. But Tanaka can give them a heads up that we're coming into their territory.*

Abby grimaced. She hadn't planned on telling Akihiro about this. Well, she would have to sooner or later — Everett, and Mei for that matter, were Tanaka pack, not Hat Island. And they were planning on giving a couple of dozen loose cannons housing in Everett? She grimaced again.

But Jake was right. She leaned her head against Jake's back, and opened up the barrier that kept information from flowing through her mate bond. So much she didn't want him to know. *Akihiro? We're going to need to go through Tulalip territory. Jake says they look to you — would you give them a heads up?*

A bit of silence: *Please tell me you're not on I-5!*

Abby was startled. *We are,* she said slowly. *But apparently there's an accident ahead, and we want to go around. We thought we might go down to Tulalip and have a boat come for us — make a nice trip, actually.*

Akihiro: *Communicating like this isn't easy for me, as you know. And there is much I need to tell you. Are you near a phone?*

Abby: *No.* She knew Akihiro struggled with talking like this over any distance. Up close worked. Emotions worked. *Sex* worked. But distance was a problem. She thought it might be because for over a century he hadn't believed it was possible.

Akihiro: *Then listen. As much as I want to know who the 'we' might be, you need information more. The Tulalip Alpha called me just an hour ago. He says yesterday there were strange shifters in his territory, but he wasn't particularly worried. Still he asked his wolves who work at the casino to keep an ear out for trouble. And there is trouble.*

Of course there was, Abby thought with a sigh. She wished she could patch Jake into this, but resistance from both of them made it impossible. She understood the resistance, but right now, she wished for exceptions.

Akihiro continued: *That accident? It's a tractor-trailer rig — two trailers, and it looks like at least one was fluid — maybe gas or some kind of fuel —and it jackknifed across all lanes, then exploded. A previous smaller accident had stopped traffic south of it, and now prevents first responders from getting to the injured. Other vehicles are also engulfed. I've been watching the news. It's bad, Abby. And the Tulalip Alpha — Norman Posey — says shifters were involved. The casino is trying to marshal some kind of first response, or even first aid, but I gather there are problems. Not relevant to you. But you need to get off that free-*

way — Arlington airport or Arlington main exit — ASAP — before it's backed up too far and you won't get off at all.

Abby: *We've already got one vehicle past that, I'm afraid.*

A pause, and then Akihiro said slowly, *Maybe you had better tell me who the 'we' is after all.*

Abby: *Let me pass on this information to Jake. And then I'll tell you. Stand by.*

She opened the flood gates.

The accident is really bad and may have been caused by shifters. People are in trouble! Akihiro says go around, but I think the bus is already past the last exit. Benny?

Benny: *I'm on the overpass at the airport exit. It is bad. And I don't see a way to turn the bus around. Alpha? I think we should use those young men to combat that blaze. There appears to be blockage south of the explosion as well — I don't see any firetrucks at the explosion.*

Abby hesitated. This was hardly the low profile she'd hoped for.

Cujo: *Mei says we're going to go on to the bus and direct the firefighting efforts. We'll be there in a moment. Benny? You should probably stick with the Alpha.*

Abby: *What? No! Don't let Mei do that, Cujo!*

Cujo: *She's driving the bike, Alpha. I'm along for the ride on this one. And she's not wrong. Shifters may have caused this. We need to help fix it. And we need to have on-the-ground damage control so that it doesn't turn into a first-rule violation.*

Okami: *I have the boats underway to Tulalip, Alpha. You need to go there. We cannot risk you. But Jason thinks he and I should assist Mei. So we will do so. David as well. We have the two vans, and David is a medic. All will be useful. But you must go on ahead to Tulalip.*

Jake: *And the women in the RVs to Tulalip as well. I would like a few of Benny's guys to go down the east route still. I'd like to round up a few of those bastards to question.*

Cujo: *Oh I'm going to find a few, don't worry.*

Abby considered it. Really, they weren't going to listen to her, so why bother arguing? She could probably exert dominance, but they weren't wrong. She sighed. *What about Ryder? How do we reach him? And what about his club? Are they behind us still?*

Cujo: *They must be. I haven't seen 30 bikers go by, have you?*

Abby: *No.*

Benny: *I'll wait for Ryder. And he can wait for the rest of the club and send them down the east route. They aren't going to Hat Island, so the ferry route isn't useful. And then Ryder can come after us to Tulalip.*

Abby considered it. *All right,* she decided. *I need to tell Akihiro the rest of the plan then. Wish me luck.*

Benny snickered. She could count on him to see the humor in that. The rest just felt grim — which was appropriate for the situation, but she needed the humor to stay sane.

Abby adjusted the barriers to the inner circle links and took a deep breath. Really she was getting better at being intentional with information floods, rather than just the overflow because she was emotional.

Jake: *Or getting laid.*

Abby laughed. *Or that,* she agreed.

And then she sighed, re-opened the link to Akihiro and began to tell him what was going on. She hoped she could hold the bond open long enough. But the more info he had — and could share with the Tulalip Alpha — the better off they would be.

Right?

***

Maggie had seen the Alpha and her Second alongside the road with Benny. They had phones out, and she hesitated. Was there a problem? "Go slow," she told Wilma. "Let's make sure there isn't a problem."

"No problem," Taisiya said in her polite soft voice. "They're planning something. I can't quite pick up what."

Wilma and Maggie exchanged glances. Yes, that was creepy, Maggie thought. And no, it wasn't normal shifter shit either. Wilma slowed down and let all the traffic buzz past them. Just one more sluggish RV clogging up I-5. They took the Arlington city exit. Maggie frowned. It was hard to tell, but there looked like there was an accident backing up traffic in the far distance. Wilma looked at her and turned on the radio.

The Seattle all-news channel was full of it — a tanker truck had lost control, jackknifed and then had a tank explode. Traffic southbound was completely backed up. There were injuries, but first responders couldn't get to the accident itself. Maggie glanced up. Yes, there was a news helicopter in the sky. Two actually.

People were being warned to use alternative routes. Maggie noted they weren't providing what those routes might be. And all the traffic that I-5 saw? There weren't alternative routes that could handle it anyway.

"Where are our people?" Maggie asked tensely. "Is the bus ahead of us or behind?"

"Ahead," Carol said, pointing it out. She was leaning between the two front seats now. "See them?"

Maggie did. "Anyone got that driver's phone number? Tell him to take the airport exit?"

No one had it, and then it was too late. They watched as the bus rolled past that exit. A handful of motorcyclists trailed along behind it. Maggie grimaced.

Her phone rang, and she answered it. Benny.

"We're sitting up at the first Arlington exit," Maggie told him. "It's bad shit, babe."

"We know," Benny said. "Caught the bus too late, but I've sent some guards along to protect it. The Alpha wants you to go west.

You'll follow the signs to Lake Goodwin, then head south to Tulalip — the town. The pack is sending boats up to meet us there."

"You going to be there?" Maggie asked, considering the plan.

"Yes," Benny said. "I'm coming in with the Alpha. But first I've got to flag down Ryder, and then the rest of the club. The club needs to go east, and then straight-shot it down to Seattle on the back roads. The Alpha wants Ryder to join her. We need to talk."

Maggie frowned. "Are you sure the overpasses are going to be available?"

Benny was silent for a moment. "Is yours open?"

"Duh," Maggie said. "I wouldn't be talking to you if it wasn't."

Benny laughed. "True," he said. "But you've got a good point. We need to hold those two overpasses open, not just for us, but for other traffic. Sit tight then, Maggie. I'm going to send Brenda on out to Tulalip. And then I'm going to flag down someone to protect the airport exit."

"Good enough," Maggie said. "I'll sit here until Ryder shows up. He's bringing up the tail end, right?"

"The Club is behind him, I think," Benny said. She could hear the frown in his voice. "They had cleanup to do before heading out. I'm stuck here on the road flagging down bikers."

She snickered. "Ryder will have his phone on vibrate," she told him. "So does Diego. Just dial the number until they've got ants in their pants, and they'll pull over and answer it."

"Phones are new since I rode with you all," Benny muttered. "OK, I'll do that. I think I'll do it from the airport overpass, however. You've got me worried."

"I'll call Brenda for you," Maggie offered.

"Thanks, babe," Benny said gratefully. "On my way."

Maggie made the call to Brenda, who just grunted and then eased her rig around Maggie's RV and turned right. Maggie almost called her back to stop and take the twins, but she didn't. Truly she didn't trust anyone to protect them as well as she would.

Maternal instincts this late in the game? Dear Lord, she hoped not.

She was so focused on watching Benny's bike make its way up the hill to the airport overpass, that she jumped when someone pounded on her door. She opened it up just as Taisiya screamed, "Don't, it's the bad guys!"

Maggie didn't second guess the girl; she shoved the door open hard, bowling the man over, and leveled her shotgun at the man behind him. Her senses told her that they were shifters, and she didn't know them. She fired once into the man's guts, then fired again and quickly reloaded the double-barrel shotgun.

She heard a growl beside her and glanced back. Two wolves stood there, amidst the clothes the twins had been wearing. She turned back to the open door.

"Pick up my phone, and hit redial until Benny picks up," Maggie told Wilma. She hopped out of the vehicle. One of the twins started to follow her.

"No," she said. "Stay with the women. You are their first line of defense, do you hear me? I'm offense. And I'm good at it. You defend."

There was a huff from one of the wolves, but they didn't follow. Maggie stepped away from the door so that she could see better. The one man she'd shot was holding his guts — he'd live, but he wasn't happy. The other had a bloody nose and was seriously pissed.

She didn't try to reason with him, she just pulled the trigger and put him down on the ground with his buddy. Nice thing about shooting shifters, you didn't have to feel guilty that you might kill one of them. It was damned hard to kill a shifter. If it was a mistake? Well, they'd heal.

She looked around. Somehow she thought there was another one somewhere. She took another step out. Just the two bikes. So maybe she was wrong. Then she heard a bike come up the ramp. The bike was familiar even if the two on it weren't — Brenda's bike. Her eyes narrowed. Yeah, that scary dude — Cujo? — and the woman who had calmed the camp last night by announcing that she was hungry. Strangest thing she'd ever seen.

But she didn't relax. No, she wasn't wrong. There was another someone.

And then he leaped from the RV's roof on top of her. He barely connected with her, although she'd feel where he raked her with his claws — was the stupid bastard in wolf form? She went down, rolled and fired at the animal's underbelly.

Cujo pulled the wolf off her and helped her stand up. "Good job," Cujo said with approval. The woman nodded her agreement.

"Wolf form," Maggie said flatly. "Are they trying for first-rule violation?"

Cujo shook his head, baffled. "I don't know," he said. Then grinned, the kind of grin that made a person want to back away slowly. Holy hell, what was he?

"Can we stash one of them in the back?" he asked.

Maggie shrugged. "The twins changed," she said. "I suspect they could stand guard."

Cujo glanced at her. "You tell them to?"

She shook her head slightly. "No," she said quietly. "This bastard wrenched the door open, and Taisiya screamed 'they're the bad guys,' about the same time my senses said 'shifters.' I pulled the trigger, and the girls had already shifted when I glanced back."

"Fast," he commented. He scowled at the one in wolf form. "Can't leave him here like that," he muttered.

He toed the wolf. He wasn't none to gentle about it either, she noted with approval. The wolf opened his eyes.

"Shift," Cujo ordered, and Maggie had to stop her own wolf from obeying. Only her Alpha had been able to do that — she didn't think even Ryder could. Automatic obedience? No. Cujo hadn't even been aiming the command in her direction.

And he wasn't even pack Second? Maggie held very still while she tried to think about what that meant about the others in the Hat island pack. Should have thought of that earlier, she chastised herself. Benny's no slouch for all that he plays the shifter playboy to the hilt.

The naked man was lying on the ground, bent over to cover his genitals. Piss-poor ones too. She sniffed.

Cujo studied the situation. "We can put you on one of their bikes," he said. "Someone else was driving the RV, I take it?"

"Wilma," she answered.

Cujo frowned. He glanced at Mei, who apparently had been driving their bike, and she was still straddling it, watching. Waiting.

"Anyone else in there know how to ride?" Cujo asked.

Maggie leaned inside and asked. They all shook their heads no. "Wouldn't mind learning," one woman said. "It looks like fun." There were murmurs of agreement.

"I'll give you lessons," Maggie promised.

Benny came across the overpass and stopped. "Well, kids, isn't this fun?" he said, observing the scene. "That looks like your work, Maggie. Still got the shotgun, I see."

"I do," she agreed, smiling at him.

"OK, then, here's how this goes," Benny said and he got off his bike, and prowled toward the men. Moved more like a cat than a wolf, she had always thought. "We don't really need the three of you alive. One will do. So we're going to load you on your bikes. And you're going to ride slowly out of here, and away from the freeway. And then we'll talk. See if any of you have something worth your measly lives."

"Fuck that," one of the men growled. Maggie raised her shotgun and blew his head off.

"Messy," Cujo observed. "Got a tarp in that rig, I hope?"

"What about the other two of you? You going to argue with the bitch with a shotgun? Or hope my Alpha is more merciful?" Benny asked, as if it were a matter of curiosity only.

Maggie leaned back into the RV. "Look in the storage bins in back," she said. "I think there's a tarp or two. We're going to need them." Carol went back to look. The two wolves let her pass. They hadn't shifted back either. Well, they see themselves as guards for the women, Maggie thought, suddenly. And they can do that best in wolf form. Enlightened as to why they'd shifted so quickly, she turned back to the men outside.

"We could wrap up all three of them, stash them on the roof," Maggie said. "They'd survive it. I think."

"We've got extra bikes, though," Cujo pointed out. You take one, I take one. And the other?"

Maggie looked the bikes over. "Leave that one — it's a piece of junk anyway."

"All right," one of the men said. "I don't want to spend the next hour wrapped up in a tarp with a dead man. I'll talk. Then you let me ride out of here."

"Depends on what you've got to say," Cujo countered. "I think we'll take the short version here, and you ride down to the shore to meet the Alpha for the rest of it."

"I'll talk too," the other man volunteered. "Really? You'd wrap us up in a tarp on the top of the RV? That's pretty brutal, man."

Cujo shrugged. "I could kill you first, I suppose."

There was silence. The second man started talking.

Chapter 19

Benny stepped away from the RV to start dialing Ryder's phone. As Maggie instructed, he let it ring until his brother answered. "What?"

"Need you to get off at the first Arlington exit," Benny said, ignoring the tone. "Maggie got jumped. And it went just as you might expect."

Ryder grunted. "Any of them alive?"

"Two of the three bad guys, although they're not in good shape," Benny said. "And Cujo is questioning them. So they're not likely to be in better shape when you get here. We need to send Diego and the club down the backroads. Then you need to join me and the Alpha going down to Tulalip. We're finishing the last leg of the trip by boat. There's a real clusterfuck up here. Fuckers rigged a tanker truck to blow and backed up traffic. The bus is snarled in the mess. Luckily, we got a heads up and we're can re-route the Alpha. Cujo and Mei are going up to take charge of the bus, and probably help with relief efforts. They can't get firetrucks or ambulances in there. They're bringing them in from I-5 north, but it's a wide meridian. They planned it well."

Ryder swore savagely. "We know what this is about yet?"

Benny let out a long sigh. "A power grab," he said. "Cujo's getting some of the details out, but not all of them. So get up here and help ride herd on these bastards. We'll take them to Abby."

"All right," Ryder said. "Call Diego. Same thing you did to me. I'll catch up to you soon."

"Shouldn't we be able to see him by now?" Benny asked, because it had been worrying at him.

Ryder was silent. "Can't see him at all?"

"No," Benny said. "Come up. If we can't see him by the time you get here, we'll go looking for him."

He called Diego's number. It rang, went to voicemail, and Benny dialed it a second time. He was about to panic when Diego finally picked up on the third try. "What? Bit busy right now!" Diego shouted into the phone.

"You need some backup?" Benny asked.

"And what do you think you can do, that I can't do with 40 men?" Diego asked with disgust.

"I don't know," Benny replied. "Bring more ammo?"

Diego laughed at that. "Might need some," he admitted. "We got everything policed up, and we were ready to ride out, and they showed up. A dozen men — shifters — in trucks. We don't have much shelter, but they can't shoot at us without getting out of a truck. So far, we're all alive. But there's going to be cops soon. Even as deserted as this campground is, someone's got to hear the gunshots."

"What happens if the cops do show up?" Benny said, considering the matter. "You're just wrapping up a ride out with the boys, and a bunch of shitkickers showed up to give you grief?"

Diego considered that. "You're thinking we should call the cops ourselves?"

"Just law-abiding citizens," Benny said. Diego laughed again. "Weekend warriors."

"You don't need to be insulting," Diego chided, still laughing. " Sure, why the hell not? Stay by your phone, then. I hope you've got an attorney you can call to bail us out of jail if this goes tits up."

Benny thought of Haru Ito, and wouldn't he love to sic the man on a rural sheriff's department. Helicopter him in with his $5,000 bespoke suit, and $1,000 Italian loafers. He snickered. Almost be worth it. "Yeah, we've got an attorney or two," Benny answered. "But listen, you can't come down I-5. South of Mount Vernon, get on SR-8 and head into Arlington, then continue on down to Marysville."

"Why? What happened?"

"Bad guys blew up a tanker on I-5," Benny said succinctly. He could hardly believe it himself. And where were all these shifters coming from? His eyes narrowed at that thought.

Where indeed?

He had a growing list of questions. And he and Ryder were going to have to be the ones to go find out. He ground his teeth. He dreaded that.

"All right," Diego said slowly. "You sure you don't need another team of guards? If we can get out of here, I mean?"

Benny laughed at that, then reconsidered. Did he? He was nervous about how few guards were protecting the Alpha, and yes, he was willing to take on a third-world country with the Hat Island team. But they were getting split up here — Okami, Jason and David were down with Alefosio and his bus load of short-fused men, and Cujo was planning to join them. Or rather, Mei was, and Cujo was going where she went.

He was momentarily diverted by considering that team, then shrugged. So there would be him, Ryder and Jessie. Jake, of course. Maggie, who was no slouch, 15 troubled women, and two teenagers who had more power than they could control. And? Had he really goofed?

"Yeah," he said, finally. "I need another team." Was that Penticton's plan? Split them to hell and gone, and pick them off? Shit. He wanted to catch up with Abby and catch up with her now!

"All right," Diego said. "I'll send a half-dozen your way — to Tulalip, because we might take a while to get out of here."

Diego was remarkably matter-of-fact about it, Benny thought with amusement. "I appreciate it," he said. "Take your men home safe, Diego."

He hung up, and then with a bit of glee, he thought of an idea. He called Sarah Johannsen, ringleader of the girls at the boarding school. "Teacher?" she said with surprise.

"I have a bit of research I need, and I figured you all are slacking down there," he teased.

"It *is* the weekend," she said, a bit affronted.

He laughed. "Look, we're being attacked," he said seriously. "I think it's driven by the Alpha in Penticton, but he can't be the brains of it."

"Couldn't lay siege to an outhouse," Sarah agreed. "That's what my father used to say." Sarah was the daughter of the former Alpha of the Bellingham pack who had also been the former Chairman of the Northwest Council. She'd run away to Hat Island when her father was going to give her to the Alpha in Kodiak. Stupid shit. The girl was a healer! And he was going to give her away.

Well, a dead stupid shit, now. He set that aside.

"Exactly," he said. "But he's able to field 50 men to attack us, Sarah. Where are they all coming from? And that's on top of the 50 who Chen had. Do we have that many lone shifters in the Northwest? Outside the Tanaka Pack?"

"There's never been a shifter census, has there?" Sarah asked thoughtfully. "I don't know how many there are. And if Dad knew, I would have heard it, I think."

Another young woman who listened, Benny mused, thinking of Jessie.

"Can I use the other girls on this?"

"Of course," Benny said. She would, anyway, might as well give her formal permission.

"And can we reach out through Girls Who Howl?"

Benny paused at that. The girls had set up a TikTok page to inform girls in the region about the serum. It had spread. He had no idea how far, or what they were up to really. But what could it hurt? Famous last words, he thought with a snort.

"Sure," he said. "Go for it. I want to know as much as you can find out about the Penticton pack — and the Okanogan pack, if there's anything out there. And I want to know where are all these young men are coming from!"

"OK, I know we've got some girls in Howl from Penticton. Not from Okanogan though."

"No, Okanogan doesn't have families," he agreed. Too bad really. As Hat Island was finding out, a pack needed families. He changed the subject. "How are the girls from Haile's pack settling in?"

"I like them a lot," she said promptly. "They're going to put up some pages in Italian for us! And some of the African languages, too. Languages we don't have. And they're going to teach us Italian. It's cool."

"Good," Benny said. "What about the teachers who were their chaperones? Have they gone home?"

"No," Sarah said, and sounded troubled. "Teacher, they're asking a lot of questions. Should they be doing that?"

No, Benny thought. Well, maybe? "What kinds of questions?" he asked cautiously.

"About why there is a boarding school? Who are all these men? Where are our parents?" The list came out in a rush.

Not unusual questions for teachers serving as chaperones, Benny thought. But something was making Sarah uneasy and she had good instincts. "What do you say?" he asked.

"What Teacher Trainer told us to say — that it's connected to the Center for the Study of Oral-Tradition Cultures. And that we share the island with an intentional community for military veterans suffering PTSD," Sarah said. "And when they ask about parents and such, the girls just giggle, and say they're at home."

Benny snorted. Good luck getting information out of those girls. He hadn't gotten anything they didn't want to give him, and he was a trained intelligencer — and a psychologist. The girls just giggled, if you pressed too hard.

It was very disconcerting.

"Joy says they smell wrong," Sarah said. "And she's got good instincts."

Joy was Okami and Yui's 12-year-old daughter. He considered the talents she might have inherited from them both. If she didn't like the two chaperones, then it was worth taking seriously. "I'll let Cujo know," he said, glancing over at the man, who was crouched down by a prone body. He grimaced. Cujo was scaring the hell out of him. "He'll talk it over with Olivia. When are the women supposed to go back?"

"Teacher Trainer convinced them to stay until Sunday night. She said it would be a shame to come all this way and not experience the Pacific Ocean."

So Olivia sensed something off too, and wanted time to evaluate things, was how Benny read that. "Good enough then," he said. "We'll be home tonight. See what you can gather by then. I'll expect a presentation after dinner."

"On it," she said cheerfully, and then was gone. Benny smiled. Working with the girls was truly a pleasure.

If he was ever given time to actually do it.

Benny waited until Cujo was done with his interrogations. Cujo was troubled by what he'd learned, but Benny was getting antsy. They shouldn't still be here. And where was Abby and Jake? They'd gone on. Were they alone? Alarmed, he considered where all of his pieces were — and wished he had a map like Abby's. Well, he could reach Abby and ask her, but.....

They weren't alone, he realized uneasily. It was worse than that. The other RV was with them, or just behind. Shit.

"We've got to go," Benny said urgently. Ryder had joined them while he was on the phone. Good. "The Alpha doesn't have the guards she should."

Cujo looked around the group, calculating who was where, and nodded. "Go," he ordered.

Benny paused. "Maggie, you riding with us? Or with the RV?"

Maggie looked torn. "Riding, but the RV needs to go with us, Benny."

Benny grimaced. He'd like to go faster than the RV could go, and catch up with Jake and Abby, but Maggie was right. "I suppose I have to give you your bike back," he grumbled.

"You do," she said. "But take your pick. Anyone of those will do."

Benny rolled his eyes and took the dead man's bike. Cujo efficiently rolled the dead man into the tarp and lifted it up onto the roof of the RV. Man was strong, he'd give him that. The other two men shakily walked to their bikes. "Remember, she's still got that shotgun," Cujo warned them. "Try anything and we'll pull over than add your body to the RV roof. I'd take my chances with the Alpha if I were you. She's more lenient than Maggie is."

"Saw what she did," one of the men muttered. "No hesitating at all."

"Nope," Maggie said cheerfully. "And there will be even less if you pull some shit."

With Maggie as their herder, they started down the ramp. Benny turned to Cujo. "Talk to Olivia," he said quickly. "Sarah thinks there's something weird about the chaperones."

Cujo nodded. He looked worried about something. Benny waited.

"I'd heard from the others about a new pack Second," Cujo said finally. "I finally got a name — Bjorn."

Benny flinched. "Isn't that Jessie's missing fiancé's name?"

Cujo nodded. "I'll leave it to you whether to tell her," he said. "But it looks like he drifted east to Penticton, and then challenged the pack Second. And there's evidence that he's driving this attack."

Benny frowned, thinking about what that told them. "You're going to make me tell her?" Benny asked. Cujo shrugged and glanced at Mei. OK, he had enough on his plate, Benny conceded. "Are you sure you shouldn't come with us?" he added. Because he would be much happier if Cujo was with the Alpha. And Cujo looked torn. But he shook his head.

"Mei wants to join up with the guys," Cujo said quietly. "Actually? I don't think she could leave them, even if she wanted to. That burst dandelion," he added succinctly.

Benny winced. "Good luck then," he said. "We'll see you on Hat Island." He straddled his bike, waved the RV driver to go ahead, and they headed out toward Lake Goodwin. Now he just had to catch up with Abby.

And he needed to think about this new wrinkle. Jessie had told Ryder she wanted to go with him to Penticton based on the earlier rumors. But would she see Bjorn as the man she loved? Or as a betrayer?

Or both? He chewed on his lip. Well, it would have to wait until they got to Tulalip. And then? Maybe he could delegate the whole question to Ryder.

She was riding pillion behind him, after all.

He settled into the ride, and headed west, catching up with Maggie and the two Penticton pack she was escorting. The RV followed behind them, and Ryder, with Jessie, bringing up the rear.

Alpha? Benny sent. *Where are you? We had a delay, but we're headed after you now. Where are you?*

***

Abby felt like she was adrift on a sea in her own mind. The soothing sounds of the motorcycle, the feel of her breasts pressed firmly against Jake, her arms wrapped tightly around him, her hands clasped at his belt buckle. Or where his belt buckle would be if he wore one.

Most shifters didn't — not unless it was a very dressy occasion, she'd found.

In case you needed to shift. Shifter were very practical about that; she just wished she could be as practical and dispense with a bra. But no.

The sea was the flooded rice field, she decided. She could sense Benny who was concerned about something and concerned about Cujo. And Cujo was a cold spot, grim. She frowned at that. Cujo hadn't felt like that before. He'd burned hot. What had changed?

Okami was pleased with Jason. She focused on him for a moment. *Jason has marshaled our young men and is working with the first responders, Alpha,* Okami informed her. *He has teams carrying the wounded across the median to the ambulances on the northbound freeway. Others are pulling the hoses across in the other direction to help put out the fire. The lads are doing well under his guidance. And he knows what he's doing.*

I'm not surprised, Abby said. *He is a very competent man.*

David is assisting with the injured. So is Alefosio. He has medic training of some kind. I'm watching from the bus. Benny's guardsmen have left their bikes here as well and went forward to pitch in. I have become the rearguard.

Abby could feel his bemusement at that. She grinned. For a man who had once been a samurai for more than one Shogun in ancient Japan, that must seem a comedown.

No Alpha, it means I have become an elder and a teacher, and I am happy with both roles.

She sent him a visual image of her conducting a low bow of respect. It amused him.

She drifted. The twins were in wolf form for some reason. She frowned at that — shouldn't she know why? And Yui was concerned about the teacher-chaperones. All these people and their concerns, all hers to care about.

Stefan was oblivious to everything. He was back from Oregon, and happily spending a long day in the labs analyzing the data he'd collected there. She smiled. He was happy, absorbed in his work. It was a feeling they both knew — she understood him, and he appreciated being understood. It was really all he asked of her.

That and more funding for more research. And that too was familiar for her. All of her faculty felt like that. Stefan was a touchstone, a common thing between her new world and her old one.

She found her mate bond. Akihiro was intent on something — spreadsheets, perhaps? He was.... satisfied. How come she never felt satisfied looking at spreadsheets? She usually felt frustrated — well, higher ed, she supposed. And next to her mate bond was a solid dot, a marble really. Haru. She got nothing from him but his presence. But even that was considered impossible. Actually all of this was supposed to be impossible.

She didn't care. She had her people here with her.

Something pinged her from Benny's corner. *Where are you?* he asked. *We're finally heading west again. And I want to catch up. I don't like it that you're alone.*

I'm not alone, Benny, Abby protested. *I have all of you. I hear your worry, and Cujo's alarm, and Okami's report on the boys at the fire, and even the twins. And I can feel Jake, wrapping me up like a blanket on a cool evening. I'm not alone.*

A moment of silence. *Abby? Where are you in the physical world?* Benny asked, and it felt like he was choosing his words carefully. *Is there a street name? Are you before the lake, or south of it?*

Oh. Abby considered that. She didn't think that was all that important, was it? She was more interested in asking Yui why she was worried about those Parisian teachers.

Abby! Listen to me! Benny ordered. *You need to raise your barriers and lower the flood of information. You've got to get back in touch with the real world here. There is danger.*

You're not the boss of me, Abby said, fretfully. *I don't want to.*

Another silent period. Maybe he was leaving her alone, and she could talk to Yui now.

Abby, Jake needs you, Benny said. *Ask Jake where you are. He needs you.*

She frowned, but she obediently opened her link with Jake. *Benny says you need me? And he needs to know where we are? In the physical world,* she added. *He's being a nag.*

Jake felt amused, she thought, somewhat indignantly. *You feel drunk, Abby,* Jake said. *You need to raise your barriers enough so that you have edges again. Tell Benny. And tell him that we're south of the lake. No problems. Just us, and a big RV rattling along here on this road. Haven't even seen any traffic. But you need to pull back, a bit, OK? Raise the barriers.*

Abby grimaced. She didn't want to. Probably all the more reason why she should, she conceded. But still. *Benny? Jake says I'm drunk,* she said grumpily. *But we're south of the lake and there's been no one. No traffic, no concerns. Just us and the RV.*

Drunk, are you? Benny said, his mind-voice teasing. But Abby thought there was real worry underneath it. *Cut yourself off then, Alpha. Raise the barriers. Dry up that flooded field a bit. You're getting too much from too many, and you won't be able to respond to an emergency. And we've had trouble.*

Abby sighed. There was always trouble. And she was tired of being the one people brought their troubles to. Well, no, not really. She didn't know what she meant. But she liked drifting on that sea.

Alpha! Benny's voice was sharp. *Raise your barriers. Do it now!*

Abby grimaced, but she did it. She was tempted to raise her barrier to Benny first, but she resisted the temptation. Instead she pulled back from Yui and the island. And then from Okami — just a narrow trickle of information. And Cujo, he needed the connection! Wait, he was with Okami now, she could tell. Well, that was good. She pulled back from them all.

Slowly she felt like she was waking up from a drugged sleep. What the heck?

You were losing your edges, Alpha, Benny said soberly. *Don't do that again.*

I don't know what I did! Abby wailed, frightened now.

You let down your guard while the flood was still in place, Jake offered. *Perhaps that's not a great idea.*

I guess not, Abby said, alarmed. *I wanted to be able to respond to whoever needed me. But you're was right, it was more like I was drunk.*

We'll talk about it, Benny said, and she could tell he was shaken by it. That scared her even more.

Benny?

When we're in a more stable environment, he promised. It sounded forced, but he added teasingly, *Where I can slap you out of it, if I need to.*

Be prepared to be punched back if you do, Jake said. Apparently those were not words he liked even as a metaphor, Abby thought. And that brought her back into better focus.

You said there was trouble, she said.

Got attacked at the overpass. Tell you when we catch up. But be on the lookout. I'm not convinced there aren't more of them.

Jake: *Understood. We need to shut down this link so I can focus, and Abby can regain her balance.*

Benny faded from her awareness. Abby struggled to raise all of her barriers tight, alarmed now at how difficult that was. All but Jake.

Even mine, Alpha, Jake said. *After all, I can always stop the bike and ask.*

Abby laughed, and she did raise even the filter to Jake. Mostly. She left enough connection for her own comfort. What the hell had she just done?

By the time they pulled into Tulalip, they'd developed quite a following. *Convoy!* Her brain sang at her. Great — she needed *that* as an ear bug? She sighed. She'd been focused on her ride behind Jake, and on looking around. Really, this was a pretty part of the country. Her parents used to bring her and her brothers here to go clamming. But she hadn't been here since.

And then the ocean — Puget Sound, actually — always made her glad to see it, even on a gray day like today. There was a poem she'd memorized in grade school: "I must go down to the sea again, to the lonely sea and the sky...." That line had stuck with her — a much better ear bug than *Convoy*. She too needed to go to the sea regularly or something withered inside her. She felt a rush of pleasure — she lived on the Sound now. She never needed to lack the sea again.

They pulled into the south end of the marina. Ryder parked his bike and started directing the two RVs where he wanted them — blocking the view of the picnic table area, she thought. Her eyes narrowed. What were they going to be doing that he didn't want others to see?

Not that there was much activity around at all. It wasn't a large marina. Jessie, who had been riding behind Ryder, disappeared into one of the RVs.

Jake parked next to Ryder, and a woman pulled up next. She appeared to be herding two men — strangers, although the woman looked familiar. Maggie, Abby thought. She'd been protecting the twins. Why was she now on a bike?

And she was pulling a double-barrel shotgun out of her pack? With a shortened barrel? The two men got off their bikes and looked warily at that shotgun.

Abby grimaced. It was never good news when a shifter pulled out a shotgun.

Benny had a guard unit with him, and they parked alongside her.

"That's it?" Abby asked him wryly.

"We could probably round up a few more to be completely conspicuous," Benny replied with a sigh. "Come on. We need to take these two into one of the RVs and question them. And you need to be there for it."

She hated that. Hated beguiling someone to talk, and then ordering their death. It didn't set well with her. But shifters didn't have jails. Probably would prefer death anyway. So how did you punish someone? Within the pack it was different. 'Community service' determined by Pete Craven usually. But attacks from another pack? What was she going to do with them?

They're eating their seed corn, Abby thought helplessly. The shifters were self-destructing. The death of so many girls at first shift. The death of all these young men in some cause that she didn't even fully understand.

"I'll do the questioning," Benny said quietly. "But you may need to use your authority as an Alpha, and Chairman of the Council. I know you hate it, but we're at war, Abby. And we've got to at least figure out why."

That about summed it up, she thought, as she followed him and the two men into the RV. The twins were hauling out a box of food as they approached. She smiled at them and gave each a one-armed hug. "You two doing OK?" she asked.

They nodded. "We were ready to protect the other women," Taisiya informed her. "We aren't going to run and hide, Alpha. I'll tell Mom so when she contacts me again."

"Sometimes running and hiding is the right thing to do," Abby cautioned her, wondering if she'd created a monster. "And sometimes staying and fighting is. That discernment is important — and you have to get good at it, by thinking about all of it. We'll talk more at the island."

Kristina smiled at her and led her sister away with their food boxes. Abby's stomach growled. She could hardly walk into a torture session with a sandwich in hand. And she didn't delude herself, that was exactly what this was. And the fact that it was mental pressure, not physical, didn't change things.

Although, as she surveyed the two men, it looked like it might have gotten physical earlier.

Twenty minutes later, she walked out of the RV, Jake and Benny behind her. The two men were tied up and gagged in the back bedroom. Ryder was standing outside the RV door. "There's someone here to meet you," he said softly, so that his voice wouldn't carry. "The head of the family pack here. Norman Posey."

Abby forced a smile. "How about you invite him to join me for a sandwich or three?"

She needed something to eat, and she needed some time to digest her food and what she'd just been told. Quite frankly it raised as many questions as had been answered —questions these two men didn't know the answers to. She wondered if it was possible to turn them loose because they were just following orders. She sighed. No, that wouldn't work.

Norman Posey was dressed in blue jeans that bagged a bit in the butt and a red-plaid, flannel shirt. Scuffed boots. A black flat-brimmed hat that had seen better days. She wondered what he did for a living — it hadn't sounded like he was working at the Casino from what Akihiro had said about him.

She shook his hand; he had a soft grip. "It's good to meet you," she said. "I'm trying to meet all the Alphas as the new Chairman of the Northwest Council of Alphas. I want to make sure there's a commitment to the Council, to the future generations of shifters, and to the girls getting the serum."

"I'm no pack Alpha," he denied. "Just the leader of an extended family. Well, there's a couple of others who have drifted in...." He trailed off at her laugh and shrugged. "Don't want to be their Alpha," he admitted. "Too much work. They pester me enough as it is."

She laughed. "I fully understand that," she admitted. "But come, eat with me, and tell me what's going on at the Casino and the freeway."

They sat at the picnic table side by side so they could look out at the harbor and the Sound beyond it. He had a younger man with him, a son, she thought. He didn't introduce him.

"So they tell me you've got two of the men who started that mess out at the freeway?" Norman Posey asked, after they'd finished their first sandwich. Abby was happily plowing into a second one. Look Ma, no limits.

"We do," she said. "I don't suppose you want them?"

"I would be delighted to take them," Posey said grimly. "There's two dead, a dozen injured. No telling how much damage to people's cars. Done by a shifter pack? What the hell?"

"If you will deal with these two, I'd be grateful," Abby said, trying not to show how grateful.

"Did you get an explanation of why?" Posey asked her. She noted that he assumed she'd questioned them. Rightly so, she conceded.

"I don't know how much you know about what Alpha Chen was up to in Vancouver," Abby began slowly. "But he was ambitious, and he had a partnership with one of the Asian Council Chairmen who wants to oust Tanaka as Chairman of the World Council. He was amassing an army of disaffected young shifters, promising them a pack, position, and a wife."

She swallowed hard at that last bit. It still was so appalling, it was hard to say. "So we have some of those young men — they're the ones out battling the fire right now — and the new Vancouver Alpha has some of the young men as well. But some apparently drifted east to the Penticton pack. And the Penticton Alpha — who has had ambitions in the past and was probably helping Chen — decided to step into Chen's role."

Posey nodded, his eyes watchful. "I had heard some of that," he said. "I must say I am impressed with the young men who are fighting the fire."

"Yes," Abby said. "I am hopeful we can repair the damage done to them." She hesitated, then added hopefully. "Impressed enough to take some of them on? Do you have need of young workers in your pack?"

"My family," he corrected absently, as he considered it. He nodded. "We have some openings at the casino that would welcome young men who come with my recommendation. But maybe five? No more."

Abby nodded. "I will make the offer to them," she promised. "And I am grateful."

"Grateful enough to give us some of the serum I'm hearing about?" he countered. "I've got two young girls who are at that age."

"The serum is free to all girls, no strings attached," Abby said firmly. "We can send a medic out with the serum as soon as we get back. Or, you can send the girls to us. It takes two days. And you need to decide whether *you* want to pull them through first shift, or if you want us to, and then you bring them into your family pack when they come home. Up to you. But there are no strings attached whatsoever."

"We may need to spread that information, then, Alpha," Posey said. "Rumor has it, it's for the packs, but not for the families and independents."

"No," Abby said. "Everyone. They can call for a medic — which might take a bit of time, depending on demand. Or they can come to the Wolf Harbor office on the Everett dock and ask to come across, if the need is more urgent. We won't even ask questions about pack or family status. All girls means all girls."

"I know some families who will be relieved to hear that," he said. "Expect calls."

"Are there that many?" Abby asked, curiosity getting the better of her — as it usually did, she admitted ruefully. "I was led to believe most shifters belonged to packs, and most packs belonged to the Council."

"Most formal packs do belong to the Council," Posey said carefully, measuring his words. "That is almost the definition of a pack, although there are a few that are not recognized by the Council. But in the past, the Northwest Council has viewed families and independents with disapproval. We learned to stay very quiet and go unnoticed. Or, as we have done, ask for the protection of a neighboring pack."

"Is that where these young men are coming from then?" Abby asked, because that question bugged her. "Chen seemed to have found quite a large number of young shifters to recruit."

I've assigned that question to Sarah Johannsen and the other students, Benny said in her mind. *She suggested tapping into the Girls Who Howl network might give us some answers. I assigned her a presentation after supper tonight.*

Abby sent wordless approval and focused back on Norman Posey.

"Perhaps," he said, considering it carefully. "And from some of the packs as well. There are so many more young men than young women, Alpha. And marrying humans is asking for heartbreak. It's done, of course, but what Chen offered was very attractive." He hesitated, then added, "We lost two of ours," he said. "But they came back earlier in the week, after Chen's death. But they are in bad shape. The snap of the pack bond hurt. And for some reason it didn't snap to the new Alpha. That strikes me as unusual."

Abby saw Jessie flinch out of the corner of her eye. It was the first time she realized the girl was standing there. No wonder Benny liked her. That ability to blend in and listen? An intelligencer in the making.

If she survived what Abby would need to tell her, she thought somberly.

We might leave that to Ryder to do, Benny suggested. Abby wanted to turn and stare at him, but she kept her focus on Posey.

Say what? she demanded. *Never mind. Later.*

"So the Penticton Alpha decided to make his move," she continued with her story. "Replace Chen in the conspiracy. But also, he's been eying the Okanogan territory and pack. And it's fallen into disarray because Alpha Garrison is traveling." Abby guessed she could call it that. Damn the man, he needed to come home to his pack!

"So he's using the drifters to take over the Okanogan pack," she continued. "He's running into a problem — there's no one to challenge for it. So he hears that one of the quote, unquote, 'heirs' of the pack Alpha is at Margarite's in Delta, and he sends a team to take him out. We're still missing some pieces to this story," she warned the man. He nodded. "They get there and make contact with someone they know from Chen's army, who's already there. And they learn the so-called dònglì diànchí are there too. Then the other 'heir' shows up with only a few of his motorcycle club. And the Penticton Alpha adds new objectives to their mission."

"Which dooms it," Jake said from his position standing behind her. "Mission creep. It's always a disaster. One mission, one agenda, one objective. Can't fail with that."

Abby glanced at him over her shoulder. "Have you ever seen an agenda for a faculty meeting?" she demanded sourly. The agenda for the meeting last week had been two pages.

"I rest my case," he said, amusement lurking.

Abby had to laugh at that.

"Dònglì diànchí?" Posey asked.

"A myth about powerful women that Chen had bought into," Abby said vaguely. "But then they followed everyone down to the campground north of Bellingham, and I showed up. This morning they tried to attack me. I killed their squad leader."

"Mission creep," Jake said with a grin. Abby could tell his swagger was faked for the theater of it — but she didn't think Posey could tell.

"I'm happy to accept your rules, Alpha," Posey said. "And my girls are in the car," he added with a grin.

Abby laughed. "You've been talking to Akihiro," she accused.

"Yu'up," he drawled it into two words. "And I'll take the two live men off your hands, and the dead one too." He nodded toward the roof of the RV. Abby raised an eyebrow at Benny, who just nodded. She'd missed that. And she shouldn't have. She should have smelled him. Her wolf sniffed. She'd smelled him — Abby just wasn't paying close enough attention.

Sorry, she told her wolf. I'll do better.

"Deal," Abby said, standing up. She needed to stretch. The white church across the road might be just a great short walk. "Benny? Perhaps you'd introduce the girls to Kristina?"

Benny nodded, but his eyes were watchful. She tipped her head slightly.

He's got something more to say.

"Shall I walk you to your car?" she asked Posey. He nodded. "The marina is mine," he said abruptly. "I think you should have a permanent slip here."

Abby considered that. Really, Tulalip marina wasn't any farther from Hat Island than Everett was. "A back door," she said slowly. And a port for the Council ship? She studied the marina, and the harbor. She'd have to ask Okami. She had an idea for that ship; this might make it work.

Posey nodded. "I'm an old man," he said quietly. "And I've never seen unrest like this. I'm not sure what's driving it. And yes, Akihiro and I talk — one old man to another. Except I'm older. Don't tell him that."

Abby's eyes widened. Akihiro was 187. Posey was older?

"Change has come to the shifter world, whether we like it or not," Posey continued. "And mostly, we don't like change much. Not us old ones. But there is a word, a phrase, in Lushootseed, that means magic in the blood. And I think it's close to that word you used. If so, be very careful, Alpha. Have you mentioned it to Akihiro?"

Abby frowned. Had she? "I think so, when it first came up?" she said doubtfully. "The changes are happening so fast, as you say, and I'm not sure what I've told whom."

"Happens," Posey agreed. "It's why we like to sit with our thoughts. But Anglos fill every space," he said with a quick grin.

"I try not to, but yes, we do," she agreed. "And I of all people should know better."

"Your linguistic tradition is just as proper as ours," Posey said, and her eyebrows raised slightly at the use of that phrase. "Just no better than ours either."

She laughed at that. "And that's the problem," she agreed. She made a mental note to ask about this man. He was intriguing.

"I asked Robert Golde if there was a similar myth in his culture," Abby said abruptly deciding to trust this man. "He hasn't returned my call since."

Posey nodded. He didn't seem surprised. "It's a phrase used these days to celebrate our connection to the earth and the sea," he said. "But originally? it was someone who could command the earth and the sea. And it foretold destruction."

Abby chewed on her bottom lip, and then nodded. "I understand." She smiled at him. "I'd like to come back sometime and talk to a man who runs a marina and uses the term linguistic traditions."

He snorted. "I'm part of the restoration of the Lushootseed language. Don't tell them I'm an actual native speaker, hey? Because they think the last native speaker died in 2004."

Abby laughed and held out her hand. "Nice to meet you, Norman Posey," she said frankly. "And we'll send you some wolves to help out around here."

"Come again," he invited, as two young girls got out of his car. He introduced them to Benny, and drove his car up alongside the RV. Another man got out of the car with him, and Ryder went to assist them. Their two prisoners were led out and a blue tarped bundle was eased off the roof of the RV and into the trunk of the car. Posey waved as he drove away.

"Well, well," Jake said softly. "That's an interesting man."

"He is," Abby agreed. "Rent us a slip."

"I will," Jake said. "I like the idea of a back door."

"I do, too."

Chapter 20

Day 156 of the re-emerged Hat Island pack, Saturday, Nov. 9, Hat Island

Supper was late, and the meeting Abby needed to have was even later. Benny insisted that Sarah's presentation kick it off. Abby would have postponed that to another day, but Benny was unusually adamant about it.

The good news was that Stefan was back from Oregon. She wanted to talk to him, but he had disappeared into his lab, and she didn't have the courage to brave him in his den. So she sighed, and sucked it up, letting Benny organize the meetings for the evening. She ate supper in the lodge so that people could see her.

She wanted to talk to Olivia about the teachers, but Benny said that was on *his* list. "Go take a nap," he suggested. "We aren't doing this until Cujo and Okami are here. And Mei."

A nap didn't sound bad at all, especially since she could drag Jake off to join her.

So it was late when everyone gathered in the conference room of the Wolf Harbor lodge. And everyone looked damned tired. The boys on the bus — a phrase that made Abby snicker but she wouldn't share publicly, she promised herself — had been sent off into Pete Craven's care. Ditto with the motorcycle shifters beyond Ryder — and Maggie for some reason. But the inner circle was here, and Abby felt some of her anxiety melt because of it.

"Go ahead, Benny," Abby said. "Run with it."

"All right, so a brief check-in. Jason? Status of the I-5 wreck?" Benny asked.

"They opened I-5," Jason said. He was standing at parade rest next to Jake — also standing like that — by the door. "The driver of the truck is one of the dead. Or at least the man in the driver's seat is dead. I'm skeptical he was actually driving the truck when it jackknifed." He sounded tired. "We were praised for our service. We'll probably be on the news — but I made Mei the media contact. She's smarter about that kind of thing than I am."

Mei rolled her eyes with a grimace, but she didn't deny it. Abby nodded her thanks.

"So there are now three dead, a dozen injured, two dozen cars damaged, probably more with minor damage. But I don't think shifters are going to be outed because of it," Jason said.

Abby glanced at Okami. He seemed in agreement.

"Ryder? Your MC? Has Diego checked in? He had problems at the campground." Benny continued, down his list.

"He did," Ryder said. "And he took your advice and called the cops for help. He'll probably laugh all the way to California about it. But it worked — the attackers took off when the cop cars pulled in. Diego thanked them profusely. They should be in Oregon somewhere. They'll check in when they stop for the night." He glanced at his phone. "Should be soon, I'd think."

"RVs have been turned in?" Benny asked.

Ryder nodded. "Might take a cleaning fee hit," he said. "Blood on the roof is hard to get out."

"Are they likely to look on the roof for blood?" Abby asked, perplexed. When Benny glared at her, she added hastily, "Never mind."

"Can we go next?" Olivia asked. "As interesting as this is, I'd like to get back to our 'guests.'" Everyone could hear the quote marks around the word guests.

"Go ahead," Benny said.

"So I think the women are plants," Olivia said bluntly. "They ask the wrong questions. Kent and I speculate that the whole attack was to send the girls off to Cujo, with female chaperones who could report back where he is."

Cujo grimaced. "Move that mission higher on the list," he muttered. He didn't explain.

Olivia nodded once. So apparently she knew what he was talking about. "So Kent and I discussed it, and we're recommending we send them back to Paris, with Kent and Tighe escorting them. No hardship — Tighe has been flirting madly. We put them under surveillance and see who shows up."

Cujo frowned and nodded his approval. "Fine."

"Any objections? Concerns?" Abby asked. No one said anything. "Good. Thank you for handling that, Olivia. No one else could do it as well."

Olivia looked gratified. "So I'm headed off to the Beach House. We've been wining and dining them. But I'm staying down there where I can keep an eye on things. I don't think that's an issue — other than some idiots who decided to race on the beach last night as wolves."

Abby winced, more for those poor idiots than anything else. She bet Olivia tore them a new one.

"The problem will be when they return to Paris," Olivia continued.

"Which is when?" Abby asked.

"We leave for the airport after lunch tomorrow," Olivia said. "All four of them."

"Thank you," Benny said. "You're welcome to stay, of course, but we won't keep you if you think you should be at Beach House."

Olivia looked at Sarah Johannsen for a moment. "No, I'll catch up with Sarah tomorrow," she said regretfully. She gathered her things and walked out — on high heels. Abby shook her head briefly. She did not know how the woman did it. She wondered if Olivia would give her lessons? She felt amusement in her brain, and hastily raised her barriers. She wasn't even sure who it was from. As she'd learned, that was dangerous.

"Cujo? The recruits?"

"After today, I think they've earned the right to be forgiven for Chen's recruitment," Cujo said somberly. "They turned a major disaster into a minor one. I don't know what we do with them, but that needs to be taken into consideration."

And why had Benny asked Cujo, Abby thought with a bit of disgust. "Mei? What is your plan for them? Did anyone tell you that the Tulalip leader will welcome five into his family?"

"That's good news," Mei said. "We have a dozen who I would like to keep here until we can free up some space in the apartment complex. Let Pete get them into some kind of disciplined form. That leaves a dozen or so. Five to Tulalip. One van load out to Odessa. That's more manageable for her as well."

"Do you still have the burst dandelion of links?" Abby asked.

"Yes." Mei didn't say any more, and Abby didn't press her on it.

"Did links form with the women?"

Mei shook her head. "No."

"What plans do you have for the women?" Maggie asked suddenly. Benny was scowling — he'd lost control of the meeting. Abby was amused. Usually it was Benny who hijacked her carefully planned meetings.

"Some will be offered space in Mei's building, and an opportunity to attend college," Abby said. "The rest? Probably out to Odessa as well."

"I'd like to propose some of them might want to come down to Horse Creek and check out our summer residence," Maggie said. "I didn't get to know the women in the other RV, but the women in mine were great. They pitched in, helped drive while I defended us against attack. I'd happily sponsor them."

"That's a big task," Ryder warned.

"Probably," Maggie agreed. "But we'd increase the number of women in the pack too."

Ryder shrugged, and nodded his approval.

"What does that mean exactly?" Abby said slowly. "No coercion right?"

Ryder looked briefly amused. "Maybe seduction? I imagine they'll get plenty of that."

Maggie looked a bit more sour. "I'll watch out for them," she promised. "Add some self-defense training too. Ryder does run a tight camp — when he knows about it."

Ryder looked at her quickly. "Maggie?"

Maggie shook her head. "We're fine," she assured him.

Ryder looked like he might have more questions for her later. And that spoke well of him, Abby thought.

"Good," Benny said, with an attempt to regain control. Good luck, Abby wished him. She was beginning to enjoy this. Maybe this should be a regular thing. She looked around the room speculatively. Who else could benefit from running the meeting on occasion?

"I asked Sarah to do some research for me," Benny said, and people straightened up. Here was the point of the meeting. They could sense it. "I wanted to know where these young men are coming from? There are so many! So, Sarah? You've got the floor."

Sarah stood up, poised as always. She was 17, their oldest student — their first. She'd come here, almost as soon as the pack was formed, pretending to be a boy. And when she was outed, she asked for sanctuary. She was the daughter of then-Alpha Johannsen of Bellingham. He was going to give her away to the new Alpha in Kodiak as a reward for his takeover of the pack.

Sarah had rightly decided that was a fate worse than death and ran away.

Really, they'd practically invented the boarding school for her, and for girls like her that Abby had anticipated would follow. She hadn't realized the girls who followed would come from Southeast Asia, but they had. And the twins from Russia. Now more from Africa? They were an international school. She felt a rush of pleasure.

Sarah was tall, slim, blonde, reflecting her Norwegian heritage. She was also smart, formidably dominant, and apparently a healer — what exactly that meant, Abby wasn't sure. But Benny had cackled with glee when it was determined that she was. Her father had thrown away a healer? She thought Benny still regretted Alpha Johannsen had died before he could rub it in.

"We determined that there were actually several research questions," Sarah began, and she listed them. How many recruits did Chen actually have? What was the chronological pattern? Where did they come from? How many more were still coming into Penticton? "What we realized is that we needed a census of shifters," she concluded. She nodded to Joy Yoshida who was sitting with her parents. Joy started the computer and projected a North America map on the screen.

"So first, we needed to figure out where the known packs were," Joy said in a clear voice. "We sent out a call through Girls Who Howl."

"Safely?" Abby asked.

Joy nodded. "Carlos worked with us to make sure it was secure."

"Good," Abby said. "So what did you find?"

"While the girls were reporting in, we mapped what we knew. And really, the girls at the school knew a lot," Joy said. "Especially Sarah. She liked to lurk and listen to her father. But first, one note. Shifters, like their wolf counterparts are not spread evenly over the world. They prefer the cooler regions. The Haile pack girls who joined us this weekend pointed out that there is only one Council of Alphas for the entire African continent, whereas here we have many such councils. The same is true for South America — one council. Even Europe — and it is a very populated area — has just one Council."

"Such as it is," Cujo muttered. Benny glared at him, and he apologized. Joy nodded and continued. "But the United States and

Canada have a lot of packs, and more Councils than any other region. Shifters moved out of Russia, into Europe and China, and then across to North America. From there we've seen exploration, and then the establishment of Councils in the Southern Hemisphere."

Joy put up an overlay showing the rough territories of the 14 Councils. Abby studied it. She'd never seen even a list of the Councils before. And the World Council was meeting in Seattle in less than a month? Her ignorance was appalling, and she needed to get up to speed fast. She considered how, until Joy put up a new map — one of the packs in the Pacific Northwest Council region. There were multiple bubbles on the map — most of them were in Washington state. Abby frowned. "Why so many in Washington?"

Benny answered. "Politics. Johannsen recognized a lot of packs in the state so that they would be loyal to him and keep him in power. So where other areas might have independents and family packs, ours are recognized as Council packs — and they can vote. Lewis pack, Craven pack — they're really just extended family packs. But they have Council status because Johannsen wanted the votes — and wanted to stack the Council in his favor."

Abby nodded, and smiled at Joy. "Sorry to interrupt. Go ahead."

"No, that's an important point," Joy said. "Washington State is pretty well lined out with pack territories. And that's rare. There are a lot of open spaces elsewhere in North America. There isn't a recognized pack from Dawson's pack eastward until you get to the Ontario pack, and south to Vancouver, Penticton and Castle packs. That's a lot of territory and there are a lot of family packs and independents."

The light dawned on Abby as to why this was important. This was where the young men were coming from. "Define independent," she asked.

Joy frowned slightly. "That's hard, and we tried. We know one when we see it, but I don't know that we still have a good definition.

But basically it's three to six guys who have drifted into a location for jobs or school or some other reason and are now cohabitating." She stumbled a bit over the word. Abby smiled encouragingly, and Joy took heart and continued on. "We often hear wolves do not do well alone. And that's true. This is a way of not being alone. They might work in the timber industry, for instance. Or go to community college. But they are a group and they usually stay together for a long time."

Abby nodded. "Usually young? Are they lone wolves?"

"Usually young, but not lone wolves," Joy said with a quick look at Benny. He nodded his agreement. "They're pack, but there was nothing there for them, and they drifted. Or they might be from a family pack and moved out for better opportunities."

Abby could cite countless ethnographies dealing with Appalachia that described similar situations. She made a mental note of the similarities. "Why don't they come to Seattle and petition the Tanaka pack, if their home packs don't have resources and opportunities?"

Joy hesitated and looked at Mei. "The Tanaka pack rarely takes outsiders," Joy said. "Most certainly it wouldn't take young drifters. It does allow them within their territory as it does lone wolves. And that's important."

Mei sighed and nodded her agreement. "Tanaka pack would be flooded, and we're already considered too big, too obvious," she said. "It sounds harsh, but we just can't take them in. We won't be able to take in these recruits either."

"Go on, Joy," Abby said. Without her support, this presentation would get derailed — probably by her. She had so many questions. She should toss the girls research questions like this and have them present weekly.

She paused. Actually, that was a very good idea.

"So then the numbers started coming back from the Girls Who Howl," Sarah said, taking control of the presentation again. "And our first conclusion is that there are more shifters than people think. A lot more."

Abby didn't know if she even knew how many shifters they thought there were. That thought needed an editor — and she needed caffeine. As the thought crossed her mind, she saw Okami slip out of the room.

"So I called my great-uncle to ask him about the numbers," Joy said. Abby blinked. Joy's great uncle was Haru Ito, a man most people found scary as hell. She wasn't even sure *she* would just call him up and ask questions.

"Uncle Haru was interested in what we were finding out," Joy said. There were equally flummoxed expressions around the room as people realized who she was talking about. Abby wanted to snicker, but Joy might think it was about her. She controlled her amusement.

"Pardon me, daughter," Okami said, somewhat formally, returning to the room with a kitchen worker behind him. At this time of night? Well, Okami ran a tight ship back there. She might need to check with Mei and make sure Okami understood the difference between modern-day workers and serfs. "But I would interrupt, if you would permit it, to serve coffee. It will help some people stay focused."

Abby laughed, and took the first cup fixed the way she liked it. Others followed, and Joy waited patiently.

When the kitchen worker left, Okami nodded at Joy, and she continued. "So Uncle Haru estimated the population of packs and Council areas. We compared his estimates with the numbers we were extrapolating from Girls Who Howl. His estimate of the Northwest Council was close to ours: 2,000 in Tanaka pack, 2,000 more in the other recognized packs, an additional 2,000 in family packs and independents, and probably 1,000 lone wolves. So, 7,000 shifters, all together."

Abby was stunned at those numbers — 7,000 shifters in her region? She just hadn't ever added them up.

"But other regions? Like most of Canada? Our projection almost doubles his of 5,000," she continued. "And you can see it on the map. The Rocky Mountain Council probably has a 1,000 additional wolves. And this was the first time that Uncle Haru had thought to add in the lone wolf population. There are other estimates from him versus our projections that might be of interest in a different presentation, but those are the two that matter to the question that Teacher Garrison asked us to pursue."

And they'd done all of this today? Well, they had dozens of researchers, and an on-the-ground collection team that would make the U.S. Census Bureau drool with envy. She considered the data, but Sarah wasn't done. She nodded to Joy who left the room, and then she continued. "Most of the wolves are male, and probably young — let's say under 30, because that's the population that Alpha Chen was pulling in. So the fact that he pulled in 200 young, unattached shifters over the last 10 years is perfectly believable."

"Why 10 years?" Abby asked.

"We used that time frame because of the number of women he's been kidnapping and turning," Sarah answered. "And because there seemed to be a growing number of his recruits who were hitting 30 and being used as guards and going on missions for the Alpha. But there had been some even before then. We talked to Alpha Margarite today as well to get her take on the numbers. She said some women she's counseling have been part of the pack for decades. So Alpha Chen was kidnapping women as a standard practice for a long time. But the increased numbers escalated about 15 years ago."

Okami grunted as if he'd been kicked, and he took Yui's hand. Abby raised her eyebrow his direction. *We're OK,* he sent. *Just didn't expect it.*

"Do we know of an inciting event at that time?" Sarah asked, looking around the room. "Because there seems to be another one this past summer. We wondered if that was formation of the Hat Island pack."

Abby looked at Benny. "Benny? You're the intelligencer."

"Former intelligencer," he corrected absently. "I think the one 15 years ago was when Alpha Johannsen and Chairman Anton Vuk of the World Council conspired to take out Alpha Tanaka, hoping the pack would dissolve into much smaller family packs. They used the Vancouver and Penticton packs — and possibly the Castle pack — as manpower. It failed."

He nodded his respect to Okami, who nodded back. Sarah's eyes widened as she realized what event Benny was referring to. She glanced anxiously at the Yoshidas, but Yui smiled at her reassuringly. Abby didn't interfere. Instead she moved them onward. "And last summer?"

"It could be our formation," Benny agreed. "But I rather think it was Tanaka's ascension to Chairman of the World Council. That has thrown the traditionalists into a tailspin."

He considered it for a moment. "I suspect the Chinese Alpha probably was involved 15 years ago, and we didn't know it. Which one? We still don't know. But my guess is that's when Chen formed that partnership."

Abby nodded slowly. "That makes sense," she said. "Thank you. Is there more, Sarah? This has been a phenomenal presentation to pull together in one day. I'm coveting all of you for students at Seattle University." Abby could almost feel Benny bursting with pride at his students. Actually, she probably was feeling his pride directly. She smiled at him and nodded her approval.

"There is more," Sarah said. "But you all may want more coffee for this. We're waiting for our next resource to arrive." She glanced anxiously toward the door.

"And dessert this time?" Abby asked. "We've earned it."

Okami nodded and went to find his workers. She glanced at Mei thoughtfully. They needed to talk.

Cookies and coffee arrived, along with Joy and Stefan Lebenev. Abby choked on her coffee in surprise.

"There was one thing that troubled us about our numbers," Sarah said, beginning the presentation again. "Most of the recruits, as people call them, are packless. They are often ignorant of shifter norms. We talked to people here on Hat Island who had knowledge of the situation in Vancouver, but in particular Security Chief Brighton and Assistant Chief Geoff Nickerson were very helpful."

Abby saw someone flinch at Geoff's name, and for the first time, she realized that Jessie Nickerson was in the room. Just listening, indeed, Abby thought, and made a mental note to discuss the girl's future with her.

"They had been struck by that ignorance when they questioned the squad that attacked Hat Island earlier this month," Sarah continued. "And that confirmed something we'd begun to wonder about." She took a deep breath, and glanced at Stefan, of all people, for reassurance.

"Go ahead," Stefan said. "You've got this." Everyone stared at the man, and Abby suddenly realized he might have been a good teacher when he was still in the classroom. Huh, she thought of him as a researcher, but really he would have been teaching faculty for even longer.

Looks like we might have a science teacher after all, Abby sent to Benny.

Who knew? he responded.

Abby grinned.

"This part isn't as well documented as we'd like," Sarah said slowly. "We probably wouldn't have added it, if Dr. Lebenev hadn't returned from Oregon today. But Pi thought we should ask him about it, in light of some of the things he'd been hearing among the research staff about recessive genes and human parents." She swallowed. "We think someone has found a way to identify and change young men who carry a shifter gene. He then sends them on to Penticton, and then on to Vancouver as needed. It isn't done through the normal way of changing someone — none of the men reported that kind of trauma, Chief Nickerson said. So he's got some other means. But we think he's working on the West Coast of Canada and then the United States, probably as far east as the Rockies."

There was stunned silence. "A Pied Piper," Abby said slowly.

"Sorry?" Sarah asked.

"The Pied Piper of Hamlin," Abby amplified. "It's a well-known fairy tale. A talented man was hired because he could pipe to the rats infesting the city and lead them out. He did it, and the town fathers refused to pay. In retaliation he changed the tune and led all of their children out and they were never seen again."

"Which is why they are called Grimm fairy tales," Benny cracked.

Abby laughed with everyone else. "Scholars think the fairy tale — and a famous epic poem — are based on a real event," she added. "So, do we have someone who can do that? Sarah? Stefan?"

Sarah gestured to Stefan and sat down. Obviously she was dumping it in his lap, Abby thought amused. But it fit. "So this is a tentative observation based on qualitative data," Stefan began. "I have a ton — and that might be literally true — of genetic data and other medical samples from the homesteads in Oregon. As you may remember, the Oregon pack strings along the I-5 corridor as a series of homesteads — extended family packs. Each homestead has a leader, called a pack Second, who answers to the Alpha in Portland."

Most people knew that, but you never knew, Abby thought, glancing around the room.

"And the samples will be rich with information for us on a number of questions," Stefan continued. "But Joy and a team of girls from Africa — when did they get here, anyway?"

"Yesterday," Cujo answered, a bit terse. Abby wanted to laugh; Cujo was feeling a bit overwhelmed.

Stefan nodded. "So they wanted to know about latent traits and recessive genes, and how do shifters with a human parent become shifters? And what about those who don't?"

Benny looked up at that. He had a human mother. Stefan himself apparently had a human father. Something clicked for Cujo, and he swore softly. He actually had his phone out to call someone before he stopped and put it away.

Cujo? Abby asked.

We've had a major problem, two actually, that this impacts, Alpha. And Haru is going to want to know — know yesterday, probably. But I should hear it all first.

Abby nodded.

"So as most of you know, I have a human father. Benny has a human mother," Stefan continued.

Ryder looked up. "I do too," he said.

Stefan looked at him. "I don't think we've met."

"I'm Alpha Garrison's son," Ryder said. He didn't give his name.

Stefan nodded. "I've heard of you, but no, we haven't met. And you are an additional example of my hypothesis. So Joy? Do you want to do your slide presentation?"

Joy nodded and returned to the computer. "So 'shifter' is a recessive gene, apparently," she said, and she showed a basic gene chart. The old fashioned kind that looked more like an organization chart or family tree rather than the gene charts as they were today. She apologized for the over-simplified chart.

"No problem," Benny said. "We wouldn't understand a real one anyway."

Stefan snorted at that, and everyone laughed. Joy watched them as if they were interesting specimens in a tide pool. Abby grinned at that.

Joy continued, "It takes two recessive genes for the characteristics to present themselves. But then, how does someone like Teacher Garrison or Dr. Lebenev even exist? We hypothesize that in actuality a shifter can present with one recessive gene, if the parent is dominant enough to pull the child into first shift, and then, of course, through it."

"But I'm a problem," Stefan said. "My mother was pack, not my father. And that's rare. But given what I've heard about her relationship with Alpha Lebenev, she was probably strong-willed and an alpha wolf. And I had a substitute parent who pulled me through." He nodded at Yui, who nodded back. "That was helped by the fact that I was raised in a pack, knew about first shift, and expected to go through it. Expectations are powerful. Benny? I haven't had time to ask, but were you raised in a pack?"

Benny nodded. "My mother was human and as is all-too-common, died during my birth. But my father, while not pack, was among the Cambodian pack, and I was raised by the women of the pack. Dad pulled me through first shift. Then the pack loaded my memory with the stories of their Keeper of Stories and sent me to safety."

Abby hadn't realized he'd been that young — 13? Quite a desperate attempt to save the stories of the Cambodians. No wonder Benny had done everything he could to protect those stories.

"So that tracks. Nurture as well as nature," Stefan said. He nodded to Joy, who went to the next slide. Abby didn't try to figure it out. She'd get the details later. For now, she was struggling to master the mind-boggling concepts here.

"So we think it might be sex-linked in some way," Joy said. "Boys of a human mother go through first shift. Girls typically don't, which is why the Oregon pack is so interested in the serum. They'll be able to have their girls shift as well."

"And their mothers," Benny muttered thoughtfully.

"And again, I'm the anomaly," Stefan said ruefully. "I had a twin — a sister."

It hit Abby why, and she blurted it out. "Because your mother was the shifter, not your father."

Stefan looked poleaxed. "Thank you, Alpha," he said. "I think you're right. Male lone wolves are the most common source of a human mother conceiving. And Oregon, of course." He added that wryly with a bow toward Okami. Okami rolled his eyes.

"However, we think girls of such a pregnancy carry the gene," Joy continued, looking at her slides. "Dr. Lebenev theorizes that it might explain what is happening in Oregon — there are a lot of such women who have that latent gene who might be marrying back into the homesteads of the pack. And that's why they don't die in first child birth, although they may die later, and why the occasional girl goes through first shift."

Stefan interjected, "I think the strength of the father is also key — or the strength of the Alpha who pulls the girls through. As we know, you have to be stronger than the new wolf to be able to pull a wolf through first shift."

Abby's gut clenched at the reminder. She felt Jake's worry, and reassured him. Yes, it still hit her, but she was getting over it. If Ricci had been more dominant, Abby would have become a shifter three years earlier — and have been in Jedediah Jones' hands. She shuddered. Dodged a bullet there.

Joy continued, "We don't know how many generations back that shifter gene could be. At least grandfather, I think, because if it was only a parent, the homestead would know of the parentage. But it could be more."

It was Sarah who drove the point home. "That means there could be a lot of people out there who think they're human but who carry the shifter gene. Think about how long a shifter can parent a child. A shifter woman is fertile for 70 years or more. And although we're taught that shifter women struggle to give birth, they still might have five or more during that span. And the men?"

She looked at Okami, who nodded. "I am 457 years old," he said steadily. "And I fathered a child five years ago."

There was silence.

Abby broke it. "So if we have a Pied Piper who can spot a latent shifter and pull them through somehow, he would have quite the pool to pull from."

"So we believe, Alpha," Sarah said, formally. She nodded to Joy who closed down the computer, and the two of them took their seats.

"Well done," Abby said, heartfelt. "We have much to think about. Stefan? Do we have any clues how the Pied Piper might be pulling the young men through?'

It was Cujo who answered. "The same way you and I have done with the young girls after the serum shots," he said slowly. "In a group. Pulling them through together, their mutual belief and support reinforcing the work of the serum."

"But not with the serum," Abby said. "He doesn't have that. And it doesn't work on boys."

"I'll bet he uses a drug though," Benny said. "A hallucinogenic drug, a group experience, perhaps after having already introduced the concept of being powerful, a shifter. And then while they're under the influence he pulls out the wolf and introduces them."

Abby blew out air through her lips. She looked at Cujo. "Then they still have a vestige link to the man, don't you think? We do to the girls we've pulled through."

Cujo nodded slowly. "And we've got dozens of them here."

"And in Delta, Bellingham, and Vancouver," Mei added. She looked sick. "And I've got a link to them too."

No one knew what to say to that. "Tomorrow," Abby said firmly. "We don't need to solve all of this tonight."

"We do need to solve one more thing," Benny said, somewhat apologetically. "Alpha, Ryder and I would like to take a squad up to Penticton and resolve things on behalf of the Okanogan pack. We cannot afford to have that large of a region in turmoil." He nodded toward the screen where they'd just seen how large that area was. "And we are alerting you, as Chairman of the Northwest Council, that a resolution may involve the overthrow of the Penticton Alpha."

And the transfer of the Okanogan pack, Benny added through their link.

Not to you, Abby said. *I need you too badly.*

No, not to me. But Ryder isn't ready to accept that realization. But you should be aware that's what I think will happen.

Abby: *Understood.*

Out loud, Abby said, "You have the blessing of the Chairman of the Northwest Council of Alphas. When do you leave?"

"As soon after breakfast as we can," Ryder answered. "The increase in his aggressiveness is dangerous."

"Alpha?" Jessie said quietly. "I'm going too."

Abby glanced at Benny and Ryder, but neither protested. "All right," she said. "Do you mind sharing why?"

"I think my fiancé I've been searching for is in Penticton," she said steadily.

You haven't told her, Abby said to Benny.

Not yet. When it's time, Ryder will. There was a pause, and Benny added, *or she'll be confronted with it when we get there. And truly that might be best.*

Coward, Abby said, but there was no hostility to it. Benny knew Jessie best; they'd worked together all week. And she thought there was something going on between Ryder and Jessie.

Possible, Benny said, responding to her thoughts even though they weren't directed at him. *But she has a lot of healing to do emotionally before she's ready for that. And Ryder knows.* There was a feeling of grimness. *He knows because I told him I'd beat the shit out of him if he hurt her.*

Big brother has spoken, she teased.

Damned right.

Abby said formally, "This meeting is closed. Sarah? Joy? You have done amazing work. Thank you. And thank you all for being here. I know it's been a long day. Benny, Jessie, and Ryder? I'll see you and your guards at breakfast."

Get me out of here, Abby ordered Jake. *I'm past done.*

Chapter 21

Day 157 of the re-emerged Hat Island pack, Sunday, Nov. 10, Hat Island

Abby walked the path to her house, guided by Jake's comforting presence behind her more than anything else. She had a headache coming on — a sign she'd overdone it. Odd that the boundaryless experience earlier hadn't left her with one. Tonight had.

Long day, Jake said.

She snorted.

There was a rustle off to her left, and Jake pushed in front of her.

"I'm sorry," a soft voice said. "It's me, Jessie. I didn't mean to startle you. But...."

Abby peered around Jake, who was still solidly between her and the young woman. "You need a place to sleep!" Abby exclaimed. "I'm sorry. I didn't think."

"I didn't know who to ask," she admitted. "I could have asked Benny, but I...."

"He would have found you a place. But I understand," Abby said. "Let me call someone."

"I don't want to be a problem," Jessie began but Abby already had her phone out. She knew who would be perfect for this issue. She paused to ask, "Jessie? Are you sure about going north with the guys?"

Jessie nodded. "I told Benny I was going with or without them. Bjorn is there. And I promised I would find him."

"He may not be the person you remember," Abby said, searching for a way to prepare her.

"I know," Jessie said softly. "I don't think he ever was."

Abby started to say something else, when she heard another sound, a more dangerous one. "Drop," she ordered Jessie, and was gratified to see she obeyed instantly.

She turned to meet the threat coming at her from the trees.

"Alpha, I chal...."

But he was close enough that Abby slashed his throat with her shifted hands, stopping the words of a challenge. He fell to the ground, bleeding out, and Jake finished his death, pulling head from body. Abby grimaced; she found it horrifying, and at the same time it annoyed her that she couldn't quite get the hang of it.

"Call Brighton," Jake said as he surveyed the surrounding area warily.

Abby nodded, looking for the phone she'd dropped when she sensed the attacker. She picked it up and brushed it off. She pinged Benjamin. "We were attacked," she said tersely, and described where they were. "We need to lock down the island."

"On my way."

Abby went to look at the dead man. Well, his head, she thought, grimacing. He was a stranger. "Too old to be one of the recruits," she said, relieved. Jessie appeared beside her and looked as well.

"He's not one of the bikers, either," Jessie murmured. "I'm not sure I could put a name to all of them, but I'd recognize them by sight."

Abby was relieved about that, too. She didn't want betrayal to muddy the waters of what Benny and Ryder needed to do in the morning.

Cujo? We've had an intruder, she sent. *He's dead. But can you run the shoreline? He had to get here somehow, and the ferry was with us most of the day. No trips.*

On it, he replied.

Brighton showed up with a half-dozen guards as well as his assistant chief, Geoff Nickerson.

Abby glanced at him, and then at Jessie. "Tell me quick," she murmured. "That's your great-grandfather. Do you want to meet him? Or is that too much for a spur of the moment thing?"

Jessie glanced at the man who was standing with Jake and the others looking at the dead man. "I've heard the stories," she said quietly. "I'd like to meet him, but will he want to meet me? I might not be back this way again. So now or never?"

Abby glanced at her, wondering where she thought she might be going next. She didn't ask. "Geoff?" she called softly. Geoff, a quiet man of about her own height, joined her, looking at her quizzically.

"This is Jessie," she introduced. "Jessie Nickerson. I thought perhaps you two might want to get acquainted. She leaves in the morning, but she could use a place to stay for the night."

Geoff and Jessie stared at each other. The resemblance was remarkable.

"Benjamin? I'm off duty for the night," Geoff called out, without looking away from Jessie. "You don't need me."

Benjamin Brighton looked startled, but a glance from Abby silenced any protest.

"Come on," Geoff said a bit huskily. "I would be delighted to host you for the night."

Jessie gave one anxious glance at Abby, and then nodded. The two of them walked away into the night, side-by-side, but not touching.

Found a boat, Alpha. No one is guarding it, so he must have come alone, Cujo sent. *But, just so you know? Pi has been out somewhere tonight. I don't think it's related to this. I found his transportation method a while back. Didn't seem like he was hurting anything, so I didn't out him. But there might be new girls at the school in the morning. Someone needs to do a headcount.*

Abby shrugged mentally. *Who is that going to be? Michil Bogun? Olivia? Because Benny is heading out right after breakfast for Penticton and the Okanogan.*

Cujo swore. *I'll tell Olivia,* he said reluctantly.

"Cujo says there's a boat, but no one is with it," Abby said. "So probably he came alone. Does anyone recognize him? He's not one of the young men, and Jessie said she didn't recognize him as being one of the bikers either."

"We'll search," Brighton said. "And we'll post guards at the Retreat House."

"Better add some to Beach House too," Abby said. "We don't want any surprises there with the two human women in residence."

Brighton nodded.

Abby glanced at Jake as they moved toward the house once more.

"Well, now that that's over," Jake said ruefully, "I wonder what Jessie already knows."

Abby glanced in the direction the young woman had gone. "Or maybe she's had time to reconsider some things," Abby agreed. "Like why did he leave the city without her? And when Chen fell, why didn't he come back to her? She's doing everything she knows to find him."

"Ouch," Jake said.

"And she listens," Abby added ruefully. "That's what she calls it. She's intelligencer material if there ever was any. She may well have pieced the story together on her own."

They crossed the bridge over the koi pond, and as always, Abby blessed Okami for the garden he'd built her. The bridge served multiple functions: beauty, defense, and most of all, it was the place she let go off all of the burdens of the day. Retreat House, indeed.

Abby pulled open the door and stepped inside. Something warned her, and she dived for the floor — just seconds ahead of when Jake would have pushed her there, she thought ruefully. She shifted her hands, again, and let her wolf come close to the surface.

Intruder. So there *was* a second one.

"I'm not here to hurt you," a voice said. Abby frowned. It tantalized her. Familiar, but not recently. "I need your help."

He turned the light of his phone so that they could see his face. Abby gasped. "You."

"Hello, Abby," the man said.

"Alpha Garrison," Jake said. "It's about time you showed up."

Who? This was Benny's father? Abby started to get up, felt Jake's caution and stayed down. What was Jake wary about him for? Well, other than Jake was wary about everyone.

And they'd just had an intruder try to challenge her.

"I'm not a threat," Garrison repeated. "But I've got an injured person in the spare bedroom, and I need your help."

"A shifter?" Abby asked, startled. She stood up, because crouching on the floor made her feel ridiculous. But a shifter who was so injured they couldn't heal on their own was rare — nearly dead, rare.

"A shifter tried to gut her," Garrison said. "I think he had toxins of some kind on his claws, because she's not healing."

Abby started moving toward the bedroom. She glanced inside. The woman on the bed was unconscious, her middle bound in something sheet-like. It looked a bit grubby. The two of them had endured some hard days. Her eyes adjusted to the dark, and she realized who this was. Nadia Vuk, the twins' mother. She looked like them.

She backed out of the room, carefully shutting her link to the twins down tight. "Nadia Vuk," she said.

Garrison nodded. "Do you know her?"

"She looks like the twins," Abby replied. "She could be their older sister instead of their mother."

"They are here, then," he said relieved. "We hoped so, but we weren't sure. And then Taisiya reached her a couple of days ago — just after Nadia was attacked, actually. Nadia has been frantic about their safety. She's delirious, and I'm afraid she communicated her fear to Taisiya. But we weren't sure where they were."

Abby snorted. "Taisiya is a powerful telepath," she said, using the term that Alpha Hiro had been so startled by. They needed to get used to it! Tom Garrison didn't seem startled at all, she noted. "She passed on that fear to two dozen women, and it was all people could do to restrain them from scattering and hiding."

Garrison looked amused, and Abby wanted to smack him. It hadn't been funny at the time! Although in retrospect....

"She probably is their older sister, in case you haven't figured that out," he replied quietly. "And their mother."

Abby nodded. She hadn't put it in those terms, but yes, she had figured that the twins were probably the result of incest and rape. "He was trying to breed a *istochnik sily.*"

"You have been busy," Garrison observed. "We've got some talking to do." He glanced at the woman with worry. "Do you have a doctor?"

Abby nodded, and pulled out her phone. "Stefan, I need you at Retreat House," she said quietly. "No, no, I'm fine, but I have a patient." She listened. "Just get here, will you? Bring supplies. Have a guard escort you. There was an attack earlier tonight."

"An attack?" Garrison said sharply.

Jake explained, while Abby paced restlessly. She watched out the front for Stefan to appear by the bridge, and then she looked in at the woman. She was so still, Abby had to watch to make sure she was still breathing.

"I wish I could have seen him," Garrison muttered. "Would help to know if the men who have been chasing us have found a way onto the island."

Jake called Brighton, asked him to take a picture of the dead man, and send it to him. A minute later he handed his phone to Garrison. Garrison grimaced. "Was he alone?"

"Seems to be," Jake said. "Found his boat, but we haven't found any other intruders. But then, we hadn't spotted you either. I assume Pi brought you over?"

"Don't want to get the lad in trouble," Garrison said.

"Stefan's here," Abby warned. The two men fell silent, and she opened the door for the doctor. The guards stayed outside.

Stefan glanced at the stranger in the room and paused for a moment. "Alpha Garrison," he said. "I don't know if you remember me — Stefan Lebenev. I was considerably younger the last time we met."

"I remember," Garrison said. Well, Abby supposed he would. Benny had at the Scout Camp that had linked Jake and Stefan and Cujo and all the others together.

"A patient?" Stefan said impatiently. That was all the niceties he was going to waste on the man, Abby thought with amusement.

"In here," Garrison answered. He looked at Abby. "Don't tell my sons I'm here. I'll explain later."

Abby nodded. She waited in the living room with Jake while Tom Garrison explained what had happened to Nadia Vuk to Stefan. Stefan listened as he unwound the sheet to look at her.

"Well?" she asked softly.

Jake shrugged. "He's known to be on the right side of things," he answered. "But, devious."

Abby snorted, thinking of the man's sons. Like that was a surprise.

Abby could hear the two men arguing in low tones, and she went into the bedroom to listen. "She's going to need a nurse," Stefan said, turning to her. "But he's refusing to let me call her."

Call Yui, Abby interpreted. "If you can't trust Yui Ito Yoshida, you're beyond help, Alpha Garrison," she said, using his formal title.

He hesitated, then nodded reluctantly, and Stefan called her. "Use guards," he cautioned her. Abby nodded her approval. This was not a night that Okami should leave his household of children and vulnerable people. She felt Okami questioning her in her mind, and she reassured him. *Details later,* she promised.

Stefan gestured them all out of the bedroom. "I cleaned out the wound," he said tiredly. "I think you're right, there was a toxin of some kind. Her body could fight it off, but not expel it completely. And the toxin would start the damage all over again."

Garrison nodded. Apparently that matched his observations. Abby considered the situation. If Nadia wasn't better in the morning, she'd see what she could do. But if conventional methods worked, she shouldn't spend herself. She knew that, even if it sat hard with her. She felt Jake's approval of that conclusion.

"I'll check back in the morning," Stefan said. "But really, Yui is better at this than I am. I haven't done any 'doctoring' in decades. Not ever, really. I'm a researcher."

"I understand," Garrison said. "And I appreciate this."

They waited in silence until Yui tapped on the door, and Jake let her in. She too recognized their uninvited guest, but she just nodded once, and then followed Stefan into the bedroom to see the patient who needed her care. Abby waited until Stefan came out and closed the bedroom door behind him. "Tomorrow," he repeated briefly, and then saw himself out of the house. Abby checked to make sure guards were waiting for him on the other side of the bridge. Satisfied that he was off safely, she turned to Garrison.

"Talk," she demanded. "Start with why I shouldn't call Benny in for this."

Garrison ran his hand over his chin. He looked exhausted. Jake went to the refrigerator, pulled out a beer and handed it to him. Then he got out the fixings to make an omelet. Abby's stomach growled. Jake looked up and grinned and mixed up more eggs.

"So, I picked up that Ryder is here too," he began. "And that they're heading north tomorrow to take care of things in Okanogan. About bloody time. So I don't want to interfere with that."

"I'd like to know how you know that," Jake said equitably.

"Pi was full of gossip when he came to pick me up," Garrison answered. "He's been lurking around the lodge all day, I gathered."

Abby was going to have to have a word with that young man. And then she might have to hire him. Him and Jessie both. And Sarah and the other girls. The thought amused her.

"It's not just Okanogan, it's Penticton too," Jake said. He updated their guest, as he slid the first omelet onto a plate and handed it to Abby. She didn't protest, although it made her uncomfortable to be served before a guest. And she could tell that amused Jake, although he didn't let it show. She took one bite and set down her fork to wait for the other two.

"Where's my pack Second in all of this?" Garrison asked, puzzled.

"Benny's first thought was that he had to be dead," Abby said. Jake got up and fixed her some coffee. Neither man took any, but Abby was grateful for the warmth and the caffeine. A long day indeed. "But he and Ryder decided he had to be alive, or you would feel his death and return. So now they believe he must be a prisoner somewhere. It's on their list of things to investigate up there."

Garrison winced. "No wonder things went sour," he muttered and sighed. "We should have taken out the Penticton Alpha a long time ago. And I'm at fault there. I could have just expanded my territory north, but I wasn't willing to do it, and there wasn't anyone else who would step into that pack as Alpha. Not anyone better anyway. I've been waiting a long time for Benny to stop playing around and come home."

"He's never going to do that, Tom," Abby said. She winced when she realized she'd used his first name. "You need another plan."

"Not me," he denied. "The two of them can sort it out. I'm done. My time up there is over. I'm needed here."

"Here, as in Seattle, or here as on Hat Island?" Jake asked.

"Here, as at the side of the Shogun," Garrison said, looking at Abby steadily.

It took her a moment to understand that he meant her. "No," she said adamantly, standing up to pace. "No. I am never going to be your Shogun or Okami's Shogun. I am no warlord, Tom Garrison!"

"A Shogun is more than a warlord," Garrison said, seemingly unfazed by her reaction. "They brought peace to their lands, established a functioning government and judiciary, and gave their people prosperity and an amazing quality of life."

"I don't care," Abby said, although she found that moderately interesting — in an academic sense. "I think you're both nuts. I'm a middle-aged faculty member! And I've been a shifter all of six months!"

"And you're the most dominant shifter in the world," Garrison said quietly. "And don't deny that. It's not something we should even say out loud. But you know it. You both do." He looked at Jake. "After all, Colonel Lewis, isn't that why you're here? Standing at the back of the next leader of the shifter world?"

Jake shook his head. "No," he said simply. "I stand at Abby's back because I love her. That's it. Nothing more. No devious political shit. But nothing less. I love her with all I've got."

Abby looked at him, and her eyes burned. She felt something settle inside of her. She loved this man fiercely, and with his love, she'd face demons. Even old men and their talk of mythical leaders. But she wasn't going to allow Tom Garrison or Okami Yoshida cast her in that role.

"No," she said again. "I won't."

She stalked toward the bedroom door. "I've had it," she announced not turning to look at them. "I'm going to bed."

"Won't?" Garrison said softly. "Not can't?"

Abby closed the door behind her.

Chapter 22

Day 157 of the re-emerged Hat Island pack, Sunday, Nov. 10, Hat Island

Jake hesitated, wanting to follow her, but the practicalities of a guest won out. "Come on Alpha Garrison," he said. "You'll have my room."

Jake went about the responsibilities of hosting an unexpected guest. He got out fresh sheets and started to make the bed. Garrison pitched in to help. Jake saw Garrison's worn knapsack leaning against the wall of the bedroom. Well, the arrangements were obvious, he thought, but he wondered how long the man had been in the house. Probably long enough to toss the place thoroughly. Not that there was anything to be found.

Abby's office might have interesting field notes, he thought with amusement. But he doubted Garrison was looking for information about the linguistic implications of how Okanogan was spelled — with an O and two As in the States, and with three As in Canada.

Well, Garrison might be interested actually. He thought the man of mythos and story among the intelligence community was probably as curious as Abby was. Given Jake's experience with Benny, it was almost a given that he was.

Jake found fresh toiletries, set out fresh towels. The very prosaic nature of the tasks amused him.

"We'll talk more in the morning," Jake said. "But Abby and I need to go to the lodge for an early breakfast or those sons of yours will be down here demanding to know what's wrong. And your plan for secrecy will be shot to hell."

Garrison nodded, and Jake turned to leave him. He could feel Abby's distress, and it called him.

"Jake?" Garrison said softly behind him. "Am I wrong?"

Jake paused. He didn't look back. "No," he said. "You're not. But for someone renowned for his ability to synthesize information and formulate a plan — to topple a government even — that was remarkably stupid."

Garrison snorted. "I'll give you that."

Jake turned back to look at him. "One question," he said. "Have you and Okami Yoshida discussed this in any fashion?" He dreaded the answer, but he needed to know.

"I would welcome any discussion Okami Yoshida wished to have with me, including this one," Garrison said slowly. "But no, he and I haven't talked in years. Not since he wanted me to take on the Penticton pack, as a matter of fact. And I'm going to have to eat crow and admit he was right. Why? Has he said something about a Shogun?"

"Freaked her out," Jake said. "They've got some kind of special link that she can pull energy through from all of the pack. She pulls from me and the inner circle, as she calls her closest advisors, too, but Okami can feed it to her from the whole pack."

"The *real* 'last samurai,'" Garrison said softly. "You know that, don't you? He's the real deal. And he thinks she's the Shogun?"

"She's *his* Shogun," Jake said. "I don't know about *the* Shogun. But know this, Garrison. Whatever she decides? I back her. Even if it means the destruction of the whole shifter species. And she needs to make those decisions free of pressure from delusional old men who have absorbed too many mystic prophecies."

"Does she know about them — the prophecies?"

Jake shook his head. "I don't know what she knows, not completely, but I don't think so. She knows about the dònglì diànchí because of Chen's obsession with it. Maybe more." Jake thought about Gene and his appearance in Vancouver, but he didn't share it with Garrison. He wasn't sure what it meant anyway — but there'd been a conversation he hadn't been privy to, one that had troubled Abby for days. "But no, I don't think she knows those myths exist."

"Prophecies," Garrison corrected. He shook his head. "Goes against all of my training and culture," he admitted. "But you spend enough time in the Orient, and you become more of a believer in things we cannot see."

Orient? Jake wondered how old was this man? He smiled to himself. Abby's linguistic curiosity was infecting him. But he hadn't heard that term used for Asia in a long time. Not ever, really. Only in treatises on war dating back a generation or more. It suddenly struck him curious that Garrison would use the term Shogun.

Garrison continued, "Or maybe it is a part of our culture too: 'There are more things in heaven and earth, Horatio, than are dreamt of.'"

Jake shrugged. "Woo woo stuff, Alpha Garrison," he said. "I live in the here and now. And I stand at Abby Stafford's back."

The older man nodded. "Good enough," he said.

Jake left him there and went to see what he could do for the woman he loved.

The room was dark when he let himself in, just the light from the moon streaming in through her window. Abby was in bed, a pillow covering her head. He chuckled. "Does that help?"

"It worked when I was a kid," she muttered, rolling over to face him. The sheet slid down, revealing her breasts. God, she was beautiful.

Jake took off his wool jacket and dropped it in the chair. He kicked off his boots and shrugged out of his shoulder harness. The ankle holster for his knife came off next. Shifters might disdain the use of weapons, but Jake was matter-of-fact about whatever got the job done. And after 40 years as a Marine, weapons were just as natural as underwear.

More so, he thought with a laugh, since he often went without. Even now. He pulled his T-shirt off over his head. Abby was watching him avidly. "Like what you see?" he teased.

She nodded. "It's like having a present unwrap itself for me," she said huskily.

Jake felt his body harden at that. He unzipped his trousers and dropped them on the floor next to the bed. It still gave him a secret thrill to be able to do that. To be a bit sloppy — although he'd have to put everything away shipshape soon enough. But now? He pounced on the bed — which was sexier in his mind than in reality. They got tangled up in the sheet, and it took both of them to get it out of the way. Abby got the giggles, but the sheet soon joined the other covers at the foot of the bed. He liked that they were comfortable enough with each other now that they could be playful, and yes, even get tangled up in a sheet and have to sort it out. It felt good.

Really good.

He was kneeling over her now, just as he had envisioned — before the sheet — straddling her on all fours. And he delighted in just looking at her. Her out-of-control red hair that came down to a peak on her forehead, the arch of her eyebrows, the creamy smoothness of her skin. He lowered his eyes, taking in her full breasts with their aroused nipples, and the smoothness of her belly. She was more muscled than when he'd first seen her, that day on the dock. Probably didn't weigh all that much less — but it was muscle, not fat. Her skin was younger looking. Her hair was brighter and wilder. But she was still the same woman who had fascinated him from the beginning, with the same half-smile that was watching him now. "Like what you see?" she asked, teasing him with the same question he'd asked of her.

"Yes," he said simply, and he kissed her.

Sex was straightforward tonight, and quick, even. Some nights, they played and teased, and arousal was long and delayed. That was good too. Really, there was no such thing as bad sex with Abby. She threw herself into it enthusiastically, meeting his passion with her own. But tonight, it was about simple release, and the reassurance that body-to-body contact gave. And when they'd both climaxed, they lay there satiated, her head on his shoulder.

He would keep her like this if he could, cocooned in a world of pleasure and safety. But that wasn't their future, and he knew it. Abby knew too. It made moments like this all the more to be treasured.

"Sleep," he whispered, and she smiled at him before drifting off. He held her, the most precious thing in his world.

But when he was sure she was sleeping soundly, he got up and pulled his pants back on. Padding back out to the main room, he shut the door carefully, so that he didn't wake her. He glanced at the other two bedrooms. Their doors were closed as well.

He called Brighton. "Lock the island down," he said tersely. "Permanently."

Brighton grunted. "You know I'm supposed to leave for California Monday, right?"

"You institute the protocol we've established, and Geoff is more than capable of managing it," Jake answered. He wished Brighton was going to be here — the old Brit was a formidable strategist — but he was also needed in California to protect Syn, Ricci and his own partner, Terry. The smaller household was even more exposed. And what Ricci was doing was important. Geoff was more than competent.

But maybe a bit more ethical or moral than Brighton. There wasn't anything Brighton wouldn't do if it was necessary. And without hesitation. Jake knew he was more like Geoff — he might hesitate to be ruthless enough, fast enough.

Well, he had Cujo. Not even Brighton matched that man, when he was in mercenary mode as Benny called it. They'd be fine without Brighton. Truthfully, Jake suspected Brighton would go anyway to be with his partner, whether Jake approved or not.

"Got a lucky ID on our attacker," Geoff said. "One of my security team recognized him. He's a hired killer out of Las Vegas. Do you know about that pack?"

Jake did. The remnant of one of the old mobsters. How a pack Alpha had pulled that off in the '20s was beyond him. But he had, and rolled in the money too. He'd been killed in a shootout with the FBI — Jake was hazy on the details — and his Second had stepped into the Alpha role. But the new Alpha could see that things were changing in Las Vegas, and he moved the pack out to the hills. Muscle for hire instead of one of the players on the Strip. It had been a smart move.

They were damned ruthless killers. And someone had sent one of them after Abby? It hadn't been a challenge then. Of course it hadn't been really anyway. A true challenger would have shown up at the office on the dock and declared himself, not attack by stealth in the night. But using the words might make some Alphas hesitate to kill outright.

Not Abby. She'd decided if she killed them before they finished the sentence, it wasn't a true challenge. Death by stupidity. Abby could be pretty ruthless herself.

Well, she'd had to be.

"Any clues as to who might have sent him?" he asked, walking to the big plate-glass windows and looking out. He could see the guards out there silhouetted by the moonlight. "Did you find anyone else?"

"No, just the boat," Brighton said. "We moved it around to the boathouse — adding it to Okami's fleet. A nice little skiff, actually."

Jake grunted. Okami seemed intent on building a fleet of boats. It had been amusing at first — and given the boat he'd been using to fish from when Jake arrived, it hadn't seemed strange. Now they had enough boats that King Davis was talking about offering guided tours and fishing excursions as part of the Beach House Hotel. And Okami has happy to work with King on that. But Jake thought Okami had something in mind, something more ominous. Not that he was sharing, of course. Okami kept his own counsel, damn the man.

Shogun, his hind brain whispered.

Jake shook his head. Damn both of the men.

But Abby was up to something about boats too. She'd talked to Okami tonight about Norman Posey's suggestion of a permanent slip in Tulalip. She wanted to bring the Council ship down from Bellingham, to have it closer. Okami agreed to take a look and see if the harbor in Tulalip made that feasible. Jake had sensed that Abby was intent on something, something to do with all these young men, but he couldn't quite pick up the specifics.

Well, she'd tell him when she had time. She didn't withhold information from him — not for long, although she'd managed to keep the baby a secret for a week, which amused him — but sometimes things had to be prioritized. And he got the feeling that whatever she was thinking was more of a long-term strategy. He set aside his curiosity. He had enough on his plate.

"Increase the guards at the boarding school," Jake said. "I'm worried about the twins, in particular, but all of those girls need careful protection, Benjamin. Cujo thinks those teachers who brought in the African girls are plants. And if so, there are traffickers who want those girls badly."

Brighton swore. Jake always got a bit of pleasure listening to the man's invective. He grinned now.

The two men talked for a while about the details of the protocol — of the island shutdown. The trick had been to design a plan that wouldn't get much notice. To tighten up the checks at the ferry, but not shut the ferry down. To increase the patrols of the shoreline, especially at night, and to use security guards in wolf form as well as human. They were going to have to stop Pi from his excursions, but now that Garrison was here instead of Southeast Asia, Jake guessed they wouldn't be getting any more girls. He'd have to ask the man about that.

This was stage one of the lockdown. Stage two would eject all the people on the island who weren't pack. There might be some exceptions made. He didn't know what to do about the women who had come back here through Cujo's mission but hadn't asked to become pack. Hell, he didn't think Olivia was pack for that matter. Or people like Mei, who were integral to the operations of Wolf Harbor and Hat Island but were members of Tanaka pack. Well, they weren't there yet. But he made a mental note to see if someone could start talking to the women about asking to become pack.

They had established priorities. Protect Abby, of course. Protect the school. Protect the women. Protect the island itself.

They were blessed with a potential fighting force of hundreds — experienced, ex-military, disciplined. He thought of all the dominance fights they'd had, especially at first, and grimaced. Mostly disciplined. But they'd already learned that bad guys could be hiding among them — especially among the lone wolves who were here on employment bonds.

"I wonder if our attacker had inside help," Jake said abruptly. "He knew right where to be, and when we'd be there."

"I'll give that some thought," Brighton promised. "Tomorrow. Get some sleep, Jake."

Jake let the call end but stood there looking out at the pond and the garden, watching the moonlight play across it. He marveled at the multifaceted person that Okami was. Thinking of him, he started to go check on Yui and her patient.

The bedroom door opened. "Jake?" Abby said quietly. "Is something wrong? What are you doing?"

"Would you believe, I'm watching the moonlight over the garden?" he said whimsically. She came out, wearing his T-shirt, which didn't cover as much as she thought it did. And he wasn't going to tell her either. He grinned.

Abby slid her arm around his waist and leaned against him. He draped his arm on her shoulders. They stood there for a long time, looking out, lost in their own thoughts, watching moonlight dance across the pond.

Finally Abby stirred. "Come to bed," she said.

And Jake followed her back inside.

Chapter 23

Day 157 of the re-emerged Hat Island pack, Sunday, Nov. 10, Hat Island

Benny Garrison was watching the door to the lodge while Ryder paced restlessly. As if that didn't sum up the differences between the two of them. Ryder had all that restless energy, while Benny taught yoga. Go figure.

They were waiting for Jessie. He couldn't believe he hadn't thought about getting her a room! He supposed she found a place to stay with the other women, but he didn't know where she was. If she didn't show up soon, he'd try to call her.

"What the fuck?" Ryder growled. Benny looked at the door to see Jessie walk in with Geoff Nickerson. He'd be what, her great-grandfather? He supposed so. He looked like her — an older brother version.

She gave him a hug, and he waved at Benny before turning around and leaving. Jessie smiled at the two of them. "Good morning," she said cheerfully.

"If I'd known you were so desperate for a room, you'd pick up a one-night stand, you could have come to me," Ryder said, all but hissing the words. Benny's eyes widened, and he started to say something. One glance at Jessie, and he settled back to watch the fireworks.

"One, you're not the boss of me, Ryder, and if I want to sleep with a dozen men, you have no say in it," Jessie said back. She got right in his face too.

Benny admired the strength that took — not many could. And the few who could, would probably reconsider the wisdom of it. Not Jessie. She wasn't having it.

"And two? That's my great-grandfather, who the Alpha introduced me to last night," Jessie said. "And we spent most of the time since then getting acquainted. He's an assistant security chief here."

Ryder started to say something, then visibly reconsidered it. "You're right," he said then. "I had no business saying that. And I'm glad you were able to connect with a relative here."

Jessie stared at him, open-mouthed. Even Benny was impressed. "Well then, kids," he said cheerfully. "Now that we've got that out of the way, let's get some breakfast. The breakfast buffet here is called the meat-lovers special." He headed toward the dining room, and the other two followed him.

Ryder gestured toward a backpack leaning against the wall. "I know you don't have much with you," he said. "So I asked Mei? She put together a kit for you."

Jessie smiled at him, his earlier assholeness forgiven. "Thank you," she said. "That's thoughtful of you. I'm down to the toothbrush Geoff gave me this morning."

Benny moved them along. It was thoughtful, and Benny was impressed. But then Ryder's mother had been a high school guidance counselor. She'd raised her son right.

She'd also been as close to a mother-figure as Benny had — she'd managed to cope with him when he landed in her high school, angry, belligerent. Got him on track and into college, even. He still called her regularly, but no visits, of course. Naomi George accepted the fact that no one stopped in to see someone in Okanogan — it wasn't exactly on the way to anywhere. And she believed the Tom Garrison she'd married was dead, so she didn't know about Benny's trips home. Really, maintaining relationships with humans was hard work. Benny was only six years younger than Naomi. But she looked like she was nearly 70 — albeit a spry, active woman — and he didn't look much older than he had when they first met and he'd been 18 pretending to be 15.

Ryder was 42. Naomi had been 26 when he was born — she'd was determined to have a child, and Tom really hadn't been consulted, if Benny had the story right. He thought it amusing, but he knew his father had feared the pregnancy would kill her. Human women often died birthing a shifter baby. Which reminded him of the presentation last night.

What the fuck had that been all about? He should be staying here, tracking it all down. A Pied Piper? Latent genes — he could barely get his mind wrapped around it. He knew that he needed to go north — they couldn't let that whole region go up in chaos, and he and Ryder were the ones who could intervene. Still....

But he wasn't going to stay, he promised his wolf. He wasn't going to become the Alpha of either pack. They would have to figure out some other solution. He was coming back to Hat Island. His wolf agreed, although the wolf liked the Okanogan just fine. Pack, the wolf said. Alpha.

Exactly, Benny approved.

Speaking of the Alpha, he looked around for Abby and Jake. He wanted to say goodbye before they left. Get their blessing or something. It didn't feel right to just slip out without that. Well, slip out wasn't exactly the right word. Benny, his brother, Jessie, and six bikers, with bikes for all? They weren't going to go unnoticed.

Benny paused in dishing up his plate and looked around. They weren't here yet, but Cujo was. He was eating breakfast with Mei Tanaka. Wasn't that interesting? "Catch you later," he murmured to his brother and Jessie. He took his plate over to join Cujo.

"Good morning?" Benny said, turning it into a question, because Cujo looked beat. And Mei still looked stressed. Having two dozen new cousins added to your family links would do that. He tried not to laugh, because it had serious implications, but her description of the young men *was* funny.

"Is it a good morning?" Cujo said sourly. "We had an intruder last night. Came at the Alpha. She killed him."

Benny sobered and sat down. "An intruder got that close?" he asked, then started to eat.

Cujo nodded. "She sliced his throat before he could finish a challenge," Cujo said, and that obviously amused him. Well, it did all of them. Abby had interesting solutions to shifter culture norms. This norm said an issued challenge had to be treated formally. Abby figured if they died before they got the words out, it didn't count. Death by stupidity, she called it.

"Jake finished him off," Cujo continued. "I found his boat, but we didn't locate any partners. But Benny? One of the guards recognized him. He was Las Vegas pack."

Benny paused at that. No that wasn't good news at all. He frowned. "Issuing a challenge?"

"Yeah, we can't figure that out," Cujo agreed. "Why force her to fight him formally? Then what? Best guess is he thought the challenge wording would make her and Jake hesitate, and he'd get the kill in before they reacted."

Could be, Benny acknowledged. Most Alpha's would stop to formally accept a challenge, and state the conditions — wolf or human, was the big one; no assistance was the other. Benny grimaced. That might be it — the attacker sought to eliminate Jake's involvement.

I need to be here, he thought again. He shook his head. "Wanted to talk to you about that theory last night, about the Pied Piper," he said. He was focused on his food, but a man should be able to multitask when necessary, right?

Cujo grunted.

"You told me about the girls you pulled through first shift in Hayden Lake," Benny began. Cujo's face froze, and he glanced at Mei. She looked like she was absorbed in her own thoughts, but Benny knew that could well be deceiving.

Not in front of her, Cujo said in his brain. *But yes, I thought of that. I'm wondering if some of Mei's new cousins might also have lingering links. I'll pursue it.*

Benny nodded. "Speaking of your family, you mentioned your sister and her husband are nearly equal in power. They don't fight? And they have a mate bond?"

"Have had one since both got through first change," Cujo answered. "Mom wouldn't let them seal it, of course. She got them through high school and down to University of Idaho. This was 40 years ago? Nearly that, anyway. And they sealed it there, got married and came home to be the school teachers." Cujo grinned, genuinely amused by something. "And they use Ruby Bridges to teach the kids about going to a human school where everyone is going to be different."

Benny frowned. Who was Ruby Bridges?

"The civil rights activist? The first Black child in the New Orleans schools?" Mei asked incredulously. "They're using her to teach the white nationalist pack of Hayden Lake?"

Cujo nodded, still smiling. "Isn't it great? Mom wants a video-conferencing book club. Olivia is interested in running it."

"Can I lurk?" Benny asked. "I think I want to meet your mother."

"Ask Olivia," Cujo said. *Why are you asking about my sister?*

Thought it might apply to someone else, Benny said, keeping it vague, but his eyes sought out his brother and Jessie.

Akihiro and Abby? That would be interesting.

Benny snorted. That hadn't occurred to him. *You get to be the one to bring it up to Akihiro.*

Not a chance, Cujo replied. But Benny picked up a whiff of Haru Ito? He considered the man across the table. Was he on that good of terms with Haru Ito? That was interesting too. So many interesting things to pursue, and he was going to the outback of nowhere.

Mei stood up and gathered her plate and silverware. "If the two of you are going to have side conversations I can't hear, I'm gone. I have work to do."

How had she known that, Benny wondered. He glanced at Cujo who was looking glum. "You playing with fire, my friend?" he asked.

"We aren't friends," Cujo said. "And if I want counseling, I'll make an appointment."

Benny was a bit hurt. He thought of Cujo as a friend. Didn't he? He considered the man. Did Cujo have friends? Kent what's his name, his business manager. Was that it? Well if Cujo made an appointment, that's where they would start.

"She knew we were having side conversations," Benny observed out loud. "How did she know that? For that matter, how were we able to do that?" Usually he and Cujo could only communicate if Abby had 'flooded the field.'

Cujo looked unhappy. "Try it now," he suggested.

Benny thought at him: *Was Mei really OK about all those new links?*

Cujo shook his head. "Nope," he said.

"What the hell?" Benny asked. "Was Mei doing something?"

Cujo shrugged his agreement. "We could talk when she was here; we can't when she is gone," he pointed out. "I don't think she knows what's she doing. But Benny? Have you paid attention to how smoothly she keeps this place running?"

Benny frowned. "Is it that difficult to run?"

Cujo looked at him like he was being a dumb shit. He guessed he was. "Juggling the needs of the lab, the kitchen, the lodge, and all the different workers? Not to mention Okami and Stefan? What do you think?"

"Oh," Benny said lamely, and he considered it. He winced. They all just took it for granted. "You think, what? That she's got some kind of superpower here?"

"I think she allows all the factions to feel what each other is feeling," Cujo said slowly. "And that when she felt the longing of those young men, she reached out for them. And just now, we translated that field into Abby's flooded field, and talked to each other." Cujo shrugged and stood up. "Or maybe it was just coincidence?"

Benny snorted. Cujo didn't believe in coincidence any more than he did.

"But you might consider this," Cujo said. "What if shifter men oppress shifter women not just because they're dominant, patriarchal assholes, but because they are afraid of the gifts shifter women possess?"

Cujo grabbed his own dishes and started away. He stopped and turned back. "Abby called what Taisiya did, broadcasting fear to the other women, telepathy, and Hiro Tanaka had a fit. No such thing as telepathy, he insisted."

Benny shrugged. "There isn't."

"Then what would you call what we just did?" Cujo said softly. "What the Alpha can do? What Taisiya did? For that matter, what would you call the emotions that flow from Alphas to their packs, and the warmth of the pack to each other? Why do you believe there is no telepathy, Benny? Why does Okami insist the 'power battery' that Chen was searching for was just a myth, and was a lie? What myths, for that matter?"

He stopped for breath, and then shook his head. "When you get back," he said wryly. "And we can start with your ideas that maybe shifter teachings on pack bonds and links are over-simplified."

Cujo left then, and Benny stared after him. Where had all those questions come from?

He spotted Abby and Jake with relief. He wouldn't have to leave without seeing them after all. He bused his dishes, and then sought them out. But the question haunted him: Why did he automatically deny telepathy? And what would he call his and Abby's communication if it wasn't that?

Abby looked at him sourly. "Not a word until I have my coffee," she announced. Jake snorted, and pressed a cup into her hand. Benny obediently waited until she took a deep gulp of it and sighed. "All right," she said, smiling at him. "Are you all ready to go?"

Benny nodded. "I'm not sure I should go," he confessed. "There are a lot of open questions I should be working on."

"I could use you here, no lie," Abby admitted. "But you and Ryder are the only two who can do this." She paused for a moment, and Jake put a plate of food in her hands. Really the two of them were so cute. But Jake was just being practical. They'd never get through the buffet line if he didn't. "Well, Cujo," she said. "But his solutions tend to be the 'blow shit up and let God count his own.' Although if you two can't get it done, that's a thought."

Benny winced. It had its appeal, he admitted. But they were talking about men he knew. Wounded, battered men who had been in his father's care for decades. No, there had to be a better solution than that.

"Are you coming to see us off?" Benny asked, sitting down at the table to watch Abby eat. She ate like a shifter these days, he thought with amusement. She was focused on the food, and to hell with his attempts at conversation.

She swallowed a last bite, took another slug of coffee. "Yes," she said. "We'll walk over."

Reassured, he went to gather up his brother, Jessie, and the biker-guards who had drifted to their table. "We're good to go," he said. "The Alpha will see us off."

The Alpha wasn't the only one who was there to see them off — Maggie met them at the ferry dock as well. She was wearing Benny's army jacket. He stopped beside her, and she kissed him on the cheek. "You bring my bike back safely," she threatened.

He grinned at her. They'd spent the night together, and he was feeling good this morning, really good. A bit sleep deprived, but good. "Does that mean you're going to stay here, and wait for me?"

"Wait for my bike, you mean," Maggie countered. "But yeah, I'll be here. These women interest me. I think I'll help out for the week and then see if some of them might want to go south with me."

Benny gestured Abby over. "She's interested in working with Chen's victims," he announced. "I figure you would want to know that."

"You are?" Abby said with interest. Benny snickered at the deer-in-the-headlights look on Maggie's face, and started to roll his bike toward the ferry. It looked like Okami was doing the piloting himself. Well, this trip wasn't on the ferry schedule, that was for sure. Nine people, eight motorcycles, nine backpacks, and that about took up all the space the small ferry had to offer anyway.

"Benny?" Maggie called to him. He turned back. "You come back, you hear?"

He smiled at her, warmed by the message. "I'll do my best," he promised.

The ferry ride was 45 minutes, and it didn't really lend itself to chitchat, anyway. The day was like the day before — and the day before that — misty, overcast, gray. And he was grateful, really, because the alternative was wind, rain and gray. He realized he hadn't checked what the weather was like in Penticton — or Okanogan for that matter. He was rusty about this — been a while since he rode out with Ryder. Well, Ryder wouldn't have forgotten to check. And for the first time in a long time, he relaxed. He wasn't in charge of this trip. He really was just along for the ride. Ryder was in charge, and the guards looked to him. Oh, if he asked something of them, they'd probably obey — all of them had been chosen because they'd ridden with Benny in the past. But they were Ryder's men, not his.

He followed Ryder out of Everett to I-5. Jessie rode behind Ryder, and she looked more comfortable there today. The other guards followed behind, stringing out in the slow lane. There was no hurry.

No hurry, Benny thought with pleasure. Two hours to Abbottsford, and then they'd be in Canada. Get lunch there — shifters, like armies, marched on their stomachs — and then head east. Beautiful rugged country along Highway 3, but the road was good. There might be snow, and that was always tricky on a bike. But that was later. Now? Just the road, and the freedom to think.

Although he found he didn't want to think either. All the questions that Cujo had posed, plus all of his own, swirled in his mind, until finally he shut them all down. Today, he would just ride. He could think later.

And if he felt like he was running away? Well, it had his Alpha's blessing, didn't it?

He carefully avoided thinking about what he was running away from.

Chapter 24

Day 157 of the re-emerged Hat Island pack, Sunday, Nov. 10, Hat Island

Abby turned away from the ferry and smiled at Jake. "They're off," she said with relief. "And we've got guests to attend to." Jake nodded.

Abby looked at the biker woman thoughtfully. And she was so going to interview her! What a chance to gain insight into a closed culture. Sure this might be a shifter biker club, but it was still a biker club. But not now. "Did someone tell you where you can find food?" she asked. "Do you have a place to stay?"

"Staying at Benny's," Maggie answered, and fell into step beside Abby as they headed back toward the lodge. "He mentioned the lodge, but I wasn't in any mood to get up as early as he did to find out. I gather that's the place we went when we got here?"

Spent the night at Benny's, had she? Abby refrained from rolling her eyes. "That's it," she said. "There's a cafeteria-style dining room. Food's really good. We'd have a mass revolt if it wasn't. Come on, I'll see if Mei's around. She'll put you to work."

Maggie nodded, and Abby thought she had something on her mind. She gave her space to think about it. "Benny's not in a good place," Maggie said finally.

Abby chewed her lip. "Want to elaborate?" she asked. "You don't have to, but Benny matters to me. Matters to us all."

"He's got holes in his memories," Maggie said. "I guess you know that? They bug him more than he wants to admit. He's jittery — for him. Anxious. I've seen him clear out a bar in a fight and never lose his serenity, never a moment of anxiety. He's lost some of the joy. What happened?"

"That's a long story," Abby said, and it hurt. Lost his joy? Shouldn't the pack have healed him? Abby gave Maggie the highlights of the Russia trip. "He saved us all — and I mean that. He saved the shifter species from extinction. But he paid a price, maybe higher than I may have realized," she finished.

Maggie chewed her lip. "I'm not surprised," she said finally. "But something's bugging him. Bugging him still, besides the missing memories. Something current. It worries me. Worries me about them going off like this." She shrugged and smiled at Abby. "Had to be done. Thank you for explaining."

Abby nodded, and took her inside to meet Mei. Mei's grin was fierce — fierce enough to make Abby want to flee — but Maggie took it in stride. She'd do, Abby thought, and then she got out of there.

Benny in a bad place? Had she neglected him?

"He's been up in Vancouver for over a week," Jake said, answering her thoughts out loud. "Something might have happened up there?"

Abby nodded, and filed it under people she worried about.

Jake had told Tom Garrison to help himself to the kitchen, before they went up to the lodge. And Tom was cleaning up when they returned. Yui had gone home, a good sign that Nadia was improving. Tom nodded.

"She's better," he said. "Coherent, which is a big plus. The woman has formidable mental abilities, and when she's trapped in a nightmare, she's dangerous. Thank you for taking us in."

"Only fair," Abby said, smiling at him. "You took me in once."

She felt Jake's curiosity, and smiled ruefully. "I wonder if I will ever know how many shifters I've encountered and never knew it," she said. She glanced at Tom teasingly. "But Tom was my hero for years. The stranger who rescued me and my research assistants when we'd been abandoned to our fates in one of the worst storms of the year. We were up in the hill country of Thailand — beyond Chang Mai. Our guide panicked. Decided he'd have a better chance of surviving without us and fled. We hunkered down — I found a sheltering spot beside a tree that had been uprooted — and hoped we'd survive. And then this big man came out of nowhere. He gathered us up, took us to a hut, and kept us there. Storm lasted three days. I probably told him my whole life story — and the stories of every culture I'd been to, and the stories of every person I met — and all I learned about him was his name — Tom."

"She does talk when she has nothing to do," Tom Garrison agreed. "Fascinating stuff, though. She knew things about the cultures of the Southeast that I didn't — and I'd lived there for decades. Didn't know enough to choose a better guide, however."

Abby rolled her eyes. "I found him when we got back," she said. "Reported him to his bosses, and when they didn't appear concerned, reported them all to the country's tourism agency. We survived, but the next tourists might not have Tom to come to their rescue."

"Why did you?" Jake asked. He was tidying up the house while he listened.

Tom shook his head. "Not entirely sure," he admitted. "Something called me to their distress, and once I'd found them, I couldn't just walk away."

Jake glanced at him but didn't say anything.

What? Abby asked.

He makes it sound like altruism wouldn't let him walk away from any stranded tourists he'd come across. But I know his rep. Yes, he could have. And would have. But something about you meant he couldn't walk away.

Abby stared at him, then stared at Tom, who was watching amused. "I'm going to talk to Nadia," she said. "Do you think she's going to want to see the girls?"

"I'm sure she would — she's not seen them since they were born, you know," Tom said soberly. "And yet, they've never been out of contact. But we all should talk about that first."

"I'd like to hear why you've been sending girls to the boarding school, in the first place," Abby said. "You had to know that it was mostly a fictional sanctuary created for Sarah Johannsen, and a dream of mine that someday we'd be able to offer sanctuary to any girl who needed it. But we were years away from being ready to do that. Then Pi showed up. And then the girls who followed."

Tom laughed. "And you made it a reality," he said. "Have Haile's girls made it in yet?"

"Yes," Abby said. "Last Friday. They've been in Monte Carlo waiting for chaperones."

"Good," Tom said. "What about Garcia's girls?"

Abby hesitated, looked at Jake. He shook his head. "Chairman of the South American Council," he said. "But no, we haven't gotten girls from there. What are you trying to do? Set up a United Nations of girls?"

"Pretty much," Tom agreed. "There's a war coming — not just the one with humans when they discover us, but among shifters. That's what pulled me out of the Okanogan. Didn't think that the Okanogan would deteriorate so fast — but the boys can take care of it."

"And what was so important that you left them?" Abby asked.

He blew out a long sigh. "Trying to prevent a shifter civil war," he said at last.

"And did you?"

"No," Tom Garrison said. "I failed. And it's coming here. I thought I sent the girls to safety, and instead I managed to put them at ground zero. The World Council of Alphas meeting? It's likely to go up in flames."

"Literal flames?" Jake asked intently.

Garrison nodded. "Afraid so. The Chinese Alpha is bringing his troops." He paused. "So Lt. Col. Lewis? Do we have troops?"

Abby looked at Jake. He morphed into something else, something besides the lover and protector she knew him to be.

"We do," he said.

Well, that was news to her. They would have words about that, she thought ominously. She felt his reaction — laughter? He thought that was funny? "I'm going to check on Nadia," she said again. "And then? We'll talk."

Also by L.J. Breedlove

A Mac Davis Thriller

Trust No One

In God's Name

Serve & Protect

When No One Came

Blood and Water

One Big Lie

Accessory After the Fact

Christmas 101

A Newspaper in Texas

Sins of Omission

Pledge Allegiance

A Virtuous Woman

Deep Cover

Weddings, Politics & Football

Salt Mine

Newroom PDX short stories

Opening Pandora's Box

Interludes
When Ryan Met Master A
Kaleidoscope of Memory
Baby Ruby
Fire Drill

Newsroom PDX
Choose
Don't Go
Hold Me
Rage
Be the Change
In Charge
When Ryan Met Ruby

Newsroom PDX Omnibus
PDX 2020 Fall
PDX 2021 Winter
PDX 2021 Spring
Truth to Power

PDX Year 2
Do the Job
Hear Me
Miss You
Memory
Hunted
Seen

Past Lives

Life in Focus

PDX Year 3

Smart Girl

Hero

A Story Well Told

Who Do I Tell?

My Body

A Literary Life

Will Anyone Hear?

Talkeetna

Everybody Lies

Somebody's Secrets

Nobody Cares

Nobody's Fool

Is Anybody Alive?

Somebody New

Dead Tourist

Talkeetna

Wolf Harbor

Woman of Hat Island

Alpha Female

Alpha's Alpha

Power Grab

Safe Haven

Missing Pieces
Beta Wolf
Girls School
Redemption Road
Battle Lines
I Love You Two

Wolf Harbor Rescue

Seek and You Shall Find
To Have and to Hold
All the Hidden Places

About the Author

L.J. Breedlove writes suspense novels of all kinds, police procedurals, historical mysteries, romantic suspense and political thrillers. And now a paranormal suspense series — Wolf Harbor.

She's been a journalist, a professor, and now a fiction writer. (And a ranch hand, oceanography lab assistant, librarian assistant, cider factory line worker, and a typesetter. Oh, and worked in the laundry of an old folks home, something that inspired her to become an over-educated adult who would never be that desperate for a pay-check again.) She covered politics, among other things, taught media and politics, among other things, and writes political novels. You've been warned.

Read more at www.ljbreedlove.com.

Milton Keynes UK
Ingram Content Group UK Ltd.
UKHW010627271123
433341UK00001B/258